The Mischief-Maker

E. PHILLIPS OPPENHEIM

The Mischief-Maker

E. Phillips Oppenheim

© 1st World Library – Literary Society, 2004
PO Box 2211
Fairfield, IA 52556
www.1stworldlibrary.org
First Edition

LCCN: 2004195294

Softcover ISBN: 1-4218-0121-3
Hardcover ISBN: 1-4218-0021-7
eBook ISBN: 1-4218-0221-X

Purchase *"The Mischief-Maker"*
as a traditional bound book at:
www.1stWorldLibrary.org/purchase.asp?ISBN=1-4218-0121-3

1st World Library Literary Society is a nonprofit
organization dedicated to promoting literacy by:

- Creating a free internet library accessible from any
  computer worldwide.
- Hosting writing competitions and offering book
  publishing scholarships.

Readers interested in supporting literacy
through sponsorship, donations or
membership please contact:
literacy@1stworldlibrary.org
Check us out at: www.1stworldlibrary.ORG
and start downloading free ebooks today.

The Mischief-Maker
contributed by Tim, Ed & Rodney
in support of
1st World Library Literary Society

CONTENTS

BOOK TWO

BOOK ONE

CHAPTER I

SYMPATHY AND SELFISHNESS

The girl who was dying lay in an invalid chair piled up with cushions in a sheltered corner of the lawn. The woman who had come to visit her had deliberately turned away her head with a murmured word about the sunshine and the field of buttercups. Behind them was the little sanitarium, a gray stone villa built in the style of a château, overgrown with creepers, and with terraced lawns stretching down to the sunny corner to which the girl had been carried earlier in the day. There were flowers everywhere - beds of hyacinths, and borders of purple and yellow crocuses. A lilac tree was bursting into blossom, the breeze was soft and full of life. Below, beyond the yellow-starred field of which the woman had spoken, flowed the Seine, and in the distance one could see the outskirts of Paris.

"The doctor says I am better," the girl whispered plaintively. "This morning he was quite cheerful. I suppose he knows, but it is strange that I should feel so weak - weaker even day by day. And my cough - it tears me to pieces all the time."

The woman who was bending over her gulped

something down in her throat and turned her head. Although older than the invalid whom she had come to visit, she was young and very beautiful. Her cheeks were a trifle pale, but even without the tears her eyes were almost the color of violets.

"The doctor must know, dear Lucie," she declared. "Our own feelings so often mean nothing at all."

The girl moved a little uneasily in her chair. She, also, had once been pretty. Her hair was still an exquisite shade of red-gold, but her cheeks were thin and pinched, her complexion had gone, her clothes fell about her. She seemed somehow shapeless.

"Yes," she agreed, "the doctor knows - he must know. I see it in his manner every time he comes to visit me. In his heart," she added, dropping her voice, "he must know that I am going to die."

Her eyes seemed to have stiffened in their sockets, to have become dilated. Her lips trembled, but her eyes remained steadfast.

"Oh! madame," she sobbed, "is it not cruel that one should die like this! I am so young. I have seen so little of life. It is not just, madame - it is not just!"

The woman who sat by her side was shaking. Her heart was torn with pity. Everywhere in the soft, sunlit air, wherever she looked, she seemed to read in letters of fire the history of this girl, the history of so many others.

"We will not talk of death, dear," she said. "Doctors are so wonderful, nowadays. There are so few diseases

E. Phillips Oppenheim

which they cannot cure. They seem to snatch one back even from the grave. Besides, you are so young. One does not die at nineteen. Tell me about this man - Eugène, you called him. He has never once been to see you - not even when you were in the hospital?"

The girl began to tremble.

"Not once," she murmured.

"You are sure that he had your letters? He knows that you are out here and alone?"

"Yes, he knows!"

There was a short silence. The woman found it hard to know what to say. Somewhere down along the white, dusty road a man was grinding the music of a threadbare waltz from an ancient barrel-organ. The girl closed her eyes.

"We used to hear that sometimes," she whispered, "at the cafés. At one where we went often they used to know that I liked it and they always played it when we came. It is queer to hear it again - like this.... Oh, when I close my eyes," she muttered, "I am afraid! It is like shutting out life for always."

The woman by her side got up. Lucie caught at her skirt.

"Madame, you are not going yet?" she pleaded. "Am I selfish? Yet you have not stayed with me so long as yesterday, and I am so lonely."

The woman's face had hardened a little.

"I am going to find that man," she replied. "I have his address. I want to bring him to you."

The girl's hold upon her skirt tightened.

"Sit down," she begged. "Do not leave me. Indeed it is useless. He knows. He does not choose to come. Men are like that. Oh! madame, I have learned my lesson. I know now that love is a vain thing. Men do not often really feel it. They come to us when we please them, but afterwards that does not count. I suppose we were meant to be sacrificed. I have given up thinking of Eugène. He is afraid, perhaps, of the infection. I think that I would sooner go out of life as I lie here, cold and unloved, than have him come to me unwillingly."

The woman could not hide her tears any longer. There was something so exquisitely fragile, so strangely pathetic, in that prostrate figure by her side.

"But, my dear," she faltered, -

"Madame," the girl interrupted, "hold my hand for a moment. That is the doctor coming. I hear his footstep. I think that I must sleep."

Madame Christophor - she had another name, but there were few occasions on which she cared to use it - was driven back to Paris, in accordance with her murmured word of instruction, at a pace which took little heed of police regulations or even of safety. Through the peaceful lanes, across the hills into the suburbs, and into the city itself she passed, at a speed which was scarcely slackened even when she turned into the Boulevard which was her destination. Glancing at the slip of paper which she held in her hand, she pulled the

E. Phillips Oppenheim

checkstring before a tall block of buildings. She hurried inside, ascended two flights of stairs, and rang the bell of a door immediately opposite her. A very German-looking manservant opened it after the briefest of delays - a man with fair moustache, fat, stolid face and inquisitive eyes.

"Is your master in," she demanded, "Monsieur Estermen?"

The man stared at her, then bowed. The appearance of Madame Christophor was, without doubt, impressive.

"I will inquire, madame," he replied.

"I am in a hurry," she said curtly. "Be so good as to let your master know that."

A moment later she was ushered into a sitting-room - a man's apartment, untidy, reeking of cigarette smoke and stale air. There were photographs and souvenirs of women everywhere. The windows were fast-closed and the curtains half-drawn. The man who stood upon the hearthrug was of medium height, dark, with close-cropped hair and a black, drooping moustache. His first glance at his visitor, as the door opened, was one of impertinent curiosity.

"Madame?" he inquired.

"You are Monsieur Estermen?"

He bowed. He was very much impressed and he endeavored to assume a manner.

"That is my name. Pray be seated."

She waved away the chair he offered.

"My automobile is in the street below," she said. "I wish you to come with me at once to see a poor girl who is dying."

He looked at her in amazement.

"Are you serious, madame?"

"I am very serious indeed," she replied. "The girl's name is Lucie Rénault."

For the moment he seemed perplexed. Then his eyebrows were slowly raised.

"Lucie Rénault," he repeated. "What do you know about her?"

"Only that she is a poor child who has suffered at your hands and who is dying in a private hospital," Madame Christophor answered. "She has been taken there out of charity. She has no friends, she is dying alone. Come with me. I will take you to her. You shall save her at least from that terror."

It was the aim of the man with whom she spoke to be considered modern. A perfect and invincible selfishness had enabled him to reach the topmost heights of callousness, and to remain there without affectation.

"If the little girl is dying," he said, "I am sorry, for she was pretty and companionable, although I have lost sight of her lately. But as to my going out to see her, why, that is absurd. I hate illness of all sorts."

The woman looked at him steadfastly, looked at him as though she had come into contact with some strange creature.

"Do you understand what it is that I am saying?" she demanded. "This girl was once your little friend, is it not so? It was for your sake that she gave up the simple life she was living when you first knew her, and went upon the stage. The life was too strenuous for her. She broke down, took no care of herself, developed a cough and alas! tuberculosis."

The man sighed. He had adopted an expression of abstract sympathy.

"A terrible disease," he murmured.

"A terrible disease indeed," Madame Christophor repeated. "Do you not understand what I mean when I tell you that she is dying of it? Very likely she will not live a week - perhaps not a day. She lies there alone in the garden of the hospital and she is afraid. There are none who knew her, whom she cares for, to take her into their arms and to bid her have no fear. Is it not your place to do this? You have held her in your arms in life. Don't you see that it is your duty to cheer her a little way on this last dark journey?"

The man threw away his cigarette and moved to the mantelpiece, where he helped himself to a fresh one from the box.

"Madame," he said, "I perceive that you are a sentimentalist."

She did not speak - she could not. She only looked

at him.

"Death," he continued, lighting his cigarette, "is an ugly thing. If it came to me I should probably be quite as much afraid - perhaps more - than any one else. But it has not come to me just yet. It has come, you tell me, to little Lucie. Well, I am sorry, but there is nothing I can do about it. I have no intention whatever of making myself miserable. I do not wish to see her. I do not wish to look upon death, I simply wish to forget it. If it were not, madame," he added, with a bow and a meaning glance from his dark eyes, "that you bring with you something of your own so well worth looking upon, I could almost find myself regretting your visit."

She still regarded him fixedly. There was in her face something of that shrinking curiosity with which one looks upon an unclean and horrible thing.

"That is your answer?" she murmured.

The man had little understanding and he replied boldly.

"It is my answer, without a doubt. Lucie, if what you tell me is true, as I do not for a moment doubt, is dying from a disease the ravages of which are hideous to watch, and which many people believe, too, to be infectious. Let me advise you, madame, to learn also a little wisdom. Let me beg of you not to be led away by these efforts of sentiment, however picturesque and delightful they may seem. The only life that is worth considering is our own. The only death that we need fear is our own. We ought to live like that."

The woman stood quite still. She was tall and she was slim. Her figure was exquisite. She was famous

E. Phillips Oppenheim

throughout the city for her beauty. The man's eyes dwelt upon her and the eternal expression crept slowly into his face. He seemed to understand nothing of the shivering horror with which she was regarding him.

"If it were upon any other errand, madame," he continued, leaning towards her, "believe, I pray you, that no one would leave this room to become your escort more willingly than I."

She turned away.

"You will not leave me already?" he begged.

"Monsieur," she declared, as she threw open the door before he could reach it, "if I thought that there were many men like you in the world, if I thought -"

She never finished her sentence. The emotions which had seized her were entirely inexpressible. He shrugged his shoulders.

"My dear lady," he said, "let me assure you that there is not a man of the world in this city who, if he spoke honestly, would not feel exactly as I do. Allow me at least to see you to your automobile."

"If you dare to move," she muttered, "if you dare -"

She swept past him and down the stairs into the street. She threw herself into the corner of the automobile. The chauffeur looked around.

"Where to, madame?" he inquired.

She hesitated for a moment. She had affairs of her

own, but the thought of the child's eyes came up before her.

"Back to the hospital," she ordered. "Drive quickly."

They rushed from Paris once more into the country, with its spring perfumes, its soft breezes, its restful green, but fast though they drove another messenger had outstripped them. From the little chapel, as the car rolled up the avenue, came the slow tolling of a bell. Madame Christophor stood on the corner of the lawn alone. The invalid chair was empty. The blinds of the villa were being slowly lowered. She turned around and looked toward the city. It seemed to her that she could see into the rooms of the man whom she had left a few minutes ago. A lark was singing over her head. She lifted her eyes and looked past him up to the blue sky. Her lips moved, but never a sound escaped her. Yet the man who sat in his rooms at that moment, yawning and wondering where to spend the evening, and which companion he should summon by telephone to amuse him, felt a sudden shiver in his veins.

E. Phillips Oppenheim

CHAPTER II

AN INDISCREET LETTER

The library of the house in Grosvenor Square was spacious, handsome and ornate. Mr. Algernon H. Carraby, M.P., who sat dictating letters to a secretary in an attitude which his favorite photographer had rendered exceedingly familiar, at any rate among his constituents, was also, in his way, handsome and ornate. Mrs. Carraby, who had just entered the room, fulfilled in an even greater degree these same characteristics. It was acknowledged to be a very satisfactory household.

"I should like to speak to you for a moment, Algernon," his wife announced.

Mr. Carraby noticed for the first time that she was carrying a letter in her hand. He turned at once to his secretary.

"Haskwell," he said, "kindly return in ten minutes."

The young man quitted the room. Mrs. Carraby advanced a few steps further towards her husband. She was tall, beautifully dressed in the latest extreme of fashion. Her movements were quiet, her skin a little pale, and her eyebrows a little light. Nevertheless, she was quite a famous beauty. Men all admired her without any reservations. The best sort of women rather mistrusted her.

"Is that the letter, Mabel?" her husband asked, with an eagerness which he seemed to be making some effort to conceal.

She nodded slowly. He held out his hand, but she did not at once part with it.

"Algernon," she said quietly, "you know that I am not very scrupulous. We both of us want success - a certain sort of success - and we have both of us been content to pay the price. You have spent a good deal of money and you have succeeded very well indeed. Somehow or other, I feel to-day as though I were spending more than money."

He laughed a little uncomfortably.

"My dear Mabel!" he protested. "You are not going to back out, are you?"

"No," she replied, "I do not think that I shall back out. There is nothing in the whole world I want so much as to have you a Cabinet Minister. If there had been any other way -"

"But there is no other way," her husband interrupted. "So long as Julien Portel lives, I should never get my chance. He holds the post I want. Every one knows that he is clever. He has the ear of the Prime Minister and he hates me. My only chance is his retirement."

Mrs. Carraby looked at the letter.

"Well," she said, "I have played your game for you. I have gone even to the extent of being talked about with Julien Portel."

Her husband moved uneasily in his chair.

"That will all blow over directly," he declared. "Besides, if - if things go our way, we shan't see much more of Portel. Give me the letter."

Still she hesitated. It was curious that throughout the slow evolution of this scheme to break a man's life, for which she was mainly responsible, she had never hesitated until this moment. Always it had been fixed in her mind that Algernon was to be a Cabinet Minister; she was to be the wife of a Cabinet Minister. That there were any other things greater in life than the gratification of so reasonable an ambition had never seemed possible. Now she hesitated. She looked at her husband and she saw him with new eyes. He seemed suddenly a mean little person. She thought of the other man and there was a strange quiver in her heart - a very unexpected sensation indeed. There was a difference in the breed. It came home to her at that moment. She found herself even wondering, as she swung the letter idly between her thumb and fore-finger, whether she would have been a different woman if she had had a different manner of husband.

"The letter!" he repeated.

She laid it calmly on the desk before him.

"Of course," she said coldly, "if you find the contents affectionate you must remember that I am in no way responsible. This was your scheme. I have done my best."

The man's fingers trembled slightly as he broke the seal.

"Naturally," he agreed, pausing for an instant and looking up at her. "I knew that I could trust you or I would never have put such an idea into your head."

She laughed; a characteristic laugh it was, quite cold, quite mirthless, apparently quite meaningless. Carraby turned back to the letter, tore open the envelope and spread it out before them. He read it out aloud in a sing-song voice.

Downing Street. Tuesday

MY DEAREST MABEL,

I had your sweet little note an hour ago. Of course I was disappointed about luncheon, as I always am when I cannot see you. Your promise to repay me, however, almost reconciles me.

The man looked up at his wife.

"Promise?" he repeated hoarsely. "What does he mean?"

"Go on," she said, with unchanged expression. "See if what you want is there."

The man continued to read:

I am going to ask you a very great favor, Mabel. When we are alone together, I talk to you with absolute

E. Phillips Oppenheim

freedom. To write you on matters connected with my office is different. I know very well how deep and sincere your interest in politics really is, and it has always been one of my greatest pleasures, when with you, to talk things over and hear your point of view. Without flattery, dear, I have really more than once found your advice useful. It is your understanding which makes our companionship always a pleasure to me, and I rely upon that when I beg you not to ask me to write you again on matters to which I have really no right to allude. You do not mind this, dear? And having read you my little lecture, I will answer your question. Yes, the Cabinet Council was held exactly as you surmise. With great difficulty I persuaded B - to adopt my view of the situation. They are all much too terrified of this war bogey. For once I had my own way. Our answer to this latest demand from Berlin was a prompt and decisive negative. Nothing of this is to be known for at least a week.

I am sorry your husband is such a bear. Perhaps on Monday we may meet at Cardington House?

Please destroy this letter at once.

Ever affectionately yours,

JULIEN.

The man's eyes, as he read, grew brighter.

"It is enough?" the woman asked.

"It is more than enough!"

Slowly he replaced it in its envelope and thrust it into

the breast-pocket of his coat.

"What are you going to do with it?" she inquired.

"I have made my plans," he answered. "I know exactly how to make the best and most dignified use of it."

He rose to his feet. Something in his wife's expression seemed to disturb him. He walked a few steps toward the door and came back again.

"Mabel," he said, "are you glad?"

"Naturally I am glad," she replied.

"You have no regrets?"

Again she laughed.

"Regrets?" she echoed. "What are they? One doesn't think about such things, nowadays."

They stood quite still in the centre of that very handsome apartment. They were almost alien figures in the world in which they moved, Carraby, the rankest of newcomers, carried into political life by his wife's ambitions, his own self-amassed fortune, and a sort of subtle cunning - a very common substitute for brains; Mrs. Carraby, on whom had been plastered an expensive and ultra-fashionable education, although she was able perhaps more effectually to conceal her origin, the daughter of a rich Yorkshire manufacturer, who had secured a paid entrance into Society. They were purely artificial figures for the very reason that they never admitted any one of these facts to themselves, but talked always the jargon of the world to which they aspired, as though they were indeed denizens therein by right. At that moment, though, a single natural feeling shook the man, shook his faith in himself, in life, in his destiny. There was Jewish blood in his veins and it made itself felt.

"Mabel," he began, "this man Portel - you've flirted with him, you say?"

"I have most certainly flirted with him," she admitted quietly.

"He hasn't dared - "

A flash of scorn lit her cold eyes.

"I think," she said, "that you had better ask me no questions of that sort."

Carraby went slowly out. Already the moment was passing. Of course he could trust his wife! Besides, in his letter was the death warrant of the man who stood between him and his ambitions. Mrs. Carraby listened to his footsteps in the hall, heard his suave reply to his secretary, heard his orders to the footman who let him out. From where she stood she watched him cross the square. Already he had recovered his alert bearing. His shoes and his hat were glossy, his coat was of an excellent fit. The woman watched him without movement or any change of expression.

CHAPTER III

A RUINED CAREER

Sir Julien Portel stood in the middle of his bedroom, dressed in shirt and trousers only. The sofa and chairs around him were littered with portions of the brilliant uniform which he had torn from his person a few minutes before with almost feverish haste. His perplexed servant, who had only just arrived, was doing his best to restore the room to some appearance of order.

"You needn't mind those wretched things for the present, Richards," his master ordered sharply. "Bring the rest of the tweed traveling suit like the trousers I have on, and then see about packing some clothes."

The man ceased his task. He looked around, a little bewildered.

"Do I understand that you are going out of town tonight, Sir Julien?" he asked.

"I am going on to the continent by the nine o'clock train," was the curt reply.

Richards was a perfectly trained servant, but the situation was too much for him.

E. Phillips Oppenheim

"You will excuse me, Sir Julien," he said, "but there is Lord Cardington's dinner tonight, and the reception afterwards at the Foreign Office. I have your court clothes ready."

His master laughed shortly.

"I am not attending the dinner or the reception, Richards. You can put those things back again and get me the traveling clothes."

The man seemed a little dazed, but turned automatically towards the wardrobe.

"Shall you require me to accompany you, sir?" he inquired.

"Not at present," Sir Julien replied. "You will have to come on with the rest of my luggage when I have decided what to do."

Richards was not more than ordinarily inquisitive, but the circumstances were certainly unusual.

"Do you mean, sir, that you will not be returning to London at present?" he ventured to ask.

"I shall not be returning to London for some time," Sir Julien answered sharply. "Get on with the packing as quickly as you can. Put the whiskey and soda on the table in the sitting-room, and the cigarettes. Remember, if any one comes I am not at home."

"Too late, my dear fellow," a voice called out from the adjoining room. "You see, I have found my way up unannounced - a bad habit, but my profession excuses everything."

The man stood on the threshold of the room opening out from the bedroom - tall, florid, untidily dressed, with clean-shaven, humorous face, ungloved hands, and a terribly shabby hat. He looked around the room and shrugged his shoulders.

"What an infernal mess!" he exclaimed. "Come along out into the sitting-room, Julien. I want to talk to you."

"I should like to know how the devil you got in here!" Sir Julien muttered. "I told the fellow downstairs that no one was to be allowed up."

"He did try to make himself disagreeable," the newcomer replied. "However, here I am - that's enough."

Sir Julien turned to his servant.

"Get on with your packing, Richards," he directed, "and let me know when you have finished."

Sir Julien followed his visitor into the sitting-room, closing the door behind him. His manner was not in the least cordial.

"Look here, Kendricks, old fellow," he said, "I don't want to be rude, but I am not in the humor to talk to any one. I have had a rotten week of it and just about as much as I can stand. Help yourself to a whiskey and soda, say what you have to say and then go."

The newcomer nodded. He helped himself to the whiskey and soda, but he seemed in no hurry to speak.

E. Phillips Oppenheim

On the contrary, he settled himself down in an easy-chair with the appearance of a man who had come to stay.

"Julien," he remarked presently, "you are up against it - up against it rather hard. Don't trouble to interrupt me. I know pretty well all about it. I said from the first you'd have to resign. There wasn't any other way out of it."

"Quite right," Julien agreed. "There wasn't. I've finished up everything to-day - resigned my office, applied for the Chiltern Hundreds, and I am going to clear out of the country to-night."

"And all because you wrote a foolish letter to a woman!" Kendricks murmured, half to himself. "By the bye, there's no doubt about the letter, I suppose?"

"None in the world," Julien replied.

"There's nothing that the Press can do to set you right?"

"Great heavens, no!" Julien declared. "No one can help me. I've no one to blame but myself. I wrote the letter - there the matter ends."

"And she passed it on to that shocking little bounder of a husband of hers! What a creature! Did it ever occur to you that it was a plot?"

Julien shrugged his shoulders.

"It makes so little difference."

"You were in Carraby's way," Kendricks continued, producing a pipe from his pocket and leisurely filling it. "There was no getting past you and you were a young man. It's a dirty business."

"If you don't mind," Julien said coldly, "we won't discuss it any further. So far as I am concerned, the whole matter is at an end. I was compelled to take part in to-day's mummery. I hated it - that they all knew. I suppose it's foolish to mind such things, David," he went on bitterly, taking up a cigarette and throwing himself into a chair, "but a year ago - it was just after I came back from Berlin and you may remember it was the fancy of the people to believe that I had saved the country from war - they cheered me all the way from Whitehall to the Mansion House. To-day there was only a dull murmur of voices - a sort of doubting groan. I felt it, Kendricks. It was like Hell, that ride!"

Kendricks nodded sympathetically.

"I suppose you know that a version of the letter is in the evening papers?" he asked.

"My resignation will be in the later issues," Julien told him. "It was pretty well known yesterday afternoon. I leave for the continent to-night."

There was a short silence between the two men. In a sense they had been friends all their lives. Sir Julien Portel had been a successful politician, the youngest Cabinet Minister for some years. Kendricks had never aspired to be more than a clever journalist of the vigorous type. Nevertheless, they had been more than ordinarily intimate.

E. Phillips Oppenheim

"Have you made any plans?" Kendricks inquired presently. "Of course, you would have to resign office, but don't you think there might be a chance of living it down?"

"Not a chance on earth," Julien replied. "As to what I am going to do, don't ask me. For the immediate present I am going to lose myself in Normandy or somewhere. Afterwards I think I shall move on to my old quarters in Paris. There's always a little excitement to be got out of life there."

Kendricks looked at his friend through the cloud of tobacco smoke.

"It's excitement of rather a dangerous order," he remarked slowly.

"I shall never be likely to forget that I am an Englishman," Julien said. "Perhaps I may be able to do something to set matters right again. One can't tell. By the bye, Kendricks," he went on, "do you remember when we were at college how you hated women? How you used to try and trace half the things that went wrong in life to their influence?"

The journalist nodded. He knocked the ashes from his pipe deliberately.

"I was a boy in those days," he declared. "I am a man now, getting on toward middle age, and on that one subject I am as rabid as ever. I hate their meddling in men's affairs, shoving themselves into politics, always whispering in a man's ear under pretence of helping him with their sympathy. They're in evidence wherever you go - women, women, women! The place reeks with them. You can't go about your work, hour by hour or day by day, without having them on every side of you. It's like a poison, this trail of them over every piece of serious work we attempt, over every place we find our way into. They bang the typewriters in our offices, they elbow us in the streets, they smile at us from the next table at our workaday luncheon, they crowd the tubes and the cars and the cabs in the streets. Why the deuce, Julien, can't we treat them like those sage Orientals, and dump them all in one place where they belong till we've finished our work?"

Julien lifted his tumbler of whiskey and soda to his lips and set it down empty.

"In a way, you're right, Kendricks," he agreed. "You go too far, of course, but I do believe that women hold too big a place in our lives. I am one of the poor fools who goes to the wall to gratify the vanity of one of them."

The journalist muttered a word under his breath which he would have been very sorry to have seen in the pages of his paper. Julien had moved to the open window. There had been a little break in his voice. No one knew better than Kendricks that a very brilliant career was broken.

"I think you're wise to go away for a time, Julien," he decided. "Look here, it's six o'clock now. I have a taxicab waiting downstairs. Come round to my rotten little restaurant in Soho and dine with me. Your fellow can meet us at Charing-Cross with your things. You won't see a soul you know where I'm going to take you."

Julien turned slowly away from the window. He was looking for the last time from those rooms at the London which he had loved. The setting sun had caught the dome of St. Paul's, was flashing from the dark, placid water of the Thames. The roar of the great city was passing from eastwards to westwards.

"You're a good chap, Kendricks," he declared. "I'll come along, with pleasure. I shall have enough solitude later on. But listen, before we go - listen, David, to a speech after your own heart."

Julien stood quite still for a moment. His pale face seemed suddenly whiter, his eyes were full of fire.

"David," he said, "if ever the time comes in the future when I find that a woman is beginning to claim a minute of my thoughts, a single one of my emotions, to govern the slightest throb of my pulses, I'll take her by the throat and I'll throw her out of what's left of my life as I would a rat that had crept into my room. I've done with them. Curse all women!"

There was a silence. Kendricks leaned over to the fireplace and knocked his pipe against the hearth. Then he suddenly paused.

"What's that?" he asked abruptly.

There was a soft knocking at the outside door.

CHAPTER IV

A BUNCH OF VIOLETS

Kendricks rose slowly to his feet. Julien was looking toward the door with a frown upon his face. While they stood there the knocking was repeated, still soft but a little more insistent. Julien hesitated no longer.

"I think," Kendricks said dryly, "that you had better see who is there."

The door was already opened. Julien seemed suddenly transformed into a graven image. He said nothing, merely gazing at the woman who walked calmly past him into the room. Kendricks, who also recognized her, withdrew his pipe from his mouth. This was a situation indeed! The woman, with her hands inside her muff, looked from one to the other of the two men.

"Am I interrupting a very important interview?" she asked calmly. "If not, perhaps you could spare me five minutes of your time, Sir Julien?"

Kendricks recovered himself at once.

"I'll wait for you downstairs, Julien," he declared.

He caught up his hat and departed, closing the door

E. Phillips Oppenheim

after him. Julienwas still motionless.

"Well?" she began.

He drew a little breath. He was beginning to regain his self-possession.

"My dear Mrs. Carraby," he said, "with your wonderful knowledge of the world and its ways, will you permit me to point out that your presence here is a little embarrassing to me and might, under certain circumstances, be a good deal more embarrassing to you?"

Mrs. Carraby smiled. She stood where the sunlight touched her brown hair and her quiet, pale face. She was one of those women who are never afraid of the light. Her face was of that strange, self-contained nature, colorless, apparently, yet capable of strange and rapid changes. Just now the last glow of sunlight seemed to have found a skein of gold in her hair, a queer gleam of light in her eyes. She stood there looking at the man whom she had come to visit.

"Julien," she said, "I wanted a few words with you."

It was impossible for him to remain altogether unmoved. Whatever else might be the truth, she had risked most of the things that were dear to her in life by this visit.

"Mrs. Carraby," he declared, "I am entirely at your service. If you think that any useful purpose can be served by words between you and me, I would only point out, for your own sake, that your visit is, to say the least of it, unwise. These are bachelor chambers."

"You know very well," she replied calmly, "that it was my only chance of speaking with you. If I had sent for you, you would not have come. If I had spoken to you in the street, you would have passed me by - quite rightly. This was my only chance. That is why I have come to you."

"If you think it worth the risk," he remarked gravely, "pray continue."

She shrugged her shoulders very slightly.

"Who can tell what is worth the risk?"

"You have at least excited my curiosity," he admitted, leaning a little towards her. "I cannot conceive what it is that you want to say to me."

She lifted her eyes to his, and though there was nothing unusual about them - there were few people, indeed, who could tell you what color they were - men seldom forgot it when Mrs. Carraby looked at them steadily.

"I do not know, myself," she said. "I do not know why I have come."

Julien laughed unnaturally.

"Pray be seated," he begged. "Would you like to examine my curios or my photographs? I must apologize for the condition of my room. You see, you happen to be the first woman who has ever crossed its threshold."

"That," she remarked, "rather interests me. Still, it is only what I should have expected. No, I do not think that I will sit down. I am trying to ask myself exactly why I have come."

"If you can answer that question," Julien said grimly, "you will appease a very natural curiosity on my part. It is not like you."

"Quite true," she assented. "It is not like me. I have run a great risk in coming here and it is not my métier to run risks. And now that I am here I do not know why I have come. This has been an impulse and this is an hour outside my life. I am trying to understand it. Come here, Julien." He came unwillingly to her side. She held out her hand, but he shook his head.

"Mabel," he said, "you and I do not need to mince words. To-night I am celebrating the ruin of my career. I am leaving England within a few hours. I have you to thank for what has happened. Yet you come to me, you hold out your hand. You must forgive me - I am afraid I am dull."

"No," she replied, "you are not dull. Your feelings towards me are obvious and very natural. Mine towards you I am not so sure of. It is not because I did not understand you that I came here to-night. It is because I did not understand myself. May I go on?"

"Why not?" he answered. "I am at your service."

"From the days of my boarding-school," she continued, "I have known only one Mabel. In her girlhood she had all that she could get out of life and turned everything she could to her own ends. A marriage was arranged for her - you see, I was half a Jewess and my husband was half a Jew, and things are done like that with us.

The marriage opened the door to a fresh set of ambitions. For the last few years I have trodden a well-worn path. It was I who advised my husband to refuse a baronetcy. It was I who won his first election. I see that my photographs are in all the illustrated papers, that his speeches are properly recorded, that my visiting list moves within the correct limits. These things have spelt life. To the fulfillment of my husband's ambitions there was one obstacle. That obstacle was you. In life one schemes. It was my husband's wish that I should make myself agreeable to you, even to the extent of a flirtation."

She raised her eyes.

"Your obedience to your husband is most touching," he said.

"It is true, I suppose," she went on, "that we have flirted. I looked upon it as the means to an end. The end came. I played my cards quite ruthlessly, I gathered in the reward. I got your letter, I handed it to my husband. Your career was finished, my husband's begun."

"This is most interesting," Julien muttered.

"Is it?" she answered. "I suppose it should have been an hour of triumph with me. It simply isn't. I have come to a place in my life which I don't understand. When I told myself that it was over, that I had flirted with you, that I had won your friendship and your confidence, betrayed you, ruined you for a peerage and that my husband should take office, I should surely have been satisfied! It was for that I had worked. I gave my husband the letter and I watched him walk off in triumph. Since then I have not been myself. I have come to you, Julien, to ask if there is no other end possible to this?"

Once more she raised her eyes. Julien came a step nearer to her. They were standing now face to face.

"All of a sudden," she murmured, "I looked back and I saw the way I have lived and the way I am living and the life that spreads itself out before me. I saw myself a peeress, I saw myself receiving my husband's guests, I saw the gratification of all those ambitions which have seemed to me so wonderful. And I locked the door and I shrieked and it seemed to me that there was a new thing and a new thought in my life. I have done you a hideous wrong, Julien. There is only one way I can set it right. There is only one moment in which it can be done, and that moment is now. Tomorrow I shall be back again. For this one hour I see the truth. I am a very rich woman, Julien. My husband's future, indeed, is largely bound up with my wealth. Remember that in all I have done I have been his agent. He hates you, has hated you from the first because you were a gentleman and he never was. This is my one moment of madness in a perfectly well-ordered life."

One of her hands stole from her muff, stole out half-hesitatingly towards him. Julien took it in his and raised it to his lips. Then he looked her in the eyes.

"Dear Mabel," he said, "you are forgiven. I understand perfectly the reasons for your coming. Go back to your husband, wear your coronet and receive his guests with a free conscience. I forgive you."

Her hand slipped back into her muff. She began to

tremble a little.

"As for me," he went on, "I played the fool and I pay willingly. I was engaged to marry a very charming girl who believed in me and whom I cared for as much as it was possible for me to care for anything outside my career. I flirted with you because it was a piquant thing to do. You were a woman whom other men found difficult, you were the wife of a man whom I despised and who was trying all the time to undermine my position. I sacrificed my self-respect every time I crossed your threshold. To-day I pay. I am willing. As for you, Mabel, your visit here shall square things between us. I wish you the best of luck. You must let me ring for my servant. He will find you a taxicab."

He moved toward the bell. Mrs. Carraby, with her hands inside her muff, stood exactly as though she were part of the furniture of the room. With his finger upon the ivory disc, he hesitated. She was not looking towards him and her eyes were half closed.

"Perhaps," he suggested, "you would rather find your way out alone? I will not offer my escort, for obvious reasons."

She turned slowly round.

"Do not ring," she ordered sharply. "Come here."

He came at once towards her. She took both his hands in hers, she leaned towards him. She was a tall woman and they were very nearly the same height.

"Julien," she whispered, "is this all that you have to say to me?"

E. Phillips Oppenheim

"It is more," Julien replied frankly, "than I expected ever to have to say to you again in this world. What do you expect? You don't think that I am the kind of man to - but that is absurd! Come. We'll part friends, if you like. Here's my hand."

"We must part, then?" she said.

He shrugged his shoulders.

"Unless a walking tour in Normandy for a month appeals to you. You see, I am going to take a holiday, and I have a fancy that our ideas on the subject of holidays might not exactly agree."

"A holiday," she repeated. "I am not sure - do you know, Julien, I sometimes believe that I have never had a holiday in my life?"

He looked at her doubtingly.

"After all," she continued, "can't you see that I have come here to ask you one question? You are different from the people I have known intimately and the people with whom I have been brought up, different from my husband. You know what my life has been. I have told you just now that the great doubt has come to me within the last few days. Won't you tell me what I want to know? Is there anything better, anything greater, anything more wonderful in life than these things which I have known, these ambitions, this social struggle? Tell me, Julien, is there anything else? Can you tell me how and where to find it?"

Once more her fingers had crept out of her muff.

Her hands were upon his shoulders, she seemed to be drawing him to her. Julien kissed her lightly on the forehead.

"For you, my dear Mabel," he decided, "I should say that there was nothing better. A leopard cannot change its spots. The life into which you have been brought and for which you have qualified so admirably, is the only life which would suit you. If you fancy sometimes in your dreams, or in your waking hours, that you hear cries and calls from another country, don't listen to them. You would never be happy outside the world you know of. You see, one who has made such a failure of life himself is yet well able to advise. Forgive me."

The telephone on his writing table was ringing. He turned aside to answer it. It was a question regarding the whereabouts of some papers at the office and it took him a few minutes to explain. When he set the receiver back and turned around, he was alone. There was nothing to remind him of her visit but a bunch of violets which seemed to have fallen from her muff, and the faint perfume from them. He took them up, smelt them for a moment, and flung them lightly into the hearth. Then he touched his bell.

"My hat, stick and gloves, Richards," he ordered. "Bring my things to Charing-Cross at half-past eight. Have them registered only to Boulogne. You understand?"

"Perfectly, sir," the man replied.

Julien glanced once more around his sitting-room. The little bunch of violets was smouldering upon the hearth. In a sense they seemed to him symbolical.

"Kendricks is right," he muttered. "It is the women who play the devil with our lives!"

CHAPTER V

A SENTIMENTAL EPISODE

Kendricks was waiting below in the taxicab, leaning back in the corner with his feet upon the opposite seat, and smoking his very disreputable pipe with an air of serene content.

"Sorry to have turned you out into the street like this," Julien remarked.

"Thank you," Kendricks replied, "under the circumstances I preferred the street."

Julien hesitated for a moment and glanced at his watch.

"There is one more call that I must pay, David," he said. "You won't mind, will you? We've plenty of time."

"Mind? Of course not," Kendricks answered, stretching himself out in the cab. "Do what you please with me, only leave an hour or an hour and a half for dinner. I am the best-tempered person in the world so long as no one interferes with my regular meal hours."

"It's just a little farewell call," Julien explained, "that I want to pay. I've told the man where to go."

E. Phillips Oppenheim

Kendricks nodded silently. He knew all about that little call, but if he felt any sympathy he was careful not to show it. They drew up in a few minutes before a large and solemn-looking house at the corner of Hamilton Place.

"Don't hurry," Kendricks advised, stretching himself out once more in the cab. "I'll smoke another pipe and thank heaven we are not in New York! You wait an hour there and take your choice of paying the fare or buying the taxicab!"

Julien ascended the steps and rang the bell at the door of the house. It was immediately opened by a man-servant, who recognized him with a bow and a smile, for which, somehow or other, he felt thankful.

"Is Lady Anne in, Robert?" he inquired.

The man stood on one side.

"Please to walk in, Sir Julien," he invited. "Lady Anne is with some young people in the drawing-room. Will you go in there to them, or would you prefer that I announce you?"

"Is there any one in the waiting-room?" Julien asked.

"No one at present, sir."

"Let me go in there, then. I want to speak to Lady Anne alone for a moment. You might let her know that I am here."

"Certainly, sir."

Julien walked restlessly up and down the small, uncomfortable apartment, the room which he had always hated. There were illustrated papers arranged in a row upon a leather-topped table, two stiff horsehair easychairs, and various views of Clonarty, the country seat of the Duke of Clonarty, around the walls. Presently he heard the laughter in the drawing-room cease. There was a short silence, then the sound of footsteps across the hall and the abrupt opening of the door of the room in which he was waiting. Julien looked up quickly. It was, after all, what he had expected! A somewhat vivacious-looking little lady in a muslin gown and elaborate hat held out both her hands to him. In the darkened light of the room she might very well have passed for a younger and less serious edition of her own daughter.

"My dear Julien!" she exclaimed, in a tone which was manifestly sympathetic. "This is terrible news we are hearing about you. But what an odd time you have chosen to come and tell us all about it!"

"I have not come to tell you all about it, Duchess," Julien assured her. "The newspapers will tell you everything that is worth knowing. They are so much better informed."

"The newspapers sometimes exaggerate," she objected.

"In my case," he replied, "I do not think that exaggeration is possible. Everything has happened to me that could possibly happen to any one in my unfortunate position."

"You mean that these stories are all true, then?"

"Every one of them. I really don't suppose that I ought to show my face here at all. I have simply come to say good-bye. There is just a single word that I want to say to Anne."

"Tell me, Julien," she demanded, "you really did write that letter to Mrs. Carraby?"

"I did."

"And she gave it to her husband?"

"Yes!"

For once the Duchess was perfectly and delightfully natural.

"That woman," she declared, "is a detestable cat! Mind, Julien," she added, "I don't mean by that that you were not hideously and entirely to blame. I can't feel that you deserve a single grain of sympathy. All the same, a woman who can do a thing like that should not be tolerated."

Julien smiled grimly. He was perfectly well aware that at that moment Mrs. Carraby was passing from the list of the Duchess's acquaintances. It was all so inconsequent.

"Can I have that one word with Anne?" he begged.

The Duchess looked doubtful.

"Why?"

"I am going abroad to-night. I should like to say

good-bye to her."

"Isn't it a little foolish?" she asked. "I don't mean your going abroad - that, I suppose, is almost necessary - but why do you want to see Anne? I can give her all the proper messages."

Julien laughed bitterly.

"There are some things," he said, "which can scarcely be altogether ignored. It may have escaped your memory that Anne was to have been my wife."

"Not at all," the Duchess replied. "The only thing I do not understand is why, as any such arrangement is of course now ridiculous, you should want to see her again. What can you possibly have to say to her?" "An affair of sentiment," he explained. "I have a fancy to say good-bye."

The Duchess shook her head.

"Those sort of things don't belong to us," she declared. "You ought to know better, my dear Julien. I can see no possible object in it. I will give her any message you like, and so far as she is concerned I can assure you that she has not the slightest ill-feeling. She is really quite angelic about it."

"Duchess," Julien said steadily, "I came here expecting that these would be your views. You are Anne's mother and of course you are in authority, but when two people of our age are engaged to marry one another, they pass just a little beyond the sphere of their parents' influence. Anne and I have been in that position. Don't think for a moment that I wish to dispute your authority when I say that I intend to see her before I leave."

She shrugged her shoulders.

"Ah! my dear Julien," she murmured, "if you had only been as firm with that foolish woman. Still, if you have really made up your mind, I am sure I don't want to be disagreeable. Perhaps it would be just as well to get the thing over."

She touched the bell.

"Ask Lady Anne to step this way," she told the servant.

The man withdrew and the door was closed again. The Duchess showed no signs of being about to take her leave.

"This matter has already, I presume, been fully discussed between you and Anne?" Julien remarked. "It will not be necessary for you even to give her a parting word of advice?"

"You amusing person!" she laughed. "There are no words of advice of mine needed in a case like this. To tell you the truth, Julien, although I always liked you, as you know, I hated your engagement to Anne. You were a very charming young man to have about the house and I was always pleased to see my girls flirt with you, but as a son-in-law I ranked you from the first amongst the undesirables. Your income, so far as I know, is a little less than nothing at all, and politics, as you are discovering to-day, are a precarious form of livelihood. Anne hasn't a copper and never will have. She ought to marry a rich man, and I intend now that she shall. Here she is. Now do get this stupid affair over quickly."

The door was opened and Lady Anne came in. She was taller than her mother, of more serious aspect, and her hair was a shade darker. There was something of the same expression about the eyes. She came straight over to Julien and gave him both her hands.

"My dear Julien," she exclaimed, "this is shocking! Run away, if you please, mother. I must see Julien for a moment alone."

The Duchess left the room. They both waited until the door was closed. Then she turned and faced him.

"I suppose it's all true?" she asked.

"Every word of it, Anne," he answered. "Please don't misunderstand the reason of my coming. I am absolutely a ruined man and I absolutely deserve everything that has come to me. But there was one thing I wanted to say to you before I went."

"There was also one thing," she remarked, looking at him intently, "which I intended to ask you, provided you gave me the opportunity."

"It is about Mrs. Carraby," he said firmly.

"So was my question," she murmured.

"The friendship between Mrs. Carraby and myself," Julien continued, "has been patent to every one for a great many years. I knew her long before I did you. It began, in fact, when we were little more than children.

E. Phillips Oppenheim

It finished - to-day. There is only one thing I want to say to you about it, and that is this. Our friendship was of that sort which is fairly well recognized and even approved of by the world in which we live. It contained, of course, certain elements of flirtation - I am not denying that. There was never at any time, however, anything in that friendship which made it an error even of taste on my part to ask you to become my wife."

She took his face between her hands and deliberately kissed him.

"That's just what I wanted to know, Julien," she declared. "Now shake hands, be off, and do the best you can for yourself. I wish you the best of luck, the very best. That's all we can say to one another, isn't it?"

"Quite all," he admitted.

"You are a dear, good fellow," she went on, "and I have been quite fond of you, although I think that I bored you now and then. I should have made you an excellent wife, perhaps a better one than I shall the next man who comes along. Don't stay any longer, there's a dear, because although I never pretended to have much heart, this sort of thing does upset one, you know, and I want to look my best to-night. Write me sometimes, if you will. I'd love to hear that you'd found some interest in life to help you gather up the threads. And here - this is for luck."

She took a little turquoise pin from her waistband and stuck it in his black tie. Then, before he could stop her, she touched the bell with one hand and gave him the other.

"Please kiss my fingers, Julien, and tell me I've behaved nicely."

He looked steadily into her eyes and then away out of the window, across the square. It was such a natural ending, this. It was foolish that his heart should shake, even for a second. And yet there had been one occasion - at Clonarty - when she had lain very close to him in his arms, and the moonlight had been falling through the pine trees in little dappled places around them, and the wind had been making faint music among the swinging boughs - for these few moments, at any rate, the other things had shone in her face. Were they illusions really, those moments of agitation, he wondered - simply one long, sensuous period passing like breath from a looking-glass and leaving nothing behind? He looked into her face. There was no sign there. Then he dropped the fingers which he had been holding. Women were wonderful!

"Do write," she begged, as she walked into the hall with him. "Dear me, what a strange-looking person you have with you in the taxicab!"

"He is a friend," Julien said quietly, "a journalist. I might say the same of the young man who is watching us from the drawing-room, Anne! Who is he?"

She made a little face at him and whispered in his ear.

"Semitic, as you see, and positively appalling. He is entirely mother's choice. He arrived ten minutes after the evening papers were out, but somehow or other I don't fancy that we shall make anything of him. It's young Harbord, you know."

E. Phillips Oppenheim

Julien made his effort. He touched her fingers once more in conventional fashion. He leaned towards her earnestly.

"My dear Anne," he said, "that young man has an income of at least a hundred thousand a year. Have you ever considered what a wonderful thing it is to possess an income like that? You could surround yourself with it like a halo. You could eat it, wear it, and breathe it every second of your life. You could even use it as a means of escaping as often as possible from the somewhat inevitable but highly objectionable adjunct who seems now to be peering at us through the door. Be a wise girl, Anne. An income like that doesn't depend upon discretions or indiscretions. Besides, as a matter of fact, I really do not think that that young man knows what it is to be indiscreet. Remember, I am quite serious. A hundred thousand a year should lift any man beyond the pale of criticism."

"Yes!" the girl replied, looking at him as he walked down the steps. "I shall remember. Good-bye!"

"We are getting on," Julien declared lightly, as he took his place in the taxicab. "Really, it is astonishing how much a man can get through in a day if he sets his mind to it. Is there any place where we could get a drink, do you think, Kendricks? I have just passed through a trying and affecting interview. I have said farewell to the lady who was to have been my wife. That sort of thing upsets one."

"You are behaving, my dear Julien," Kendricks admitted, "like a man of sense. In a moment or two we shall pass Véry's, on our way to the restaurant where I am going to entertain you at dinner. It will probably be such a dinner as you have never eaten before in your life! You will not need an *apéritif*. I am not sure, indeed, that it is not tempting providence and inviting indigestion to offer you a mixed vermouth here. However, come along. One experience more or less in such a day will not disturb you."

They entered the café and sat down at a small, marble-topped table. Julien lit a cigarette and Kendricks affected not to notice that the hand which held the match was shaking. A crowd of people, mostly foreigners, were sitting about the place. Julien, as he sipped his vermouth, noticed a familiar face nearly opposite him - a young, somewhat sandy-complexioned man, quietly dressed, insignificant, and yet with some sort of personality.

"I wonder who that fellow is?" he remarked. "I seem to know his face."

Kendricks looked incuriously across the room.

"One knows every one by sight in London," he said. "The fellow is probably a clerk in some office where you have been, or a salesman behind the counter at one of the shops you patronize. It's odd sometimes how a face will pursue you like that. That's a pretty little girl with whom he's shaking hands."

Julien watched the two idly for a moment. The man had risen to greet his newly-arrived companion, who was chattering to him in fluent French. All the time Julien was aware that now and then the former's eyes strayed over towards him. It was odd that, notwith-standing his somewhat disturbed state of mind, he was conscious of a distinct curiosity as to this young man's identity.

"Come along," Kendricks suggested. "We shan't get a table at all at the place where I am going to take you to dine, unless we are punctual."

They finished their vermouth and left the café. Kendricks knocked out the ashes from his pipe and leaned a little forward in the taxicab.

"We go now," he continued, "into a foreign land - foreign, at least, to you, my young Exquisite - the land of journalists, of foreigners, of hairdressers and anarchists, and cutthroats of every description. Nevertheless, we shall dine well, and if you will only drink enough of the chianti which I shall order, I can promise you a nap on your way to Dover. You look as though you could do with it."

Julien suddenly remembered that his eyes were hot, and almost simultaneously he felt the weight that was dragging down his heart. He laughed desperately.

"I'll eat your dinner, David," he promised, "and I'll do justice to your chianti. From what you tell me about our expedition, I should imagine that we are going into the land to which I shall soon belong."

"It's a wonderful country," Kendricks muttered, looking out of the window. "It may not be flowing exactly with milk and honey, but its sinews are supple and its blood is red. For absolute vitality, I'd back the Café l'Athénée against the Carlton any day. Here we are."

CHAPTER VI

AT THE CAFÉ L'ATHÉNÉE

The Café L'Athénée was in a narrow back street and consisted of a ground floor apartment of moderate size, and a number of small rooms, most of which were already crowded with diners. There were no smooth-faced *maîtres d'hôtel* to conduct new arrivals to a table, no lift to the upper rooms, no palm-lined stairways, or any of the modern appurtenances of restaurant life. Kendricks, taking the lead as an habitué, pushed his way up to the first floor, pushed his way past the hurrying and perspiring waiters, who did not even stop to answer questions, and finally pounced upon a table which was just being vacated by three other people. The two men sat down before the débris and waited patiently for its removal.

"Don't turn your nose up yet," Kendricks begged. "Wait till you've tasted the spaghetti. And don't look at the tablecloth as though it would bite you. They'll put a clean napkin over it directly and you'll forget all about those stains. This is where one takes off the kid gloves and deals with the realities of eating and drinking. I am inclined to think sometimes, Julien, as a humble admirer from a long way off, that you've worn those kid gloves a little too long."

Julien looked across at his friend. Kendricks was still smoking his pipe and he was evidently in earnest. It was obvious, too, that he had more to say.

"You know," he continued, loudly summoning a waiter and pointing to the table before them, "you know, Julien, I have always had this feeling about you. I think that life has been made a trifle too easy for you. You have slipped with so little effort into the polished places. You never had to take your coat and waistcoat off and try a rough-and-tumble struggle with life. No man is the worse for it. Prosperity and smooth-traveling along the easy ways, even though they come to one as the reward of brainwork, lead to a certain flabbiness in life, lead to many moments when you have to stop and ask whether things are worth while, lead sometimes, I think, to that curious neuroticism from which clever, successful people suffer as well as the butterflies of fashion. You are up against it now, Julien, real and hard. You don't feel that you've got a day to live that you care a snap of the fingers about. You look at what you think are the pieces of your life and you imagine yourself a gaunt spectator of what has been, gazing down at them, and you've quite made up your mind that it isn't a bit of good trying to collect the fragments. Such d - d nonsense, Julien! You may have made a jolly hash of things as a Cabinet Minister, but that isn't any reason why you shouldn't make a success of life as a man. Look here, Carlo," he added, addressing the waiter, "the table d'hôte dinner - every-thing, and serve it hot. Bring us fresh butter with our spaghetti, and a flask of chianti."

"Si, signor!" the man replied, gazing for a moment in wonder at this shock-headed individual who spoke his own language so perfectly.

Kendricks laid down the menu and glanced across the table at Julien's face with its slightly weary smile.

"Of course, I know how you're feeling now," he went on, - "rotten! - so would any one. Try and forget it, try and forget yourself. Look about you. What do these people do for a living, do you think? They weren't born with a title. There's no one in this room who went to Eton and Oxford, played cricket for their university, and lolled their way into life as you did. Look at them all. The thin chap in the corner is a barber, got a small shop of his own now. I go there sometimes for a shave. He lived on thirteen shillings a week for six years, while he saved the money to start for himself. It was touch and go with him afterwards. In three months he'd nearly lost the lot. He'd married a little wife who stood behind the counter and had worked almost as hard as he, but somehow or other the customers wouldn't come. Then she had a baby, was laid up for a time, he had to engage some one to take her place, and at that time he had about fifteen shillings left in the world. I used to be shaved there every day then. I knew all about it. I used to hear him, when he thought no one was listening, go and call a cheerful word up the stairs - 'Shop full of customers!' 'Sold another bottle of hair restorer!' or something of that sort. Then some one lent him a fiver, and, by Jove, he turned the corner! He's doing well now. That's his wife - the plump little woman who's straightening his tie. They come here every Wednesday night and they can afford it. Yet he was up against it badly once, Julien. That's right, look at him, be interested. He's a common-looking little beast, isn't he? - but he's got a stout heart."

"I think," Julien said, "that I could guess the name of the man who lent him the fiver."

"You'd be a mug if you couldn't," Kendricks retorted. "It's doing that sort of thing that helps you to smile sometimes when the knocks come. I tell you, Julien, some of the people - these small shopkeepers, especially - do have the devil of a fight to get their ounce of pleasure out of life. Nothing's made easy for them. They don't know anything about that big west-end world, with pleasures tuned up to the latest pitch, where you do even your work with every luxury at hand to make it easy. There's a little chap there - an Italian. See him? He's sitting by the side of the old man with the gray beard. That man's his father. They both landed over here with scarcely a copper. The young fellow worked like a slave - sixteen shillings a week I think he was getting, and he kept the old man on it. Then he lost his job, couldn't get another. The old man had to go to the workhouse, the young man slept on the Embankment, ate free soup, picked up scraps, lived on the garbage heap of life. He pulled himself together, though, got another job, improved it, saved a few shillings, drove up in a cab and took the old man out. Look at them now. He's got a little tailor's shop not a hundred yards from here, and somehow or other one or two people on the stage - they're a good-hearted lot - have taken him up He gets lots of work and brings the old man here now and then for a treat. How are you, Pietro?" he called across the room. "When are you going to send me that coat along?"

The young man grinned.

"Too many orders to make you that coat, sir," he declared.

Kendricks smiled.

"No one can deny that I need a new coat," he said. "I told Pietro when things were slack that he could make me one, but he gets lots of orders now. See the little girl in the corner? She's going out - no, she's going to stay here; they've found her room at that table. I suppose you'd turn your nose up at her because she has a lot too much powder on her cheeks, and you don't like that lace collar around her neck. It isn't clean, I know, and the make-up on her face is clumsy. Must be uncomfortable, too, but she's done her best. She's been dancing at the *Hippodrome* this afternoon, probably rehearsing afterwards. She's got an hour now before she goes back to the evening performance. She's taking the eighteenpenny dinner, you see. She'll get a glass of chianti free with it. I am in luck to-night. I can tell you about nearly all these people. Her name is Bessie Hazell - Sarah Ann Jinks, very likely, but that's what she calls herself, anyway. She married an acrobat two years ago and they started doing quite well. Then he got a cough, had to give up work, the doctors all shook their heads at him, wanted to tell him it was consumption. Bless you, she wouldn't listen to it! She got him down to Bournemouth somehow and they patched him up. He came back and started again, caught cold, and had another bad spell. Still, she wouldn't have it that there was anything serious the matter with him! He'd be all right, she said, if it weren't for the climate, and every night she danced, mind - danced twice a day. She's quite clever, they say - might have done well if she'd only herself to think of and could spare a little of her money for lessons. Not she! She sent him to Davos, paid for it somehow. He's back again now. He can't go on the stage, but he's got a light job somewhere. I don't know that he's earning anything particular. They've got a baby to keep, but they do it all right between them. She isn't pleasant to look at, is

E. Phillips Oppenheim

she? What's that matter? She's a bit of real life, anyhow."

"Why didn't you bring me here before, Kendricks?" Julien asked.

The man leaned back and laughed.

"Ask yourself that question, not me," he replied. "You - Sir Julien Portel, caricatured as the best-dressed man in the House of Commons, member of the most fashionable clubs, brilliant debater, successful politician, future Prime Minister, and all that sort of twaddle. You were living too far up in the clouds, my friend, to come down here. You see, I am not offering you much sympathy, Julien. I don't think you need it. You were soaring up to the skies just because of your gifts and your position and your opportunities. You are down now. Well, you're thundering sorry for yourself. I don't know that I'm sorry for you. I'll tell you in ten years' time. By Jove, here's your sandy-headed little friend!"

The man, with the girl upon his arm, had entered the room and had taken seats at a table in the corner, for which, apparently, they had been waiting. Julien looked at them curiously.

"Why," he exclaimed suddenly, leaning across the table, "I remember him now! He's at the shop - I mean he's an Intelligence man."

Kendricks nodded.

"Just the sort of inconspicuous-looking person who could go anywhere without being noticed."

"I recollect him quite well," Julien continued. "It's not in my department, of course, but I remember being told he was a very useful little beggar."

"I should say, without a doubt," Kendricks declared, "that he was at present working hard for the safety and welfare of the British Empire. If you've suddenly recognized the man, I'll tell you who the girl is. She's a manicurist at the Milan."

Julien looked round and watched them for a moment curiously. Again he noticed that his interest in the young man was at least reciprocated.

"The fellow has recognized me, of course," he said. "You know, Kendricks, I remember two or three years ago a most amazing item of news was brought to us - one that made a real difference, too - through a manicurist."

"Shouldn't be a bit surprised," Kendricks replied.

"Things drop out in the most unexpected places, as you'd find out if you'd been a journalist."

"She was sent for into the room of some princess - at Claridge's, I think it was, or one of the west-end hotels - and while she was there a man came from one of the inner rooms and said a few words in Russian. The girl had been in St. Petersburg and understood. It made quite a difference. I remember the story."

"Might have been the same man and the same manicurist," Kendricks remarked.

Julien shook his head.

"There was trouble about the manicurist," he said, "and she had to leave the country. She's in South Africa now."

"I can't say that I like the appearance of the fellow," Kendricks declared. "Don't funk the soup, Julien - it's better than it looks. He's a slimy-looking sort of chap. I have a theory that the modern sort of Secret Service agent ought to be a person like myself - breezy and obvious. Julien, if that girl doesn't stop gazing at you sideways, you'll be in trouble with your late employee."

Julien looked across at the opposite table. The girl, as he had noticed before, was stealing frequent glances at him. For some reason or other, she seemed anxious to attract his attention.

"Quite a conquest!" Kendricks murmured. "Drink some more of that chianti, man, and bring some color to your cheeks. There's a charming little manicurist wants to flirt with you. What teeth and what a smile!"

"Considering that she has been listening to my history for the last quarter of an hour, I imagine that her interest is of a less sentimental nature," Julien said. "I have probably been pointed out to her as the biggest fool in Christendom."

"Not you," Kendricks declared. "I assure you that I am a critic in such matters. She looks when the young man who is with her is engaged upon his dinner, or speaking to the waiter. I am not positive, even, that she wants to flirt, Julien. I think she wants to say something to you."

Julien laughed.

"What shall I do? Present myself? Bah!" he added, almost fiercely. "I wish the girl would keep her black eyes to herself. I want to tell you this, Kendricks. You've talked some splendid common sense to me without going out of your way to do it. I am not going to whine, now or at any other time, but as long as I live I never want anything more to do with a woman. That sounds about the most futile and empty-headed thing a man can say - I know that. But there it is. I tell you the very thought of them makes me shudder. They're like pampered, highly-groomed animals, with their mouths open for the tit-bits of life. They have to be fed with whatever food it may be they crave for, and that's the end of it."

Kendricks motioned with his head across the room to where the little woman with the blackened eyebrows was eating her dinner.

"What about that?" he asked.

"I don't know anything about that sort," Julien admitted. "What you told me sounded like one of the things you read of in newspapers and never believe. I don't believe it. Mind you, I don't say it's false, but I don't believe it because I have never spoken to the woman whom I could imagine capable of such unselfishness. If I patch up the pieces again, Kendricks," he added, and his face was suddenly very dark and very set - the face of an older man, "whatever cement I use, it won't be the cement of love or any sentiment whatsoever connected with women."

Kendricks nodded.

"It's my belief," he began, then he stopped short. "Julien," he continued kindly, "you're nothing but a big baby. You think you've moved in the big places. So you have, in a way. But there was a hideous mistake about your life. You've never had to build. No one can climb who doesn't build first. These ready-made ladders don't count. Now," he added, dropping his voice and glancing quickly across the room, "you will have an opportunity to put into force your new and magnificent principles of misogyny. Our little sandy-headed friend has been summoned from the room. I saw the *commissionaire* come up and whisper in his ear. Mademoiselle is writing a note. A hundred to one it is to you!"

Julien frowned. He, too, turned his head, and he met the girl's eyes. She was looking at him curiously. It was not the look of the woman who invites so much as the look of the woman who appeals for an understanding, who has something to say. She smiled ever so faintly and touched with her finger the scrap of paper which she thrust into the waiter's hand. Then she bent once more over her plate. The man came across to Julien.

"For you, monsieur," he announced, and laid it by the side of Julien's plate.

"Read it," Kendricks whispered across the table, for he had been quick to see his companion's first impulse.

"Why should I?" Julien said coldly. "I have no desire to have anything to do with that young person. What can she have to say to me?"

"Nevertheless, read it," Kendricks repeated.

Julien unrolled the scrap of paper with reluctant fingers. There were only a few words written there in hasty pencil:

Monsieur, there is a friend of mine whom you must see. Call at number 17, Avenue de St. Paul and ask for Madame Christophor. Do not attempt to speak to me. This is for your good.

Julien's fingers were upon the note to destroy it, but again Kendricks stopped him.

"Julien," he insisted, "don't be an idiot. The little girl knows who you are. She can't imagine that you are in the humor just now for flirtations. Put the note in your pocket and call. One can't tell. Your life has been so artificial that you've probably left off believing in any adventures outside story-books. My life leads me into different places and I never neglect an opportunity like that."

"A sister manicurist, I expect," Julien replied scornfully; "a palmist, or some creature of that sort."

Kendricks hammered upon the table for the waiter.

"One takes one's chances," he agreed, "but I do not think that the little girl over there would send you upon a fool's errand. There are other things in life, you know, Julien. You carry in your head political secrets which would be worth a great deal. There may be danger in that call."

Julien looked at him with faintly curling lip.

"Tell me exactly what you mean?" he asked.

Kendricks shrugged his shoulders. The waiter had arrived and he gave him a vociferous order.

"Listen," he said, "I could hand you out a hundred surmises and each one of them ought to be sufficient to induce you to keep that appointment. You leave here - shall we say under a cloud? - presumably disgusted with life, with the Government which gives you no second chance, with your country which discards you. And you have been Under-Secretary of State for Foreign Affairs. Can't you conceive that this woman on whom you are to call might make suggestions to you which would at least be amusing? Don't look so incredulous, Julien. Remember you've lived in the stilted places. I haven't. I believe in the underground world. You must know for yourself that a great deal of the truth leaks up through the gratings."

"That is true enough," Julien admitted, "but somehow or other -"

"Let it go at that," Kendricks interrupted. "Promise me that you will call at that address."

Julien laughed.

"Yes, I'll call!" he promised.

"Then look across at the little girl and nod," Kendricks suggested. "She's watching you all the time anxiously. The man hasn't come back yet."

Julien turned his head half unwillingly. The girl was leaning across the table, her eyes fixed steadfastly upon his. Her lips were parted, her eyebrows were slightly raised, as though in question. She had been holding a menu before her face to shield her from the casual observer, but the moment Julien turned his head she lowered it. He inclined his head slowly. A curious expression of relief took the place of that appearance of strained anxiety. Her face became natural once more. She laid down the menu and took a sip of wine from her glass. Kendricks looked across at Julien and raised his glass to his lips.

"We will drink, my dear Julien," he said, "to your visit to Madame Christophor, and what may come of it!"

CHAPTER VII

COFFEE FOR THREE

"Admit," Kendricks insisted, "that you have dined well?"

"I have dined amply," Julien replied.

Kendricks frowned.

"I am not satisfied," he declared.

"The *entrecôte* was wonderful, also the omelette," Julien admitted. "I will supplement 'amply' with 'well,' if you wish, but the insistent note about this dinner is certainly its amplitude. I have not eaten so much for ages."

Kendricks was filling his pipe.

"Cigars or cigarettes you must order for yourself," he said. "I know nothing of them. The coffee is before you. I will be frank with you - it is not good. The brandy, however, is harmless."

Julien lit a cigarette and leaned back in his chair. Just then the sandy young man re-entered the room. He hastened to his place, but instead of resuming it stood by the side of the girl, talking. He seemed to be suggesting some course of which she disapproved, pointing to her unfinished dinner. Kendricks nodded his head slowly.

"The young man has to leave," he remarked. "He wishes mademoiselle to accompany him. She declines. He is annoyed. Behold, a lover's tiff! He has placed the money for the dinner upon the table. He shakes her hand very politely. Behold, he goes! Mademoiselle shrugs her shoulders. She orders from the menu. She remains alone. My dear Julien, if you will you can prosecute your conquest. The young man has departed."

Julien glanced across the room. He met the girl's eyes and once again he saw in them that curious, almost impersonal invitation.

"She wants something," Kendricks declared. "I am going over to see what it can be. Carlo!"

He summoned the waiter and asked him a question quickly in Italian.

"The man says that her companion is not returning," he remarked, rising. "I am going to interview the young lady."

Julien shrugged his shoulders.

"As you will."

Kendricks crossed the room, his pipe still in his hand. The girl watched him come, for a moment, and then looked down upon the tablecloth. She was at the end of a table laid for four or five people, but only two men were left at the extreme end.

"Mademoiselle," Kendricks said, "my friend thanks you for your message. His curiosity, however, is piqued. Is there not an opportunity now for explaining further?"

She regarded her questioner a little doubtfully.

"Who are you?" she asked.

Kendricks sighed.

"My dear young lady," he answered, "I flattered myself that I possessed a personality which no one could mistake. Furthermore, I am a constant patron here."

"I have never been here in my life before," the girl told him.

"Then your ignorance shall be pardoned," Kendricks declared. "My name is David Kendricks. I am a journalist. I ought to be an editor, but the fact remains that I am a mere collector of news, a bringer together of those trifles which go to make such prints as these," he added, touching her evening paper, "interesting."

"A journalist," she repeated, glancing up at him. "Yes! I might have guessed that. Are you a friend of Sir Julien Portel?"

"I think I may call myself a friend," Kendricks admitted. "We were at college together."

She rose composedly to her feet.

"Then I will take my coffee at your table," she decided. "You may present me. I am Mademoiselle Senn."

Kendricks hesitated.

"You may not find my friend in the most amiable of moods," he began.

The girl waved her hand.

"It is to be explained," she declared. "To tell you the truth, I was surprised to see him even in so out of the way a restaurant as this."

"He leaves to-night for the Continent," Kendricks told her.

"So I heard," the girl replied. "Come."

Sir Julien watched their approach and the frown upon his aristocratic forehead, though thin, was distinct. Kendricks, however, took no notice of it, and the girl pretended that she had not seen.

"Julien," the former announced, holding a chair for mademoiselle, "I am permitted the pleasure of presenting you to Mademoiselle Senn, who already knows your name. Mademoiselle sent you a message a few minutes ago. If she is good-natured, she may choose to explain it. If not, what does it matter? Mademoiselle will take her coffee with us."

Julien rose to his feet and bowed very slightly.

"We have only a moment or two to spare," he said, "as I am leaving London to-night."

She looked at him and smiled oddly. She was a very typical young Frenchwoman of her class - round-faced, with trim little figure, black eyes, and smart but simple hat; not really good-looking except for the depth of her clear eyes, and yet with a command of her person and movements which was not without its charm.

"Monsieur is not too gallant," she murmured, "but one is inclined to forgive him. If I may take my coffee, I will go. Monsieur has promised me that he will call and see Madame?"

"Your friend in Paris?" Julien remarked, a little doubtfully.

"Ah! I dare not call her that," the girl continued. "Madame is different. But I know that it is her wish that you call, and I know that it would be for your welfare."

"Is it necessary," Julien asked coldly, "that you should be so mysterious? After all, you know, the thing, on the face of it, is impossible. Madame probably does not know of my existence, and why should you take it for granted that I am going abroad?"

"Oh, la, la!" the girl interrupted. "But you amuse one! Madame knows everything which she desires to know. As to your going to France, monsieur over there," she added, moving her head backwards, "told me so some minutes ago."

"And how the dickens did he know, and what right had he to talk about my affairs?" Julien demanded, with all an Englishman's indignation at his movements having been discussed by strangers.

"I suppose that it is his business to know those things," she replied, sipping her coffee. "He is a very mysterious young man. He takes a room sometimes at the Milan Hotel and he sends for me to manicure his hands. Then he asks me very clever questions and I look down and I give him - very clever answers. Then he thinks, perhaps, that his methods are not quite the best, and he sends me a great box of chocolates, some stalls for the theatre, some flowers - why not? Then he comes again to be manicured and he asks more questions, but I know so little. Then sometimes, not very often, he brings me out to dine. Imagine for yourself, monsieur," she went on, with a wave of the hand, "the excitement, the wonder of all this to a poor French girl! And again he asks questions, but again I know so little. And then, in the midst of our dinner, his employer has sent for him. He has to go on a journey. It is sad, is it not? He would like me to go with him to the station, to see him off, but I -" she shrugged her shoulders. "Why should I leave before I have finished my dinner? In truth, he wearies me, that young man. I do not think, Sir Julien Portel, that Englishmen are very clever."

"As a race," Julien declared grimly, "I agree with you. I think that most men are unutterable fools. But this young admirer of yours - what are these questions which he asks you so often, and what business is he in that he should be compelled to leave you to hurry away?"

"Ah, monsieur!" she answered, "it is you now who ask questions. Why should I tell you, indeed, more than I tell him?"

Julien smiled.

E. Phillips Oppenheim

"Perhaps because it was a matter of moment to him whether you replied or not, whereas, frankly, I only ask you these questions out of the idlest curiosity."

"Also a little," she remarked, "to make conversation, is it not so? Very well, then, Sir Julien Portel, let me tell you this. If you do not know who that young man is, I do not wonder that you find it necessary to catch the nine o'clock train to the Continent to-night and to give up that delightful work of yours, where you try to keep the peace between all these wicked nations, and to get the lion's share of everything for your great, greedy country. If you do not know who that young man is, you have not the head for detail, the memory, which goes to the making of politicians."

Julien leaned back in his chair and laughed, softly but genuinely. Even Kendricks seemed a little taken aback.

"Upon my word!" the latter exclaimed. "This is an interesting young person! Mademoiselle, I congratulate you. You have the gifts."

"Interesting, indeed!" Julien agreed, sitting up in his place. "Mademoiselle, to save my reputation with you I must confess. I do know who the young man is. He is in the Intelligence Branch of the Secret Service of the British Foreign Office - Number 3 Department."

The girl nodded several times.

"What you call it I do not know," she said. "He is just one of those ordinary people who go about to collect little items of information for your Government. That is why I have received from him four pounds of chocolate, at least a sovereign's worth of roses, four stalls for the theatre - which I do believe that he had given to him because they were for plays that no one goes to see, and to-night a dinner - such a dinner, messieurs, with chianti that burned my tongue!"

"This," Kendricks declared, "is quite a bright young lady! Mademoiselle, I trust that we shall become better acquainted."

"And in the meantime," Julien inquired, "what are these wonderful items of information which you carry with you, and which this unfortunate young man fails so utterly to elicit?"

"Ah! well," she sighed, "I am by profession a manicurist, but some freak of nature gave me the power of keeping my mouth closed, of looking as though I knew a good deal, but of saying so little. Now, messieurs, what could a poor girl know in the way of secrets for which that young man would get credit if he had succeeded in eliciting them? What could I know, indeed? I sit on my little stool and sometimes there are great people who give me their hands, and they are thoughtful. And sometimes I ask questions and they answer me absently, because, after all, what does it matter? - a manicurist from the shop downstairs, earning her thirty shillings a week, and anxious to be agreeable for the sake of her tip! And then sometimes while I am there they dictate letters, or a caller comes, or the telephone rings. One does not think of the manicure girl at such a time. Fortunately, there are some like me who know so well how to keep silent, to say nothing, to be dumb."

"The methods of that young man," Kendricks asserted, "were crude. Now, young lady, consider my position. I represent a power greater than the power of Governments. I represent a Press which is greedy for personal news. Have you trimmed lately the nails of a duchess? If so, tell me what she wore, her favorite oath, any trifling expression likely to be of interest to the British public! And instead of roses I will send you carnations; instead of dead-head tickets I will take you myself to the *Gaiety*; instead of a dinner at the Café l'Athénée, I will take you to supper at the Milan."

"Your friend," mademoiselle declared, smiling at Julien, "is quite an intelligent person. I like him very much. But I wish he would not smoke that pipe and I should like to buy him a necktie."

"Julien," Kendricks sighed, "the Bohemian has no chance against such a model as you."

"I do not think," she remarked, looking Julien in the eyes, "that Sir Julien Portel cares very much for women - just now, at any rate."

Julien frowned. He absolutely declined to answer the challenge in her dark eyes.

"Mademoiselle," he said, "when I present myself to this Madame Christophor, do I deliver any message from you? Do I explain my visit?"

The girl shook her head slowly.

"It will not be necessary," she told him. "Madame Christophor will know all about you. She will be expecting you."

He smiled scornfully.

"It would be a pity to disappoint a lady with such a remarkable knack of foretelling things. Supposing, however, I change my mind and visit St. Petersburg instead?"

She raised her hands - an expressive gesture.

"There is no Madame Christophor in St. Petersburg. I think that you will be very ill-advised if you go there. Many of the elements which go to the making of life wait for you in Paris. In St. Petersburg you would be a stranger. The life is not there."

She rose to her feet briskly.

"Good night, Monsieur le Bohemian!" she said. "Remember that you have only to accept my little gift of a necktie, to let me take you to a coiffeur whom I know of, and I will dine with you when you choose. Good night, Sir Julien! I think I envy you."

Julien laughed. The idea seemed odd to him.

"I fancy you would be in a minority, mademoiselle," he declared.

"At least," she reminded him, "you are going to see Madame Christophor!"

She nodded and left them a little abruptly. Kendricks paid their bill and they descended into the street a few minutes later. The *commissionaire* called a taxi for them and they drove toward Charing-Cross.

"My friend," Kendricks said, "if I had you here for another week, cut off from your old life, I'd show you some things that would astonish you. It's good fortune and these well-ordered ways that keep a man a prig, even after he's finished with Oxford. The man who lives in the clouds of Mayfair knows nothing of the real life of this city."

"Some day I'll come back and be your pupil," Julien promised. "You're a good fellow, David. You've given me something to think about, at any rate, something to think about besides my own misfortunes."

"That's just what I set out to do," Kendricks declared. "There are plenty of bigger tragedies than yours loose in the world. Watch the people, Julien - the people whom such men as you glance over or through as of no account, the common people, the units of life. Strip them bare and they aren't so very different, you know. Try and feel for a moment what they feel. Look at the little dressmaker there, going over to Paris to buy models, hanging on to her husband's arm. She's probably got a shop in the suburbs and this trip is a daring experiment. See how earnestly they are talking about it. I don't think that they have too easy a time to make ends meet. Do you see that old lady there, clinging to her daughter? How she hates to part with her! She is going to a situation, without a doubt, and Paris isn't too easy a place for a girl with hair and eyes like hers. In her heart I think that the old lady is remembering that. Then look at that little old man with the tired eyes, carrying his two valises himself to save the hire of a porter. Can't you tell by the air of him that he has had an unsuccessful business journey? Poor fellow! It's a hard struggle for life, Julien, if you get in the wrong row. You've no one dependent upon you, you don't know the worst agony that can wring a man's heart.... Got your ticket and everything, eh? And that looks like your servant. Are you taking him with you?"

Julien shook his head.

"I shall have to do without a manservant. I never had much money, you know, David."

"So much the better," Kendricks declared heartily. "It gives you a final chance. The gutters of the world are full of good fellows who have been ruined through stepping into a sufficient income."

They found a carriage and arranged Julien's few belongings. Presently mademoiselle's companion came hurrying up the platform, followed by a porter carrying his dressing-case. A short distance behind, mademoiselle, too, was walking, humming to herself.

"Company to Boulogne for you, Julien," Kendricks pointed out. "Your little man from Number 3 Branch is on your track."

Julien smiled. The young man never glanced towards their carriage as he passed, but mademoiselle, who was still a few steps behind, made a wry face at Kendricks.

"I believe she knew that he was going across," the latter declared.

"I wonder if he, too," Julien murmured, "has to call on Madame Christophor?"

The whistle sounded. Kendricks put out his great hands.

"Good luck to you, Julien, old fellow!" he said. "Stand

up to life like a man and look it in the face. I tell you I haven't been gassing to-night. I'd hate to pose as a moralist, but I do believe that misfortunes are often blessings in disguise. And I tell you I've a sort of faith in that little French girl. She gives one to think, as she herself remarked. Look up Madame Christophor. Don't be surprised to see me at any moment. I generally turn up in Paris every few weeks or so. Good luck to you!"

Julien leaned out of the window and waved his hand to Kendricks as the train moved slowly around the curve. The last face he saw upon the platform, however, was the face of mademoiselle.

CHAPTER VIII

IN PARIS

For exactly a month Julien disappeared. At the end of that time, looking very brown, a shade thinner, and possessed of a knowledge of the older towns of Normandy which would not have disgraced a guidebook, he arrived one cold, gray morning at the Gare du Nord. During all this time he had scarcely seen one familiar face. It was an unpleasant shock for him, as he waited for his baggage in the Customs House, to realize that he was being watched from behind a pile of trunks by the little man who had shown so much interest in him at the Café l'Athénée on the night he had left England. The sight somehow annoyed him. He crossed the room and accosted his late subordinate.

"What is your name?" he asked coldly. "You are in the Intelligence Department, I believe?"

"My name is Foster, Sir Julien," the young man replied, after a moment's hesitation.

"What are you doing over here?"

The young man hesitated.

"You will excuse me, Sir Julien," he said slowly, "but I am responsible only to the permanent officials in control of my office. Besides, - "

"You can tell me at least how long you have been in Paris?" Julien interrupted.

"Since the night, Sir Julien, when you came as far as Boulogne."

"May I ask," Julien demanded, "whether I am going to be subject to your espionage?"

The young man whose name was Foster looked blandly at a pile of luggage which was just arriving.

"I am not at liberty, Sir Julien," he said, "to explain my instructions."

Julien shrugged his shoulders.

"Do as you like, of course. At the same time, let me tell you that you irritate me. Keep out of my sight as much as possible. It will be better for you."

Julien turned and left him there, declared his luggage, and was driven to a quiet hotel in the Rue de Rivoli. There he had a bath, changed his clothes, and strolled up the Champs Élysées towards the Bois. The sun had come out and the avenue was crowded with auto-mobiles and carriages. He walked steadily on until he reached the first of the cafés in the Bois. He took a chair and watched the crowd. A peculiar sensation of loneliness oppressed him, a loneliness of which he had been scarcely conscious during this last month's wanderings among the quiet places. Paris had seemed so different to him on his last visit. He was surrounded by friends and people who were anxious to become his friends. He was in charge of a difficult mission which he was conscious of conducting with skill. Everywhere he was meeting English people of his own order, all delighted to see him, all pleased with his notice. His few days in Paris were merely a change in the kaleidoscope from London. The life - everything else - was the same. This time he was like a man cast upon a desert island. He sat at his little table, sipping a glass of vermouth, and conscious that no man in Paris had fewer friends. The clubs were closed to him, there were no official visits to pay, no calls to make, no familiar faces to look for. He was a man who had had his day, a man disgraced, a man in whom the people had lost faith, who was dead politically and socially. He thought his position over carefully from every point of view. It was ruin, utter and complete. He had disclosed a valuable political secret to a woman who had not hesitated to make use of it. Nothing could be more ignoble. He tried to fancy for himself some new life under altered conditions, but everywhere he seemed to run up against some possibility, some combination of circumstances which included a share in things which were absolutely finished. His brain refused to fashion for him the thought of any life which could leave outside everything which had been of account to him up till now. Even in London, among the working classes, it might have been easier. He remembered those few vivid speeches of Kendricks'. What a gift the man had! Always he seemed to see big things in life smouldering underneath the lives of these ordinary people - big things unsuspected, invisible. There was nothing of the sort to be found here. The only Paris Julien had ever known was closed to him. Paris the vicious repelled him instinctively. He was

E. Phillips Oppenheim

here, he had even looked forward to coming, but now that he had arrived there was nothing for him to do. After all, he had better have found some far distant corner in Switzerland or Italy. There was no club for him to go to, no interest in perusing the newspapers, no visits from ambassadors to think about. The puzzles of his daily life were ended. There was nothing for him to do where he was but to eat and to drink and to sleep!

He lunched at a restaurant of which he had never heard before, and there, to his anger, almost at the next table, he found Foster. With a trace of his former imperiousness of manner, he summoned him. The young man rose, after a moment's hesitation, and obeyed the mandate.

"What are you doing here?" Julien demanded.

"Lunching, sir," the young man replied. "The place has been recommended to me. I do not know Paris well."

"You lie," Julien declared. "Unless you knew Paris well, you wouldn't be here for Number 3 Branch. Tell me, are you still watching me?"

"That is a question, Sir Julien, which, as I said before, I am not at liberty to answer."

Julien drew a little breath between his teeth.

"Look here," he continued, "I want to warn you that I am a bad-tempered man. You can write home if you like and tell them that you met me coming out of the German Embassy and the Russian Embassy and the Italian Embassy, with a list of prices in my hands for different pieces of information. Is that what you're afraid of, eh?"

"Sir Julien," the young man answered, "I have to make reports only. It is not my business to question the necessity for them."

Julien laughed. After all, the little man was right.

"Well, perhaps I do need looking after. Is there any particular place where you would like me to dine? I don't want to bring you out into the byways if I can help it."

The young man excused himself politely. Julien finished his luncheon and then took a carriage back to his hotel. He found half-a-dozen visiting cards in his box and glanced at them eagerly. Every one of them was from the representative of a newspaper. He tore them into pieces, left a curt message for their bearers, and went up to his room. A telegram was lying upon his bureau. He tore it open and read:

Call on Madame Christophor this afternoon.

He frowned and threw the unsigned telegram into a wastepaper-basket.

"That decides it," he muttered to himself. "I will not call upon Madame Christophor."

Nevertheless, he changed into calling attire and presently strolled out once more into the sunshine. From habit he turned into the Champs Élysées. The sight of a group of acquaintances drove him into a side street. He walked for a short distance and then paused to see his whereabouts. He was in the Avenue de St.

Paul. He studied the numbers. Exactly opposite was Number 17. He stood there, gazing at the house, and at that moment a large automobile glided up to the front door. The footman sprang down and a lady descended, passing within a few feet of him. She was tall, very elegant, and her eyes, gaining, perhaps, a little color from the pallor of her cheeks, were the most beautiful shade of violet-blue which he had ever seen. She was a woman whom it was impossible not to notice. Julien stood quite still, watching her. The footman who had stepped down in advance had rung the bell, and the postern door already stood open. The lady did not at once enter. She was looking at Julien. This, then, was Madame Christophor! He was aware at that moment of two distinct impressions - one was that she knew perfectly well who he was; the other that at any cost, however *gauche* it might seem, it was better for him to ignore the faint gleam of recognition which already lent the dawn of a gracious smile to her lips.

The woman was certainly expecting him to speak. Every second her hesitation seemed more purposeful. Julien, however, with an effort which was almost savage, set his teeth and walked on. She looked after him for a moment and began to laugh softly to herself. Julien walked steadily on till he had reached the corner of the street. Then he turned away abruptly and without glancing around. He was angry with himself, angry at the sound of that faint, musical laugh. He had quite made up his mind not to call upon Madame Christophor. It would, in fact, now be impossible. He would never be able to explain his avoidance of her.

He was in a part of Paris of which he knew nothing, but he walked on aimlessly, anxious only to escape the vicinity of the clubs and of the fashionable thoroughfares. Suddenly he was conscious that an automobile had drawn up close to the curbstone by his side. The footman sprang lightly down and accosted him.

"Monsieur," he announced, "Madame Christophor has sent her automobile. She would be happy to receive you at once."

Julien glanced inside the automobile. It was daintily upholstered in white. A pile of cushions lay on the seat, there was a glove upon the floor, the faint fragrance of roses seemed to steal out. Almost he fancied that the woman's face was there, leaning a little towards him, with the curious smile about the lips, the wonderful eyes glowing into his. Then he set his teeth.

"You had better inform your mistress," he said, "that there is some mistake. I have not the honor of the acquaintance of Madame Christophor. You have followed the wrong person."

The man hesitated. He seemed perplexed.

"But, monsieur," he persisted, "madame pointed you out herself. It was only because of a block in the roadway that we were not able to catch you up before. We have, indeed, never lost sight of you."

Julien shook his head. "Pray assure madame," he said, "of my most respectful regrets. I have not the honor of her acquaintance."

He walked on. The two men sat for a moment on the box of the car, watching him. Then they turned around and the car disappeared. Julien jumped into a little carriage and drove back to his hotel. As he passed through into the office, the clerk leaned forward.

"Monsieur is desired upon the telephone," he announced.

Julien frowned.

"Who is it?"

The man shrugged his shoulders and pointed to the booth. Julien hesitated. Then he stepped inside and held the receiver to his ear.

"Who is this?" he asked.

A very slow, musical voice answered him. He never for a moment had a doubt as to whose it might be.

"Is this Sir Julien Portel?"

"This is Julien Portel," he answered. "Who is it speaking?"

"I am Henriette Christophor," the voice replied. "I had word from England, Sir Julien Portel, that you were coming to see me."

"I shall do myself that honor," Julien assured her, "before I leave Paris."

"You were not polite," the voice continued, "that you did not come this afternoon."

"Madame," Julien said, "I am not here to make acquaintances. It is true that I promised to call upon you; I do not know why, I do not know whom I promised, I do not know for what reason I was asked to come. Since I have promised, however, and you are kind enough to desire it, I will come."

"And why not now?" the voice persisted. "You are alone in Paris, are you not? I have something to say to you, something which is best said quickly."

Julien hesitated.

"You will come?" the voice begged. "My automobile will be at your hotel in ten minutes. You shall come, and if you dislike, after all, to make that call, you shall drive with me, if you prefer it. Monsieur, if you please!"

"I will be ready," Julien answered.

He hung up the receiver and walked out into the hall. He was angry with himself because only an hour ago he had told himself that he would not make that call. He was angry, too, because the fact of his making it or not making it had assumed a ridiculous importance in his eyes.

He walked to the bar and filled his case with cigarettes. Then he took up a monthly magazine and read. His own official resignation was dealt with in a political article of some significance. It interested him curiously. One sentence in particular he read several times:

It is not our desire to play the alarmist, but we would point out to Great Britain that she may at any time within the next few weeks be called upon to face a situation of great gravity, and we cannot help expressing our regret that when that time comes the country should be deprived of the advice, sound judgment and experience of a man who, notwithstanding his youth, has already made his mark in European politics.

Julien flung the paper down. What that situation might be he knew, perhaps, better than any man!

The porter hurried up to him.

"There is a lady outside who inquires for monsieur," he announced.

CHAPTER IX

MADAME CHRISTOPHOR

She held out an ungloved hand to him as he stepped up to the automobile. Having gained her ends, she was disposed to be merciful.

"This is very kind of you, Sir Julien," she murmured. "I really was most anxious to have you visit me. Will you step in, please, and drive with me a little way? One converses so easily and it would perhaps amuse you more than to sit in my rooms."

"You are very thoughtful," Julien replied. "I will come, with pleasure, if I may."

He seated himself by her side.

"You must put your stick and gloves in the rack there," she continued, "and make yourself quite comfortable. We drive a short distance into the country, if you do not mind."

"I am entirely at your service," he answered.

He was firmly determined to remain wholly unimpressed by whatever she said or did, yet, even in those first few moments, the sweetness of her voice and the

E. Phillips Oppenheim

delicate correctness of her English sounded like music to him. There was a suspicion of accent, too, which puzzled him.

"We are not altogether strangers, you know," she went on. "I have seen you before several times. I think the last time that you were in Paris you sat in a box at Auteuil with some friends of mine."

Somehow or other, he was conscious of a certain embarrassment. He was not at his best with this woman, and he found it hard, almost impossible, to escape from commonplaces.

"It was my misfortune that I did not see you," he remarked. "My visit was rather a momentous one. I dare say I paid less attention than usual to my surroundings."

"Tell me," she asked, "it was my little friend Emilie, was it not, who persuaded you to come and see me?"

"It was a little girl with whose name, even, I was unacquainted," Julien replied. "I must admit that I scarcely took her request seriously. I could not conceive anything which you might have to say which could justify the intrusion of a perfect stranger."

"But you," she reminded him, "are not a perfect stranger. You have been a public man. You see, I am not afraid of hurting you because I think that you will soon get over that little sensitiveness. I know all about you - everything. You trusted a woman. Ah! monsieur, it is dangerous, that."

"Madame," he said, looking into her wonderful eyes,

"one makes that mistake once, perhaps, in a lifetime - never again."

"The woman who deceives," she sighed, "makes it so difficult for all those who come after! I suppose already in your mind I figure as a sort of adventuress, is it not so?"

"Certainly, madame," he answered calmly. "It never occurred to me to doubt but that you were something of the sort."

She half closed her eyes and laughed softly to herself, moving her head like a child, as though from sheer pleasure.

"It is delicious, this frankness!" she exclaimed. "Ah! what a pity that you did not come before that other woman had destroyed all your faith! We might, perhaps, have been friends. Who can tell?"

"It is possible," he assented.

"So you believe that I am an adventuress," she continued. "You think that I sent for you probably to try and steal one by one all those wonderful secrets which I suppose you have stored up at the back of your head. One cannot be Under-Secretary of State for Foreign Affairs without knowing things. Keep them to yourself, Sir Julien. I ask you no questions."

"Then why," he demanded, "did you insist upon this visit from me, and why did the little manicurist, who is a perfect stranger to me, insist also that I should come to you?"

She smiled, and looked down at her hands for a moment.

"Now if I answer all your questions, Sir Julien," she said, "you will have no more curiosity left, and when your curiosity is gone, perhaps some measure of your interest may go, too. Can you not bring yourself to believe that I may have had personal reasons for desiring your acquaintance?"

"Madame," he answered, "no! I cannot bring myself to believe that."

Again she laughed.

"I think," she declared, "that it is your candor which makes you Englishmen so attractive. Do you believe that I am a dangerous person, Sir Julien?"

He looked at her coldly and dispassionately.

"I think," he decided, "that you might be very dangerous indeed to a susceptible person."

"But not to you?"

"Certainly not to me," he admitted. "As you have already told me, it is within your knowledge that I am paying the price for having trusted a woman."

She nodded.

"It is a fine sort of ruin, after all. Not to trust is generally proof of a mean and doubting disposition."

"You are probably right, madame," he agreed. "Is it

permitted to remind you that we have been together for some time and you have not yet enlightened me as to your reasons for seeking my acquaintance?"

"Can't you believe that it was a whim?" she asked.

"No!"

"Remember that I saw you when you were here before," she persisted.

"I have no recollection of having met you."

"Yet I can tell you nearly all that you did on that last visit of yours. You dined one night at the Embassy, one night at the Travelers' Club with a party of four, one night with the Minister - Courcelles. You were two hours with him on the afternoon of the day you dined with him. You managed to snatch an hour at the races and to lunch at the Pré Catelan on your way. You lunched, I believe, with Monsieur le Duc de St. Simon and his friends."

"Your knowledge of my movements," he declared, "is very flattering. It suggests an interest in me, I admit, but I have yet to be convinced that that interest is in any way personal."

She looked at him from under the lids of her eyes.

"What is it, Sir Julien, that you possess, then, which you fear that I might steal?"

He returned her gaze boldly. "I am a discarded Minister," he said. "I might reasonably be supposed to be suffering from a sense of wrong. Why should it not

E. Phillips Oppenheim

occur to a clever woman like you that it might be a favorable moment to obtain a little information concerning one or two political problems of some importance? Are you interested in such matters, madame?"

She leaned back in her seat and laughed. He sat and watched her. Distinctly she was, in certain ways, the most beautiful woman he had ever seen. It was true that she was pale and that her neck was a trifle thin, but her face was so aristocratic and yet so piquant, the color of her eyes so delightful, her mouth so soft and yet so humorous. She laid her hand upon his arm.

"Oh! my dear, dear Englishman," she exclaimed, "Heaven indeed has sent you to me that I should not die of ennui! You do not know who I am - I, Madame Christophor?"

"I have no idea who you are," he assured her. "I have never seen you before. I know of no other name than the one by which I was told to ask for you."

She leaned a little closer to him.

"Come," she said, "you see me for what I am. I shall not rob you, I shall not drug you, I shall not try to tear secrets out of your throat by any medieval methods. We are neither of us of the order of those who seek adventures in vulgar fashion and expect always a vulgar termination. Can't we be friends for a time - companions? Paris is an empty city for me just now. And for you - you must avoid those whom you know. It follows that you must be lonely. Let me show you my Paris."

Julien looked steadfastly out at the country, at the flying hedges, the tall avenues of poplar trees in the distance, the clumsy farm wagon coming across the hayfield, the blue-petticoated women who marched by its side - anywhere to escape for a moment or two from her eyes. It was absurd that he should feel even this faint interest in her proposition! It was only a month since the blow had fallen, only a month since the girl to whom he had been engaged had sent him away with a sigh and a little handshake. It was only a month since life lay in splinters around him. It was much too soon to feel the slightest interest in the things which she was proposing!

"Madame Christophor," he said, "you are very kind, but I tell you frankly that I should accept your proposition with more pleasure if you had been of my own sex."

"You have become a woman-hater?"

"I cannot trust a woman," he answered coldly. "All the time I have the feeling of insecurity. I fear that it must sound ungallant if I tell you what is the sober truth - that your sex for the present has lost all charm for me."

She closed her eyes. Perhaps from behind the mask of her still face she was laughing at him!

"Do you think I don't understand that a little?" she murmured. "Never mind, for to-night, at least, I will be sexless. You can believe that I am a man. I think you will find that I can talk to you about most of the things that men know of. Politics we will leave alone. You would mistrust me at once. Art - I can tell you of our modern French painters; I can tell you about these two wonderful Russians who are painting in their studio here; I can tell you what to look for at the new exhibitions, what studios to visit - I can take you to them, if you will. Or old Paris - does that interest you? Have you ever seen it properly? I know my old Paris very well indeed. Or would you rather talk of books? There have been many years when I have done little else but read. Tell me that we may be companions for a time. You have nothing to lose, indeed, and I have so much to gain."

"Madame," Julien replied, "I do not trust you. You are doubtless an agreeable companion, and as such I am willing to spend a short time with you. This is an ungracious acceptance of your suggestion, but it is the best I am capable of."

She clapped her hands.

"It is something, after all," she declared, "and let me tell you this, my friend," she added, leaning over. "You have been frank with me. You have told me that you hated my sex, that you distrusted us all. Very well, I will share your frankness. I will tell you this. Neither am I any friend of your sex. I, too, have my grievance. I, too, have something in my heart of which I cannot speak, which, when I think of it, makes me hate every male creature that walks the earth. Perhaps with that in my heart and what you have in yours, we may meet and pass and meet again and pass, and do one another no harm. Is that finished?"

"By all means," he agreed.

Her expression changed.

"Come," she said, "now you shall see that I have begun my plots. I have brought you away from Paris into the country places. For what, I wonder? Are you terrified?"

"Not in the least," he assured her.

"Brave fellow! Perhaps when you know the truth, your heart will shake with fear. You are going to dine in a country restaurant."

"That does not terrify me in the least," he replied, smiling. "I think that it will be charming."

"It is a tiny place," she told him, "not very well known as yet; soon, I fear, likely to become fashionable. One sits at little tables on a lawn of the darkest green. If the sun shines, an umbrella of pink and white holland shades us. Quite close is the river and a field of buttercups. There are flowers in the garden, and so many shrubs that one can be almost alone. And behind, an old inn. They cook simply, but the trout comes from the river, and it is cool."

"It sounds delightful," Julien admitted; "but, madame, indeed it is I who must be host."

She shook her head.

"On the contrary, it is by subtlety that I have brought you here and that I claim to be the giver of the feast. You see, you dine with me to-night. You must ask me back again. It is the custom of your country, is it not?"

He smiled. The automobile had turned in now up a short drive, and stopped before a long, low building.

Down in the gardens they could see fairylights swinging in the faint breeze. A short man, with close-cropped hair and a fierce black moustache and imperial, came hastening out to greet them. When he recognized Madame Christophor, he bowed low.

"Monsieur Léon," she said, "I bring an Englishman to try your river trout. You must give me a table near that great tree of lilac that smells so sweetly. I order nothing - you understand? But you must remember that monsieur is English. He will want his champagne dry and his brandy very old. Is it not so, my friend? Now I will give you into charge of *monsieur le propriétaire* here. He shall show you where you can drink a little *apéritif*, if you will. He shall show you, too, where to find me presently."

A trim maid came hurrying up and took possession of Madame Christophor. Julien followed his guide into a small reception room, all pink and white.

"If monsieur desires to wash," the proprietor explained, "he passes beyond there. And for an *apéritif*?"

"I will take anything you send me," Julien declared. "What is the name of this place, monsieur?"

"They call it the Maison Léon d'Or, monsieur," the man replied. "It is my own idea - a country house I purchased once for myself, but found it too far, alas! from Paris. In the fine weather we could, if we chose, have half Paris here. When the cold days come, there is nobody. Monsieur permits?"

He departed and Julien strolled to the window. In the portion of the gardens over which he looked were smaller tables, set out simply for those who desired to take their coffee and liqueurs or *apéritif* out of doors. Julien glanced out idly enough at the little group of people dotted about here and there. Then his face suddenly darkened. At a table within a few yards of where he stood were seated Foster and a man whose back was turned towards him.

Julien's first impulse was to retire out of sight, for the window was open and he himself imperfectly concealed by the muslin blind. Then, as he was on the point of retiring, he distinctly heard the sound of his own name. The two men were speaking in a low tone, but a slight breeze was blowing into the room. Julien stood still and listened. The man who was a stranger to him was speaking to Foster.

"The woman is first, it is true," he muttered. "She will pump him dry, no doubt. But what matter? She may even put him on his guard, but I say again, what matter? There is a price for everything, a price or - "

The man's voice died away and Julien heard nothing for some time. Then he saw Foster shake his head.

"Our service," Foster declared, "does not protect us in such a position. It does not allow us to go to extremes. I am supposed to be here to watch him, but I am really powerless. He might become your man or hers or any one else's. I could do nothing but report."

His companion leaned across the table.

"What you call your Secret Service," Julien heard him say, "is a farce. You have no authority, no scope. You are too proud to ferret about as the others do. You sit in

E. Phillips Oppenheim

dignified ease and wait for information to be brought to you. My good Foster, you must learn to be a man. We must teach you."

Again their voices became inaudible. Julien drew back into the room. His heart was beating faster, his brain was full of new thoughts. From a place where he was absolutely secure he sat and gaze d at Foster andhis companion. Presently the waiter entered with the *apéritif.* Julien gave him five francs.

"Listen," he said, "you see those two gentlemen sitting there?"

"*Parfaitement*, monsieur," the man replied.

"Have you ever seen the elder one before - the dark one with the glasses?"

The waiter hesitated.

"Monsieur," he said, looking at the five francs in his hand, "*monsieur le propriétaire* here has strange notions. He objects that we mention ever the name of any of his clients."

"Why is that?" Julien asked.

"How should one know, monsieur?" the waiter answered. "Only it seems that this place is a little distance from Paris, it is retired, one finds seclusion here. People meet, I think, in these gardens who do not care to be seen in Paris. There are some come here who whisper at the door to *monsieur le propriétaire* that their names must never be mentioned."

"One can understand that, perhaps," Julien agreed, "but these are surely affairs of gallantry? It is when the gentlemen bring ladies, perhaps?"

The man shook his head and gesticulated an emphatic negative.

"Monsieur," he declared, "there are other things. There are other things, indeed. This place is well-known because there meet here often men who are interested in discussing serious matters. I can tell monsieur, alas! the name of no one among the guests here. If I attempted it, it would mean my dismissal, and there is no place in Paris, monsieur, where the salaries are so good as here." Julien hesitated. Then he drew a louis from his pocket.

"Listen," he said, "you may rely upon my word. No mention of it shall go outside this room. Take this louis for just the name of that gentleman with his back to you."

The waiter took the louis.

"His name, monsieur, I cannot tell you, but I will tell you what perhaps will do for monsieur as well. The German Ambassador comes sometimes here with a party of friends; somewhere in the distance you will find the gentleman about whom you ask. The German Ambassador rides through the streets when Paris is troubled; somewhere close at hand you will find monsieur there. The German Ambassador he attends the races; feeling, perhaps, is running a little high. Somewhere amongst the crowd who watch the races, and very close to *Monsieur l'Ambassadeur*, you will find monsieur there with the shoulders."

Julien drank his *apéritif* thoughtfully.

"Thank you," he said to the waiter. "You have earned your money. You need have no fear."

There was a knock at the door. *Monsieur le propriétaire* presented himself.

"Monsieur," he announced, "it is my honor to conduct you to the table reserved for madame and yourself. Madame awaits you."

CHAPTER X

BETTER ACQUAINTANCE

The gardens of the Maison Léon d'Or were, in their way, unique. There was no extent of open space, but the walks threaded everywhere a large shrubbery, and in all sorts of corners and quiet places little dining tables had been placed. Scarcely any one was in sight of any other person, although they were so close together that all the time there was a hum of voices. In the distance, down by the river, a large gondola was passing slowly backwards and forwards, on which an orchestra played soft music. Julien and Madame Christophor crossed the narrow strip of lawn together and followed Monsieur Léon into the graveled path bordered with fairy lamps.

"I have arranged for madame and monsieur," he announced, looking backwards, "a table near the lilac tree of which madame is so fond. The perfume, indeed, is exquisite. If madame pleases!"

They turned from the path on to another strip of lawn, which they gained by rounding a large lilac bush. Here a small table was laid with the whitest of cloths and the most dazzling of silver. An attentive waiter was already arranging an ice-pail in a convenient spot. From here the gardens sloped gently to the river, which was barely forty yards distant. Although it was scarcely twilight, the men on the gondola were lighting the lamps.

"Madame and monsieur will find this table removed from all chance visitors," the proprietor declared. "If the dinner is not perfect, permit that I wait upon you again. A word to the waiter and I arrive. Madame! Monsieur!"

He retreated, with a bow to each. Julien, with a little laugh, took his place at the table.

"Madame," he said, "your entertainment is charming."

"The entertainment is nothing," Madame replied, "but here at least is one advantage - we are really alone. I do not know how you feel, but the greatest rest in life to me is sometimes the solitude. There is no one over-looking us, there is no one likely to pass whom we know. We are virtually cut off from all those who know us or whom we know. My friend, I would like you to remember this our first evening. Talk, if you will, or be silent. For me it is equal. I, too, have thoughts which I can summon at any time to bear me company. And there is the river. Do you hear the soft flow of it, and the rustle of the breeze in the shrubs, the perfumes, and - listen - the music? Ah! Sir Julien, I think that we give you over here some things which you do not easily find in your own country."

"You are right," he agreed slowly. "You give us a better climate, more sympathetic companionship, a tenderer chicken, a more artistic salad."

"At heart you are a materialist, I perceive," she declared.

"We all are," he admitted. "Everything depends upon our power of concealment."

The service of dinner commenced almost at once. There was something excessively peaceful in the scene. The tables were so arranged that one heard nothing of the clatter of crockery. The murmur of voices came like a pleasant undernote. They talked lightly for some time of the English theatres, of the stage generally, some recent memoirs - anything that came into their heads. Then Julien was silent for several minutes. He leaned slightly across the table. Their own lamp was lit now and through the velvety dusk her eyes seemed to glow with a new beauty.

"Tell me," he begged, "you spoke of yourself a little time ago as though you might have a personality at which I ought to have guessed. Are you a woman of Society, or an artist, or merely an idler?"

"I have known something of Society," she replied. "I believe I may say that I am something of an artist. It is very certain that I am not an idler. Why ask me these questions? Let us forget to be serious tonight. Let us remember only that we are companions, and that the hours, as they pass, are pleasant."

"It is a philosophy," he murmured, "which brings its own retribution."

She shrugged her shoulders.

"All happiness is lost," she declared, "the moment you

E. Phillips Oppenheim

begin to try and define it. It is a sensation, not a state of being. Let us drift. The waters are not dangerous for you or for me."

Her words chilled him with a sudden memory. Then, in the act of helping himself to wine, he paused. Some one had taken the table nearest to them, dimly visible through the laurel bushes. He heard the voice of the man who had been with Foster, giving the orders.

"Listen!"

There was no need for him to have spoken. Curiously enough, Madame

Christophor seemed also to have recognized the voice. Her hand fell upon Julien's. He looked at her in surprise. Her cheeks were blanched, her eyes blazing.

"You hear that voice?" she whispered.

Julien nodded.

"It is the voice of the only person in the world," she continued, "whom I absolutely hate."

"You know whose it is, then?"

"Of course!" she replied.

"So do I," he muttered. "I have never seen the man's face, but I know a little about him."

She shivered.

"Come," she said, "let us have our coffee later. We

have finished dinner and the moon is coming up. If we walk to the bottom there, we shall see it from the bend of the river, and we shall escape from those men."

He rose hastily to his feet. She led the way down the path. Here and there they caught a glimpse of other tables as they passed - little parties of two or four, all very gay. Madame breathed more freely as they progressed. Presently they passed through an iron gate into a field, already half-mown. The perfume of the fresh-cut grass came to them with an almost over-powering sweetness. Her hand fell upon his arm.

"Forgive me," she begged, "I am not really a weak woman. I do not think that there is any other sound in life which I hate so much as the sound of that voice."

They walked in silence along the narrow path. Soon they reached the edge of the river. A few steps further on was a seat, of which they took possession. In the distance the gondola, on fire now with lamps, was playing a waltz. A bat flew for a moment about their heads. Somewhere in the woods a long way down the river a nightingale was singing.

"I am not often so foolish," she murmured. "Once - let me tell you this - once I had a dear little friend. She was very sweet, but a little too trusting, too simple for the life here. She found a lover. She thought she had found the happiness of her life. Poor child! For a month, perhaps, she was happy. Then he forced her to give up her little home and her savings and go upon the stage. He preferred a mistress from the theatres. She worked hard, but, sweetly pretty though she was, she was not very successful. Then she caught cold. She began to lose her health - and she lost her lover."

"Brute!"

"The child got worse," madame went on. "Presently they told her that it was consumption. She went to a hospital and she wrote a pathetic little note to the man. He tore it up. There had been an article in the papers a few weeks before proving that consumption was among the diseases which were more or less infectious. He sent her a few brutal lines and a trifle of money, with a warning that there was to be no more. He never went to see her. The child grew worse. I used to sit with her sometimes. I saw her look down upon the river, almost as we are looking now, and her eyes would grow soft and wet with tears, and she would tell me in whispers of the evenings she had spent with him, when the love had first come, and how sweet and tender he was. There must be something wrong, she was sure. He did not understand, he could not know how ill she really was. She prayed for the sight of him. I put her off with one excuse after another, but one day the fear of death was in her eyes, the terror came to her, she was afraid. She was afraid of dying alone, of going into a strange country, no one to hold her. I went to the man, I begged him to come and see her. He scoffed at me. If she had consumption, she was better dead. He would have flirted with me if I had let him. I can hear his voice now - brutal, jeering, hideous! It was the voice, Sir Julien, which we heard ten minutes ago at the next table. Do you wonder that I hate it?"

"And the little girl?" he asked.

"When I returned without him," she answered, "the little girl was dead."

They were both silent, listening to the splash of the

water and to the distant music.

"Life is like that," she went on. "We pass through it lightly enough, but Heaven only knows the number of little tragedies against which our skirts must brush. Sometimes they leave impressions, sometimes we grow callous, but the horror of that man's voice will stay with me always.... Shall we go back now? You would like your coffee."

"Sit here for five minutes more," he begged. "Tell me, did you know that the man was a spy?"

She looked at him curiously.

"How is it that you know so much about him?"

"He is sitting there with an Englishman who comes from our Intelligence Department," Julien explained. "They were speaking together of some one - I believe it was myself - speaking in none too friendly terms. There was a woman, too, whose name they coupled with mine, but I could not hear that. I made some inquiries about the man. I was told that he was in the suite of the German Ambassador."

She nodded.

"Whoever or whatever he is," she said, "he is some-thing to be abhorred. Hush! There is some one coming down the footpath."

They sat quite silent. Some instinct seemed to tell them who it was. Suddenly they heard the voice - rasping, unpleasant.

"You have bungled the affair, Foster. It is not well-managed; it is not clever. You were to have brought him to me, to have let me know the instant he reached Paris. I would have seen him. Just as he was, I should have succeeded. Now it may be that this woman has warned him already. She is very clever. If she has him, he will not escape."

Foster's voice was inaudible, but whatever he said seemed to anger his companion.

"Thunder and lightning!" they heard the man exclaim. "Am I a fool that you talk to me like this? Yes, I go to him - I go to him to-night, but I tell you that it is too late! If it is too late, there is but one thing to be done. You are a coward, Foster!"

They came out into the open, on the path which fringed the river, and they were immediately silent. They came strolling along and noticed for the first time the two figures upon the seat. Instantly they began to talk upon some local subject. No escape was possible. In a few minutes they were opposite the bench. Foster started a little. The other man's face darkened. He ventured upon a bow. Madame Christophor looked at him as one might look upon some strange animal. Foster hesitated for a moment, but his companion pushed him along.

"I think," she whispered, "that that man would like to do me an injury."

Julien was watching their retreating forms.

"I don't understand what Foster is doing there, or what the dickens they were talking about," he said thoughtfully. "I think if you don't mind," he added, "we will return."

"Why are you so suddenly uneasy?" she asked.

He shrugged his shoulders.

"Apparently," he answered, "you know who I am and everything about me. I, on the other hand, am ignorant almost of your very name. There are certain circumstances connected with my late career which make it inadvisable - "

"Oh, I know all that you are going to say!" she interrupted. "But ask yourself. Have I made any attempt whatever to ask you a single unbecoming question?"

"You certainly have not," he confessed.

"Your little friend returns," she whispered. "See!"

Foster came back to them, slowly, with reluctant footsteps. He had the appearance of a man bent upon a mission which he dislikes.

"Sir Julien," he said, as he drew near, "would you grant me a moment's interview?"

Julien looked at him.

"You probably know my address," he replied coldly. "You can call there and see me. At present I am engaged."

"Sir Julien, the matter is of some importance," Foster

E. Phillips Oppenheim

persisted. "I have a friend who is anxious to meet you. It would be an affair of a few words only, and perhaps an appointment afterwards."

"Is the friend to whom you refer the person with whom you were walking just now?" Julien inquired.

"Yes!" Foster admitted. "If you can spare me a moment I can explain - "

"You need explain nothing," Julien interrupted. "Understand, please, that I decline absolutely to make that person's acquaintance."

Foster looked away from Sir Julien to the woman who stood by his side.

"Am I to take this as final?" he asked.

Julien turned on his heel.

"Absolutely," he said. "The little I know of the person with whom you seem to be spending the evening makes me feel more inclined to pitch him into the river than to make his acquaintance. As a matter of fact, Foster, I don't know, of course, under what instructions you are acting over here, but I should not have considered him exactly a companion for you."

Foster started. A new fear had suddenly broken in upon him.

"I am doing my best to carry out instructions, sir," he declared. "I do not understand why you should take so prejudiced a view of my friend."

"It is, perhaps," Julien replied, "because I know more about him than you seem to. Good night!"

They walked slowly back to the gardens. The woman was thoughtful.

"I am sorry," she said, "that those people came along to spoil our first evening together. I am glad, though, that you refused to meet the German. All that he would have done would have been to try and fill your mind with suspicions of me. Haven't you found me harmless?"

"I am not sure," he answered.

She laughed softly.

"Ah, me!" she exclaimed, "I gave you an opening, didn't I, and one must remember that of late years the men of your nation have established a reputation over here for gallantry. Harmless, at least, so far as regards tearing political secrets from your bosom?"

"As a matter of fact," Julien remarked, "there are not so many secrets between France and England, are there?"

"Thanks in some measure to you," she reminded him. "You take it for granted, I notice, that I am a Frenchwoman."

He looked at her in great surprise.

"Why, indeed, yes! Is there any doubt about it?"

"My mother was an American," she told him.

"Tell me your real name?" he asked suddenly.

"On the contrary, I am going to beg you not to try and discover it. Let us remain as we are for a little time. You are lonely here and you need companionship, and I am very much in the same position. You are a hater of women and I have sworn eternal enmity against all men. We are so safe, and solitude is bad for us."

He smiled.

"You are very kind," he said, "but as for me, I am only starting my wanderings. I want to go on through Algiers to Morocco, to Egypt, and later to the east. I never meant to stay long in Paris."

"I do not blame you," she declared. "Sooner or later you must find your way where the battle is. Paris is not a city for men. One loiters here for a time, but one passes on always. Never mind, while you stay here I shall claim you."

They drove back to Paris through the perfumed stillness of the long spring night. Madame had instructed her chauffeur to drive slowly, and more than one automobile rushed past them, with flaring lights and sounding horn. In one they caught a glimpse of Foster and his companion, whispering together as they raced by. Madame half closed her eyes with a little shiver.

"Those men again!" she exclaimed, "They say that Estermen never abandons a chase. You may still find him waiting for you in your hotel!"

CHAPTER XI

THE TOYMAKER FROM LEIPZIG

In the front row of balcony tables at the Café des Ambassadeurs was one which had been transformed into a veritable bower of pink roses. The florists had been at work upon it since early in the afternoon, and their labors were only just concluded as the guests of the restaurant were beginning to arrive. Henri, the chief *maître d'hôtel*, had personally superintended its construction. He stood looking at the result of their labors now with a well-satisfied aspect.

"But it is perfect," he declared. "The orders of Monsieur Freudenberg have indeed been delightfully carried out. You will present the account as usual, mademoiselle," he directed the florist, who in her black frock, a little hot and flushed with her labors, was standing by his side. "Remember monsieur is well able to pay."

"It is, perhaps, a prince who dines in such state?" the girl inquired.

The *maître d'hôtel* smiled.

"It is, on the contrary," he told her, "a maker of toys from Germany."

E. Phillips Oppenheim

She made a little grimace.

"And to think that my back aches, that I have pricked myself so," she exclaimed, showing the scarred tips of her fingers, "for the sake of a toymaker from Germany! But it is not like you, Henri, to disturb yourself so for anything less than a prince."

Henri, who was a sleek and handsome man, with black moustache and imperial, shook his head sadly.

"Ah! mademoiselle," he said, "when you have lived as long as I, you will know that the times indeed have changed. It is no longer the princes of the world to whom one gives one's best service. It is those who carry the heaviest money bags who command it."

"Well, well," she replied, "that is perhaps true. Yet in our little shop in the Rue de la Paix we do not always find that it is those with the heaviest money bags who pay us most generously for our flowers. I would sooner serve a bankrupt aristocrat than a wealthy shopkeeper. If they pay at all, these aristocrats, they pay well."

Henri stretched out his hands.

"Mademoiselle, there are shopkeepers who are also princes. My client of this evening is one of those. Behold, he comes! Pardon!"

The man for whom these great preparations had been made stood in the entrance of the restaurant, waiting for the woman who was giving her cloak to the *vestiaire*. He was tall and thin, dressed rather severely, with a black tie and short coat, a monocle which hung from his neck with a black ribbon. His face was unusually long, his eyes deep-set, his mouth set firm on a somewhat protuberant jaw, with lines at the corners which somehow suggested humor. When he saw Henri he nodded.

"Once more, Henri," he remarked, with a little smile, "once more in my beloved Paris!"

"Monsieur is always welcome," Henri declared, bowing to the ground. "Paris is the gayer for his coming."

"You are indeed a nation of courtiers!" Herr Carl Freudenberg exclaimed. "What German *Oberkellner* would have thought of a speech like that to a Frenchman finding himself in Berlin! Ah! Henri, you try, all of you, to spoil me here. Is it not so, mademoiselle?" he added, turning with a bow and a smile to the girl who stood now by his side. "Henri here speaks honied words to me always. The wonder to me is that I am ever able to tear myself away from this city of fascination."

"If we could keep monsieur," the girl murmured, smiling at Henri, "I think that we should all be very well content."

Herr Freudenberg made a little grimace.

"But my toys!" he cried. "Who is there in Germany could make such toys as I and my factory people? The world would be sad indeed - the world of children, I mean - if my factory were to close down or my designers should lose their cunning."

"Is it the greatest ambition of monsieur," the girl

asked, "to amuse and make happy the world of children? Have not the world of grown people some claims?"

"Monsieur will, I trust, and madame," Henri declared, as they moved slowly forward, "find much to admire in the table which has been prepared for them this evening. It is by the orders of monsieur so enclosed that here one may talk without fear of observation. And the perfume of these roses, every one of which has been selected, is a wonderful thing. It is indeed a work of art."

Herr Freudenberg turned deliberately on one side where the little flower girl was still lingering.

"Mademoiselle," he said, "something tells me that it is you whom we have to thank for this adorable creation. It is indeed a work of supreme art. If mademoiselle would permit!"

He slipped a crumpled note into her fingers, so quietly and unostentatiously that it was there and in her pocket before any one had time to notice it. She went out murmuring to herself.

"He is a prince, this monsieur - a veritable prince!"

"For your dinner," Henri announced, as they seated themselves in their places, "I have no word to tell you. I spare you, as you see, the barbarity of a menu. What will come to you, monsieur and madame, is at least of our best. I can promise that. And the wine is such as I myself have selected, knowing well the taste of monsieur."

"And of madame also, I trust?" Herr Freudenberg remarked.

"Ah! monsieur," Henri continued, "when monsieur is not in Paris, madame is invisible. Not once since I last had this pleasure of waiting upon you, have I had the joy of seeing her."

Herr Freudenberg looked across the table at his companion with twinkling eyes.

"This is a city of conspirators," he declared. "You make a man vain and happy and joyous at the same time. Let your dinner be served, then, Henri. Since I was in Paris last I have eaten many times, but I have not dined."

The *maître d'hôtel* departed, but for the next hour or so his eyes were seldom far away from the table where sat his most esteemed client. Once or twice, others of the diners sent for him.

"Henri," one asked, and then another, "tell us, who is it that dines like a prince under the canopy of pink roses?"

Henri smiled.

"Monsieur," he replied, "it is Herr Carl Freudenberg of Leipzig."

"Herr Carl Freudenberg of Leipzig - but who is he?"

"He is a great manufacturer of toys, monsieur."

"A German!" one muttered.

"It is they who are spoiling Paris," another grumbled.

"They have at least the money!"

One woman alone shook her head.

"It is not money only," she murmured, "which buys these things here from Henri."...

The companion of Herr Carl Freudenberg was, without doubt, as charming as she appeared, for Herr Freudenberg certainly enjoyed his dinner as a man should. Nor were those lines of humor engraven about his mouth for nothing, to judge by the frequent peals of laughter from mademoiselle. Towards the close of dinner, Henri himself carried to them a superb violet ice, with real flowers around the dish and an electric light burning in the middle.

"For two days, madame," he announced, "our chef has dreamed of this. It is a creation."

"It is exquisite!" mademoiselle cried, with a gesture of delight. "Never in my life have I seen anything so wonderful."

"Henri," Herr Freudenberg said in an aside, "you will present my compliments to the chef. You will shake him by the hand from me. You will double the little affair which passes between us. Tell him that it comes from one who appreciates the work of a great artist, even though his French thickens a little in his throat."

Henri bowed low.

"If monsieur's body is German," he declared, "his soul

at least belongs to the land of romance."

They were alone again and the girl leaned across the table.

"Monsieur," she murmured, "it is cruel of you to come so seldom. You see what you do? You spoil the keepers of our restaurants, you steal away the hearts of your poor little companions, and then - one night or two, perhaps, and it is over. Monsieur Freudenberg has gone. The earth swallows him."

"Back to my toys, mademoiselle," he whispered. "One has one's work."

She looked at him long and tenderly.

"Monsieur," she said, "it is two months, a week and three days since you were in Paris. Since then I have sung and danced, night by night, but my heart has never been gay. Come oftener, monsieur, or may one not sometimes cross the frontier and learn a little of your barbarous country?"

For the first time the faintest shadow of gravity crossed his face.

"Mademoiselle," he replied, "alas! The world is full of hard places. Behold me! When I am here, I am your devoted and admiring slave, but believe me that when I leave Paris and set my face eastwards, I do not exist. Dear Marguerite, it hurts me to repeat this - I do not exist."

She looked down into her plate.

E. Phillips Oppenheim

"I understand," she murmured. "You said it to me once before. Have I not always been discreet? Have I ever with the slightest word disobeyed you?"

"Nor will you ever, dear Marguerite," he declared confidently, "for if you did it would be the end. In the city where I make my toys, life as we live it here is not known. It is not recognized. And there is one's work in the world."

She looked up from her plate. Her expression had changed.

"It was foolish of me," she whispered. "To-night is one of those nights in Heaven for which I spend all my days longing. I think no more of the future. You are here. Tell me, from here - where?"

"To the Opera. I have engaged the box that you prefer. We arrive for the last act of 'Samson et Dalila' and for the ballet."

"And afterwards?"

"To the Abbaye. After that, there is the Rat Mort - Albert must not be disappointed - and a new place, they tell me. One must see all these new places."

"And we leave here soon?"

"You are impatient!"

"Only to be alone with you," she answered. "Even those few moments in the automobile are precious."

He smiled at her across the table. She was very pretty

with her fair hair and dark eyes, very Parisian, and yet with a shade of graceful seriousness about her eyes and mouth.

"Dear Marguerite," he said, "I wait only for one of my agents who comes to speak to me on a matter of business. He is due almost at this moment. After he has been here, then we go. Cannot you believe," he whispered, dropping his voice a little and leaning slightly across the table, "that I, too, will love to feel your dear fingers in mine, your lips, perhaps, for a moment, as we pass to the Opera?"

"It is a joy one must snatch," she murmured.

"There is no joy in life," he replied, "which is not the sweeter for being snatched, and snatched quickly."

"And you a German!" she sighed.

Henri appeared once more, and after him Estermen. Herr Freudenberg, with a word of excuse to his companion, turned to greet the newcomer.

"Well?"

Estermen stood quite close to the table. He was distinctly ill at ease.

"Herr Freudenberg," he said, "I have done my best. It was impossible for me to obtain an introduction to this customer."

"Impossible?" Herr Freudenberg repeated, his face suddenly becoming stony.

E. Phillips Oppenheim

"Let me explain," Estermen continued hastily. "This customer arrived in Paris last night or early this morning. He was called upon at once by a lady who lives in the Avenue de St. Paul. She has told him a little story about me - I am sure of it. He has refused to make my acquaintance."

"And you were content?"

Estermen spread out his pudgy hands.

"What can one do?" he muttered. "The man is quick-tempered. He dined tonight in the country at the Maison Léon d'Or with madame. It was there that I sought an introduction with him. It was impossible for me to force myself."

"You know where to find him, I suppose?"

"I know the hotel at which he is staying."

"Make it your business to find him," Herr Freudenberg ordered. "Bring him with you, if before one o'clock to the Abbaye Thelème; if afterwards, to the Rat Mort."

Estermen looked stolidly puzzled.

"Am I to mention the subject of the toys of Herr Freudenberg's manufacture?"

Herr Freudenberg tore a corner from the programme which lay on the table between them, and wrote a single word upon it.

"Study that at your leisure, my friend," he said. "Pay attention to the task I impose upon you. Nothing is more important in my visit to Paris than that I should make the acquaintance of this person. Much depends upon it. I rely upon you, Estermen."

Estermen thrust the morsel of paper into his waist-coat pocket. Then he leaned a little closer to this man who seemed to be his master.

"Herr Freudenberg," he began, "I spoke of a lady in the Avenue de St. Paul, the companion to-night of the person whose acquaintance you are anxious to make."

"What of her?" Herr Freudenberg asked calmly. "There are many ladies, without a doubt, who live in the Avenue de St. Paul."

"The name of this one," Estermen continued slowly, "is Madame Christophor."

Herr Freudenberg sat quite still in his place. His eyes seemed fixed upon a cluster of the roses which hung down from the other side of the sweet-smelling barrier by which they were surrounded. Yet something had gone out of his face, something fresh had arrived. The half contemptuous curl of the lips was finished. His mouth now was straight and hard, his eyes set, the deep lines upon his forehead and around his mouth were suddenly insistent. He sat so motionless that his face for a moment seemed as though it were fashioned in wax. Then his lips moved, he spoke in a whisper which was almost inaudible.

"Henriette!"

From across the table his companion watched him. At first she was puzzled. When she heard the woman's name which came so softly from his lips, she turned pale. Herr Freudenberg recovered from his fit of abstraction almost as quickly as he had lapsed into it.

"I thank you, Estermen," he declared. "It is a coincidence, this. I am obliged for your forethought in mentioning it. Until later, then."

The man made a somewhat clumsy bow, glanced admiringly at Herr Freudenberg's companion, and departed. Herr Freudenberg was shaking his head slowly.

"I fear," he said softly to himself, "sometimes I fear that I am not so well served as might be in Paris. However, we shall see. For the moment let us banish these dull cares. If you are ready, Marguerite, I think I might suggest that the nearer way to the Opera is by the Champs Élysées."

She rose to her feet and gave him her hand for a moment as she passed.

"If one could only find as easily the way to your heart, dear maker of toys!" she murmured.

CHAPTER XII

AT THE RAT MORT

Julien had been back in the hotel about half an hour and in his room barely ten minutes when he was disturbed by a knock at the door. Immediately afterwards, to his amazement, Estermen entered.

"What the devil are you doing up here?" Julien asked angrily. "How dare you follow me about!"

"Sir Julien," his visitor answered, "I beg that you will not make a commotion. It was perfectly easy for me to gain admission here. It will be perfectly easy for me, if it becomes necessary, to leave without trouble. I ask you to be reasonable. I am here. Listen to what I have to say. You are prejudiced against me. It is not fair. You have spoken with a woman who is my enemy. Give me leave, at least, to address a few words to you. You will not be the loser."

Julien was angry, but underneath it all he was also curious.

"Well, go on, then."

"You are reasonable," said Estermen, laying his hat and stick upon the bed. "Listen. Your story is known at

E. Phillips Oppenheim

Berlin as well as in Paris. There is only one opinion concerning it and that is that you have been shamefully treated."

"I am not asking for sympathy, sir," Julien answered coldly.

"Nor am I offering it," the other returned. "I am stating facts. There are many who do not hesitate to say that you have been made the victim of a political plot, conceived among the members of your own party; that you are suffering at the present moment from your masterly efforts on behalf of peace."

"Pray go on," Julien invited. "I consider all this grossly impertinent, but I am willing to listen to what you have to say."

"The greatest man in Germany," Estermen continued, "when he heard of your misfortune, declared at once that the peace of Europe was no longer assured. I am here to-night, Sir Julien, without credentials, it is true, but I am the spokesman of a very great person indeed. He is anxious to know your plans."

"I have no plans."

"Your political future, then -"

"I have no political future," Julien interrupted. "That is finished for me."

"But the thing is absurd!" protested Estermen. "There is no other man but you capable of dealing tactfully and diplomatically with my country. Your blundering predecessors brought us twice within an ace of war. If the man takes your place to whom rumor has already given it, I give Europe six weeks' peace - no more. We are a sensitive nation, as you know. You learned how to humor us. No one before you tried. You kept your alliance with France, but you were not afraid to show us the open hand. There are those in Berlin, Sir Julien, who consider you the greatest statesman England ever possessed."

"I listen," Julien said. "Pray proceed."

"It cannot be," Estermen went on, "that you mean to accept the situation?"

"I have no alternative," Julien answered.

"It is not, then, a question of money?" Estermen ventured slowly. "The Press tell us that you are poor."

"Money, in this case, would scarcely help," Julien remarked.

"There is no man in the world who can afford to despise the power of money," Estermen said quietly.

"Are you here to offer me any?"

"I am not. Have you anything to give in exchange for it?"

Julien laughed a little shortly.

"I imagined," he declared, "that with your first remarks you had climbed to the dizziest heights of imperti-nence. I perceive that I was mistaken. I am a discarded minister," - dryly. "I may be supposed to have in my

E. Phillips Oppenheim

possession secrets for which your country would pay. Is it not to those facts that I am indebted for the honor of this visit?"

"Not in the least," answered Estermen. "Our own Secret Service keeps us supplied with such information as we desire. My object in seeking you is this. The Prince von Falkenberg is in Paris for a few hours only. He wants to meet you. I have been ordered to arrange this meeting, if possible."

Julien did not attempt to conceal his interest.

"Why on earth didn't you say so at once?" he exclaimed. "What does he want of me?"

Estermen shrugged his shoulders.

"Who knows? Who knows what Falkenberg ever wants? He is here, there and everywhere - today in Paris, tomorrow in Berlin, next week in Moscow. Yet it is he, as you know well, who shapes the whole destinies of my country. It is he alone in whom the Emperor has blind and absolute confidence. If he holds up his hand, it is war. If he holds it down, it is peace."

"What does he do in Paris?" Julien inquired.

Estermen shook his head.

"He arrived this morning and disappeared. Tonight he sent me orders that I was to search for you."

"Where is he now?" Julien asked.

"At eight o'clock tonight," Estermen said, "he declared

himself to be Herr Carl Freudenberg, dealer in German toys. He dressed, dined at the Ambassadeurs with Mademoiselle Ixe from the Opera, sent for me, learned that I was at the Maison Léon d'Or, telephoned there, and all for this one thing - that I should bring you to him without a moment's delay."

"But where is he now?" Julien asked again.

Estermen glanced at the clock and at a piece of paper which he took from his pocket.

"It is one o'clock within a few minutes," he remarked. "Herr Freudenberg is either at the Abbaye Thelème or the Rat Mort."

Julien scarcely hesitated.

"When you first came in," he admitted, "I felt like throwing you out. How you got here I don't know. I suppose it is no use complaining to the hotel people. But there is no man on the face of this earth in whom I am more interested than Falkenberg. I shall change my clothes, and in a quarter of an hour I am at your service. Wait for me downstairs."

Estermen drew a little sigh of relief. "I shall await you, Sir Julien," he declared.

All Paris seemed to be seeking distraction as they drove in the automobile along the Boulevard des Italiens. Julien sat with folded arms in the corner of the automobile. He had no fancy for his companion. He was anxious so far as possible to avoid speech with him. Estermen, on the contrary, seemed only too desirous of removing the impression of dislike of which he was acutely conscious. He talked the whole of the time of the cafés and the women, of everything he thought might be interesting to his companion. Julien listened in grim silence. Only once he interrupted.

"What brings Herr Freudenberg to Paris?" he inquired once more.

Estermen was suddenly reticent.

"He has affairs here," he said. "He is also like us others - a man who loves his pleasure. You will find him tonight with a most charming companion - Mademoiselle Ixe of the Opera. Before the coming of Herr Freudenberg, I remember her well - the companion at times of many. To-day she is changed, *triste* when he is not here, faithful in a most un-Parisianlike manner."

They swung round to the left.

"Herr Freudenberg," Estermen continued, "is a great lover of the night life of Paris. He goes from one café to the other. He is untired, sleepless. He seems to find inspiration where others find fatigue."

Julien raised his eyebrows, but he said nothing. These were not his impressions of the man whom they were seeking!

They drew up presently at the doors of the Abbaye Thelème. There were crowds of people trying to gain admission. Estermen elbowed his way through.

"Herr Freudenberg?" he asked of the man who stood at the door.

The man's forbidding face changed like magic.

"Herr Freudenberg left but ten minutes ago for the Rat Mort. Those who inquired for him were to follow."

Estermen nodded and touched Julien on the arm.

"We will walk," he said. "It is at the corner there."

They presented themselves at the doors of a smaller and dingier café. Estermen elbowed the way up the narrow stairs. They emerged in a small room, brilliantly lit and filled with people. The usual little band was playing gay music. A corpulent *maître d'hôtel* bowed as they appeared.

"Herr Freudenberg," Estermen began.

The waiter's bow by this time was a different affair.

"Monsieur will follow me," he invited.

At the corner table at the far end of the room - the most desired of any - sat Herr Freudenberg with Mademoiselle Ixe by his side. They met the flower girl coming away with empty arms. The table of Herr Freudenberg was smothered with roses. There was a shade more color in the cheeks of Mademoiselle Ixe, in her eyes a light as soft as any which the eyes of a woman who loved could know. Herr Freudenberg, unruffled, had still the air of a man who finds life pleasant. As the two men came up the room, he rose and held out both his hands.

"Ah!" he exclaimed, "it is indeed my friend of Berlin! Welcome, dear Sir Julien! We meet on neutral ground, is it not so? We meet now in the city of pleasures. Let us sit for a little time and talk, and forget that you and I once wrote a chapter together in the history - of toy-making. But first," he added, turning to Mademoiselle Ixe, "mademoiselle permits me to introduce a very dear and cherished acquaintance to an equally dear and cherished friend. This gentleman, dear Marguerite, and I make toys in different countries, and there was a time when it was necessary for us to consult together. So he came to Berlin and I have never forgotten his visit. For the present, join us, dear Julien. You permit that I call you by your first name? It is after midnight, and after midnight in Paris one permits everything. Now we drink together, we three, for Estermen must leave us, I know. We drink together to the making of toys, the building of toy palaces, and the love of one another. Come, Monsieur Albert, see that your *sommelier* opens that bottle that you have chosen for us so carefully," he continued, turning to the manager who was hovering close at hand. "This is a meeting and we need the best wine that ever came from the vineyards of France. A dear friend, Albert. Bow low to him, indeed, for he is worthy of it. Afterwards we will perhaps eat something. Send your waiter. But above all, monsieur, see to it that mademoiselle with the fair curls dances once more. My friend, I think, would like to see her. And we must have music. Let the band never cease playing. Ah! it is here, dear Albert, that one learns to forget how strenuous life really is. It is here that one may unbend. The wine!"

While Herr Freudenberg talked the *sommelier* had gravely served the champagne in some tall and wonderful glasses brought from a private cabinet by Monsieur Albert himself to honor his most treasured visitors. Herr Freudenberg raised his glass, clinked it against the glass of mademoiselle, clinked it against Julien's glass.

"Come," he cried, "to our better acquaintance, to our better understanding! Mademoiselle," he added, lowering his tone, "to the eternal continuance of those things which lie between you and me!"

Estermen had departed and Julien breathed the freer for it. Mademoiselle Ixe chattered to him for a few moments, and Herr Freudenberg whispered in the ears of Albert, who withdrew at once.

"One must eat," Herr Freudenberg declared. "Albert has some peaches, wonderful peaches from the gardens where the sun always shines. Peaches and macaroons - afterwards coffee. Ah! my friend, you remember those somber banquets when we all hated one another because we all fancied that the other wanted what we had a right to? Ugh! When I think of Berlin in those days, when no one smiled, when one's sense of humor was there only to be kept down with an iron hand, why, it gives one to weep! Mademoiselle, I have a prayer to make."

"It is granted," she assured him softly.

"Presently the orchestra shall play the music of Faust. You will sing to us? Tonight is one of my nights, never really perfect unless some minutes of it move to the music of your voice."

She laughed softly.

"Yes, monsieur, I will sing," she answered, "but not the Jewel Song tonight. Send the *chef d'orchestre* to me."

E. Phillips Oppenheim

At the merest signal he was there with his violin under his arm. Mademoiselle whispered a word in his ear and he departed, all smiles. The selection which they were playing suddenly ceased. *Monsieur le chef* alone played some Italian air, which no one wholly recognized but every one found familiar. Slowly he walked around the tables, playing still, always with his eyes upon Mademoiselle Ixe, and when at last he stood before her, she threw her head back and sang.

The clatter of crockery diminished, the waiters paused in their tasks or crept on tiptoe about the place. Men and women stood up at their tables that they might see the singer better; conversation ceased. And all the time the *chef d'orchestre* drew music from his violin, and mademoiselle, with half-closed eyes, her head thrown back, filled the whole room with melody. Even she herself knew that she was singing as she never sang at the Opera, as she had never sung when a great impressario had come to try her voice, as one sings only when the heart is shaking a little, and as she finished, the fingers of her left hand slowly crept across the table into the hand of Herr Freudenberg, the toymaker, and her last notes were sung almost in a whisper into his ears. The room rose up to applaud. The *chef d'orchestre* went back to his place, bowing right and left. Herr Freudenberg raised the fingers that lay between his hand to his lips.

"Ah, mademoiselle," he murmured, "I have no longer words!"

Albert came back. Scarcely more than a look passed between him and Herr Freudenberg. Then the latter rose to his feet.

"Come," he said, "a little surprise for you. You, too, dear Julien. I insist. This way."

They passed from the room. As mademoiselle rose to her feet, people began once more to applaud.

"Mademoiselle will sing again presently, perhaps," Herr Freudenberg answered a man who leaned forward. "We do not depart."

He led the way to the head of the staircase and they passed into the back regions of the place - dim, ill-lit, mysterious. Albert, who had preceded them, threw open the door of a room. There was a small supper table laid for three, more flowers, more wine.

"It is that one may talk for five minutes," Herr Freudenberg explained. "Mademoiselle!"

But mademoiselle had already flitted away. The door somehow was closed, the two men were alone.

E. Phillips Oppenheim

CHAPTER XIII

POLITICS AND PATRIOTISM

Herr Freudenberg shrugged his shoulders and glanced at the softly-closed door.

"Mademoiselle is a paragon," he declared. "Always she understands. Sir Julien, will you not sit down for a moment? Let me confess that this little supper-party is a pretense. For five minutes I wish to talk to you."

Julien seated himself without hesitation.

"My dear host," he said, "I left Berlin a year ago with only one hope - or rather two. The first was that I might never have to visit Berlin again! The second was that I might have the pleasure of meeting you as speedily and as often as possible."

Herr Freudenberg smiled - a quiet, reminiscent smile.

"Even now," he remarked, "when I would speak to you for a moment on more serious subjects, the strange humor of that round-table conference comes home to me. There were you and I and our big friend from Austria, and that awful dull man from here, and the Russian. Shall you ever forget that speechless Russian, who never opened his lips except to disagree?

Sometimes I caught your eye across the table. And, Sir Julien, you know, I presume, whose was the triumph of those days?"

Julien smiled doubtfully.

"Yours, of course," Herr Freudenberg continued. "The Press even ventured to find fault with me. England, as usual, they declared, had gained all she desired and had given the very minimum. However, we will not waste time in reminiscences. To-day the only pleasure I have in thinking of that conference is the fact that you and I came together. When you left Berlin - I saw you off, you remember - I told those who stood around that there went the future Prime Minister of England. I believed it, and I am seldom mistaken. Tell me, what piece of transcendental ill-fortune is this which brings you here an exile?"

"I committed an act of transcendental folly," Julien replied. "I have no one to blame but myself. I not only wrote an indiscreet letter, but I put my name to it. I was deceived, too, in the character of the woman to whom it was sent."

"It is so trifling an error," Herr Freudenberg said thoughtfully, "made by many a man without evil results. One learns experience as one passes on in life. It is a hard price that you are paying for yours. Come, that is finished. Now answer me. What are you going to do?"

Julien laughed, a little bitterly.

"My friend," he answered, stretching out his hand and taking a cigarette from the open box upon the table, "you ask rather a hard question. My resignation was accepted, was even required of me. Politics and diplomacy are alike barred to me. There is no return. What is there left? I may write a book. So far as my means permit, I may travel. I may play games, take a walk in the morning, play bridge in the afternoon, eat heavily and sleep early. What is there left, Herr Freudenberg - tell me of your wisdom - for a man about whose ears has come crashing the scaffolding of his life?"

Herr Freudenberg looked across at his companion, and in that dimly-lit room his eyes were bright and his lips firm.

"To rebuild, my friend," he declared. "Choose another foundation and rebuild."

"You recognize, I presume," Julien said, "that I require a few more details if your advice is to be of value?"

"The details are here in this room," Herr Freudenberg replied firmly. "Be my man. I cannot offer you fame, because fame comes only, nowadays, to the man who serves his own country. You see, I make no pretense at deceiving you, but I offer you a life of action, I offer you such wealth as your imagination can have conceived, and I offer you revenge."

"Revenge," Julien repeated, a little vaguely.

"Upon the political party by whose scheming that letter was first of all elicited from you and then made public," Herr Freudenberg said slowly. "Do you imagine that it was a thoughtless act of that woman's? Do you know that her reward is to be a peerage for her husband?"

"You, too, believe that it was a trap, then?" Julien remarked.

"Of course. Don't you know yourself that you were a thorn in the flesh to your own party? They hated you because you were not afraid to preach war when war might have saved your country from what is to come. They hated you because you were a strong man in a strong place, and because the people believed in you. They hated you because the policy which would have been yours in the four or five years to come, would have been the policy which would have brought the country around you, which alone would have kept your party in power. You were the only figure in politics which the imperialist party in England had to fear. Mrs. Carraby - I believe that was the lady's name - is ill-paid enough with that peerage. Leave out the personal element - or leave it in, if you will, for when I speak of my country I know no friendships - but, my dear friend, let me tell you that I myself would have given more than a peerage - I would have given a principality - to the person who threw you out of English politics."

Julien's eyes were bright. Somehow or other, his old dreams, his old faith in himself had returned for a moment. And then the bitterness all swept in upon him.

"I think, Herr Freudenberg," he said, "that you are talking a little in the skies. At any rate, it makes no difference. Those things have passed."

"Those things have passed," Herr Freudenberg assented. "There is no future for you in England. That is why I wish to rescue you from the ignominy of which you yourself have spoken. I repeat my offer. Be my man. You shall taste life and taste it in such gulps as you wish."

Julien shook his head slowly.

"My friend," he said, "it is the cruel part of our profession that one man's life can be given to one country alone."

"Wrong!" Herr Freudenberg declared briskly. "I am not going to decry patriotism. The welfare of my country is the religion which guides my life. But you - you have no country. There is no England left for you. She has thrown you out. You are a wanderer, a man without ties or home. That is why I claim you as my man. I want to show you the way to revenge."

"You puzzle me," Julien admitted. "You talk about revenge. I know you far too well to believe that you would propose to me any scheme which would involve the raising even of my little finger against the country which has turned me out."

"Naturally," Herr Freudenberg agreed. "You do me no less than justice, my dear Sir Julien. What I do hope that you have firmly fixed in your mind is that I, despite your halfpenny papers, your novelists seeking for a new sensation, and your weird middle class, I, Carl Freudenberg, maker of toys, am the honest and sincere friend of England. The work which I ask you to do for me would be as much in the interests of your country as of my own, only when I say your country, I mean your country governed by the political party in which I have faith and confidence. I tell you frankly that an England governed as she is at present is a country I loathe. If I raise my hand against her - not in war, mind, but in diplomacy - if I strive to humble her to-day, it is because I would cover if I could the political party who are in power at this moment with disrepute and discredit. Why should you yourself shrink from aiding me in this task? They are the party in whose ranks - high in whose ranks, I might say - are those who stooped with baseness, with deceit unmentionable, to rid themselves of you. Therefore, I say strike. Come with me and you shall help. And when the time comes, I think I can promise you that I can show you a way back, a way which you have never guessed."

Julien looked across the table long and earnestly.

"Herr Freudenberg," he said, "if I answer you in the negative, it is because of your own words. The love of your country, you told me not long ago, is your religion. For her good you would make use even of those you call your friends. Now I am sincere with you. I do not know whether to trust you or not. For that reason I cannot attempt to discuss this matter with you. I do not ask even that you explain yourself."

"You mean that at any rate you cannot trust me entirely?" Herr Freudenberg replied. "Well, if you had, I should have been disappointed in you. Still, I have said things that were in my heart to say to you. We send now for Mademoiselle Ixe. Before very long we talk together again."

Herr Freudenberg touched the bell. A waiter appeared almost immediately.

"Find mademoiselle," he ordered. "Tell her that we wait impatiently."

Mademoiselle was not far away. Herr Freudenberg passed his arm through hers.

"We return, I think," he said. "This little room has served its purpose."

Julien on the landing tried to make his adieux, but his host only laughed at him. Mademoiselle Ixe held out her hand and led him into the room by her side.

"He wishes it," she murmured softly. "He has so few nights here, one must do as he desires."

The little party returned to their table in the corner. Somehow or other, their coming seemed to enliven the room. There was more spirit in the music, more animation in the conversation. Albert walked with a sprightlier step. Then Julien, in his passage down the room, received a distinct shock. He stopped short.

"Kendricks, by Jove!" he exclaimed.

Kendricks, sitting alone at a small table, with a bottle of champagne in front of him and a huge cigar in his mouth, waved his hand joyfully. Then he glanced at his friend's companions, frowned for a moment, and gazed fixedly at Herr Freudenberg.

"Julien, by all that's lucky!" he called out. "And I haven't been in Paris four hours! I called at your hotel and they told me you were out. Sit down."

"I am not alone," Julien began to explain, -

Herr Freudenberg turned round.

"You must present your friend," he declared. "He must join us."

Julien hesitated for a moment.

"Kendricks," he said, "this is my friend, Herr Freudenberg."

The two men shook hands. Kendricks as yet had scarcely taken his eyes off Herr Freudenberg's face.

"I am glad to meet you, sir," he remarked. "It is odd, but your face seems familiar to me."

Herr Freudenberg leaned over the table.

"My friend, Mr. Kendricks," he said, "you are, I believe, a newspaper man, and you should know the world. When you see a face that is familiar to you in Paris, and in this Paris, it goes well that you forget that familiarity, eh?"

Kendricks nodded.

"It is sound," he agreed. "I will join you, with pleasure."

"Mademoiselle," Herr Freudenberg continued, "permit me to introduce my new friend, Mr. Kendricks. Mr. Kendricks - Mademoiselle Ixe. We will now begin, if it is your pleasure, to spend the evening. There is room in our corner, Mr. Kendricks. Come there, and presently Mademoiselle Ixe will sing to us, mademoiselle with the yellow hair there will dance, the orchestra shall play their maddest music. This is Paris and we are young. Ah, my friends, it comes to us but seldom to live like this!"

They all sat down together. Herr Freudenberg gave reckless orders for more wine. The *chef d'orchestre* was at his elbow, Albert hovered in the background. Kendricks leaned over and whispered in his friend's ear.

"Julien, who is our friend?"

"A manufacturer of toys from Leipzig," Julien answered grimly.

"The toys that giants play with!" Kendricks muttered. "I have never forgotten a face in my life."

"Then forget this one for a moment," Julien advised him quickly. "This is not a night for memories. I have lived with the ghosts of them long enough."

Their party became larger. The little dancing girl came to drink wine with them and remained to listen to Herr Freudenberg. A friend of Mademoiselle Ixe - a tall, fair girl in a blue satin gown - detached herself from her friends and joined them. Herr Freudenberg, with his arm resting lightly around Mademoiselle Ixe's waist, talked joyously and incessantly. It was not until some one lifted the blind and discovered that the sun was shining that they spoke of a move. Then, as the *vestiaire* came hurrying up with their coats and wraps, Herr Freudenberg lifted his glass.

"One last toast!" he cried. "Dear Marguerite, my friends, all of you - to the sun which calls us to work, to the moon which calls us to pleasure, to the love that crowds our hearts!"

He raised his companion's hand to his lips and drew her arm through his.

"Come," he cried, "to the streets! We will take our coffee from the stall of Madame Huber."

E. Phillips Oppenheim

CHAPTER XIV

THE MORNING AFTER

Kendricks and Julien drove down from the hill in a small open victoria. The sun had risen, but here and there were traces of a fading twilight. A faint mauve glow hung over the sleeping streets. The sunlight as yet was faint and the morning breeze chilly. As they passed down the long hill, tired-looking waiters were closing up the night cafés. Bedraggled revelers crept along the pavements with weary footsteps.

With every yard of their progression, the meeting between the two extremes of life seemed to become more apparent. The children of the night - the weary, unwholesome products of dissipation, rubbed shoulders with the children of the morning - girls, hatless, in simple clothes, walking with brisk footsteps to their work; market women, brown-cheeked and hearty, setting out their wares upon the stalls; the youth of Paris, blithe and strenuous, walking light-footed to the region of warehouses and factories. Julien and Kendricks looked out upon the little scene with interest. Both had been sleepy when they had left the café, but there was something stimulating in the sight of this thin but constant stream of people. Kendricks sat up and began to talk.

"Julien," he declared, "this Paris never alters. It's a queer little world and a rotten one. We are here just at the ebbing of the tide. Don't you feel the hatefulness of it - the thin-blooded scream for pleasure which needs the lash of these painted women, these gaudy cafés, this yellow wine all the time? My God! and they call it pleasure! Look at these people going to their work, Julien. There's where the red blood flows. They're the people with the taste of life between their teeth. Can't you see them at their pleasures - see them sitting in a beer-garden with a girl and a band, their week's money in their pocket, and the knowledge that they've earned it? Perhaps sometimes they look up the hill and wonder at the craze for it all. Did you see the stream coming up to-night - automobiles, victorias, carriages of every sort; pale-faced men who had lunched too well, dined too well, flogging their tired systems in the craze for more excitement, more pleasure; eating at an unwholesome hour, smoking sickly cigarettes, kissing rouged lips, listening to the false music of that hard laughter? Look at those girls arm in arm, off to their little milliner's shop. Hear them laugh! You don't hear anything like that, Julien, on the top of the hill."

"Of course," Julien remarked, stifling a yawn, "if you've come to Paris to be moral -"

"Not I!" Kendricks broke in roughly. "Bless you, I'm one of the worst. A wild night in Paris calls me even now from any part of the world. But Lord, what fools we are! And, Julien, we get worse. It's the old people who keep these places going."

"The older we get," Julien replied, "the harder we have to struggle for our joys."

Kendricks wheeled suddenly in his place.

"Tell me how long you have known Herr Freudenberg?" he insisted. "How many times have you been seen with him? Is it the truth that you met him to-night for the first time?"

Julien laughed.

"My dear David!" he protested, -

"To tell you the truth, Julien," Kendricks interrupted, "there's some hidden trouble, some mysterious influence at work which seems to be upsetting the relations just now between France and England. To be frank with you, I know that Carraby, at a Cabinet meeting yesterday, suggested that you were at the bottom of it."

Julien's eyes suddenly flashed fire.

"D - n that fellow!" he muttered. "Does anybody believe it?"

Kendricks shrugged his shoulders.

"Scarcely. And yet, Julien, it pays to be careful. You can't afford to be seen in public places with the enemies of your country."

"Is Carl Freudenberg an enemy of my country?"

Kendricks leaned back in his seat and laughed scornfully.

"Julien," he exclaimed, "there are times when you are

very simple! Do you indeed mean that you would try to deceive even me? You would pretend that I, David Kendricks, of the *Post*, don't know that Herr Freudenberg and the Prince von Falkenberg, ruler of Germany, are one and the same person? Maker of toys, he calls himself! Maker of fools' palaces, if you like, builder of prison houses, if you will. No man was ever born with less of a conscience, more solely and wholly ambitious both for his country and for himself, than the man with whom you talked to-night. You knew him?"

"Naturally," Julien answered. "We met at Berlin."

"The man is a great genius," Kendricks continued. "No one will deny him that. They speak of his weaknesses. They talk of his drinking bouts, of his plunges into French dissipation. The man hasn't a single dissipated thought in his mind. He moves through this world - this little Paris world - with one idea only. He gets behind the scenes. He comes here secretly, drops hints here and there as a private person, lets himself be considered a Parisian of Parisians. All the time he listens and he drops his cunning words of poison and he works. What are his ambitions? Do you know, Julien?"

"Do you?" Julien asked.

"It seems to me that I have some idea," Kendricks answered. "This is your hotel, isn't it?"

Julien nodded.

"Are you going to stay here?"

Kendricks shook his head.

"I stay at a little hotel in the Rue Taitbout. I stay there because it is full of the weirdest set of foreigners you ever knew. This morning we breakfast together?"

"Come and see me when you will," Julien invited, "or I will come to you; not to breakfast, though - I am engaged."

"To Herr Freudenberg?" Kendricks asked quickly.

"To the lady whom your little friend, the manicurist, sent me to visit," Julien replied. "Perhaps now you will tell me that she is an ambassadress in disguise?"

"I'll tell you nothing about her this morning," Kendricks said. "I'll tell you nothing which you ought not to find out for yourself."

"Do you think I may breakfast with her safely?" Julien inquired.

"Heaven knows - I don't!" Kendricks replied. "No man is safe with such a woman as Madame Christophor. But let it go. We dine together to-night. I'll tell you some news then. I'm going to unroll a plan of campaign. There's work for you, if you like it; - nothing formulated as yet, but it's coming - perhaps hope - who knows?"

The sun rose higher in the heavens, the mauve light faded from the sky. Morning had arrived in earnest and Paris settled herself down to the commencement of another day. Julien, for the first time since he had left England, was asleep five minutes after his head had touched the pillow. Herr Freudenberg, on the contrary, made no attempt at all to retire. In the sitting-room of his apartments in the Boulevard Maupassant he sat in his dressing-gown, carefully studying some letters which had arrived by the night mail. Opposite to him was a secretary; by his side Estermen, who appeared to be there for the purpose of making a report.

"Not a document," Estermen was saying, "not a line of writing of any sort in his trunk, his bureau, or anywhere about his room."

Herr Freudenberg nodded thoughtfully.

"But these Englishmen are the devil to deal with!" he said. "The luncheon is ordered to-day in the private room at the Armenonville?"

"Everything has been attended to," Estermen replied.

Herr Freudenberg was thoughtful for several moments. Then with a wave of his hand he dismissed Estermen.

"You, too, can go, Fritz," he said to his secretary. "You have had a long night's work."

"You yourself, Excellency, should sleep for a while," his secretary advised.

Herr Freudenberg shook his head.

"Sleep," he declared, "is a waste of time. I need no sleep. As you go, you can tell my servant to prepare a warm bath. I will rest then for an hour and walk in the Champs Elysées."

The secretary withdrew and Herr Freudenberg was alone. He picked up a crumpled rose that lay upon the

E. Phillips Oppenheim

table and twirled it for a moment or two in his fingers. The action seemed to be wholly unconscious. His eyes were set in a fixed stare, his thoughts were busy weaving out his plans for the day. It was not until he was summoned to his bath that he rose and glanced at the withered flower. Then he smiled.

"Poor little Marguerite!" he murmured. "What a pity!"

He touched the rose with his lips, abandoned his first intention, which seemed to have been to throw it into the fireplace, and put it back carefully upon the table, side by side with an odd white glove.

"Queer little record of the froth of life," he said softly to himself. "One soiled evening glove, a faded rose, a woman's tears, - they pass. What can one do - we poor others who have to drive the wheels of life?"

He sighed, shrugged his high shoulders, and passed out.

CHAPTER XV

BEHIND CLOSED DOORS

Very soon after mid-day on the same morning, Herr Carl Freudenberg was the host at a small luncheon party given in a private room of the most famous restaurant in the Bois. His morning attire was a model of correctness, his eyes were clear, his manner blithe, almost joyous. There was no possible indication in his appearance of his misspent hours. He was at once a genial and courteous host. Monsieur Décheles sat at his right hand; Monsieur Felix Brant on his left; Monsieur Pelleman opposite to him. The three men had arrived in an automobile together and had entered the restaurant by the private way, but that they were guests of some distinction was obvious from their reception by the manager himself.

The luncheon was worthy of the great reputation of the place. It was swiftly and well served. With the coffee and liqueurs the waiters withdrew. Herr Freudenberg, with a smile, rose up and tried the door. Then he returned to his place, lit a cigarette, and leaned back in his chair.

"My dear friends," he announced, "now we can talk."

Monsieur Pelleman smiled.

E. Phillips Oppenheim

"Yes," he admitted, "we can talk. In this excellent brandy, Monsieur Carl Freudenberg, I drink your very good health. Long may these little visits of yours continue."

Herr Freudenberg smiled his thanks.

"Monsieur Pelleman," he said, "and you, too, my dear friends, let me assure you that there is nothing in the world which I enjoy so much as these brief visits of mine to your delightful capital. No more I think of the pressures and cares of office. I let myself go, and on these occasions, as you know, I speak to you not in the language of diplomacy, but as good friends who meet together to enjoy an hour or two of one another's company, and who, because there is no harm to be done by it, but much good, open their hearts and speak true words with one another."

Monsieur Décheles smiled.

"It is a pleasure which we all share," he declared. "It is more agreeable, without a doubt, to take lunch with Monsieur Carl Freudenberg, and to speak openly, than to exchange long-winded interviews, the true meaning of which is too much concealed by diplomatic verbiage, with the excellent gentleman to whose good offices are intrusted the destinies of Herr Freudenberg's great nation."

"Monsieur," Herr Freudenberg said, "to-day shall be no exception. To-day I speak to you, perhaps, more openly than ever before. To-day I perhaps risk much - yet why not speak the things which are in my heart?"

Monsieur Felix Brant took a cigarette from the box by

his elbow, but he felt for it only. His eyes never left the face of his host. Of the three men, he seemed the one least in sympathy with the state of affairs to which Herr Freudenberg had alluded so cheerfully. He watched the man at the head of the table all the time as though every energy of which he was possessed was devoted to the task of reading underneath that suave but impenetrable face.

"Gentlemen," Herr Freudenberg continued, "there have been many misapprehensions between your country and mine. Ten years ago we seemed indeed on the highroad to friendship. It was then - I speak frankly, mind - that your country made the one fatal mistake of recent years. Great Britain, isolated, left behind in the race for power, a weakened and decaying nation, having searched the world over for allies, held out the timorous hand of friendship to you. What evil genius was with your statesmen that day! When the history of these times comes to be written, it is my firm belief that it will be then acknowledged that the genius of the man who reigned over Great Britain at that time was alone responsible for the commencement of what has become a veritable alliance."

Herr Freudenberg paused.

"There is no doubt," Monsieur Décheles asserted calmly, "that the influence of the late king was immense among the people of France. He appealed somehow to their imaginations, a great monarch who was also a *bon viveur*, who had lived his days in Paris as the others."

Herr Freudenberg nodded thoughtfully.

E. Phillips Oppenheim

"He is dead," he said, "and history will write him down as a great king. Do you know that it is one of my theories that morals have nothing to do with government? I doubt whether a more sagacious monarch has ever reigned over that unfortunate country than the one we speak of. So sagacious was he that he even saw the beginning of the end, he saw the things that must come when he looked across the North Sea; and notwithstanding his descent, notwithstanding all the ties which should have allied him with Germany, he hated our people and he hated our country with a prophetic hatred. But we gossip a little, gentlemen. Let me proceed. I want you to realize that the policy of Germany for the last five years has been wholly directed towards securing the friendship of your country. I want you to realize that but for the continual interference of Great Britain you would even now be in a far more favorable position with us than you are to-day. Germany wants nothing in Morocco. Germany's first and greatest wish is for a rich and prosperous France. On the other hand, Germany is loyal to her friendships, and fervent in her hatreds. The country whose humiliation is a solemn charge upon my people is Great Britain and not France."

Monsieur Décheles leaned back in his chair. Monsieur Felix Brant never moved.

"I want," Herr Freudenberg continued, "to have you think and consider and weigh this matter. Why do you, a great and prosperous country, link yourselves with a decaying power, against whom, before very long, Germany is pledged to strike? These are the plainest words that have ever been spoken by a citizen of one country to three citizens of another. Herr Freudenberg, the maker of toys, speaks to his three French friends as a thoughtful merchant of his country who has had unusual facilities for imbibing the spirit of her politicians. Gentlemen, you do not misunderstand me?"

"It is impossible, Herr Freudenberg," Monsieur Décheles said, "to misunderstand you for a single moment. Your hand is too clear and your methods too sagacious."

"Then let me repeat," Herr Freudenberg declared, "that before many years are passed - perhaps, indeed, before many months - it is the intention of my country either to inflict a scathing diplomatic humiliation upon Great Britain, or to engage in this war the fear of which has kept her in a state of panic for the last ten years. Keep that in your minds, my friends. Friendship is a great thing, honor is a great thing, generosity is a great thing, but I would speak to you three citizens of France to-day as I would speak to her rulers had I access to them, and I would say, 'Do you dare, for the sake of an alliance out of which you have procured no single benefit, do you dare to drag your country into unnecessary, fruitless and bloody war?' You have nothing to gain by it, you have everything to lose. Let Germany deal with her traditional enemy in her own way. And as for France, let France believe what is, without doubt, the truth - that she has nothing whatever to fear from Germany. I will not speak of the past, but the greatest thinkers in Germany to-day regret nothing so much in the history of her splendid rise as that unfortunate campaign of Bismarck's. It is the one blot upon her magnificent history. Let that go - let that go and be buried. I bring you timely warning. I come to the city I love, for her own sake, for the sake of her people whom I also love. I beg you to listen to these words of mine, to adjust your policy so that little by little you weaken the joints which bind you to England, so that when the time comes you yourself may not be dragged into a hopeless and pitiless struggle."

There was a moment's silence. Then Monsieur Décheles spoke.

"Herr Freudenberg," he began, "what you have said we have been in some measure prepared for. The more amicable tone of all the correspondence between our two countries has been marked of late. Yet there have been times, and not long ago, when your country has shown wonderful readiness to treat with a rough hand the claims of France in many quarters of the world. The more powerful your country, the greater she is to be feared. Supposing France stood on one side while Great Britain fell before your arms, what then would be the relations between France and Germany?"

Monsieur Brant spoke for the first time.

"Herr Freudenberg, you remind me of the fable of the Persian who had two men to fight, both as strong as himself. To the one he sent ambassadors, with the key of his favorite gardens; the other he fought. It is a great policy to deal with your enemies one at a time."

Herr Freudenberg stretched out his arms across the table.

"My friend," he pronounced, "without faith there is no genius. Without genius there is no government. I only ask you to believe this one thing. Germany is not and never has been the traditional enemy of France. I ask you to study the whole question for but one single half-hour, I ask you to read the commercial records of these days. Help yourself to all the statistics that throw light upon this question, and I swear that you will find that whereas Great Britain and Germany stand opposed to one another under every condition and in every quarter of the world, there is no single bone of contention anywhere between France and Germany. Their aims are different, their destinies are written. I ask you to apply only a reasonable measure of philosophy and common sense, a reasonable measure of faith, to the things I say."

There was a cautious tap at the door, a whispered message. Monsieur Pelleman rose.

"It is my secretary," he announced. "I fear, gentlemen, that we are due elsewhere."

"Herr Freudenberg, your luncheon has been delightful," Monsieur Décheles declared, holding out his hand. "You have given us, as usual, something to think of. These informal meetings between citizens of two great countries will do, I am sure, more than anything else in the world, to ripen our budding friendship."

"Your words," Herr Freudenberg replied, grasping the hand which had been offered to him, "are a happy augury. When we meet again, I shall be able to prove the coming of the things of which I have spoken."

They left him on the threshold of the room. The giver of the feast was alone. Very slowly he retraced his steps and stood for a moment with folded arms, looking down on the table at which they had lunched. His natural urbanity, the smile half persuasive, half humorous, which had parted his lips, had gone. His

E. Phillips Oppenheim

face seemed to have resolved itself into lines of iron. As he stood there, one seemed suddenly to realize the presence of a great man - a greater, even, than Carl Freudenberg, maker of toys!

CHAPTER XVI

HAVE YOU EVER LOVED?

Nothing which he had heard or imagined of Madame Christophor had prepared Julien for the subdued yet manifest magnificence of her dwelling. He passed through that small postern gate beneath the watch of a butler who relieved him of his stick and gloves and handed him over to a sort of major-domo. Afterwards he was conducted across a beautiful round hall, lit with quaint fragments of stained-glass window, through a picture gallery which almost took Julien's breath away, and into a small room, very daintily furnished, entirely and characteristically French of the Louis Seize period. A round table was laid for two in front of an open window, which looked out upon a lawn smooth and velvety, with here and there little flower-beds, and in the middle a gray stone fountain. Madame Christophor came in almost at the same moment from the garden. She was wearing a long lace coat over the thinnest of muslin skirts, and a hat with some violets in it which seemed to match exactly the color of her eyes.

"So you have come, my friend of a few hours," she said, smiling at him. "The fear has not seized you yet? You are not afraid that over my simple luncheon table I shall ask you compromising questions?"

E. Phillips Oppenheim

"I am neither afraid of your asking questions, madame," he assured her, "nor of my being tempted to reply to them."

"That," she murmured, "is ungallant. Meanwhile, we lunch."

Such a meal as he might have expected from such surroundings was swiftly and daintily served. There was cantaloup, cut in halves, with the faintest suspicion of liqueur, and a great globule of ice; an omelette, even for Paris a wonderful omelette, - a *mousse* of chicken, some asparagus, a bowl of peaches, and coffee. After the latter had been served, madame, with a little wave of her hand, dismissed the servants from the room.

"Sir Julien," she said, "I am not pleased with you."

He sighed.

"I regret your displeasure the more," he declared, "because I find myself indebted to you for a new gastronomic ideal."

"You are really beginning to wake up," she laughed. "When you first arrived here, less than twenty-four hours ago, you thought yourself a broken-spirited and broken-hearted man. You were very dull. Soon you will begin to realize that life is a matter of epochs, that no blow is severe enough to kill life itself. It is only the end of an epoch. But I am displeased with you, as I said, because you have told me nothing. This morning I have letters from London. I learn that through a single indiscretion not only were you forced to relinquish a great political career, but that you were forced also to give up the lady for whom you cared."

"You have ingenious correspondents," he remarked.

"Truthful ones, are they not?"

"I was engaged to marry Lady Anne Clonarty," he admitted. "It was, if I may venture to say so, an alliance."

Madame Christophor's eyes twinkled.

"Once," she declared, "I met the Duke of Clonarty. I also met the Duchess, I also saw Lady Anne. They were traveling in great state through Italy. It was in Rome that I came across them. The Duchess was very affable to me. I think you have rightly expressed your affair of the heart, my friend. It was to have been an alliance!"

Julien was thoughtful. Madame Christophor in a moment continued.

"You know, my friend," she said, tapping the ash from her cigarette into her saucer, "your misfortune came just in time to save you from becoming what in English you call a great, a colossal prig."

His eyebrows went up. Suddenly he smiled.

"Perhaps," he admitted. "To be a successful politician one must of necessity be a prig."

"Not in the least," she reminded him swiftly. "There is the Prince von Falkenberg."

"The maker of toys," he murmured.

"The maker, alas! of toys which the world were better without," she replied. "But never mind that. For the sake of your ambitions you were content, were you not, to marry a young woman with whom you had not the slightest sympathy, in order that she might receive your guests, might add the lustre of her name to the expansion of her husband's genius?"

"Madame," he said, "we live a very short time. We live only one life. Only certain things are possible to us. The man who tries to crowd everything into that life fails. He is a dilettante. He may find pleasure but he reaches no end. He strikes no long sustained note. In the eyes of those who come after him, he is a failure."

"This," she murmured, "is interesting. Please go on."

"The man who means to succeed," he continued, "to succeed in any one position, must sacrifice everything else - temperament, if necessary character - for that one thing. When I left college, the study of politics was almost chosen for me. It became a part of my life. As my interest developed, it is true that my outlook upon life was narrowed. I was content to forget, perhaps, that I was a man, I strove fervently and desperately to develop into the perfect political machine. From that point of view, nobody in England would have made me a better wife than Lady Anne Clonarty."

She nodded.

"What a blessing that you wrote that letter!"

"I don't know," he replied. "I still think it was a great

misfortune. Frankly, I have no idea what to make of my life. I don't know how to start again, to deal with the pieces in any intelligent fashion. Now that I am outside the thing, I see the narrowness of it all, I see that I was giving up many things which are interesting and beautiful, many friendships that might have been delightful, but on the other hand there was always the pressing on, the big, vital side, the great throb of life. I miss it. I feel to myself as a great factory sounds on Sundays and holidays, when the engine that drives all the machinery of the place is silent. I wander among the empty, quiet places, and I am lonely."

"Have you ever loved a woman?" she asked.

Her voice had suddenly dropped. He looked across the table. Her lips were slightly parted, her eyes fixed upon his. There was something shining out of them which he did not wholly understand. He only knew that the question seemed to have stirred him in some new way. An intense sense of pleasurable content, a feeling as though he were listening to music, stole through his senses. This was a new thing. He was bewildered. He leaned a little further across the table. He found himself watching the faint blue veins of her delicate fingers, noticing the curious perfume of roses that seemed to come to him from the flutter of the lace around her neck.

"You are a man, Sir Julien. You must be thirty-five - perhaps older. Yet somehow you have the look to me of one who has never cared at all."

"It is true," he admitted.

"Life," she declared, "is a strange place. A few months

ago your whole career was one of ambition. Misfortune came, or what you counted a misfortune. You reckoned yourself ruined. It is simply a change of poise. You turn now naturally to the other things in life. Do you know that you will find them greater?"

He shook his head.

"It is too early for me to believe that," he said. "I will admit that now and then in my forced solitude I have sometimes realized that one may become too engrossed in a career of ambition. One may shut out many things in life that are sweet and wholesome. But it is too early yet for me to look back upon what has happened with equanimity and say that I am glad to be a wanderer on the face of the earth, a homeless man, a waif."

She shrugged her shoulders.

"You know that people are talking about you in London?" she asked abruptly.

He looked a little startled.

"I know nothing of the sort," he replied. "I have scarcely looked at a newspaper for weeks. Kendricks is over here with some story -"

"Who is Kendricks?" she interrupted.

"A journalist, an old friend of mine. What he told me, though, I looked upon as simply a little more malice from my friend Carraby."

"Tell me exactly his news?"

"He told me," Julien continued, "that there is a good deal of unrest over in London concerning our relations with France. The absolute candor and completely good understanding which existed a short time ago seems to have become clouded. Carraby is trying to suggest in English circles that I have been using my influence over here against the present government. The absurd part of it is that although I have been in France for a month, I arrived in Paris only yesterday."

"I was not alluding to that at all," she said. "It is in the country places, at the by-elections, and twice in the House itself lately, that things have been said which point to a certain impatience at your having been dropped so completely. You know Brentwood?"

"A strong, firm man," Julien replied, "but scarcely a friend of mine."

"Well, in your House of Parliament, the night before last," she continued, "he said that your country needed men at the Foreign Office who, however great might be their love of peace, still were not afraid of war, and your name was mentioned."

Julien smiled.

"They used to call me the fire-brand. I suppose I am in a great minority. I have never been able to see that a wholesome war, in defense of one's territory and one's honor, is an unmixed curse. It is the natural blood-letting of a strong country."

"No wonder you are unpopular in radical circles," she remarked, raising her eyebrows; "but anyhow, what I really want to say to you is this. Don't do anything

E. Phillips Oppenheim

rash. You have made the acquaintance of the most dangerous man in Europe. Don't let him control your actions, don't let him influence you. I want you always, whatever you do, to leave the way open for your return."

He shook his head.

"I do not think that my return is ever possible."

"Have you talked with your friend Kendricks?" she asked.

"Not yet," he replied.

"Hear what he has to say," she continued. "Bring him to see me if you will."

"I will try," he promised.

They were silent for a moment, listening to the splashing of the fountain outside and the distant hum of the city.

"Do you know that you are very kind to me?" he said.

"You were very much afraid of me yesterday," she reminded him.

"Had I any cause?"

She smiled.

"I shall not tell you my secrets. You must find them out. I have dabbled in politics, I have dabbled in diplomacy. I have not as a rule very much sympathy with your sex, as I think you know. It has never interested me before even to give good advice to a man. If I were you, Sir Julien, beyond a certain point I would not trust Madame Christophor, for when the time comes I have always the feeling that if a man's career lay within my power, I would sooner wreck it than help him."

"Of course you are talking nonsense," he declared.

"Am I?" she replied. "Well, I don't know. I can look back now to a half-hour of my life when I loathed every creature that could call itself a man."

"But it was a single person," he reminded her, "who sinned."

"His crime was too great to be the crime of a single man," she asserted, with a quiver of passion in her tone. "It was the culmination of the whole abominable selfishness of his sex. One man's life is too light a price to pay for the tragedy of that half-hour. I have never spared one of your sex since. I never shall."

"So far you have been kind to me," he persisted.

"Up to a certain point. Beyond that, I warn you, I should have no pity. If you were a wise man, I think even now that you would thank me for my luncheon and take my hand and bid me farewell."

"Instead of which," he answered, smiling, "I am waiting only to know when you will do me the honor to come and dine with me?"

She shook her head.

"I will make no appointment," she said. "Send me your telephone number directly you move into your rooms. If I am weary of myself I may call for you, but I tell you frankly that you must not expect it. If I see a way of making use of you, that will be different."

"May I come and see you again?" he begged. "You are dismissing me rather abruptly."

She shrugged her shoulders. She was looking weary, as though the heat of the day had tried her.

"I care very little, after all," she answered, "whether I ever see you again. I wish I could care, although if I did the result would be the same."

"You asked me a question a short time ago," he remarked. "Let me ask you the same. Have you never cared for any one?"

"I cared once for my husband."

"You have been married?"

"Most certainly. I lived with my husband for two years."

"And now?" he persisted.

"We are separated. You really do not know my other name?"

"I have never heard you called anything but Madame Christophor."

"Well, you will hear it in time," she assured him. "You

will probably think you have made a great discovery. In the meantime, farewell."

She gave him her hands. He held them in his perhaps a little longer than was necessary. She raised her eyes questioningly. He drew them a little closer. Very quietly she removed the right one and touched a bell by her side.

"If my automobile is of any service to you, Sir Julien," she said, "pray use it. It waits outside and I shall not be ready to go out for an hour at least."

"Thank you," he replied. "Your automobile, empty, has no attractions."

The butler was already in the room.

"See that Sir Julien makes use of my automobile if he cares to," she ordered. "This has been a very pleasant visit. I hope we may soon meet again."

She avoided his eyes. He had an instinctive feeling that she was either displeased or disappointed with him. He followed the butler out into the hall filled with a vague sense of self-dissatisfaction.

CHAPTER XVII

KENDRICKS IS HOST

"You are going to spend," Kendricks declared, "a democratic evening. You are going to mix with common folk. To-night we shall drink no champagne at forty francs the bottle. On the other hand, we shall probably drink a great deal more beer than is good for us. How do you find the atmosphere here?"

"Filthy!"

"I was afraid you might notice it," Kendricks remarked. "Never mind, presently you will forget it. You have never been here before, I presume?"

"I have not," Julien agreed. "I daresay I shall find it interesting. You wouldn't describe it as quiet, would you?"

"One does not eat quietly here," Kendricks replied. "Four hundred people, mostly Germans, when they eat are never silent. The service of four hundred dinners continues at the same time. Listen to them. Close your eyes and you will appreciate the true music of crockery."

"If that infernal little band would keep quiet," Julien

grumbled, "one might hear oneself talk!"

"Let us have no more criticisms," Kendricks begged. "To-night you are of the working class. You may perhaps be a small manufacturer, the agent of a manufacturing firm in the country, a clerk with a moderate salary, or a mechanic in his best clothes. Remember that and do not complain of the music. You do not hear it every day. Let us hear no more blasé speeches, if you please.... Good! The dinner arrives. We dine here, my friend, for two francs. You will probably require another meal before the evening is concluded. On the other hand, you may feel that you never require another meal as long as you live. That is a matter of luck. In any case, you had better squeeze a little further up. Madame and her two daughters are going to sit next to you, and opposite there will be monsieur, and I judge the fiancé of one of the young ladies. It will be a family party. If there is anything in that dish of *hors d'oeuvres* which you fancy particularly, help yourself quickly. In a moment or two there will be no opportunity."

The two men were seated opposite one another at a long table in a huge popular restaurant in the heart of the city. It was Kendricks' plan - Kendricks, in fact, had insisted upon it.

"You know, my dear Julien," he continued, "a certain education is necessary for you. If only I had a little more time I should be invaluable. You have taken all your life too narrow a view. That wretched Eton training! You would have been better off at a board-school. We all should."

"You were at Winchester yourself," Julien reminded

E. Phillips Oppenheim

him, trying some of the bread and approving of it.

"For a short time only," Kendricks admitted, "and then you forget the years after which I spent in the byways. Oh, I know my people! I know the common people of America and England and France and Germany. I know them and love them. I love the middle classes, too, the honestly vulgar, honestly snobbish, foolishly ambitious, yet over-cautious middle class. The extreme types of every nation lose their racial individuality. You find the true thing only among the bourgeoisie. Oh, if I only knew whether these people," he added, "understood English!"

"You must not risk it," Julien warned him. "Madame has already her eye upon you."

"As a possible suitor for that unmated daughter on her right, I suspect," Kendricks declared. "The young lady has looked at me twice and down at her plate. Julien, you must change places."

"I shall do nothing of the sort," Julien retorted.

"If I ingratiate myself with this family and trouble comes of it," Kendricks continued, "the fault will be yours. Madame," he added, standing up and bowing, "will you permit me?"

Madame had been looking at the bread. Kendricks gallantly offered it. Madame's bows and smiles were a thing delightful to behold. Mademoiselle, too, would take bread, if monsieur was so kind. When Kendricks sat down again, the way was paved for general conversation. Julien, however, practically buttonholed his friend.

"Kendricks," he said, "you have told me nothing about England."

"There is little to tell," Kendricks replied. "The little there is will filter from me during the evening. We are spending a long evening together, you know, Julien."

"Heavens alive!" Julien groaned. "I am not sure that I am strong enough."

"Eat that soup," Kendricks advised him. "That, at least, is sustaining. Never mind stirring it up to see what vegetables are at the bottom. Take my word for it, it is good. And leave the pepper-pot alone. How the people crowd in! You perceive the commercial traveler with a customer? How they talk about that last order! The fat man facing you puzzles me. I wish I could know the occupation of our neighbors. I am curious."

"I should ask them," Julien suggested dryly.

"An idea!" Kendricks assented approvingly. "Let us wait until they have drunk the free wine. You understand, my dear Julien, that you pay nothing for that flask which stands by your side? It comes with the dinner. It is free."

Julien helped himself, and sipped it thoughtfully.

"At least," he murmured, as he set his glass down, "one is thankful that we do not pay for it!"

"There are some," Kendricks remarked, "who prefer beer. Personally, I like to preserve my local color. *Vin ordinaire* in Paris, beer in Germany. Madame!"

Kendricks had caught madame's eye with the glass at his lips. He rose at once and bowed. Madame acknowledged his graciousness with a huge smile, which spread even to her double chin. Monsieur leaned forward and joined in the ceremony. Mademoiselle, after a timid glance at her mother, also responded. Kendricks' character as an Englishman of gallantry was thoroughly established.

"I am doing our national character good," he declared to Julien, as he set down his glass empty. "As to my own constitution - but let that pass. We will drown this stuff in honest beer, later on. How are you getting on with the fish?"

"It is excellent - really excellent," Julien proclaimed. "Do you mean to say seriously that you are going to pay only two francs each for this repast?"

"Not a centime more," Kendricks assured him. "Do you know why I brought you here?"

"Part of my education, I suppose," Julien replied resignedly.

"Quite true. Further than that, I am here on business for my paper. I am here to study the effect of the German invasion of Paris. This place is being spoken of as being the haunt of Germans. It still seems to me that I find plenty of the real French people."

"Do we pursue your investigations elsewhere during the course of the evening?" Julien inquired.

"The whole of our evening," Kendricks told him, "is devoted to that purpose, and incidentally," he added, "to your education. We are going for red-blooded pleasure to-night, for the real thing, - for the hearty laughs, for the wholesome appetites; no caviare sandwiches, over-dry champagne, rouged lips and Rue de la Paix hats for us. If we make love, we make love honestly. Mademoiselle may permit a clasp of her hand - no more."

"So far," Julien remarked, "mademoiselle -"

"That is for later," Kendricks interrupted briskly. "We shall go to a singing-hall - a German singing-hall. The mademoiselles whom we meet will probably have their own sweethearts. Somehow, to-night I fancy that we shall be lookers-on. What does it matter? We shall at least see life. We shall catch the shadows of other people's happinesses. It is, I believe, the sincerest form. The chicken, dear Julien, - what of the chicken?"

Julien hesitated.

"There is little to be said against it," he confessed. "The only trouble is that it fails to arrive."

Kendricks summoned a waiter, a task of no inconsiderable difficulty, for the service was automatic - the dishes were set upon the table and the waiter disappeared for the next lot. Anything intervening was almost impossible. Monsieur, Kendricks declared, pointing indignantly across the table, had not been served with chicken! The waiter shook his head. It was unheard of! Monsieur had probably had his chicken and forgotten it. The chicken had been brought, two portions. There was no doubt about it. But where then had the chicken been hidden? Kendricks became fluent. He looked under the table. He pointed to his

E. Phillips Oppenheim

friend's empty plate. The waiter, only half convinced, departed with a vague promise. Kendricks sipped his wine.

"It is a regrettable incident," he declared, "but in the excitement of conversation, Julien, I ate both portions of chicken."

He had lapsed into French, the language in which he had argued with the waiter. Madame was overcome with the humor of the affair. Mademoiselle tittered as she leaned across and told her fiancé. The unattached mademoiselle looked her sympathy with Julien. Monsieur saw the joke and laughed heartily. They looked reproachfully at Kendricks. To them it was indeed a tragedy!

"Madame," Kendricks explained, "it is not my custom to be so greedy. The waiter set both portions before me, meaning, without doubt, that I should pass one to my friend. Alas! in the pleasure of conversation in these delightful surroundings," - he bowed low to mademoiselle - "something, I don't know what it was, carried me away, and I ate and ate until both portions were vanished. Ah!" he exclaimed. "Triumph! The waiter returns. He brings chicken, too, for my friend. Garçon, you have done well. You shall be rewarded. It is excellent."

The waiter, still with a protesting air, passed up the chicken. The little party was convulsed with merriment. They all watched Julien eat his tardy course. Kendricks, with an air of recklessness, sipped more wine.

"I flatter myself," he said, "that before very long I shall

have taught you to forget that you were ever a Cabinet Minister, that you were ever at Eton, that you were ever at Oxford. One does not live in those places, you know, Julien. One shrivels instead of expands.... My friend, we have dined."

"Is there nothing more?" Julien asked.

"There is fruit," Kendricks admitted. "It was in my mind to spare you the fruit. I see it to right and left of us being handed around - nuts, a banana, apples whose exterior I trust is misleading. Never mind, you have desired fruit and you shall have it. Waiter, monsieur desires his fruit."

The waiter disappeared and in a moment or two Julien was served.

"Coffee, if you will?"

"No coffee, thanks," Julien decided. "If we are really going to spend the evening visiting places of entertainment of a similar class, let us reserve our coffee. A large cigar, I think."

Kendricks sighed.

"I hate to go. Mademoiselle opposite is pleased with me. I have made a good impression upon madame. Monsieur is ready to extend to me the right hand of fellowship. One of those pleasing little romances one dreams about might here find a commencement. In a week's time I might be accepted as a son-in-law of the house. I see all the signs of assent already beaming in madame's eye. Perhaps we had better go, Julien!"

E. Phillips Oppenheim

They took their leave, not without the exchange of many smiles and bows with the little family party they left behind. They walked slowly down the room, arm in arm.

"We were fortunate, you see, in our neighbors," Kendricks declared. "There are Germans everywhere here. One is curious about these people. One wonders how far they have imbibed the manners and customs of the people among whom they live. Are they still absolutely and entirely Teutons, do you suppose? Do they intermarry here, make friends, or do they remain an alien element?"

"To judge by appearances," Julien remarked, "they remain an alien element. It is astonishing how seldom you see mixed parties of French people and Germans here."

"It is exactly to make observations upon that point that I am in Paris," Kendricks asserted. "My people are curious. They want me to watch and write about it. Do you know that there is a feeling in London, Julien, that we are reaching the climax?"

Julien nodded.

"I can quite believe it," he replied. "Falkenberg seems to show every desire to force our hand."

"May the Lord deliver us from a Germanized Paris!" Kendricks prayed. "They may have the Ritz, if they will, and the Elysées Palace. They may have all the halls of fashion and gilt and wealth. They may swamp the Pré Catelan and the Armenonville, so long as they leave us the real Paris. Come, we take our coffee here.

This is a German café, if you like. Never mind, let us see if by chance any French people have wandered in."

They drank coffee at a little table in a huge building, hung with tobacco smoke, with the inevitable band at one end, and crowded with people. Kendricks smiled as the waiter brought them sugared cakes with their coffee.

"It is Germany," he declared. "Look! An odd Frenchman or two, perhaps; no French women. Look at the hats, the women's faces. The hats looked well enough in the shop-windows here. What an ignoble end for them! From an aesthetic point of view, Julien, nothing is more terrible than the domesticity of the German. If only he could be persuaded to leave his wife at home! Think how much more attractive it would make these places. He would have more money to spend upon himself, upon his own beer and his own pretzels, and in time, no doubt, a lonely feeling, a feeling of sentiment, would overpower him, and the vacant chair would be filled by one of these vivacious little women who might teach him in time that blood was meant to flow, not to ooze like mud."

"I shall begin to think," Julien remarked, "that you don't like Germans."

"There you are wrong," Kendricks replied. "In their own country I like them. They have all the good qualities. Germany for the Germans, I should say always, and me for any other country. We have drunk our coffee. Let us go."

They passed on to a music-hall, where they listened to a mixed performance and drank beer out of long

E. Phillips Oppenheim

glasses, served to them by a distinctly Teutonic waiter. Greatly to Kendricks' annoyance, however, they were surrounded by English and Americans, and were too tightly packed in to change their seats. On the way out, however, he suddenly beamed.

"Behold!" he exclaimed.

He swept his hat from his head. It was their companions at the dinner table. Madame was pleased to remember him, also mademoiselle.

"I shall invite them to supper," Kendricks declared.

"If you do," Julien retorted, "I shall go home."

Kendricks heaved a long sigh as he regretfully let them pass by.

"It's just a touch of Oxford left in you," he complained. "For myself, I know that madame would be excellent company, and I am perfectly certain that mademoiselle would let me whisper - discreetly - in her ear. Alas! it is a lost opportunity, and from here we go - to who knows what?"

He was suddenly serious. Julien looked at him in surprise. They were standing on the pavement outside. Kendricks consulted his watch.

"You have courage, I know, my friend," he said. "That is one reason why I choose you for my companion to-night. I have two tickets for a German socialist gathering here. The tickets were obtained with extraordinary difficulty. I know that your German is pure and I can trust to my own. From this minute, not a word in any other language, if you please."

"I am really not sure," Julien objected, "that I want to go to a German socialist meeting. In any case, I am hungry."

"Hungry!" Kendricks exclaimed. "Hungry! What ingratitude! But be calm, my friend," he added, taking Julien's arm, "there will be sausages and beer where we are going."

"In that case," Julien agreed, "I am with you. Which way?"

"Almost opposite us," Kendricks declared. "Come along."

They paused outside a brilliantly lit café with a German name. Julien looked at it doubtfully.

"Surely they don't hold meetings in a place like this?" he muttered.

Kendricks lowered his voice.

"We go into the café first," he said. "The meeting is in a private room. Come."

They pushed open the swinging doors and entered the place.

E. Phillips Oppenheim

CHAPTER XVIII

A MEETING OF SOCIALISTS

The *brasserie* into which the two men pushed their way was smaller and less ornate than the one which they had last visited. Many of the tables, too, were laid for supper. The tone of the place was still entirely Teutonic. Kendricks and his companion seated themselves at a table.

"You will eat sausage?" Kendricks asked.

"I will eat anything," Julien replied.

"It is better," Kendricks remarked. "Here from the first we may be watched. We are certainly observed. Be sure that you do not let fall a single word of English. It might be awkward afterwards."

"It's a beastly language," Julien declared, "but the beer and sausages help. How many of the people here will be at the meeting?"

"Not a hundredth part of them," Kendricks answered. "It was a terrible job to get these tickets and I wouldn't like to guarantee now that we have them that we get there. Remember, if any questions are asked, you're an American, the editor or envoy of *The Coming Age*."

"The dickens I am!" Julien exclaimed. "Where am I published?"

"In New York; you're a new issue."

Julien ate sausages and bread and butter steadily for several minutes.

"To me," he announced, "there is something more satisfying about a meal of this description than that two-franc dinner where you stole my chicken."

"You have Teutonic instincts, without a doubt," Kendricks declared, "but after all, why not a light dinner and an appetite for supper? Better for the digestion, better for the pocket, better for passing the time. What are you staring at?"

Julien was looking across the room with fixed eyes.

"I was watching a man who has been sitting at a small table over there," he remarked. "He has just gone out through that inner door. For a moment I could have sworn that it was Carl Freudenberg."

Kendricks shook his head.

"Mr. Carl Freudenberg takes many risks, but I do not think he would care to show himself here."

"It is no crime that he is in Paris," Julien objected.

"In a sense it is," Kendricks said. "These incognito visits of his must soon cease if they were talked too much about. Then there is another thing. This café is the headquarters of German socialism in Paris, and

Herr Freudenberg is the sworn enemy of socialists. He fights them with an iron hand, wherever he comes into contact with them. This is a law-abiding place, without a doubt, and the Germans as a rule are a law-abiding people, but I would not feel quite sure that he would leave unmolested if he were recognized here at this minute."

"You think he knows that?" Julien asked.

"Knows it!" Kendricks replied scornfully. "There is nothing goes on in Paris that he does not know. He peers into every nook and corner of the city. He knows the feelings of the aristocrats, of the bourgeoisie, of the official classes. Not only that, he knows their feelings towards England, towards the Triple Alliance, towards Russia. He never seems to ask questions, he never forgets an answer. He is a wonderful man, in short; but I do not think that you will see him here to-night."

The long hand of the clock pointed toward midnight. Kendricks called for the bill and paid it.

"We go this way," he announced, "through the billiard rooms."

They left the café by the swing-door to which Julien had pointed, passed through a crowded billiard room, every table of which was in use, down a narrow corridor till they came face to face with a closed door, on which was inscribed "Number 12." Kendricks knocked softly and it was at once opened. There was another door a few yards further on, and between the two a very tall doorkeeper and a small man in spectacles.

"Who are you?" the doorkeeper demanded gruffly.

Kendricks produced his tickets. The tall man, however, did not move. He scrutinized them, word for word. Then he scrutinized the faces of the two men. Kendricks he seemed inclined to pass, but he looked at Julien for long, and in a puzzled manner.

"Of what nationality is your friend?" he asked Kendricks.

"I am an American," Julien replied.

"And your profession?"

"A newspaper editor. I edit *The Coming Age*."

"This is not altogether in order," the tall man declared. "The meeting which we are holding to-night is not one in which the Press is interested. We are here to discuss one man, and one man only. I do not think that you would hear anything you could print, and as you do not belong to our direct association here I think it would be better if you did not enter."

Kendricks stood his ground, however.

"I must appeal," he said, "to your secretary."

The little man in spectacles came forward. Kendricks stated his case with much indignation.

"Here am I," he announced, "editor of the only socialist paper in London worthy of the title. I come over because I hear of this meeting. I bring with me my American friend, the editor of *The Coming Age*. For no

E. Phillips Oppenheim

other reason have we visited Paris than for this. If you refuse us admission to this meeting, the whole of the English branch will consider it an insult."

"And the American," Julien put in firmly.

The two men whispered together. The taller one, still grumbling, stood on one side.

"Pass in," he directed. "It is not strictly in order, but our secretary permits."

The two men passed on. The room in which they found themselves was a small one and there were not more than fifty people present. It was very dimly lit and they could barely make out the forms of the row of men who were sitting upon chairs upon the platform. They contented themselves with seats quite close to the door. No drinks were being served here. Although one or two men were smoking, the general aspect seemed to be one of stern and serious intensity. A man upon the platform was just finishing speaking as they entered, and he apparently called upon some one else. A large and heavy German stood up on the centre of the slightly raised stage. He wore shapeless clothes and horn-rimmed spectacles. His face was benevolent. He had a double chin and a soft voice.

"My brothers," he said, "at these our meetings we have many things to discuss. We have little time to waste. Why beat about the bush? I am here to speak to you of the greatest enemy our cause has in the world - Prince Adolf Rudolf von Falkenberg."

He paused. There was an ugly little murmur through the room. It was very easy indeed to understand that the man whose name had been mentioned was unpopular.

"The cause of socialism," the speaker continued, "is the one cause we all have at heart. In our Fatherland it flourishes, but it flourishes slowly. The reason that we are denied our just and legitimate triumphs is simply owing to the vigorous opposition, the brutal enmity, of Prince Adolf Rudolf von Falkenberg. My brothers, this man has been warned. His only answer has been a fresh and more diabolical measure. He fights us everywhere with the fierceness of a man who hates his enemy. It is our duty, brethren, that we do not see our cause retarded by the enmity of any one man. Therefore, it is my business to say to you to-night that that man should be removed."

There was a murmur of voices, one clearer than the others.

"But how?"

The man on the platform adjusted his spectacles.

"My brother asks how? I will tell him. Falkenberg loves war. We others hate it. We work always to infuse throughout the army our own principles and theories. Falkenberg falls upon them with all his might and main. There are orders posted in every barracks in Germany. Our literature is confiscated. Any man preaching our doctrines is drummed out upon the streets. I say that these things cannot last. I say that Falkenberg must go. A friend in the audience has asked how. I will answer you. There is a body of men whose beliefs are somewhat similar to ours, but who go further. It is possible they see the truth. But for us at

E. Phillips Oppenheim

present it is not possible to accept their general principles. This case is an exception. The anarchists of Berlin, one of whom, Franz Kuzman, is here to-night, will dispose of Falkenberg for us if we provide sufficient funds to make an escape possible, and an annuity for the executioner should he live, or for his wife should he die."

There was a slow, ominous murmur of voices. The fat man on the platform beamed at everybody.

"Kuzman is here upon the platform," he announced. "Does any one wish to hear him?"

Kuzman stood up - an awkward, rawboned, dark-featured man. In a coat that was too short for him, he stood rather like a puppet upon the platform.

"If you delegates of the socialist societies decide that it is just," he said, in a hoarse, unpleasant tone, "I am willing to see that Falkenberg meets his reward. I can say no more. I do not fail. I move against no one save those who deserve death and against whom the death sentence has been pronounced. But when I do move, that man dies."

He resumed his seat. The fat man went on.

"Is it your wish," he asked, "that Kuzman be authorized by you to arrange this affair?"

The murmur of voices was scarcely intelligible.

"Into the hands of every one of you," the fat man continued, "will be placed a strip of paper. You will write upon it 'Yes' or 'No.' Kuzman will be instructed according to your verdict."

Some one on the platform bustled around. Kendricks and Julien were both supplied with the long strips. In a few minutes these were collected. The man upon the platform turned up the lights a little higher. He drew a small table towards him and began sorting out the papers into two heaps. One was obviously much larger than the other. Towards the end he came across a slip, however, at which he paused. He read it with knitted brows, half rose to his feet and stopped. Then he went on with his counting. Presently he got up.

"My brothers," he said, "there are forty-two papers here. Of these, thirty-five agree to the appointment of Kuzman for the purpose we have spoken of. Six are against it. One paper I will read to you. The writer has not troubled to put 'Yes' or 'No.' This is what I find:

"Falkenberg has served his Emperor and his country to the whole extent of his will and his capacity. He has given his life to make his country great. If he has been stern upon the cause of socialism, it is because he does not believe that socialism, as it is at present preached, is good for Germany. I vote, therefore, that Falkenberg live.

"We desire to know," the speaker continued, "who wrote those words. They do not sound like the words of one of our delegates. Johann and Hesler, stand by the door. Turn up the lights. Let us see exactly who there is here to-night, unknown to us."

There was a little murmur. A man who sat only three or four places off from Kendricks and Julien rose silently to his feet and moved towards the door. It was

E. Phillips Oppenheim

as yet locked, however. From the other end of the room the lights were suddenly heightened. The faces of the men were now distinctly visible. A light in the body of the hall flared up. A man was discovered with his hand upon the door handle. There was a hoarse murmur of voices.

"Who is he? Hold fast of the door! Let no one pass out!"

The man turned quickly round. The light flashed upon his face. Julien was the first to recognize him and he gripped Kendricks by the arm.

"My God!" he muttered, "it's Falkenberg himself! Who is the man with the key?"

Kendricks pointed to him. They crept closer. Then that hoarse murmur of voices turned suddenly into a low, passionate cry.

"Falkenberg! Falkenberg himself!"

The toymaker made no further attempt at concealment. He drew himself up and faced them. They were creeping towards him now from all corners of the room - an ugly-looking set of men, men with an ugly purpose in their faces.

"Yes, I am Falkenberg!" he cried. "I am here to spy upon you, if you will. Why not? Kill me, if you choose, but I warn you that if you do the whole of Germany will rise against you and your cause."

"Don't let him escape!" some one shouted from the platform.

"Gag him!"

"It is fate!"

"He is ours!"

"A rope!"

There was no mistaking the feeling of the men. Julien whispered swiftly in Kendricks' ear. Simultaneously his right arm shot out. The man who guarded the door felt his neck suddenly twisted back. Kendricks snatched the key from his hand and thrust it in the lock. Some one struck him a violent blow on the head. He reeled, but was still able to turn the key. They came then with a howl from all parts of the room. Julien felt a storm of blows. Falkenberg, with one swoop of his long arm, disposed of their nearest assailant.

"Get off, man," Kendricks ordered. "You first!"

The door was wide open now. They half stumbled, half fell into the outer café. The orchestra stopped playing, people rose to their feet. Before they well knew what was happening, Falkenberg had slipped through their midst and passed out of the door. One of the pursuers, with a howl of rage, sprang after him, but he tripped against an abutting marble table and fell. Kendricks and Julien stepped quietly to one side, threading their way among the throng of customers in the cafe. Loud voices shouted for an explanation.

"It was a pickpocket," some one called out from among those who came streaming from the room, - "a tall man with a wound on the forehead. Did no one see him?"

E. Phillips Oppenheim

They all looked towards the door.

"He passed out so swiftly," they murmured.

Several of them had already reached the door of the café and were rushing down the street in the direction which Falkenberg had taken.

"There were two others," a grim voice shouted from behind.

A waiter, who had seen the two men sit down, looked doubtfully towards them. Kendricks pushed a note into his hand.

"Serve us with something quickly," he begged.

The man pocketed the note and set before them the beer which he was carrying. Kendricks, whose knuckles were bleeding, laid his hand under the table. Julien took a long drink of the beer and began to recover his breath.

"So far," he declared, "I have found your evening with the masses a little boisterous."

Kendricks laughed.

"Wait till my hand has stopped bleeding," he said, "and we will slip out. That was a narrow escape for Falkenberg. What a pluck the fellow must have!"

"It seems almost like a foolhardy risk," Julien muttered. "If those fellows could have got at him, they'd have killed him. Have they gone back to their room, I wonder? Let us hear what the people say about the affair."

"What was the disturbance?" he asked.

The man shrugged his shoulders.

"It was a meeting in one of the private rooms of the café," he declared, "a meeting of some society. They were taking a vote when they discovered a pickpocket. He bolted out of the room. They say that he has got away."

"Did he steal much?" Julien inquired.

The man shook his head.

"A watch and chain, or something of the sort," he told them. "The excitement is all over now. The gentlemen have gone back to their meeting."

Julien smiled and finished his beer.

"Is our evening at an end, Kendricks?" he asked.

Kendricks shook his head.

"Not quite," he replied, binding his handkerchief around his knuckles. "If you are ready, there is just one other call we might make."

"More German *brasseries*?"

Kendricks smiled grimly.

"Not to-night. We climb once more the hill. We pay our respects to Monsieur Albert."

E. Phillips Oppenheim

"The Rat Mort?"

"Exactly!"

CHAPTER XIX

AN OFFER

Kendricks, as they entered the café, recognized his friends with joy openly expressed.

"It is fate!" he exclaimed, striking a dramatic attitude.

"It is the gentleman who ate both portions of chicken!" mademoiselle cried.

"It is the gallant Englishman of the Café Helder," madame laughed, her double chin becoming more and more evident.

"And yonder, in the corner, sits Mademoiselle Ixe," Kendricks whispered to Julien. "For whom does she wait, I wonder?".

"For Herr Freudenberg?" suggested Julien.

"For Herr Freudenberg, let us pray," Kendricks replied.

The husband of madame, the father of mademoiselle, the rightly conceived future papa-in-law-to-be of the attendant young man, rose to his feet in response to a kick from his wife.

"If monsieur is looking for a table," he suggested, "there is room here adjoining ours. It will incommode us not in the slightest."

"Of all places in the room," Kendricks declared, with a bow, "the most desirable, the most charming. Madame indeed permits - and mademoiselle?"

There were more bows, more pleasant speeches. A small additional table was quickly brought. Kendricks ignored the more comfortable seat by Julien's side and took a chair with his back to the room. From here he leaned over and conversed with his new friends. He started flirting with mademoiselle, he paid compliments to madame, he suddenly plunged into politics with monsieur. Julien listened, half in amusement, half in admiration. For Kendricks was not talking idly.

"A man of affairs, monsieur," Kendricks proclaimed himself to be. "My interest in both countries, madame," he continued, knowing well that she, too, loved to talk of the affairs, "is great. I am one of those, indeed, who have benefited largely by this delightful alliance."

Alliance! Monsieur smiled at the word. Kendricks protested.

"But what else shall we call it, dear friends?" he argued. "Are we not allied against a common foe? The exact terms of the *entente*, what does it matter? Is it credible that England would remain idle while the legions of Germany overran this country?"

Monsieur was becoming interested. So was madame. It was madame who spoke - one gathered that it was usual!

"What, then," she demanded, "would England do?"

"She would come to the aid of your charming country, madame."

"But how?" madame persisted pertinently.

Kendricks was immediately fluent. He talked in ornate phrases of the resources of the British Empire, the perfection of her fleet, the wonder of her new guns. Julien, who knew him well, was amazed not only at his apparent earnestness, but at his insincerity. He was speaking well and with a wealth of detail which was impressive enough. His little company of new friends were listening to him with marked attention; Julien alone seemed conscious that they were listening to a man who was speaking against his own convictions.

"Monsieur! Monsieur Julien!"

It was the voice of Mademoiselle Ixe. She was leaning slightly forward in her place. Julien turned quickly around and she motioned him to a seat by her side. He rose at once and accepted her invitation.

"I do not disturb you?" she asked. "It seemed to me that your friend was talking with those strange people there and that you were not very much interested. It is dull when one sits here alone."

"Naturally," Julien agreed. "My friend talks politics, and for my part it is very certain that I would sooner talk of other things with mademoiselle."

She was a born flirt - a matter of nationality as well as temperament, and not to be escaped - and her eyes flashed the correct reply. But a moment later she was gazing wistfully at the door.

"You expect Herr Freudenberg?" Julien inquired.

"I cannot tell," she replied. "I must not say that I am expecting him because he did not ask me to meet him here. But I thought, perhaps, that he might come - so I risked it. I was restless to-night. I do not sing this week because Herr Freudenberg is in Paris, and without any occupation it is hard to control the thoughts. I sat at home until I could bear it no longer. *Eh bien!* I sent for a little carriage and I ventured here. There is a chance that he may come."

"Mademoiselle permits that I offer her some supper?" Julien suggested.

She hesitated and glanced at the clock.

"You are very kind, Sir Julien," she answered. "I have waited because I have thought that there was a chance that he might come, and to sup alone is a drear thing. If monsieur really - Ah! Behold! After all, it is he! It is he who comes. What happiness!"

It was indeed Herr Freudenberg who had mounted the stairs and was yielding now his coat to the attentive *vestiaire* - Herr Freudenberg, unruffled and precisely attired in evening clothes. He showed not the slightest signs of his recent adventure. He chatted gayly to Albert and waved his hand to mademoiselle. He came towards them with a smile upon his face, walking lightly and with the footsteps of a young man. Yet mademoiselle shivered, her lip drooped.

"He is not pleased," she murmured. "I have done wrong."

There was nothing apparent to others in Herr Freudenberg's manner to justify her conviction. He raised her fingers to his lips with charming gayety.

"Dear Marguerite," he exclaimed, "this is indeed a delightful surprise! And Sir Julien, too! I am enchanted. Once more let us celebrate. Let us sup. I am in time, eh?"

"With me, if you please," Julien insisted, taking up the menu.

Herr Freudenberg smiled genially.

"Host or guest, who cares so long as we are joyous?" he cried, sitting on mademoiselle's other side. "Although to-night," he added, with a humorous glance at Julien, "it should surely be I who entertains! Dear Marguerite!"

He patted her hand. She looked at him pathetically and he smiled back again.

"Be happy, my child," he begged. "It is gone, that little twinge. It was perhaps jealousy," he whispered in her ear. "Sir Julien has captured many hearts."

She drew a sigh of content. She raised his hand to her lips. Then she dabbed at her eyes with the few inches of perfumed lace which she called a handkerchief. It was passing, that evil moment.

"There is no man in the world," she told him softly, "who should be able to make you jealous. In your heart you know."

He laughed lightly.

"You will make me vain, dear one. Give me your little fingers to hold for a moment. There - it is finished."

He looked around the room with the light yet cheerful curiosity of the pleasure-seeker. Then he leaned over towards Julien.

"What does our shock-headed friend the journalist do in that company?" he asked, with a backward motion of his head.

Julien smiled.

"He is devoted to madame with the double chin. He is apparently also devoted to mademoiselle, the daughter of madame with the double chin. He is contemplating, I believe, an alliance with the bourgeoisie."

Herr Freudenberg watched the group for a moment with a slight frown.

"They are types," he said under his breath, "absolute types. Kendricks is studying them, without a doubt."

He continued his scrutiny of the room. Then he leaned towards mademoiselle.

"Dear Marguerite!"

"Yes?"

"There is Mademoiselle Soupelles there," he pointed out, "sitting with an untidy-looking man in a morning coat and a red tie. You see them?"

"But certainly," mademoiselle agreed. "They are together always. It is an alliance, that."

"It would please me," Herr Freudenberg continued, still speaking almost under his breath, "to converse with the companion of Mademoiselle Soupelles. From you, dear Marguerite, I conceal nothing. I made no appointment with you to-night because it was my intention to speak with that person, and I could not tell where he would be. All has happened fortunately. We spend our evening together, after all. See what you can do to help me. Go and talk to your friend, Mademoiselle Soupelles. Bring them here if you can. Sir Julien thinks he is ordering the supper, but he is too late; I ordered it from Albert as I entered."

Mademoiselle rose at once and shook out her skirts. She kissed her hand across the room to her friend.

"I go to speak to her," she promised. "What I can do I will. You know that, dear one. But he is a strange-looking man, this companion of hers. You know who he is? His name is Jesen. If I were Susanne, I would see to it that he was more *comme-il-faut*."

Herr Freudenberg laughed.

"Never mind his appearance," he said. "He can drive the truth into the hearts of this people as swiftly and as surely as any man who ever took up a pen. Bring him here, little sweetheart, and to-morrow we visit Cartier together."

She glanced at him almost reproachfully.

"As if that mattered!" she murmured, as she glided away.

Julien turned discontentedly to his companion.

"This fellow will take no order from me," he objected. "Do you own this place, Herr Freudenberg, that you must always be obeyed here?"

"By no means," Herr Freudenberg replied. "To-night is an exception. I ordered supper as I entered. You see, there are others whom I may ask to join. You shall have your turn when you will and I will be a very submissive guest, but to-night - well, I have even at this moment charged mademoiselle with a message to her friend and her friend's companion. I have begged them to join us. On these nights I like company - plenty of company!"

"In that case, perhaps," Julien suggested, "I may be *de trop*."

Freudenberg laid his hand upon his companion's shoulder.

"My friend," he said earnestly, "it is not for you to talk like that, to-night of all nights. If I say little, it is because we are both men of few words, and I think that we understand. You know very well what you and your shock-headed friend have done for me. Not that I believe," he went on, "that it would ever come to me to be hounded to death by such a gang. I am too fervent a believer in my own star for that. But one never knows. It is well, anyhow, to escape with a sound skin."

"Why did you run such a risk?" Julien asked him.

"Partly," Freudenberg answered, "because I was really curious to know what those fellows were driving at; and partly," he added, "because, alas! I am possessed of that restless spirit, that everlasting craving for adventures, which drives one on into any place where life stirs. I knew that these people were plotting something against me. I wanted to hear it with my own ears, to understand exactly what it was against which I must be prepared. But now, Sir Julien, I question you. As for me, my presence there was reasonable enough; but what were you doing in such a place? What interests have you in German socialism?"

Julien shrugged his shoulders.

"I cannot say that I have any," he admitted. "It was Kendricks who took me. He is showing me Paris - Paris from his own point of view. He took me first to a restaurant, where we dined for two francs and sat at the same table with those people to whom he is now making himself so agreeable. Kendricks has democratic instincts. His latest fad is to try and instil them into me."

Herr Freudenberg looked thoughtfully across at the journalist, still deep in argument with his friends.

"I am not sure that I understand that man," he declared. "In a sense he impresses me. I should have put him down as one of those who do nothing without a set and fixed purpose. But enough of other people. Listen. I wish to speak with you - of yourself. I am glad that we have met to-night. I have another and altogether a different proposition to make to you."

Julien remained silent for several moments. Herr Freudenberg watched him.

"A proposition to make to me," Julien repeated at last. "Well, let me hear it?"

Herr Freudenberg leaned towards him.

"Sir Julien," he said, "there has happened to you, as to many of us, a little slip in your life. It is a wise thing if for a few months you pass off the stage of European affairs. You are of an adventurous spirit. Will you undertake a commission for me? Listen. I will guarantee that it is something which does not, and could not ever, by any chance, affect in the slightest degree the interests of your country. It is a commission which will take you a year to execute, and it will lead you into a new land. It will require tact, diplomacy and some courage. If you succeed, your reward will be an income for life. If you fail, the worst that can happen to you is that you will have passed a year of your life without effective result. Still, you will at least have traveled, you will at least have seen new phases of life."

Julien was puzzled.

"You cannot seriously propose to me," he protested, "to undertake a diplomatic errand for a country which has absolutely no claims upon me - to which I am not even attracted?" he added.

Herr Freudenberg tapped with his forefinger upon the table. Upon his lips was a genial and tolerant smile. He had the air of a preceptor devoting special pains upon the most backward member of his kindergarten class.

"My friend," he said, "there is no political question involved whatever. The mission which I ask you to undertake would lead you into a remote part of Africa, where neither your country nor mine has at present any interests. More than this I cannot tell you unless you show signs of accepting my invitation. The negotiations which you would have to conduct are simply these. Four years ago a distinguished German scientist who was in command of a somewhat rash expedition, was captured by the ruler of the country to which I wish you to travel. For some time the question of a mission to ascertain his fate has been upon the carpet. It is true that we have received letters from him. He professes to be happy and contented, to have been kindly treated, and to have accepted a post in the army of his captor. We wish to know whether these letters are genuine or not. If they are genuine, all is well, but a suspicion still remains among some of us that the person in question is being held in torture as an example to other white men who might penetrate so far. This is the first object in the journey which I propose to you. There is nothing political about it at all, as you perceive. It is purely a matter of humanity.... Ah! I see that our party is to be increased. Here are some new friends who arrive."

Mademoiselle Ixe had succeeded. She returned now to her place, followed by the girl with the chestnut-colored hair and her companion. At close quarters the latter, at any rate, was scarcely prepossessing. He was a man of middle age, untidily dressed, whose clothes were covered with cigar ash and recent wine stains, whose linen was none of the cleanest, and whose eyes behind his pince-nez were already bloodshot. Herr Freudenberg, however, seemed to notice none of these unpleasant defects. He grasped him vigorously by

E. Phillips Oppenheim

the hand.

"It is Monsieur Jesen!" he exclaimed. "Often you have been pointed out to me, and I have long wished to have the pleasure of making your acquaintance. Sit down and join us, monsieur. Your little friend, too, - ah, mademoiselle!"

He bent low over the girl's hand and placed a seat for her. The party was now arranged. Their host beamed upon them all.

"Come," he continued, "this is perhaps my last night in Paris for some time! We have had adventures, too, within these few hours. You find us celebrating. My English friend here is one of us. I will not introduce him by name. Why should we trouble about names? We are all friends, all good fellows, here to pass the time agreeably, to drink good wine, to look into beautiful eyes, mademoiselle, to amuse ourselves. It is the science of life, that. Monsieur Jesen, mademoiselle, dear Marguerite, my English friend here, let me be sure that your glasses are filled. To the very brim, garçon - to the very brim! Let us drink together to the joyous evenings of the past, to the joyous evenings of the future, to these few present hours that lie before us when we shall sit here and taste further this very admirable vintage. To the wine we drink, to the lips we love, to this hour of life!"

For the moment there was no more serious conversation. Herr Freudenberg had started a vein of frivolity to which every one there was quick to respond. Only every now and then he himself, the giver of the feast, had suddenly the look of a different man as he sat and whispered in the ear of Monsieur Jesen.

CHAPTER XX

FALKENBERG ACTS

At two o'clock, with obvious reluctance, Kendricks' new friends departed. Their leave-taking was long and ceremonious. Kendricks, indeed, insisted upon escorting mademoiselle to the door. Madame left the place with the assured conviction that a prospective son-in-law was soon to present himself - it could be for no other reason that the English gentleman had so sedulously attached himself to their party. Monsieur, having less sentiment, was not so sure. Mademoiselle had both hopes and fears. They discussed the matter fully on their homeward drive.

Kendricks strolled over to the table where Julien was and touched him on the shoulder.

"Is this to be another all-night sitting?" he asked.

Herr Freudenberg was deep in conversation with Monsieur Jesen - the friend of mademoiselle's friend. He glanced up, but his greeting was almost perfunctory. Kendricks looked keenly at the man who was leaning back in his padded seat. The eyes of Monsieur Jesen were a little more bloodshot now. He had spilt wine down the front of his waistcoat, cigar ash upon his coat-sleeve. He was by no means an

E. Phillips Oppenheim

inviting person to look at. Yet about his forehead and mouth there was an expression of power. Herr Freudenberg, with obvious regret, abandoned his conversation for a moment.

"You are taking your friend away?" he remarked suavely. "We shall part from him with regret. Sir Julien," he added, whispering in his ear, "I must have your answer to my proposition. I will put it into absolutely definite shape, if you like, within the next few days."

"I move into my old rooms - number 17, Rue de Montpelier - to-morrow morning, or rather this morning," Julien replied. "You might telephone or call there at any time."

"Tell me, is what I have proposed in any way attractive to you?" Herr Freudenberg asked, still speaking in an undertone.

"In a sense it is," Julien answered. "It needs further consideration, of course. I must also consult my friend."

Herr Freudenberg glanced at Kendricks and shrugged his shoulders. He had the air of one slightly annoyed. Kendricks was bending over Mademoiselle Ixe. Herr Freudenberg whispered in Julien's ear.

"You take too much advice from your boisterous friend, dear Sir Julien," he asserted. "Mark my words, he will try to keep you here, cooling your heels upon the mat. He will prevent you from raising your hand to knock upon the door of destiny. These men who write are like that. They do not understand action."

Kendricks turned from mademoiselle.

"You are ready, Julien?" he asked.

"Quite," Julien answered.

They made their adieux. Herr Freudenberg watched
them leave the room. The man by his side - Monsieur
Jesen - also watched a little curiously.

"An English journalist," Herr Freudenberg remarked,
"some say a man of ability. I find him a trifle boisterous and uncouth. Monsieur Jesen, our conversation
interests me immensely. I feel sure - "

Jesen looked suspiciously around.

"We have talked enough of business," he declared. "It
is an idea, this of yours. For the rest, I cannot tell. A
wonderful idea!" he continued. "And as for me, am I
not the man to embrace it?"

"You have but to say a single word," Herr Freudenberg
reminded him softly, "and all is arranged."

Monsieur Jesen puffed furiously at a cigarette. The
fingers which had held the match to it were shaking.
The man himself seemed unsteady on his seat. Yet it
was obvious that his brain was working.

"Herr Freudenberg," he said, "there is but one weak
point in all your chain of arguments. To do as you ask,
it will be necessary that I - I, Paul Jesen, so well-
known, whose opinions are followed by millions of my
country people - it would be necessary for me to
abandon my convictions, to turn a right-about-face.

Ask yourself, is it not like selling one's honor when one writes the things one does not believe?"

Herr Freudenberg smiled.

"My friend, you ask me a question the reply to which is already spoken. I tell you that behind, at the back of your brain, you know and realize the truth of all these things. Think, man! Call to mind the arguments I have used. Remember, I have lifted the curtain, I have shown you the things that arrive, the things that are inevitable."

Mademoiselle, the companion of Monsieur Jesen, had had enough of this. It was her weekly holiday. She yawned and tapped her friend upon the arm.

"My dear Paul," she protested, "while you and Herr Freudenberg talk as two men who have immense affairs, Marguerite and I we weary ourselves. If I am to be alone like this, very good. I speak to my friends. There is Monsieur de Chaussin there. He throws me a kiss. Do you wish that I sit with him? He looks, indeed, as though he had plenty to say! Or there is the melancholy Italian gentleman, who raises his glass always when I look. And the two Americans -"

"You have reason, little one," Monsieur Jesen interrupted. "Herr Freudenberg, this is no place for such a discussion."

"Agreed!" Herr Freudenberg exclaimed. "We owe our apologies to mademoiselle, your charming friend, and mademoiselle, my adored companion," he added, turning to Marguerite. "Come, let us drink more wine. Let us talk together. What is your pleasure, mademoiselle, the friend of my good friend, Monsieur Jesen? Will you have them dance to us? Is there music to which you would listen? Or shall we pray Marguerite here that she sings? Let us, at any rate, be gay. And for the rest, Monsieur Jesen, time has no count for us who live our lives. When we leave here, you and I will talk more."

It was daylight before they left. The whole party got into Herr Freudenberg's motor.

"I drive you first to your rooms, Monsieur Jesen," he said. "I take then the liberty of entering with you. The little conversation which we have begun is best concluded within the shelter of four walls."

Monsieur Jesen was excited yet nervous.

"It is too late," he muttered, "to talk business."

Herr Freudenberg smiled.

"Ah!" he cried, "you jest, my friend. Look out of that window. You see the sunshine in the streets, you breathe the fresh, clear air? Too late, indeed! It is morning, and the brain is keenest then. Don't you feel the fumes of the hot room, of the wine, of the tobacco smoke, all pass away with the touch of that soft wind?"

Monsieur Jesen stared. He was conscious of a very bad headache, an uncomfortable sense that he had, as usual on his weekly holiday, eaten and drunk and smoked a great deal more than was good for him. He gazed with wonder at this tall, spare-looking man, who had drunk as much and smoked as much and eaten as much as any one else, and yet appeared exactly as he had done four hours ago. Even his linen was still spotless. His eyes were bright, his manner buoyant.

"Monsieur," he murmured, "you are marvelous. I have never before met a German merchant like you."

Herr Freudenberg sat quite still for a moment. He looked at mademoiselle, the friend of Monsieur Jesen, and he realized that theirs was no casual acquaintance. In both he recognized the characteristics of fidelity. As he had always the genius to do, he took his risks.

"Monsieur Jesen," he announced, "I am no German maker of toys. Let me ascend with you to your room and you shall hear who I am and why I have said these things to you."

Monsieur Jesen held his hand to his head. Something in the manner of this new friend of his was, in a sense, mesmeric.

"You shall ascend, monsieur," he said. "I do not know who you are, but you are evidently a very wonderful person. We will ascend and you shall wait while I place my head in cold water and Susanne mixes me some absinthe. Then I will listen."

The automobile came to a standstill about halfway down a shabby street in a somewhat shabby neighborhood. Herr Freudenberg noticed this fact without change of countenance, but with secret pleasure. He turned to Marguerite.

"Dear Marguerite," he whispered, "for an hour or so I must leave you. You will permit that my man takes you to your apartments and returns for me here?"

"May I not wait for you here in the automobile?" she asked timidly.

Herr Freudenberg shook his head kindly.

"Dear little one," he murmured, "not this morning. Indeed, I have important affairs on hand. As soon as I am free, I will telephone. Sleep well, little girl."

He stepped out on to the pavement. The postern door in front of them was opened, in response to Monsieur Jesen's vigorous knocking, from some invisible place by a string. The three of them climbed four flights of rickety stairs. They reached at last a stone landing. Monsieur Jesen threw open a door and led the way into an untidy-looking salon.

"Monsieur will forgive the fact," he begged, "that I am not better housed. If it were not for little Susanne here," he added, patting her upon the shoulder, "I doubt whether I should keep a roof above my head at all."

"It is not like this," Herr Freudenberg declared, "that genius should be treated."

"Indeed," Mademoiselle Susanne intervened, "it is what I tell him always. Monsieur, they pay him but a beggarly three hundred francs a month - he, who writes all the editorials; he, who is the spirit of the papers! It is not fair. I tell dear Paul that it is wicked, and, as he says, the money, if it were not for me, he would squander it in a minute. I have even to go with him to the office, for there are many who know when Paul draws his little cheque."

Herr Freudenberg set down his hat upon the table. He

looked around at all the evidences of unclean and sordid life. Then he looked at the man. It was a queer housing, this, for genius! His face remained expressionless. Of the disgust he felt he showed no sign. In the building of houses one must use many tools!

"Monsieur Jesen," he said, "and mademoiselle - I speak to you both, for I recognize that between you there is indeed a union of sympathy and souls. Mademoiselle, then, I address myself to you. On certain terms I have offered to purchase for Monsieur Paul here a two-thirds share of the newspaper upon which he works, that two-thirds share which he and I both know is in the market at this moment. I am willing at mid-day to-morrow, or rather to-day, to place within his hands the sum required. I am willing to send my notary with him to the office, and the affair could be arranged at half-past twelve. From then he practically owns *Le Jour*. Its politics are his to control. I make him this offer, mademoiselle, and it is a greater one than it sounds, for the money which I place in his hands to make this purchase - five hundred thousand francs - is his completely and absolutely. You move at once into apartments befitting your new position. Monsieur Paul Jesen is no longer a struggling and ill-paid journalist. He is the proprietor of an important journal, through whose columns he shall help to guide the policy of your nation."

Monsieur Jesen sat down. His fingers were clutching one another. Mademoiselle stared at Herr Freudenberg. Her color was coming and going.

"Monsieur, I do not understand!" she cried. "Are you a prince in disguise? Why do you do this?"

"Mademoiselle," Herr Freudenberg replied, "your question is the question of an intelligent woman. Why do I do this? Not for nothing, I assure you. It is my custom to make bargains, indeed, but I make them so that those with whom I deal shall never regret the day they met Herr Freudenberg. I offer you this splendid future, you and Monsieur Jesen there, on one condition, and it is a small one, for already the truth has found its way a little into his brain. *Le Jour* has supported always, wholly and entirely, the *entente* between Great Britain and your country. I have tried to point out to Paul Jesen here what all far-seeing people must soon appreciate - that the *entente* is doomed."

The girl glanced at Jesen. Jesen was looking away out of the dusty window.

"Mademoiselle," Herr Freudenberg continued, "I will not weary you at this hour in the morning with politics. I have talked long with Monsieur Jesen and I think that I have shown him something of the truth. You came to the rescue of Great Britain when she lay friendless and powerless. You saved her prestige; you saved her, without doubt, from invasion. What have you gained? Nothing! What can you ever gain? Nothing! Her army of toy soldiers would be of less use to you than a single corps from across the Elbe. Her fleet - you have no possessions to guard. It is for herself only that she maintains it. I ask you to think quietly for yourself and ask yourself on whose side is the balance of advantage. You can reply to that question in one way, and one way only. France has been carried away on a wave of enthusiasm, a wave of sentiment - call it what you will. But France is a far-seeing people. The moment is ripe. I propose to Paul Jesen that his should be the hand and *Le Jour* the vehicle which shall bring the French

E. Phillips Oppenheim

people to a proper understanding of the political situation."

"Who, then, are you?" Mademoiselle Susanne persisted.

Herr Freudenberg barely hesitated.

"Mademoiselle," he said, "we speak of great things, we three, in this little chamber of yours. I, who have often talked of great things before, have learned in life one lesson at least, and that is when one may trust. It is not my desire that many people should know who I am. It suits my purpose better to move in Paris as a private citizen, but to you two let me tell the truth. I am Prince Falkenberg."

There was a silence. The man looked at him, sober enough now, in amazement. The girl's hands were clasped together. She was watching the man - her man. She crept to his side, her arm was around his neck.

"Dear Paul," she whispered, "think! Think how sweet life might be. There is so much truth in all this. I know little of politics, but think of the hard times we have lived through. Think how glorious to have you ride in your automobile to the offices of your newspaper, to see you pass into the editor's sanctum instead of waiting outside, to have me call for you, perhaps, and take you out to lunch - no, never at Drevel's any more - at the Café de Paris, or Henry's, or Paillard's, or out in the Bois! And the excursions, dear Paul. Think of them! The country - how we both love the country! You remember when we first went out together to the little town on the river, where no one ever seemed to have come from Paris before? How sleepy and quiet the long afternoon, when we lay in the grass and heard the birds sing, and the murmur of the river, and we had only a few francs for our dinner, and we had to leave the train and walk that last four miles because you had drunk one more *bock*. Dear Paul, think what life might be if one were really rich!"

The man's eyes flashed.

"It is true," he muttered. "All my life I have been a straggler."

"You have done your genius an ill turn, my friend," Herr Freudenberg said slowly. "No man can be at his best who knows care. I, Prince Falkenberg, I promise you that it is the truth which I have spoken, the truth which I shall show you. You lose no shadow of honor or self-respect. There will come a day when the millions of readers whom you shall influence will say to themselves - 'Paul Jesen, he is the man who saw the truth. It is he who has saved France.' You accept?"

"Monsieur le Prince," Susanne cried, "he accepts!"

Jesen rose to his feet. He had become a little unsteady again. He struck the table with his fist.

"I accept!" he declared.

BOOK TWO

CHAPTER I

THE FLIGHT OF LADY ANNE

It was exactly nine forty-five in the evening, about three weeks later, when the two-twenty from London steamed into the Gare du Nord. Julien, from his place among the little crowd wedged in behind the gates, gazed with blank amazement at the girl who, among the first to leave the train, was presenting her ticket to the collector. At that moment she recognized him. With a purely mechanical effort he raised his hat and held out his hand.

"Lady Anne!" he exclaimed. "Why - I had no idea you were coming to Paris," he added weakly.

She laughed - the same frank, good-humored laugh, except that she seemed to lack just a little of her usual self-possession.

"Neither did I," she confessed, "until this morning."

He looked at her blankly. She was carrying her own jewel-case. He could see no signs of a maid or any party.

"But tell me," he asked, "where are the rest of your people?"

She shook her head.

"Nowhere. I am quite alone."

Julien was speechless.

"You must really forgive me," he continued, after a moment's pause, "if I seem stupid. It is scarcely a month ago since I read of your engagement to Harbord. The papers all said that you were to be married at once."

She nodded.

"That's exactly it," she said. "That's why I am here."

"What, you mean that you are going to be married here?" asked Julien.

"I am not going to be married at all," she replied cheerfully. "Between ourselves, Julien," she added, "I found I couldn't go through with it."

"Couldn't go through with it!" he repeated feebly.

Lady Anne was beginning to recover herself.

"Don't be stupid," she begged. "You used to be quick enough. Can't you see what has happened? I became engaged to the little beast. I stood it for three weeks. I didn't mind him at the other end of the room, but when he began to talk about privileges and attempt to take liberties, I found I couldn't bear the creature anywhere near me. Then all of a sudden I woke up this morning and remembered that we were to be married in a week. That was quite enough for me. I slipped out after lunch, caught the two-twenty train, and here I am."

"Exactly," Julien agreed. "Here you are."

"With my luggage," she continued, swinging the jewel-case in her hand and laughing in his face.

"With your luggage," Julien echoed. "Seriously, is that all that you have brought?"

"Every bit," she answered. "You know mother?"

"Yes, I know your mother!" he admitted.

"Well, I didn't exactly feel like taking her into my confidence," Lady Anne explained, smiling. "Under those circumstances, I thought it just as well to make my departure as quietly as possible."

"Then they don't know where you are?"

"Really," she assured him, "you are becoming quite intelligent. They do not."

"In other words, you've run away?"

"Marvelous!" she murmured. "I suppose it's the air over here."

A sudden idea swept into Julien's mind. Of course, it was ridiculous, yet for a moment his heart gave a little jump. Perhaps she divined his thought, for her next words disposed of it effectually.

"Of course, I knew that you were in Paris, but I had no idea that we should meet, certainly not like this. I have a dear friend to whose apartments I shall go at once. She is a milliner."

"She is a what?" Julien asked blankly.

A smile played about Lady Anne's lips.

"My dear Julien," she exclaimed, "you know, you never did understand me! I repeat that she is a milliner and that she is a dear friend of mine, and I am going just as I am to tell her that I have come to spend the night. She will have to find me rooms, she will have to help me find employment."

Kendricks, who had come by the same train, and whom Julien was there to meet, was hovering in the background. Julien, seeing him, could do no more than nod vaguely.

"Lady Anne," he began, -

"You needn't bother about that," she interrupted. "We were always good friends, weren't we?" she added carelessly. "Besides, to call me 'Lady' anything would be rather ridiculous under the present circumstances."

"Well, Anne, then," he said, "please let me get my bearings. I understand that you were engaged to Harbord - you weren't forced into it, I suppose?"

"Not at all. I tried to run along the usual groove, but I came up against something too big for me. I don't know how other girls do it. I simply found I couldn't. Samuel Harbord is rather by way of being something outrageous, you know."

"Of course he is," Julien agreed, with sudden appreciation of the fact.

"You needn't be so vigorous about it. I remember your almost forcing him on to me the day you called to say good-bye."

"I was talking rubbish," Julien asserted. "You see, I was in rather an unfortunate position myself that day, wasn't I? No one likes to feel like a discarded lover. I can understand your chucking Harbord all right, but I can't quite see why it was necessary for you to run away from home to come and stay with a little milliner."

She laughed.

"My dear Julien, you don't know those Harbords! There are hordes of them, countless hordes - mothers and sisters and cousins and aunts. They've besieged the place ever since our engagement was announced. If the merest whisper were to get about among them that I was thinking of backing out, there's nothing they wouldn't do. They'd make the whole place intolerable for me - follow me about in the street, weep in my bedroom, hang around the place morning, noon and night. Besides, mother would be on their side and the whole thing would be impossible."

"I have no doubt," Julien admitted, "that the situation would be a trifle difficult, but to talk about earning your own living - you, Lady Anne -"

"Lady fiddlesticks!" she interrupted. "What a stupid

old thing you are, Julien! You never found out, I suppose, that at heart I am a Bohemian?"

"No, I never did!" he assented vigorously.

"Ah, well," she remarked, "you were too busy flirting with that Carraby woman to discover all my excellent qualities. We mustn't stay here, must we? Are you very busy, or do you want to drive me to my friend's house? Of course, meeting you here will be the end of me if any one sees us. Still, I don't suppose you object to a little scandal, and the more I get the happier I shall be."

"I'll take you anywhere," Julien promised. "You don't mind waiting while I speak to the man whom I have come to meet?"

"Not at all," she replied. "You are sure he won't object?"

"Of course not," Julien assured her. "Kendricks is an awfully good sort."

The two men gripped hands. Kendricks was carrying his own bag and smoking his accustomed pipe. He had apparently been asleep in the carriage and was looking a little more untidy than usual.

"I got your wire all right," Julien said, "and I am thundering glad to see you. Are you just in search of the ordinary sort of copy, or is there anything special doing?"

"Something special," Kendricks answered, "and you're in it. When can we talk? No hurry, as long as I see you some time to-night."

"I am entirely at your service," Julien declared. "I have been bored to death for the last few weeks and I am only too anxious to have a talk. You don't mind if I see this young lady to her friend's house first? I don't know exactly where it is, but it won't take very long. She is all alone, and as long as we have met I feel that I ought to look after her."

"Naturally," Kendricks agreed. "I can go to my hotel and meet you anywhere you say for supper."

Julien glanced at his watch.

"It is ten o'clock within a minute or two," he announced. "Supposing we make it half-past eleven at the Abbaye?"

Kendricks nodded.

"That'll suit me. So long!"

He strode away in search of a cab. Julien returned to Lady Anne and took the jewel-case from her fingers.

"It's all arranged," he said. "You are quite sure that you have no more luggage?"

She laughed.

"Not a scrap! Have you ever traveled without luggage, Julien? It makes you feel that you are really in for adventures."

"Does it!" he replied a little weakly. Somehow or other, he had never associated a love for adventures with Lady Anne.

"Isn't it fun to be in Paris once more?" she continued. "I want a real rickety little *voiture* and I want the man to have a white hat, if possible, and I want to drive down into Paris over those cobbles."

"Any particular address?"

She handed him a card. He called an open victoria and directed the man. Together they drove out of the station yard. Lady Anne leaned forward, looking around her with keen pleasure.

"Julien," she cried, "this is delightful, meeting you! I hope I shan't be a bother to you, but really it is rather nice to feel that I have one friend here."

"You couldn't possibly be a bother to me," he declared. "I'm rather a waif here myself, you know, and I am honestly glad to see you."

She looked at him quickly and breathed a little sigh of relief.

"Now that's sweet of you," she said. "Of course, I don't see why you shouldn't be. We were always good friends, weren't we? and it makes me feel so much more comfortable to remember that we never went in for the other sort of thing."

"There was just one moment," he murmured ruminatingly, -

She turned her head.

"Stop at once," she begged. "That moment passed, as you know. If it hadn't, things might have been

E. Phillips Oppenheim

different. If it hadn't, I should feel differently about being with you now. We are forgetting that moment, if you please, Julien. Do, there's a good fellow. If you wanted to be good-natured, you could be so nice to me until I get used to being alone."

"Forgotten it shall be, by all means," he promised cheerfully. "Do you know that the address you gave me is only a few yards away?"

"Oh, bother!" she exclaimed. "I knew that it was somewhere up by the Gare du Nord."

They turned off from the Rue Lafayette and pulled up opposite a milliner's shop.

"Mademoiselle Rignaut lives up above," Lady Anne said, alighting. "It's sweet of you to have brought me, Julien."

"I am going to wait and see that you are all right," he replied, ringing the bell.

There was a short delay, then the door was opened. A young woman peered out.

"Who is it?" she asked quickly.

A little of Lady Anne's confidence for the moment had almost deserted her. The girl's face was invisible and the interior of the passage looked cheerless. Nevertheless, she answered briskly.

"Don't you remember me, Mademoiselle Janette? I am Lady Anne - Lady Anne Clonarty, you know."

There was a wondering scream, an exclamation of delight, and Julien stood on the pavement for fully five minutes. Then Lady Anne reappeared, followed by her friend.

"Sir Julien," she said, "this is Mademoiselle Rignaut. I am awfully lucky. Mademoiselle Rignaut has a room she can let me have and we are going to raid her shop and get everything I want. She has costumes as well as hats."

Julien shook hands with the little Frenchwoman, who had not yet recovered from her amazement.

"But this is wonderful, monsieur, is it not," she cried, "to see dear Lady Anne like this? Such a surprise! Such a delight! But, miladi," she added suddenly, "you must be hungry - starving!"

"I am," Lady Anne admitted frankly.

The little woman's face fell.

"But only this afternoon," she explained, "my servant was taken away to the hospital! What can we -"

"What you will both do," Julien interrupted, "is to come and have supper with me."

"Do you really mean it?" Lady Anne asked doubtfully. "What about your friend?"

"He won't mind," Julien assured her. "You shall take your first step into Bohemia, my dear Anne. We had arranged to sup in the Montmartre. You and Mademoiselle Rignaut must come. I can give you half an hour to get ready - more, if you want it."

"What larks!" Lady Anne exclaimed. "Can I come in a traveling dress?"

"You can come just as you are," Julien replied. "One visits these places just as one feels disposed. I'll be off and get a taximeter automobile instead of this thing, and come back for you whenever you say."

"You are a brick," Lady Anne declared. "I shall love to go."

"Monsieur is too kind," Mademoiselle Rignaut agreed, "but as for me, it is not fitting - "

"Rubbish!" Lady Anne interrupted briskly. "You've got to get all that sort of stuff out of your head, Janette, and to start with you must come to supper with us. Bless you, I couldn't go alone with Sir Julien! I was engaged to be married to him three months ago."

Mademoiselle shook her head feebly.

"But indeed, Miladi Anne," she protested, "you are a strange people, you English! I do not understand."

Lady Anne took her by the arm and turned towards the open door.

"Don't bother about that. We'll be ready in half an hour, Julien."

Julien returned to the Gare du Nord and treated himself to a whiskey and soda. He was surprised at the pleasurable sense of excitement which this meeting had given him. During the last few weeks in Paris he had found little to interest or amuse him. He had been, in fact, very distinctly bored. The newspapers and illustrated journals, although they were always full of interest to him, had day by day brought their own particular sting. Although his affection for Lady Anne had been of a distinctly modified character, yet he had found it curiously unpleasant to read everywhere of her engagement, of her plans for the future, and to look at the photographs of her and her intended bridegroom which seemed to stare at him from every page. Somehow or other, although he told himself that personally it was of no consequence to him, he yet found the present situation of affairs far more to his liking.

He lounged about the Gare du Nord, smoking a cigarette and thinking over what she had told him. There was a good deal in the present situation to appeal to his sense of humor. He thought of the Duke and the Duchess when they discovered the flight of their daughter, - their efforts to keep all details from the papers; of Harbord and his horde of relations - Harbord, who had neither the dignity nor the breeding to accept such a reverse in silence. He could imagine the gossip at the clubs and among their friends. He himself was immensely surprised. He had considered himself something of a judge of character, and yet he had looked upon Lady Anne as a good-natured young person, brimful of common sense, without an ounce of sentiment - a perfectly well-ordered piece of the machinery of her sex. The whole affair was astonishing. Perhaps to him the most astonishing part was that he found himself continually looking at the clock, counting almost the minutes until it was possible for him to start on this little expedition!

CHAPTER II

TO OUR NEW SELVES

Julien found a taximeter automobile and, punctually at the time appointed, drove to the little milliner's shop in the Rue St. Antoine. Lady Anne and her companion were waiting for him and they drove off together in high good humor. The manager at the Abbaye bowed before them with special deference. He recognized Julien as an occasional customer, and Lady Anne, even in her traveling gown, was a person to inspire attention.

They chose a table and ordered supper for four. Kendricks had not yet arrived, but it was barely half-past eleven and the place was almost empty. Lady Anne was in high spirits and chattering all the time. Julien looked at her occasionally in amazement. They had seldom been alone together in London, but on those few occasions when the conventions had demanded it, he had been inclined to find her rather stupid. She was certainly nothing of the sort this evening!

"I suppose I am a baby," she exclaimed, laughing, "but to-night I feel as though I were beginning a new life! Tell me, mademoiselle, have you a place for me as a seamstress? Or will you have me for a model? My figure is good enough, isn't it?"

"Miladi," Mademoiselle Rignaut declared deprecatingly, "there is no girl in my shop with a figure like yours, but it is not well for you to talk so, indeed. It is shocking."

Lady Anne laughed gayly.

"Now, my little friend," she said, "let us understand one another. There is no more 'miladi.' I am Anne - Anne to you and Anne to Julien here. I've finished with the 'miladi' affair. I dare say I shouldn't care about being a model, but all the same I am going to earn my own living."

"Earn your own living!" Mademoiselle Rignaut echoed, in something like horror.

She had met the Duke and the Duchess - she had traveled even to London and had passed the night beneath the ducal roof. Lady Anne's mother had very sound ideas of economy, and Mademoiselle Rignaut was cheap and yet undoubtedly French.

"Earn my own living, without a doubt," Lady Anne repeated, helping herself to a roll. "You don't mind my eating some bread and butter, do you, Julien? I couldn't lunch - I was much too excited, and the tea on the train was filthy. Why, of course I am going to earn my own living," she continued. "I've only got a few thousand francs with me, and some jewelry. I believe I have got a small income, but Heaven knows whether they will let me have it!"

Julien's eyes were suddenly lit with humor.

E. Phillips Oppenheim

"Why, the Duke will be here for you to-morrow," he exclaimed, "to take you back!"

She leaned back in her seat with an air of deliberation.

"I'm free," she insisted. "I'm twenty-six years old, thank Heaven! Twenty-six years I've had of it - enough to crush any one. No more! You know, I like this sense of freedom," she went on. "It's perfectly amazing how young I feel. Julien, do you remember when mother wouldn't let us lunch together at the Ritz without a chaperon?"

"I do," he assented. "I'm sure we didn't need one, either."

She smiled reminiscently.

"What sticks we were! What a silly life! I really have the most delightful feeling, as though I were starting things all over again, as though there were all sorts of wonderful adventures before me."

Julien looked at her quickly. There was no woman in the place half so good-looking or with any pretensions to such style. He was conscious of an odd twinge of jealousy.

"You'll have no trouble in finding adventures," he remarked a little grimly.

Her eyes flashed back an answer to his thought.

"Bless you, I don't want anything to do with men! Fancy having been engaged to you and to Samuel Harbord! What further thrills could possibly be in store for me?"

"Well, I don't know," Julien retorted. "I suppose if I was a stick, there must have been something about you which induced me to be one."

"Not a bit of it," she objected. "You were a solemn, studious, gentlemanly, well-behaved, well-conducted prig - very much a male edition of what I was myself. What a life we should have lived together!... Here's your friend. You know, I rather like the look of him. He's so delightfully untidy. I should think he belongs round about the new world, doesn't he?"

"He's a working journalist," Julien answered, "a very clever fellow and a good friend of mine."

"Then I shall adore him," Lady Anne decided, - "not because he is a good friend of yours, but because he is a working journalist. Why, I saw him sitting waiting for you the day you came and wished me that touching good-bye," she added. "I liked him even then. It seemed so sweet of him to come and help you through that terrible ordeal."

She held out her hand to Kendricks very charmingly when he was presented.

"Don't be terrified at finding us here, please," she begged. "I know you have some business to talk over with Julien, but you see we were starving, and Julien had to be polite to me because we were once engaged to be married. I promise you that when we have eaten we will go home."

Kendricks looked at her for a moment and smiled.

"You know," he said, "I believe you've run away."

She laughed.

"I felt sure that I was going to like your friend, Julien!" she exclaimed. "He understands things so quickly."

"I am a newspaper man, you see," he told her. "Just as I left, I was reading all sorts of things about your wedding, and the presents, and the rest of it. I saw you in the train and recognized you."

"Don't think I've come over after Julien," she continued cheerfully. "I never dreamed of seeing him - not just yet, at any rate. I had no idea where to run to, but Paris seemed to me so easy and so natural, and somehow or other it must be more difficult to worry any one into going back from a foreign country. Not that I've any idea of going back," she broke off. "I think I'm going to enjoy life hugely out here."

"But it is most astonishing!" Mademoiselle Rignaut declared with a gasp.

"My little friend here," Lady Anne went on, "hasn't got over it all yet. She doesn't understand the sheer barbarity of being a duke's daughter. The worst of it is she'll never have an opportunity of trying it for herself. Heaven save the others! Julien, I hope we are going to have some champagne. Mother never liked me to drink champagne at a restaurant. You see," she explained, "we weren't rich enough to be in really the smart set, or else I should have been allowed to do any mortal thing, and if you aren't in the very smart set, it is best to turn up your nose at them and to ape propriety. That's what we did. It suited father because it was cheap, and mother because she said it went with my style."

"Champagne, by all means," Julien agreed. "I ordered it some time ago. And here comes the lobster."

"Julien, tell him to give me some wine," Lady Anne begged. "I am thirsty."

Julien gave the order to the *sommelier*. She raised the glass to her lips and looked at him.

"To our new selves," she exclaimed, laughing, "and to the broken bonds!"

Julien raised his glass at once.

"To our new selves!" he echoed.

CHAPTER III

WORK FOR JULIEN

The new Anne had not forgotten her natural stubbornness. At half-past twelve she rose from the supper table and declined absolutely to allow Julien to escort her home.

"My dear Julien," she declared, "the thing is ridiculous. We have finished with all that. I am a Bohemian. I expect to walk about these streets when and where and at what hour I choose. You have business with Mr. Kendricks and I am glad of it. You certainly shall not waste your time gallivanting around with me. Janette and I together could defy any sort of danger."

"But, my dear Anne," Julien protested, "you cannot make these changes so suddenly. To drive you home would take, at the most, half an hour."

"I shall enjoy the drive immensely," Lady Anne answered coolly, "but we shall take it alone. Don't be foolish, Julien. Come and find us a little carriage and say good night nicely."

He was forced to obey. He found a carriage and helped her in. She even stopped him when he would have paid for it.

"For the present," she said, "I prefer to arrange these matters for myself. Thanks ever so much for the supper," she added, "and come and see me in a day or two, won't you?"

She gave him her hand and smiled her farewells at him. The lamplight flashed upon her as she leaned forward to say good-bye, and Julien for the first time realized that her hair was a beautiful shade of brown, and that there was a quiet but very effective beauty about her face which he had never appreciated. She waved her hand and laughed at him in frank good-fellowship which he somehow felt vaguely annoying. The carriage rolled away and he went back to Kendricks.

"My friend," the latter exclaimed, "pay your bill and let us depart! I am in no humor for the cafés to-night. Let us go to your rooms and sit quietly, or drive - whichever you choose."

"You have news?" Julien remarked.

"I have news and a proposition for you," Kendricks replied. "I am not sure that we do ourselves much good by being seen about Paris together just now. I am not sure, even, whether it is safe."

Julien stared at him.

"You are making fun of me!"

"Not I," Kendricks assured him. "We are both being drawn into a queer little cycle of events, events which perhaps we may influence. When we get back to your rooms, I will tell you about it. Until then, not a word."

They drove down the hill, talking of Lady Anne.

"Somehow," Kendricks remarked, "she doesn't fit in, in the least, with your description of her. I imagined a cold, rather stupid young woman, of very moderate intelligence, and certainly no sense of humor. Do you know that your Lady Anne is really a very charming person?"

"She puzzles me a little," Julien confessed. "Something has changed her."

Kendricks nodded.

"Whatever has done it has done a good thing. She gave you your congé quite calmly, didn't she?"

"Absolutely," Julien admitted. "She brushed me away as though I had been a misbehaving fly."

"After all," Kendricks said, "you were of the same kidney - a prig of the first water, you know, Julien. I am never tired of telling you so, am I? Never mind, it's good for you. Have you seen Herr Freudenberg this week?"

Julien shook his head.

"Not since we were all at the Rat Mort together nearly a month ago. Did I tell you that he made me an offer then?"

"No, you told me nothing about it," Kendricks replied, leaning forward with interest. "What sort of an offer? Go on, tell me about it?"

"He wanted me," Julien continued, "to undertake the command of an expedition to some place which he did not specify, to discover whether a German who was living there was being held a prisoner -"

"Oh, là, là!" Kendricks interrupted. "Tell me what your reply was?"

"I told him that I must consult you first. As a matter of fact, I never thought seriously about it at all. The whole affair seemed to me so vague, and it didn't attract me in the least. I don't know whether you can understand what I mean, but to me it appeared to be an entirely artificial suggestion. If such a thing had been reasonable at all, I should have said that it was an offer invented on the spur of the moment by Herr Freudenberg, to get me out of Paris."

"Really, Julien," declared Kendricks, "I am beginning to have hopes of you. There are times when you are almost bright."

"What are you here for?" Julien asked. "Is there anything wrong in London?"

"Anything wrong!" Kendricks growled. "You and your foolish letters, Julien! You left the way open for that little bounder Carraby and he'll do for us. Lord, how they love him in Berlin!"

"They are not exactly appreciating him over here, are they?" Julien remarked. "I don't understand the tone of the Press at all. There's something at the back of it all."

"There is," Kendricks agreed grimly. "Sit tight, wait till we are in your rooms. I'll tell you some news."

　　　　E. Phillips Oppenheim

"We are there now," Julien replied, as the little carriage pulled up. "Follow me, Kendricks, and take care of the stairs. I hope you like the smell of new bread? You see, the ground floor is occupied by a confectioner's shop. It keeps me hungry half the time."

"Delicious!" Kendricks murmured. "Are these your rooms?"

Julien nodded and turned on the electric light.

"Not palatial, as you see, but comfortable and, I flatter myself, typically French. Don't you love the red plush and the gilt mirror? Of course, one doesn't sit upon the chairs or look into the mirror, but they at least remind you of the country you're in."

Kendricks threw open the window. The hum of the city came floating into the room. They drew up easy-chairs.

"Whiskey and soda at your side," Julien pointed out. "You can smoke your filthy pipe to your heart's content. I won't even insult you by offering you a cigar. Now go ahead."

Kendricks lit his pipe and smoked solemnly.

"Your remarks," he declared, "are actuated by jealousy. You haven't the stomach for a man's smoke. Now listen. There's the very devil of a mischief abroad and Falkenberg's at the bottom of it. Do you know what he's doing?"

"I know nothing."

"You remember the night that we were up at the Rat

Mort? He was talking with a dirty-looking man in a red tie and pince-nez."

"I remember it quite well," Julien admitted.

"Well, he was the leader writer in *Le Jour*, - Jesen - a brilliant man, an absolutely wonderful writer, but shiftless. Do you know what Falkenberg has done? The paper was in the market, the controlling share of it, and he bought it, or rather he put the money into Jesen's hands to buy it with. The whole tone of the paper with regard to foreign affairs has turned completely round. Every other day there is a scathing article in it attacking the *entente* with England. You've read them, of course?"

"So has every one," Julien replied gravely. "The people here talk of little else."

"It is known," Kendricks continued, "that Falkenberg has made every use of his frequent visits to this city to ingratiate himself with certain members of the French Cabinet, and to impress them with his views. To some extent there is no doubt that he has succeeded. The German Press - the inspired portion of it, at any rate - is backing all this up by articles extremely friendly towards France and deriding her friendship with England."

"This, too, I have noticed," Julien admitted.

"Carraby is in hot water already," Kendricks went on. "He had a chance on Monday in the House, when he was asked a question about the German gunboat which is reported to have gone to Agdar. The fool muddled it. He gave the sort of suave, methodist reply one expected, and the German Press jeered at him openly. Julien, it's serious. The French people are honest enough, but they are impressionable. A Liberal Government was never popular with them. You were the only Liberal Foreign Minister in whom they believed. This man Carraby they despise. Besides, he has Jewish blood in his veins and you know what that means over here. Jesen's articles come thundering out and already other papers are beginning to follow suit. The poison has been at work for months. You remember monsieur and madame and mademoiselle, with whom I talked so earnestly? Well, they were but types. I talked to them because I wanted to find out their point of view. There are many others like them. They look upon the *entente* with good-natured tolerance. They doubt the real ability of Britain to afford practical aid to France, should she be attacked. This good-natured tolerance is being changed into irritation. Falkenberg's efforts are ceaseless. The moment he has the two countries really estranged, he will strike."

"Against which?" Julien asked quickly.

"Heaven only knows!" Kendricks answered. "For my part, I have always believed that it would be against England. There is no strategic reason for a war between France and Germany. Germany needs more than France can give her. She does not need money, she needs territory. Falkenberg is a rabid imperialist, a dreamer of splendid dreams, a real genius. He is fighting to-day with the subtlest weapons the mind of man ever conceived. Now, Julien, listen. I am here with a direct proposition to you."

"But what can I do?" Julien exclaimed.

"This," Kendricks replied. "It is my idea. I saw Lord Southwold this morning and he agreed. We want you to write for our paper a series of articles, dated from Paris and signed in your own name, and we want you to attack Falkenberg and the game he is playing. We will arrange for them to appear simultaneously in one of the leading journals here. We want you to write openly of these German spies who infest Paris. We want you first to hint and then to speak openly of the purchase of *Le Jour* by means of German gold. We want you to combat the popular opinion here that our army is a wooden box affair, and that we as a nation are too crassly selfish to risk our fleet for the benefit of France. We want you to strike a great note and tell the truth. Julien, those articles signed by you and dated from Paris may do a magnificent work."

Julien's eyes were already agleam.

"Splendid!" he muttered, rising to his feet. "If only I can do it!"

"Of course you can do it," Kendricks insisted firmly. "Before you spoke so often you used to write for the *Nineteenth Century* every month. You haven't forgotten the trick. Some of your sentences I remember even now. I tell you, Julien, they helped me to appreciate you. I liked you better when you took up the pen sometimes than I liked you in those perfect clothes and perfect manner in your office at Downing Street. Your tongue had the politician's trick of gliding over the surface of things. Your pen scratched and spluttered its way into the heart of affairs. Get back to it, Julien. I want your first article before I leave Paris to-night."

"I'll do my best," Julien promised. "It's a great scheme. I'm going to commence now."

"I hoped you would," Kendricks replied. "You've got the atmosphere here. You're sitting in the heart of the France that belongs to the French. It isn't for nothing that I've taken you round a little with me since we were here. Chance was kind, too, when it brought us up against Freudenberg. Remember, Julien, journalism isn't the gentlemanly art it was ten or twenty years ago. You can take up your pen and stab. That's what we want."

"It's fine," Julien declared. "It is war!"

Kendricks rose to his feet.

"I'm going to bed," he announced. "The last month has been exciting and there's plenty more to come. I need sleep. Julien, just a word of caution."

"Fire away," Julien sighed. He was already gazing steadfastly out of the window, already the sentences were framing themselves in his mind.

"The day upon which your first article appears," Kendricks said, "Freudenberg will strike. Your life here will never be wholly safe. You will be encompassed with spies and enemies. Why, this wild-cat scheme of his of sending you off on some expedition was solely because you are the one man of whom he is afraid. He feared lest Carraby might make some hideous blunder in a crisis and that the country might demand you back. That is why he wanted you out of the way."

"You may be right," Julien admitted. "What's that striking - one o'clock? Till to-night, David!"

Kendricks nodded and left the room. Julien sat for a moment before the open window. It was rather an impressive view of the city with its millions of lights, the fine buildings of the Place de la Concorde in clear relief against the deep sky, the Eiffel Tower glittering in the distance, the subtle perfume of pleasure in the air. Julien stood there and raised his eyes to the skies. Already his brain was moving to the grim music of his thoughts. He looked away from the city to the fertile country. Some faint memory of those once blackened fields and desolate villages stole into his mind. He turned to his desk, drew the paper towards him and wrote.

E. Phillips Oppenheim

CHAPTER IV

A STARTLING DISCLOSURE

Julien was driving, a few afternoons later, with Madame Christophor. She had picked him up in the Bois, where he had gone for a solitary walk. In her luxurious automobile they passed smoothly beyond the confines of the Park and out into the country. After her brief summons and the few words of invitation, they relapsed into a somewhat curious silence.

"My friend," Madame Christophor remarked at length, glancing thoughtfully towards him, "I find a change in you. You are pale and tired and silent. It is your duty to amuse me, but you make no effort to do so. Yet you have lost that look of complete dejection. You have, indeed, the appearance of a man who has accomplished something, who has found a new purpose in life."

Julien to some extent recovered himself.

"Dear Madame Christophor," he exclaimed, "it is true! My manners are shocking. Yet, in a way, I have an excuse. I have been hard at work for the last few days. I was writing all night until quite late this morning. It was because I could not sleep that I came out to sit under the trees - where you found me, in fact."

"Writing," she repeated. "So you are changing your weapons, are you? You are going to make a new bid for power?"

Julien shook his head.

"It is not that," he answered. "I have no personal ambitions connected with my present work. It was an idea - a great idea - but it was not my own. Yet the work has been an immense relief."

She looked away, relapsing once more into silence. He glanced towards her. The weariness of her expression was more than ever evident to-day, the weariness that was not fretful, that seemed, indeed, to give an added sweetness to her face. Yet its pathos was always there. Her eyes, which looked steadily down the road in front of them, were full of the fatigue of unwelcome days.

"You men so easily escape," she murmured. "We women never."

Julien was conscious of a certain selfishness in all his thoughts connected with his companion. He had been so ready always to accept her society, to accept and profit by the stimulus of her intellect. Yet he himself had given so little, had shown so little interest in her or her personal affairs. He sat a trifle more upright in his place.

"Dear Madame Christophor," he said earnestly, "you have been so kind to me, you have shown so much interest always in my doings and my troubles. Why not tell me something of your own life? I have felt so much the benefit of your sympathy. Is there nothing in the world I could do for you?"

She sighed.

"No person in the world," she declared, "could help me; certainly not one of your sex. I start with an instinctive and unchanging hatred towards every one of them."

"But, madame," Julien protested, "is that reasonable?"

"It is the truth," she replied. "I do my best when we are together to forget it so far as you are concerned. I succeed because you do not use with me any of the miserable devices of your sex to provoke an interest whether they really desire it or not. You treat me, Sir Julien, as it pleases me to be treated. It is for that reason, I am sure - it must be for that reason - that I find some pleasure in being with you, whereas the society of any other man is a constant irritation to me."

Julien hesitated.

"You know," he began, "I am not naturally a curious person. I have never asked a question of you or about you from the few people with whom I have come in contact over here. At the same time, -"

"Do you mean," she interrupted, "do you seriously mean that you are ignorant as to who I really am, as to any part of my history?"

"Entirely," Julien assured her.

She was thoughtful for several moments.

"Well, that is strange," she declared. "You are upsetting one of my pet theories. All the men whom I have ever known have been more curious than women. Are you interested in me, by any chance, Sir Julien?"

"Immensely," he replied.

"I am glad to hear it. Do you know, that is a great concession for me to make, but it is the truth? I like you to be interested in me. Yet I must confess that your ignorance as to who I really am astonishes me. Perhaps," she added gravely, "if you knew, you would not be sitting by my side at the present moment."

"I cannot believe," he said, smiling, "that you are such a very terrible person."

"Terrible? Perhaps that is not the word," she admitted.

"There is one thing," he went on, "concerning which I have always been curious."

"And that?"

"The little manicure girl whom I met in the Soho restaurant," he replied promptly, "what on earth was her reason for wishing me to come and see you? Why did you want me to come?"

"I thought," she murmured, "that we had agreed not to speak of those matters for the present."

"That was some time ago. Things are changing around us every day. It is possible that within a very short time I may find myself in such a position here that I am forced to know exactly who are my friends and who my enemies."

"Can you believe," she asked, "that you would ever find me among the latter?"

Julien thought for several moments.

"I shall not ask you," he proceeded, "not to be offended with me for what I am going to say. It was a chance remark I heard - no more. It certainly, however, did suggest some association. There is a man who comes often to Paris, who calls himself a maker of toys. He says that he comes from Leipzig and that his name is Herr Freudenberg."

She sat as still as a statue. Not a line of her features was changed. Julien turned a little in his seat. As he watched, he saw that her bosom underneath the lace scarf which she wore was rising and falling quickly. Her teeth came suddenly together. He saw the lids droop over her eyes as though she were in pain.

"Herr Freudenberg," she repeated, "what of him?"

"I knew him in the days when I counted for something in the world," Julien explained. "Don't you remember that on the night when we dined together at the Maison Léon d'Or he sent one of his emissaries for me? He was a man in whom I had always felt the greatest, the most complete interest. I went to him gladly. Since then, as you will know if you read the papers, events have moved rapidly. I am beginning to realize now how completely and absolutely that man is the enemy of my country."

"It is true, that," she murmured.

"For some reason," Julien continued, "he seemed

anxious to remove me from Paris. He made me a somewhat singular offer. He wanted me to go to some distant country on a mission - not political and yet for Germany."

"And do you go?"

"No," he replied, "I have found other work. I don't think that I seriously considered it at any time, yet I have always been curious as to why he should have made such an offer to me."

She had the air now of a woman who had completely recovered control of herself.

"Sir Julien," she asked, "I beg of you to tell me this. If you do not know who I am, why have you mentioned Herr Freudenberg's name to me?"

"Madame," Julien answered, "because the man who brought me the message from Herr Freudenberg, the man who conducted me to him, the man concerning whom you told me that strange, pathetic little story - he let fall one word. I asked him no question. I wished for no information except from you. Yet I am only human. I have had impulses of curiosity."

"Herr Freudenberg is my husband," Madame Christophor declared.

Julien looked at her in amazement. For the moment he was speechless.

"I say what is perhaps literally but not actually true," she went on. "He was my husband. We are separated. We are not divorced because we were married as

Roman Catholics. We are separated. There will never be anything else between us."

Julien remained silent. It was so hard to say anything. The woman's tone told him that around her speech hovered a tragedy.

"Now you know that Herr Freudenberg is my husband," she asked, "are you not a little afraid to be sitting here by my side?"

"Why should I be?"

"Don't you know," she continued, "that he is your enemy?"

Julien looked grave.

"No, I have scarcely realized that," he answered. "I think, perhaps, when he reads yesterday's papers he may be feeling like that. At present, so far as he knows, what have I done?"

"You," she said, "were the only man who ever stood up to him, who ever dealt a blow at his political supremacy. At the Conference of Berlin you triumphed. German papers politely, and in a very veiled manner, reminded him of his defeat. It was not a great matter, it is true, but none the less the Conference of Berlin was the first diplomatic failure in which he had ever been concerned, and you were responsible for it."

"You think, then," Julien remarked, "that he still harbors a grudge against me for that?"

"Without a doubt. Now tell me what you mean when

you speak of yesterday's papers?"

"I am writing a series of articles," Julien told her. "They commenced yesterday. They will appear in a French paper - *Le Grand Journal* - and in the English *Post*. They are written with the sole idea of attacking Herr Freudenberg. When he reads the first, he will understand - he will be my enemy."

She held out her hand.

"Then say good-bye to me now, my friend," she murmured, "for you will die."

Julien laughed scornfully.

"We do not live in those days," he reminded her. "We fight with the pen, with diplomacy, with all the weapons of statecraft and intrigue, if you will. But this is not now the Paris of Dumas. One does not assassinate."

"My friend," she said earnestly, "you do not know Herr Freudenberg. If indeed you have become during these last few days his enemy, by this time next week you will surely have passed into some other sphere of activity. There are no methods too primitive for him, no methods too subtle or too cruel. He can be the most charming, the most winning, the most generous, the most romantic person who ever breathed; or he can be a Nero, a cruel and brutal butcher, a murderer either of reputations or bodies - he cares little which."

"Presently," Julien declared, "I shall begin to feel uncomfortable."

"Oh! you have courage, of course," she admitted, with a scornful little shrug of the shoulders. "No one has ever denied that to your race. But you have also the unconquerable stupidity which makes heroes and victims of your soldiers."

Julien smiled.

"Well, I am at least warned, and for that I thank you. Now let me ask you another question. You have told me this very strange thing about yourself and Herr Freudenberg. You have told me of your feelings concerning him. Yet you have not really told me exactly on what terms you are with him at present? Forgive me if I find this important."

"I do not receive him," she replied. "I have no interest in his comings or his goings. I have a solemn promise, a promise to which he has subscribed upon his honor, that he shall not seek to cross the threshold of my house. He sent me an ambassador once quite lately to make me a certain proposition connected with you."

"With me?" Julien repeated.

She nodded.

"He has great faith in my powers," she went on, looking him full in the face, "also, apparently, some belief in your susceptibility. Is that unkind of me? Never mind, it is the truth. He imagined, perhaps, that I might help him to rid Paris of your presence. There was just one thing he could offer me which I desired. He came to offer it."

"You refused?" Julien exclaimed.

Her eyes rested upon his. Her expression was faintly provocative.

"How could I accept an offer," she asked, "to deal with a thing which did not belong to me? You have shown no signs at present, Sir Julien, of becoming my abject slave."

The car rushed through a straggling village. All the time she was watching him. Then she threw herself back among the cushions with a little laugh.

"A week or so ago," she murmured, "I had a fancy that if I had tried - well, that perhaps you were not so different from other men. I should have loathed my conquest, I should probably have loathed you, but I think that I should have expected it. At the present moment," she went on, glancing into a little gold mirror which she had picked up from a heap of trifles lying on the table before her, "at the present moment I am disillusioned. My vanity is wounded though my relief is great. Nevertheless, Sir Julien, tell me what has happened to you during the last few days?"

"Work," Julien replied, "the sort of work I was craving for."

"Not only that," she insisted, setting down the mirror with a sigh. "There is something else."

"If there is," Julien assured her, "I am not yet conscious of it."

They had emerged from the country lane along which they had been traveling and were returning now to Paris along the broad highroad. They were going at a fair speed when suddenly a huge racing car came flashing by them, covered with dust, and with all the indications of having come a great distance. Madame Christophor leaned forward in her seat and clutched her companion's arm. Her eyes were fixed upon the figure of the man leaning back by the side of the driver.

"You see?" she muttered.

"Herr Freudenberg!" Julien gasped.

She nodded. Already the car had vanished in a cloud of dust.

"He is just from Germany or from the frontier. He very seldom comes all the way by rail. The car is always waiting."

"I shall see him, then, to-night," Julien declared. "Already, without a doubt, he knows. Already he is my enemy. What about you, Madame Christophor?"

"My friend," she promised, "you will have nothing to fear from me. So long as I can forget your sex, I rather like you."

"Are you going to answer my question about the little girl who sent me to you?" he asked.

"I will tell you, if you like," she said. "Mademoiselle Senn was once in my service. She occasionally executes commissions for me in London. She knows everybody. It was in obedience to my wishes that she gave you that message."

"But why?" Julien demanded. "What interest had you in me?"

"None," she answered a little coldly, - "no personal interest. I sent that message because I discovered that the individual who has just passed us in the automobile was framing certain schemes in connection with you if you should come to Paris. Politically as well as personally he and I are enemies. He hates America and the whole Anglo-Saxon race. It has amused me more than once to thwart his schemes. I intended to set you upon your guard. You see, it is very simple. Mademoiselle Senn wrote me at first that she did not know you and that she feared you were inaccessible. Then she wired me of an accidental meeting and that she had delivered my message. The whole affair is simpler than it seemed, is it not so?... Now listen. I have satisfied your curiosity. You now shall answer a question. Who is Miss Clonarty?"

Julien gazed at her in astonishment.

"Miss Clonarty?" he repeated.

Madame Christophor nodded.

"The name seems to surprise you. A young English woman called on me to-day in answer to my advertise-ment for a secretary who could write and speak English. She said that her name was Miss Anne Clonarty and she referred me to you."

"If she is the lady whom I suppose she is," Julien replied, "you will be perfectly safe in engaging her."

Madame Christophor looked at him from underneath

the lids of her eyes.

"Do you think that I do not know?" she asked, with a shade of contempt in her tone, - "that I do not sometimes read the papers? Do you think that I have not seen that Lady Anne Clonarty, the girl whom you were engaged to marry, disappeared from her home the other day, on the eve of her marriage to another man? It is this girl who comes to me for my situation, is it not so?"

Julien was silent.

"I knew nothing of her coming. I did not even know that you wanted a secretary."

"I wonder why she came to Paris," Madame Christophor remarked. "Is she in love with you?"

"There was never any question of anything of the sort," Julien declared fervently.

"You have seen her since she arrived in Paris?"

"Entirely by accident. I saw her alight from the train. I was at the Gare du Nord to meet Kendricks."

Madame Christophor leaned back in her seat.

"Is it your wish that I engage her?"

"Certainly," Julien replied. "I am sure that you will find her competent. At the same time, I don't know how long she will keep this thing up."

"As a rule I do not care for handsome women around

me," Madame Christophor said composedly. "Lady Anne is much too good-looking to please me. She has all the freshness and vitality," she added, dropping her voice a little, "which seem to have left me forever."

"You have experience," Julien reminded her. "Experience in itself is wonderful, even though one has to pay for it."

They were in the streets of Paris now. Madame Christophor shrugged her shoulders and sat up.

"It is one of the misfortunes of my sex," she said, a little bitterly, "that without experience we lack charm - in the eyes of you men, that is to say. It is your own folly.... Are you coming home with me, my friend, or shall I set you down somewhere?"

"As near the Gare du Nord as possible, if you please," Julien begged. "I have wearied you enough for one afternoon."

Madame Christophor looked at him thoughtfully. There was a slight frown upon her forehead.

"Somewhere near the Gare du Nord!" she repeated.

CHAPTER V

THE FIRST ARTICLE

Julien found Lady Anne in a small, stuffy apartment on the third floor of the house in the Rue St. Antoine. Before her was a sewing-machine, and the floor of the room was littered with oddments of black calico. She herself was seated apparently deep in thought before an untrimmed hat.

"What on earth, my dear Anne," he exclaimed, "are you doing?"

She merely glanced up at his entrance. Her eyes were still far away.

"Don't interrupt," she begged. "I am seeking for an inspiration. In my younger days I used to trim hats. I don't suppose anything I could do would be of any use here, but one must try everything."

"But I thought," he protested, "that you were going to be a lady's secretary, or something of that sort?"

"I have applied for a situation," she admitted. "I am not engaged yet. By the bye, I gave your name as a reference. I wonder if there is any chance for me."

"As a matter of fact," he told her, "I have just left the lady whose advertisement you answered."

"Madame Christophor?"

"Madame Christophor. If you are really anxious for that post, I can assure you that it is yours."

She flung the hat to the other end of the room.

"Good!" she exclaimed. "I don't think this sort of thing is in my line at all. Tell me, is Madame Christophor half as charming as she looks?"

"I have known her only a short time," Julien replied, "but she is certainly a very wonderful woman."

"What does she do," Lady Anne asked, "to require a secretary?"

"She is a woman of immense wealth, I believe," Julien answered, "and she has many charities. She is married, but separated from her husband. I think, on the whole, that she must have led a rather unhappy life."

"I think it is very extraordinary," Lady Anne remarked, "that she should be willing to take a secretary who knows nothing of typewriting or shorthand. I told her how ignorant I was, but she didn't seem to mind much."

Julien sat down by the side of the sewing-machine.

"Anne," he began, "do you really think you're going to care for this sort of thing?"

"What sort of thing?" she demanded.

"Why, life on your own. You have been so independent always and a person of consequence. You know what it means to be a servant?"

"Not yet," Lady Anne admitted. "I think, though, that it is quite time I did. I am rather looking forward to it."

Julien was a little staggered. She looked over at him and laughed scornfully.

"After all," she said, "I am not sure, Julien, whether you are a person of much understanding. You proposed to me because I happened to be the sort of girl you were looking for. My connections were excellent and my appearance, I suppose, satisfactory. You never thought of me myself, me as an independent person, in all your life. Do you believe that I am simply Lady Anne Clonarty, a reasonable puppet, a walking doll to receive some one's guests and further his social ambitions? Don't you think that I have the slightest idea of being a woman of my own? What's wrong with me, I wonder, Julien, that you should take me for something automatic?"

"You acted the part," he reminded her.

"With you, yes!" she replied scornfully. "I should like to know how much you encouraged me to be anything different. A sawdust man I used to think you. Oh, we matched all right! I am not denying that. I was what I had to be. I sometimes wonder if misfortune will not do you good."

"Misfortune is lending you a tongue, at any rate,"

he retorted.

"As yet," she objected, "I know nothing of misfortune. The impulse which led me to chuck things was just the most wonderful thing that ever came to me in life. I awoke this morning feeling like a freed woman. I sang while I got up. It seemed to me that I had never seen anything so beautiful as the view of Paris from my poky window. And I got up without a maid, too, Julien. I had no perfectly equipped bathroom to wander into. Not much luxury about these rooms of Janette's."

He glanced at her admiringly.

"You certainly look as though the life agreed with you," he answered. "Put on your hat and come out to dinner."

She rose to her feet at once.

"I have been praying for that," she confessed. "You know, Julien, I should starve badly. The one thing I can't get rid of is my appetite. You don't expect me to make a toilette, because I can't?"

"Nothing of the sort," he assured her. "Come as you are."

She kept him waiting barely five minutes. She was still wearing her smart traveling suit and the little toque which she had worn when she left home. She walked down the street with him, humming gayly.

"Have you read the English papers this morning, Julien?" she asked.

"Not thoroughly," he admitted.

"Columns about me," she declared blithely. "The general idea is that I am suffering from a lapse of memory. They have found traces of me in every part of England. Not a word about Paris, thank goodness!"

"But do you mean to say that no one has an idea of where you are? Won't your mother be anxious?"

"Not a bit of it," Lady Anne laughed. "I left a note for her, just to say that she wasn't to worry. She knows I'll take care of myself all right. Julien, don't you love these streets and their crowds of people? Every one looks as though they were on a holiday."

"So they are," Julien replied. "Life is only a holiday over here. In England we go about with our eyes fixed upon the deadliest thing in life we can imagine. Over here, depression is a crime. They call into their minds the most joyous thing they can think of. It becomes a habit. They think only of the pleasantness of life. They keep their troubles buried underneath."

"It is the way to live," she murmured.

"This, at any rate," he answered, leading the way into Henry's "is the place at which to dine. Just fancy, we were engaged for three months and not once did I dine with you alone! Now we are not engaged and we think nothing of it."

"Less than nothing," she agreed, "except that I am frightfully hungry."

They found a comfortable table. Julien took up the

menu and wrote out the dinner carefully.

"In this country," he said, leaning back, "we are spared the barbarity of table d'hôte dinners. Therefore we must wait, but what does it matter? There is always something to talk about."

"I am glad to hear that you feel like that, Julien. I remember sometimes when we were alone together in England, we seemed to find it a trifle difficult."

"Since then," he replied, "we have both burst the bonds - I of necessity, you of choice."

"I don't believe," she declared, helping herself to *hors d'oeuvres*, "that we are either of us going to be sorry for it."

"One can never tell. So far as you are concerned, I haven't got over the wonder of it yet. You never showed me so much of the woman throughout our engagement as you have shown me during the last few days."

"My dear Julien," she protested, "you didn't know where to look for it. Why does this funny little man with the mutton-chop whiskers hover around our table all the time?"

"He is distressed," Julien explained, "to see you eating so much bread and butter. He fears that you will not have an appetite for the very excellent dinner which I have ordered."

"He is right," she decided. "Never mind, I will leave the rolls alone. I am still, I can assure you, ravenous."

She leaned back and, looking out into the room, began to laugh. People who passed never failed to notice her. She was certainly a striking-looking girl and she had, above all, the air.

"Julien," she cried, "this is really too amusing! Did you see who went by just then? It was Lord Athlington - my venerable uncle - with the lady with the yellow hair. He saw you here with me - saw us sitting together alone, having dinner - me unchaperoned, a runaway! Isn't it delicious?"

Julien looked after his companion's elderly relative with a smile.

"I wonder," he remarked, "whether your uncle's magnificent unconsciousness is due to defective eyesight or nerve?"

"Nerve, without a doubt," she insisted. "We all have it. Besides, don't you see he's changed their table so as to be out of sight? I wonder what he really thinks of me! If we'd belonged even to the really smart set in town, it wouldn't have been half so funny. They do so many things that seem wrong that people forget to be shocked."

"I can conceive," he murmured, "that your mother's ambitions would scarcely lead her in that direction."

Lady Anne shrugged her shoulders.

"I don't think she could get in if she tried. The really disreputable people in Society are so exclusive. I wonder, Julien, if I shall be allowed to come out and dine with you when I am Madame Christophor's secretary?"

"Once a week, perhaps," he suggested, - "scarcely oftener, I am afraid."

"Ah! well," she declared, "I shall like work, I am convinced. Julien, you are spoiling me. I am sure this is a *cuisine de luxe*. I told you to take me to a cheap restaurant."

"We will try them all in time," he answered. "I had to start by taking you to my favorite place."

"You really mean, then," she asked, "that you are going on being nice to me? Of course, I haven't the slightest claim on you. I suppose, as a matter of fact, I treated you rather badly, didn't I?"

"Not a bit of it," he assured her. "I was a failure, that was all. But of course I am going on being nice to you. There aren't too many people over here whom one cares to be with. There aren't very many just now," he continued, "who care to be with me."

"Idiotic!" she replied. "Tell me about this work of yours?"

He explained Kendricks' idea. Her eyes glistened.

"It's really splendid," she declared. "How I should love to have seen your first article!"

"You shall read it afterwards," he told her. "I have a copy of *Le Grand Journal* in my overcoat pocket."

She beckoned to the *vestiaire*.

"I will not wait a moment," she insisted. "I shall read it while dinner is being served. It's a glorious idea, this, to fight your way back with your pen. There are those nowadays who tell us, you know, Julien, that there is more to be done through the Press than in Parliament. Your spoken words can influence only a small number of people. What you write the world reads."

She explained what she desired to the *vestiaire*. He reappeared a minute or two later with the newspaper. She spread it out before her. Julien read it over her shoulder. He himself had seen it before, but his own eyes were the brighter as he reread it. When she had finished she said very little. They ate the first course of their dinner almost in silence. Then she laid her hand suddenly upon his.

"Julien, dear," she said, "I have done you a wrong. I am sorry."

"A wrong?" he repeated.

She looked at him almost humbly. There was something new in her eyes, something new in her expression.

"I am afraid," she continued, "that I never looked upon you as anything more than the ordinary stereotyped politician, a skilful debater, of course, and with the chessboard brains of diplomacy. This," - she touched the newspaper with her forefinger - "this is something very different."

"Do you like it, then?"

"Like it!" she repeated scornfully. "Can't you feel yourself how different it is from those precise, cynical little speeches of yours? It is as though a smouldering bonfire had leapt suddenly into flame. There is genius in every line. Go on writing like that, Julien, and you will soon be more powerful than ever you were in the House of Commons."

He laughed. It was absurd to admit it, but nothing had pleased him so much since the coming of his misfortune! She was thoughtful for some time, every now and then glancing back at the newspaper. Over their coffee she broke into a little reminiscent laugh.

"Did I tell you about Mrs. Carraby?" she asked. "Mother and I met her at Wumbledon House, two or three days after her husband's appointment had been confirmed. I can see her now coming towards us. There were so many people around that she had to risk everything. Oh, it was a great moment for mother! She never troubled even to raise her lorgnettes. She never attempted any of that glaring-through-you sort of business. She just looked up at Mrs. Carraby's hand and looked up at her eyes and walked by without changing a muscle. Of course I did the same - very nearly as well, too, I believe. Cat!"

Julien frowned slightly.

"You can imagine," he said, "that I am not very keen about discussing Mrs. Carraby. Yet, after all, her husband and his career were, I suppose, the most important things in life to her."

"Then she's going to have a pretty rocky time," Lady Anne decided. "I don't understand much about politics, but I know it's no use putting a tradesman into the Foreign Office. He's wobbly already, and as for Mrs. Carraby - well, I don't know if she ever went on with you like it, Julien, but you remember Bob Sutherland - the one in the Guards, I mean? - well, she's going an awful pace with him."

"I think," he declared, "that Mrs. Carraby can take care of herself."

"Perhaps," Lady Anne replied, looking thoughtfully at her cigarette. "You see, the woman knows in her heart that she's impossible. She copies all our bad tricks. She sees that we all flirt as a matter of course, and she tries to outdo us. It's the old story. What one person can do with impunity, another makes an awful hash of. We can go to the very gates because when we get there we know how to shrug our shoulders and turn away. I am not sure that Mrs. Carraby has breeding enough for that. She'll go through, if Bob has his way."

"You are becoming rather an advanced young person," Julien remarked, as he paid the bill.

"My dear Julien," she said, "I've told you before that you never knew me. If you had appreciated me as I deserved, when you came that cropper you wouldn't have called on me to say good-bye. You'd have left that red-headed friend of yours at home and told me that the empty place in the taxicab was mine."

He laughed and then suddenly became grave.

"Supposing I had?" he whispered.

She looked at him, startled. In that moment he seemed

to see a new thing in her face, a new and marvelous softness. It passed like a flash - so swiftly that it left him wondering whether it was not indeed a trick of his imagination.

"Absurd!" she murmured. "Tell me, what is there we can do now? Must I go home?"

"On the contrary," he declared, "you are engaged to me for the evening. Only I must call at my rooms. Do you mind?"

"I mind nothing," she assured him. "Let us take a carriage and drive about the streets. Julien, what a yellow moon!"

They clambered into a little *voiture*, and with a hoarse shout and a crack of the whip from the *cocher*, they started off. Lady Anne leaned back with an exclamation of content.

"If only it weren't so theatrical!" she sighed. "The streets seem so clean and the buildings so white and the sky so blue and the people so gay. Yet I suppose the bitterness of life is here as in the other places. Why do you want to call at your rooms, Julien?"

"There is just a chance," he explained, "that there may be a telegram from Kendricks. I want to know what they think of my article."

She laughed scornfully.

"I can tell you that. There is only one thing they can think. How these people will hate you who are trying to make mischief between France and England!"

Julien smiled grimly.

"I shouldn't be surprised," he admitted. "It may come to a tussle between us yet."

They pulled up before the door of his rooms. She, too, alighted.

"I want to see what your quarters are like," she said calmly. "I may come up, mayn't I?"

"By all means," he assented.

She followed him up the dark stairs and into his room. He turned on the lights. She looked around at his little salon, with its French furniture, its open windows with the lime trees only a few feet away, and threw herself into an easy-chair with a sigh of content.

"Julien, how delightful!" she exclaimed. "Is there anything for you?"

He walked to the mantelpiece. There was a telegram and a note for him. The former he tore open and his eyes sparkled as he read it aloud.

Magnificent. Be careful. Am coming over at once.

KENDRICKS.

He passed it on to her. Then he opened the note.

I am coming to your rooms for my answer to-night.

CARL FREUDENBERG.

Even as he read it there was a knocking at the door. She looked up doubtfully.

"Who is that?"

"It may be the man who writes me here," he told her.

She rose softly to her feet and pointed to the door which divided the apartments. He nodded and she passed through into the inner room. Julien went to the outside door and threw it open. It was indeed Herr Freudenberg who stood there.

"Come in," he invited.

Herr Freudenberg removed his hat and entered.

CHAPTER VI

FALKENBERG FAILS

Herr Freudenberg was dressed for the evening with his usual fastidious neatness. He had the air of a man who had been engaged for many nights in some arduous occupation. There were dark rims under his eyes, the lines upon his forehead were deeper. Nevertheless, he smiled with something of his old gayety as he accepted the chair which Julien placed for him.

"My dear Sir Julien," he said, "I have come a good many hundred miles at a most inconvenient moment for the sake of a brief conversation with you."

Julien raised his eyebrows.

"You surprise me!" he exclaimed. "I had no idea that the mission you spoke of was so urgent."

"Nor is it," Herr Freudenberg replied. "As a matter of fact, it scarcely exists at all, or if it did exist, it was created simply as a means of removing you from within the reach of practical politics for some months. I have foresight, you see, Sir Julien. I saw what was coming. Permit me to tell you that I do not like your letter in *Le Grand Journal* yesterday, a letter which I understand appeared also in the London *Post*."

"I am sorry," Julien said calmly. "Still, to be perfectly frank, it wasn't written with a view of pleasing or displeasing you. It was written in a strenuous attempt to preserve the friendship between France and England."

"It is to be followed, I presume, by others?" Herr Freudenberg asked.

"It is the first of a series," Julien admitted.

"You know," Herr Freudenberg remarked, glancing at his finger-nails for a moment, "that it is most diabolically clever?"

"You flatter me," Julien murmured.

"Not at all. I have spoken the truth. I am here to know what price you will take to suppress the remainder of the series."

Julien considered.

"I will take," he replied, "the exact amount of the last war indemnity which was paid to you by France."

Herr Freudenberg smiled.

"A mere trifle to the war indemnity we shall be asking from England before very long."

"I am not avaricious," Julien declared. "Those are my terms."

Herr Freudenberg sighed.

"My friend," he said, "it would be better if you talked of this matter reasonably. There are other ways of securing the non-continuance of those letters than by purchase."

"Precisely," Julien answered, "but Paris, in its beaten thoroughfares, at any rate, is a law-abiding city. I don't fancy that I shall come to much grief here."

"A brave man," Herr Freudenberg remarked, "seldom believes that he will come to grief."

"If the blow falls, nevertheless, it is at least considerate of you that you bring me warning!"

"Rubbish!" Herr Freudenberg interposed. "Listen, Sir Julien, I ask you to consider this matter as a reasonable person. We don't want war. We don't mean to have war. But the desire of my Ministers - my own desire - really is to inflict a crushing diplomatic humiliation upon the present Government of Great Britain. It is composed of incompetent and objectionable persons. We desire to humiliate them. Yet who is it that we find taking up the cudgels on their behalf? You - the man whom they drove out, the man whom from sheer jealousy they ousted from their ranks. Why, you should be with us, not against us."

"I have no grudge whatever against my party," Julien said. "You seem to have been misinformed upon that subject. Besides, I am an Englishman and a patriot. The whole series of my articles will be written, and I shall do my best to point out exactly the means by which this present coolness between our two countries has been engineered."

"I will give you," Herr Freudenberg offered, "a million francs not to write those articles."

Julien pointed to the door.

"You are becoming offensive!"

Herr Freudenberg rose slowly to his feet. There was a little glitter in his eyes.

"I have gone out of my way," he declared, "to be friendly with you, most obstinate of Englishmen. That now is finished. You shall not write those articles."

"You threaten me?"

"I do!"

"There are times," Julien remarked quietly, "when I scarcely know whether to take you seriously. There is surely a little of the burlesque about such a statement?"

Herr Freudenberg shrugged his shoulders slightly.

"You think so? Nevertheless, no man whom I have ever threatened has done the thing against which I have warned him."

Julien turned towards the door to open it. Herr Freudenberg, with footsteps like a cat, came up behind him. Suddenly he threw his long, sinewy arm around the other's neck. Taken utterly unprepared, Julien was powerless. Herr Freudenberg swung him round upon his back and knelt upon his chest.

"This," he said calmly, "distresses me extremely. Yet

what am I to do?"

He whistled softly. The door was opened. Estermen came in with suspicious alacrity. There was scarcely any need of words. In a moment Julien's legs and arms were bound and a gag thrust between his teeth. Herr Freudenberg moved before the door and listened.

"Estermen has reported to me," he remarked, "that you keep no manservant. Any intrusion here, therefore, is scarcely to be feared. You will permit me?"

He took one of the tumblers from the tray, rinsed it out with soda-water, and poured the contents of a small phial into it. Then he came and stood over Julien.

"My obstinate Englishman," he proceeded, "this tumbler contains the waters of forgetfulness. Let me assure you upon my honor that the liquid is harmless. Its one effect is to reduce those who take it to such a state that for the space of a week or two their mental faculties are impaired. You will drink this in a few minutes. You will awake feeling weak, languid, indisposed for exercise, incapable of mental effort. The doctor will prescribe a tonic, you will go away, but it will be months before you are able to set yourself to any task requiring the full use of your faculties. At the end of that time, I trust that you will have found wisdom. Will you swallow the draught?"

Julien shook his head violently. Herr Freudenberg sighed.

"I was hoping," he continued, "that you would not force me to mention the alternative. I should dislike exceedingly having to inflict any more lasting injury upon you, but you stand in my path and I permit no one to do that. Drink, and in a month or two all will be as it is now. Refuse, and I shall leave Estermen to deal with you, and let me warn you that his methods are not so gentle as mine. More men than one who have been foolish have disappeared in Paris."

"If you move a step this way," a calm voice said from the other end of the room, "I shall shoot."

Herr Freudenberg turned his head. Estermen, whose nerves were less under control, gave a little cry. Lady Anne was standing upon the threshold of the doorway between the two rooms, and in her very steady hand was grasped a small revolver. The two men were speechless.

"It has taken me some time to find this," Lady Anne went on, "and longer still to find the cartridges. I do not understand in the least what has happened, but I am perfectly serious when I tell you that I shall shoot either of you two if you move a step towards me."

Herr Freudenberg looked into the revolver, looked at Lady Anne and made her a little bow.

"Mademoiselle," he said, "who you may be I do not, alas! know. Sir Julien, however, is indeed to be congratulated that he possesses already so charming and courageous a friend with the entrée to his bedroom."

Lady Anne lifted the revolver a few inches and fired. The bullet struck the wall barely a foot over Herr Freudenberg's head. A faint puff of blue smoke floated up towards the ceiling.

E. Phillips Oppenheim

"I do not like impertinence," she remarked. "If you have any more such speeches to make -"

"Mademoiselle, I have none," Herr Freudenberg interrupted, bowing. "Allow me, on the contrary, to offer you my apologies and to express my admiration for your bearing. I must, alas! acknowledge myself, for the moment, vanquished. I shall leave you to release our dear friend, Sir Julien. But, if you are wise, mademoiselle, if you are really his friend, you will advise him to obey the injunction which I have sought to lay upon him to-day. A little affair like this which goes wrong, is nothing. I have a dozen means of enforcing my words, not one of which has ever failed."

"I do not know who you are," Lady Anne said calmly, "or what it is against which you are warning Sir Julien, but I am perfectly certain of one thing. He will do what is right and what he conceives to be his duty, without fear of threats from you or any one."

Herr Freudenberg bowed low. Estermen, who had been glancing more than once uneasily towards the revolver, was already at the door.

"Mademoiselle," Herr Freudenberg declared, "bravery is a splendid gift, discretion a finer. Sir Julien knows who I am and he knows that I have yet to admit myself vanquished in any scheme in which I engage. He will use his judgment. Meanwhile, mademoiselle!"

He bowed low, turned and left the room. Lady Anne listened to his retreating footsteps. Then she crossed the room quickly and bent over Julien.

"Are you hurt?" she asked breathlessly.

He shook his head. She fumbled for a few minutes with the gag and removed it.

"Not a bit," he assured her. "Don't put the revolver down yet, but fetch me a knife. You'll find one on the mantelpiece in the bedroom."

She did as he told her. In a few minutes he was free. He stood up, gasping.

"The fellow came up behind me," he explained, "while I was walking to the door. Anne, what a brick you are!"

He held out his hand. She took it, laughing frankly.

"My dear Julien," she exclaimed, "what else could any one do? I heard the row and, - shall I admit it? - peeped through the keyhole. I couldn't see anything, so I opened the door softly and heard something of what was going on. This old revolver was lying on your dressing-table, but I had an awful hunt for the cartridges. Whoever were those men?"

Julien smiled.

"When I tell you," he said, "you will think that I am mad. Yet this is the truth. The man with whom you talked was Prince von Falkenberg."

"What, the German Minister?"

Julien nodded.

"It seems incredible, doesn't it? Falkenberg is a man possessed of one idea - to upset the relations between

France and England. For that purpose he has been paying secret visits to Paris for the last year. He has corrupted the Press here. He has wormed his way into the confidence of one or two of the Ministers. The thing is a perfect mania with him. He has taken it into his head that the articles which Kendricks has made me promise to write, and the first one of which appeared in *Le Grand Journal* yesterday - the one you read at dinner-time - are going to be exploited as an exposure of his methods. For that reason he came ostensibly to confirm an offer which he made me some time ago. When I refused, he offered me a large sum of money - anything to get rid of me and to stop my writing these articles. Of course I declined, and there you are."

Lady Anne began to laugh once more.

"Well," she said, "I suppose I'm not dreaming. It sounds like a page out of an opera-bouffe. That man who was here, whom I threatened to shoot, was really Prince Falkenberg?"

"There's no doubt whatever about it," Julien assured her. "The very first night I was in Paris he sent for me. Anne," he went on, turning once more towards her, "I haven't thanked you half enough. What a nerve you have! You were splendid!"

"Don't talk rubbish, Julien," she protested. "The stroke of luck was that I happened to be there. It must have been quite a surprise for him to see an apparently respectable young woman step out of your bedroom. I am inclined to fear, Julien, that I am compromised. Anyhow, mother would say so!"

"Between ourselves," Julien remarked, "I don't think

that Falkenberg will mention the occurrence. Just wait while I put on another collar and we'll go to that music-hall."

She glanced at the clock.

"I think you shall take me home instead."

He looked at her quickly.

"This affair has upset you!"

"My dear Julien," she said dryly, "what an absurd idea! Of course I am quite used to these little affairs, to seeing you lie bound and gagged, and pointing a revolver at that unpleasant-looking Prince, with a horrible fear inside me all the time that if I did aim at anything I shouldn't hit it! Nevertheless, I think I'll go home, if you don't mind."

They descended the stairs and he called a little *voiture*.

"I suppose it would sound silly," he ventured, after a time, "if I said anything more about thanking you?"

"Ridiculous!" she replied. "But what are you going to do? Are you going to the police?"

He shook his head.

"I think that Herr Freudenberg, as he calls himself, would be too clever for me if I tried anything of that sort. You see, I have put this revolver into my pocket. I am going to avoid the lonely places, and have Kendricks with me as much as possible."

She nodded.

"Take care of yourself," she advised, in a matter-of-fact tone, as they turned into the street where Mademoiselle Rignaut lived. "I don't want to hear of any tragedies."

"When shall I see you again?" Julien asked.

"It depends upon what reply I get from Madame Christophor," she answered. "She may want me at once, and I don't know yet whether I'll get an evening out or not! I shall have to leave you to discover that. Good night!"

She vanished within the dark doorway. Julien stepped back into the carriage more than a little puzzled. To him Anne had always seemed the prototype of all that was serene and matter-of-fact. To-night he had found her unrecognizable. There was something, too, in her face as she had turned away, a slight tremble in her voice, that bewildered him. As he drove back to his rooms through the lighted streets, it was strange that, notwithstanding the exciting adventure through which he had passed, his thoughts were chiefly concerned with the problem of this unfamiliar Lady Anne!

CHAPTER VII

LADY ANNE DECLINES

"My dear Julien!"

The Duchess was very impressive indeed. From the depths of an easy-chair in her sitting-room at the Ritz Hotel she held out both her hands, and in her eyes was that peculiar strained look which Julien had only been privileged to observe once or twice in his life. It indicated, or rather it was the Duchess's substitute for, emotion. Julien at once perceived, therefore, that this was an occasion.

"First of all," she went on, motioning him to a chair, "first of all, before I say a single word about this strange thing which has brought me to Paris, let me congratulate you. I always knew, dear Julien, that you would do something, that you would not allow yourself to be altogether crushed by the machinations of that hateful woman."

"Really," Julien began, "I am not quite sure -"

"I mean your letters, of course," she interrupted. "The Duke, when he finished the first one, said only one thing - 'Wonderful!' That is just how we all feel about them, Julien. I met Lord Cardington only a few hours

292   E. Phillips Oppenheim

before I left London, and he was absolutely enthusiastic. 'If one thing,' he said, 'will save the country, it is this splendid attack upon the new diplomacy!' - as you so cleverly called it. The Duke tells me that that first article of yours is to be printed as a leaflet and distributed throughout the country."

"I am very glad," Julien said, "to hear all this. Tell me, what brings you to Paris? Is the Duke with you?"

The Duchess smiled at him reproachfully.

"You ask me what brings me to Paris, Julien? Come, come! You and I mustn't begin like that. I want you to tell me at once where she is."

"Where who is?"

"Anne, of course! Please don't play with me. Consider what a terrible time we have all been through."

Julien did not at once reply. His very hesitation seemed to afford the Duchess a lively satisfaction.

"There!" she declared. "You are not going to pretend, then, that you don't know? That is excellent. Julien, tell me at once where to find her. Take me to her."

"I am afraid I can't do that," Julien objected.

"My dear - my dear Julien!" the Duchess protested. "This is all so foolish. Why should there be any mystery about Anne's whereabouts? I am not angry. I ought to be, perhaps, but you see I have guessed my dear girl's secret. I've felt for her terribly during the last few weeks, but it was so hard to know what to do. It seemed shocking at the time, but perhaps, after all, the course which she adopted was the wisest."

"I am very glad to hear that you are taking it like that," Julien remarked, "and I am sure Anne will be. I think the best thing I can do is to go and see her and tell her that you are here -"

"She does not know, then?" the Duchess interrupted.

"Why, of course not," Julien replied. "I received your note early this morning - before I was up, in fact - and you begged me so earnestly to come round at once that I came straight here without calling anywhere."

The Duchess coughed.

"Very well, Julien, I will leave you to go and fetch Anne whenever you like. I shall await you here impatiently. Tell me how it was that you both managed to deceive us so completely?"

Julien shook his head.

"I haven't the slightest notion what you mean."

The Duchess shrugged her shoulders.

"For my part," she said, "I always looked upon dear Anne as the most unemotional, unsentimental person. Naturally I thought that she was a little attracted towards you, but on the other hand I had no idea that she looked upon marriage as anything but a reasonable and necessary part of life. I had no idea, even, that she had any real affection for you."

"Affection for me!"

Julien looked up. The Duchess was regarding him as a mother might look at a naughty child whom she intended to pardon.

"I did notice," she continued, "that Anne seemed very silent for some time after your departure, and there was a curious lack of enthusiasm about her preparations for the wedding with Mr. Samuel Harbord. She scarcely looked, even, at the pearls he gave her. You know that I found them on the floor of her bedroom after she had gone away? Well, well, never mind that," the Duchess went on. "When I got her hurried note and understood the whole affair, I must say that on the whole it was a relief to me. Dear Anne - she is only like what I was at her age, before I married the Duke. You ought to be very proud and happy, Julien."

"I should be very happy," Julien declared, "to understand in the least what you are talking about."

The Duchess stared at him.

"My good man," she cried, "my own daughter runs away on the eve of her marriage, throws all Society into a commotion, comes to Paris to join the man whom she cares for - you - you, Julien - and then you affect to misunderstand!"

Julien was speechless for several moments. He was conscious of a little wave of strange emotion. The walls of the hotel sitting-room fell away. He was standing on the edge of the wood behind the shrubbery of laurels. The smell of the country gardens, the distant music, the delicious stillness, the queer, troubled look in Anne's eyes, her suddenly quickened breath, that moment which had passed so soon! It came back to him with a peculiar insistence during those few seconds!

Then he brushed it away.

"My dear Duchess," he said slowly, "you are laboring under some extraordinary mistake. Anne and I were very good friends and I think that we should have made a reasonably contented couple. That, however, was naturally broken off at once owing to my misfortune. Anne's visit to Paris, her sudden flight from London, had nothing whatever to do with me. I met her here entirely by accident. No word has passed between us which would suggest for a single moment that she looked upon this matter any differently!"

The Duchess listened to him steadily. At first there were signs of a coming storm. Like a skilful general, however, she abandoned her position and changed her tactics. She got up and walked to the window, produced a handkerchief from her pocket, and stood dabbing her eyes. She looked out over the Place Vendôme. Julien, who had not the least idea what to say, kept silent.

"Julien," she said at last, turning around, "this - this is a blow to me. If what you say is true, and of course it is, dear Anne's life is ruined. At present every one sympathizes with her. You know, Samuel Harbord, notwithstanding his enormous wealth - you have no idea, Julien, how horrid he was about the settlements - is very unpopular. There wasn't a soul except his own people who didn't thoroughly enjoy his position. Anne had run away to Paris, they all said, because she declined to give up her old sweetheart. You know what they will all say now? She came and you would have none of her! I ask you, Julien, as a man of the world, isn't that the view people are bound to take?"

"It is a very stupid view," Julien declared. "Anne cares no more for me than for any other man. She isn't that sort. Even if I were in a position to marry any one, I am quite sure that she would refuse me."

The Duchess began to see her way. She tried, however, to banish the look of relief from her face.

"My dear Julien," she said very gently, "you men, however well you mean, sometimes make such mistakes. I want to show you what I am sure you will see to be your duty. Things, of course, can never be as we had once hoped. On the other hand, I am a mother, Julien, and I want to see my daughters happy. We are very, very poor, but a little privation is good for all of us. The Duke will settle two thousand a year upon Anne, and I am quite sure that you can earn money with that wonderful pen of yours, and then, of course, there is your own small income."

"Anne doesn't want to marry me, and," he added, after a moment's hesitation, "I don't want to marry Anne. You forget that I am an outcast from life. I have to start things all over again. What should I do with a wife who has been used to the sort of life Anne has always led?"

"Dear Julien," the Duchess repeated, "I want to show you your duty. If you do not marry Anne, every one in London will say that she came to you and you refused her. It is your duty at least to give her the opportunity.

It is unfortunate that she came here, perhaps, but we have finished with all that. She is here, every one knows that she is here, and you have been seen together."

Julien rose from his chair and walked up and down the room.

"I haven't talked very much with Anne," he said, pausing after a while, "but it seems to me that she is making a bid for liberty. She is an independent sort of girl, you know, after all, although she was very well content, up to a certain point, to take things as they came. I don't believe for a moment that she would marry me."

"At least," the Duchess persisted, "do your duty and ask her. If necessary, even let people know that you have asked her. It is your duty, Julien."

Julien hesitated no longer.

"Very well," he decided, "since you put it like that I will ask Anne, but I warn you, I think she will refuse me."

"She will do nothing of the sort," the Duchess declared; "but oh! Julien, it would make me so happy if you would take me to her, if I could have just a few minutes' talk with her first, before you said anything serious."

Julien smiled.

"Dear Duchess, I think not. I will go to see Anne alone. I will ask her to marry me in my own way. I will tell

E. Phillips Oppenheim

her that you are here, and whether she consents to marry me or not, I will bring her to see you. But my offer shall be made before you and she meet."

"You are a little hard, dear Julien," the Duchess murmured, "but let it be so. Only remember that the poor dear child may be feeling very sensitive - she must know that she has placed herself so completely in your power. Be nice to her, Julien."

The Duchess offered him a tentative but somewhat artificial embrace, which Julien with great skill evaded.

"We shall see," he remarked, "what happens. I shall find you here, I suppose?"

The Duchess nodded.

"I have traveled all night," she said, half closing her eyes. "Directly I saw that it was my duty, I came here without waiting a single second. I shall lie down and rest and hope, Julien, until I see you both. I shall hope and pray that you will bring Anne here to luncheon with me and that we shall have a little family gathering."

Anne was seated before the wide-open window in the little back room leading from Mademoiselle Rignaut's workshop. A sewing-machine was on the table in the middle of the apartment, the floor was strewn with fragments of material. Anne, in a perfectly plain black gown, similar to those worn by the other young ladies of the establishment, was making bows. She looked at Julien, as he entered, in blank amazement. Then a shadow of annoyance crossed her face.

"My dear Julien," she exclaimed, "fancy letting you climb these four flights of stairs! Besides, these are my working hours. I am not receiving visitors."

"Rubbish!" Julien interposed. "There's surely no need for you to pose as a seamstress?"

She laughed.

"Don't be foolish! Why not a seamstress? I am absolutely determined to do work of some sort. I am tired of living on other people and other people's efforts. Until I hear from Madame Christophor, or find another post, I am doing what I am fit for here. Don't make me any more annoyed than I am at present. I am cross enough with Janette because she will make me sit in here instead of with the other girls."

He came across the room and stood by her side before the window. The slight haze of the midsummer morning rested over the city with its tangled mass of roofs and chimneys, its tall white buildings with funny little verandas, the sweep of boulevards and statelier buildings in the distance. She looked up and followed his eyes.

"Don't you like my view?" she asked. "One misses the roar of London. Do you notice how much shriller and less persistent all the noises are? Yet it has its own inspiration, hasn't it?"

"Without a doubt," Julien answered. "Of course, you can guess what I came for?"

"If it were to ask me to lunch," she said, composedly threading her needle, "I am sorry, but I can't come. I have to make twenty-five of these bows and I am rather slow at it."

"Luncheon might have followed as an after-thought," he replied. "My real mission was to suggest that you should marry me."

Lady Anne's fingers paused for a moment in the air. She sat quite still. Her eyes were half closed. There was a curious little quiver at her heart, a little throb in her ears. On the whole, however, she kept her self-control marvelously.

"Whatever put that into your head?" she inquired, going on with her work.

He hesitated. It was in his mind to tell her of that evening at Clonarty, to speak of it, to recall that one wave of emotion on which, indeed, they might have floated into a completer understanding. He looked at her steadfastly. She was very graceful, very good to look upon. She sat upright in her poor cane chair, bending over her foolish little task. But he missed any inspiration which might have guided his tongue. She looked so thoroughly self-possessed, so splendidly superior to circumstances.

"Isn't it natural?" he asked. "You and I were always good friends. We have come together here and we are both a little lonely. I have never known any one else in the world, Anne," he continued, "with whom I have been able to think of marriage with more - more content. One might live quite a pleasant life here. We should not be paupers. At any rate, there would be no reason for you to sit in this stuffy room making bows, or to go and write Madame Christophor's letters."

"Is that all?"

Again he was tempted. For a single moment she had raised her eyes and he had fancied that in that swift upward glance he had seen the light of an almost eager questioning, an almost pathetic search. He bent towards her, but she refused obstinately to look at him again.

"Dear Anne," he said, "I have always been fond of you."

Again her fingers were idle. An idea seemed to have occurred to her. She asked him a question.

"How long is it since you have seen my mother?"

He did not at once reply. She raised her head and looked at him. Then she knew the truth. She set her teeth and fought. A little sob was strangled in her throat.

"I left your mother a few minutes ago," he told her. "She arrived in Paris this morning and sent for me."

Lady Anne worked for a time in silence. Then she laid the bow, which she had finished, upon the table, and leaned back in her chair, clasping her right knee with her hands.

"You really are the queerest person, Julien," she declared. "How you were ever a success as a diplomatist I can't imagine! You came in with the air of one charged with a high and holy mission. It was so obvious and yet for a moment it puzzled me. How I would love to have been with you this morning - with you and my mother, I mean - somewhere behind a curtain! Never mind, you've done the really right and honorable thing - you have given me my chance. I am very grateful, Julien."

She looked frankly enough into his face now and laughed. Julien remained silent.

"Can't you see, both of you," Anne went on, "you silly people, that something quite alien to us and our set has found its way into my life - a sort of middle-class complaint - Heaven knows what you would call it! - but it came just in time to place me in a most awkward position. I still haven't any doubt that marriage is a very respectable and desirable institution, but to me the idea of it as a matter of convenience has suddenly become - well, a little worse than the thing which we all shudder at so righteously when we pass along the streets of Paris. Of course, I know," she added, "that's a shocking point of view. My mother would hold, and you, too, that a legalized sale is no sale at all, that matrimony is a perfectly hallowed institution, a perfectly moral state, and all the rest of it. You see, I very nearly admitted it myself - I very nearly sold myself!"

She shuddered. Then she rose to her feet, straight and splendid, with all the grace of her beautiful young womanhood.

"Men don't think just as we do about this," she continued. "You are all much too Oriental. But a woman has at least a right to keep what she doesn't choose to sell, even if in the end she chooses to give it."

Julien moved a step nearer to her.

"Anne," he said, "supposing one cared?"

Every fibre of her body was set in an effort of resistance. The mocking laugh rose readily enough to her lips, the words were crushed back in her throat. Only the faintest shadow shone for a moment in her eyes.

"Ah, Julien," she murmured lightly, "if one cared! But does that really come, I wonder? Not to such men as you. Not often, I am afraid, to such women as I."

The door was suddenly opened. Little Mademoiselle Rignaut was covered with confusion.

"But, miladi," she exclaimed, "a thousand pardons -"

"Janette," Anne interrupted, "if I hear that once more I leave - I seek another situation."

"But, mademoiselle, then," Mademoiselle Rignaut corrected, "a thousand pardons indeed! I had no idea -"

"My dear Janette," Lady Anne protested, "why do you apologize for entering your own workshop? It is foolish, this. I go now, dear Julien, to put on my hat. You shall drive me to where my mother is staying - the Ritz, I suppose? Afterwards you shall leave us. Wait in the street below. I shall be less than two minutes."

Mademoiselle Rignaut was still apologetic as she conducted Julien down the narrow stairs.

"But indeed," she declared, "there never was a young

E. Phillips Oppenheim

lady so strange, with such charming manners, so sweet, as dear Miladi Anne. All the time she smiles, inconveniences are nothing, one would imagine that she were happy. And yet at night - "

"At night what?" Julien asked.

Mademoiselle shook her head.

"Miladi Anne is not quite so cheerful as she seems. At night I fancy that she does not sleep too well. One hears her, and, alas! Monsieur Sir Julien, last night I heard her sobbing quietly."

"Lady Anne sobbing?" Julien exclaimed. "It seems impossible."

"Indeed, but women are strange!" Mademoiselle Rignaut sighed.

CHAPTER VIII

A DECLARATION OF INDEPENDENCE

Lady Anne came gayly down to the street a few minutes later. She was still wearing the plain black gown and the simplest of hats. Nevertheless, she looked charming. Her fresh complexion with its slight touch of sunburn, her wealth of brown hair, and the distinction of her carriage, made her everywhere an object of admiration in a city where the prevailing type of beauty was so different.

"Poor mother!" she exclaimed, as they crossed the Place de l'Opéra. "Tell me, was she very theatrical this morning, Julien?"

Julien smiled.

"I am afraid I must admit that she was," he declared. "I found her very interesting."

"I hate to talk about her," Anne continued, "it makes one feel so unfilial, but really she is the most wonderful marionette that ever lived the perfect life. You see, I have been behind the scenes so long. Every now and then a little of the woman's nature crops up. Her cut to Mrs. Carraby, for instance, was quite one of the events of the season. It was so perfectly

E. Phillips Oppenheim

administered, so utterly scathing. I hear that the poor creature went to bed for a fortnight afterwards. Gracious, I hope I am not distressing you, Julien!" she added hastily.

"Not in the least," Julien assured her grimly. "I have no interest in Mrs. Carraby."

Lady Anne sighed.

"That's how you men talk when your little feeling has evaporated. Julien, you're a selfish crowd! You make the world a very difficult place for a woman."

"I think," he said, "that your sex avenges itself.'

"I am not sure," she replied. "Men so often place the burden of their own follies upon a woman's shoulders."

"You rebuke me rightly," Julien declared bitterly.

"I was not thinking of you," she told him reproachfully. "I am sorry, Julien. I should not have said that."

"It was the truth," he confessed, "absolutely the truth. Still, I have never blamed Mrs. Carraby for my disasters. It was my own asinine simplicity. Tell me, when shall I see you again? I think I ought to leave you here."

She laughed.

"You want to know about my interview with mother? Well, you shall know all about that, I promise you, because I have changed my mind. I intend to make you an auditor. Don't desert me, Julien, please. Remember, this is really a trying moment for me. I have to face an irate and obstinate parent. If friendship is worth anything, come and help me."

"I can't help thinking," he objected, "that your mother would rather talk to you alone."

"Then you will please to consider me and not my mother," Anne insisted, as they drew up before the door of the hotel. "I wish you to remain."

The Duchess received them perfectly. She did not attempt anything emotional. She simply held out both her hands a little apart.

"You dear, sensible people!" she cried. "Anne, how dared you give us such a shock!"

Anne leaned over and kissed her mother.

"Mother," she announced, "I am not going to marry Julien."

The Duchess started. The expression which flashed from her eyes was unmistakably genuine.

"Don't talk nonsense, Anne!" she exclaimed sharply.

"No nonsense about it," Anne retorted. "I can't bear to talk when any one is standing up. Sit down, and in a few sentences I'll let you know how hopeless it all is."

There was real fear in the Duchess's eyes.

"Anne," she gasped, "is there a man, then?"

"You idiotic person, of course there isn't!" Anne replied. "Why on earth you should all talk about a man directly a girl breaks away for a time, I can't imagine. Now sit down there and listen. I brought Julien along because if you bully me too much I shall make him take me away. We are excellent friends, Julien and I, and he has been very kind to me since I came here; but I met him entirely by accident, and if I hadn't I am quite sure that we might have lived here for years and never come across one another."

"But I have told every one in London!" the Duchess protested. "I have explained everything! I have told them how you always loved Julien, what a terrible blow his troubles were, and how you suddenly found that it was impossible for you to marry any other man, and like a dear, romantic child that you are you ran away to him."

"Yes," Lady Anne said dryly, "that's a very pretty story! That's just what I imagined you would tell everybody when you knew that I'd come here. That is just," she continued slowly, "what you have been rubbing into poor Julien this morning before he came to see me. Very well, mother, up to a certain point it came off, you see. Julien called most dutifully, found me sitting in an attic - 'attic' is the correct word, isn't it? - and made his declaration. No, I don't think he declared anything, on second thoughts! He effectually concealed any feelings he might have had. It was a suggestion which he made."

"My manner of expressing myself," Julien began a little stiffly -

"Your manner of expressing yourself was perfect,"

Anne interrupted. "It was a great deal too perfect, my *preux chevalier*. Only you see, Julien, only you see, mother, Julien offered me exactly what I left home to escape from. I have come to the conclusion," she went on, smoothing her skirt about her knees, "that it is most indecent and wholly improper even to think of marrying a man who does not love you and whom you do not love."

The Duchess closed her eyes.

"Anne, what have you been reading?" she murmured.

"Not a thing," Anne went on. "I never did read half enough. I'm simply acting by instinct. Julien and I were engaged for three months and at the end of that time we were complete strangers. The idea of marrying a stranger was not attractive to me. Let that go. Julien went. Along came Samuel -"

"We will not talk about Mr. Harbord," the Duchess interposed hastily.

"Oh, yes, we will! Now so far as Julien was concerned," Anne continued, "I dare say I should have smothered my feelings because there is nothing revolting about him. He is quite an attractive person, and physically everything to be desired. But when it came to a man who was not a gentleman, whose manners were odious, who offended my taste every time he opened his mouth - why, you see, the thing couldn't be thought of! Day by day it got worse. Towards the end he began to try and put his hands on me. That made me think. That's why I came to Paris."

"Anne," the Duchess declared severely, "you

are indecent!"

"On the contrary," Anne insisted, "I think it was the most decent thing I ever did. Now please listen. I will not come back to England, I will not marry Julien, I will not think of or discuss the subject of marriage with any one. I am a free person and I haven't the least intention of spending my life moping. I am going to have a pleasant time and I am going to have it in my own way. You have two other daughters, mother - Violet and Lucy. Unless they change, they are exactly what you would have them. Be satisfied. Devote your energies to them and count me a black sheep. You can make me a little allowance, if you like - a hundred a year or so - but whether I have it or not, I am either going to make bows in Mademoiselle Rignaut's workshop, or I am going to be secretary to a very delightful lady - a Mrs. Christophor, or something of the sort."

The Duchess rose - she had an idea that she was more dignified standing.

"Anne," she said, "I am your mother. Not only that, but I ask you to remember who you are. The women of England look for an example to us. They look to us to live regular and law-abiding lives, to be dutiful wives and mothers. You are behaving like a creature from an altogether different world. You speak openly of things I have never permitted mentioned. I ask you to reflect. Do you owe nothing to me? Do you owe nothing to your father, to our position?"

"A great deal, mother," Anne replied, "but I owe more to myself than to any one else in the world."

The Duchess felt hopeless. She looked toward Julien.

"There is so much of this foolish sort of talk about," she complained. "It all comes of making friends with socialists and labor people, and having such terrible nonsense printed in the reviews. What are we to do, Julien? Can't you persuade Anne? I am sure that she is really fond of you."

"I wouldn't attempt to influence her for a single moment," Julien declared. "I won't say whether I think she is right or wrong. On the whole, I am inclined to think that she is right."

"You, too, desert me!" the Duchess exclaimed.

"Well, it all depends upon one's conception of happiness, of course," Julien replied, "but so far as I am concerned, let me tell you that the idea of a girl like Anne married to an insufferable bounder like Harbord, just because he's got millions of money, simply made me boil."

Anne, for some reason or other, was looking quite pleased.

"I am so glad to know you felt like that, Julien. It's really the nicest thing you've said to me all the morning. Well, that's over now. Mother, why don't you give us some lunch and take the four o'clock train back? It's the Calais train, which I know you always prefer."

The Duchess reflected for a moment. There were advantages in lunching at the Ritz with Julien on one side of her and Anne on the other. She gave a little sigh and consented.

CHAPTER IX

FOOLHARDY JULIEN

The luncheon in the beautiful restaurant of the Ritz was a meal after the Duchess's own heart. She was at home here and received the proper amount of attention. Not only that, but many acquaintances - mostly foreign, but a few English - paused at her table to pay their respects. To every one of these she carefully introduced her daughter and Sir Julien. The situation was not without its embarrassments. Lady Anne, however, dissipated them by an unaffected fit of laughter.

"Mother thinks she is putting everything quite right by lending us the sanctity of her presence," she declared. "We have been seen lunching at the Ritz. After this, who shall say that I ran away from home to meet a riding master in Paris, or some other disreputable person? I may perhaps be pitied as the victim of a hopeless infatuation for you, Julien, but for the rest, if we only sit here long enough I shall be whitewashed."

The Duchess was a little uneasy.

"I must say, Anne," she protested, "that you seem to have developed a great deal of levity during the last few days. It's not a subject to be alluded to so lightly.

Ah! now let me tell you who this is. A wonderfully interesting person, I can assure you. She was born in Paris of American parents, very wealthy indeed, married when quite young to Prince Falkenberg, and separated from him within two years. They say that she lives a queer, half Bohemian sort of life now, but she is still a great person when she chooses. My dear Princess!"

Madame Christophor, who had entered the room on her way to a luncheon party, paused for a moment and shook hands. Then she recognized Julien.

"Really," she murmured, "this is most unexpected. My dear Duchess, you have quite deserted Paris. Is this your daughter - Lady Anne? I scarcely remember her. And yet - "

"We met yesterday," Lady Anne interrupted promptly. "You know, I want to be your secretary, Madame Christophor, if you will let me. My mother has entirely cast me off, so it doesn't matter."

The Duchess made a most piquant gesture. It was really an insufferable position, but she was determined to remain graceful.

"My dear Madame Christophor," she said, "you have no grown-up children, of course, so I cannot ask for your sympathy. But I have a daughter here who is giving me a great deal of trouble. I flatter myself that I have modern views of life, but Anne - well, I won't discuss her."

Madame Christophor smiled.

"Young people are different nowadays, Duchess," she remarked. "If Lady Anne really wants to come into life on her own, why not? She can be my secretary if she chooses. I shall pay her just as much as I should any one else, and I shall send her away if she is not satisfactory. There are a great many young people nowadays, Duchess," she continued, "in very much your daughter's position, who do these odd things. I always think that it is better not to stand in their way. Sir Julien, I want to speak to you before you leave this restaurant. I have something important to say."

The Duchess was a little taken aback. To her it seemed a social cataclysm, something unheard of, that her daughter should propose to be any one's secretary. Yet this woman, who was certainly of her own order, had accepted the thing as entirely natural - had dismissed it, even, with a few casual remarks. Julien, who since Madame Christophor's arrival had been standing in his place, was somewhat perplexed.

"You are lunching here?" he asked.

"With the Servian Minister's wife. I shall excuse myself early. It is a vital necessity that we talk for a few minutes before you leave here. Five minutes ago I sent a note to your rooms."

"I shall be at your service," Julien replied slowly.

"I shall expect you in the morning," Madame Christophor said, smiling at Lady Anne. "Don't be later than ten o'clock. I am always at home after four, Duchess, if you are spending any time in Paris," she added.

They watched her as she passed to the little group who were awaiting her arrival. She was certainly one of the most elegant women in the room. Lady Anne looked after her with a faint frown.

"I wonder," she murmured, "if I shall like Madame Christophor?"

"I had no idea, Julien," the Duchess remarked, "that you were friendly with her."

Julien evaded the question.

"At any rate," he said, turning to Anne, "this will be better for you than making bows."

"I suppose so," she assented. "All the same, I am very much my own mistress in that dusty little workshop. If Madame Christophor - isn't that the name she chooses to be called by? - becomes exacting, I am not even sure that I shan't regret my bow-making."

"Tell me exactly how long you have known her, Julien!" the Duchess persisted.

"Since my arrival in Paris this time," Julien answered. "I had - well, a sort of introduction to her."

"She is received everywhere," the Duchess continued, "because I know she visits at the house of the Comtesse Deschelles, who is one of the few women in Paris of the old faction who are entirely exclusive. At the same time, I am told that she leads a very retired life now, and is more seen in Bohemia than anywhere. I am not at all sure that it is a desirable association for Anne."

"Well, you can leave off troubling about that," Anne said. "Remember, however much we make believe, I have really shaken the dust of respectability off my feet. Hamilton Place knows me no longer. I am a dweller in the byways. Even if I come back, it will be as a stranger. People will be interested in me, perhaps, as some one outside their lives. 'That strange daughter of the poor dear Duchess, you know,' they will say, 'who ran away to Paris! Some terrible affair. No one knows the rights of it.' Can't you hear it all? They will be kind to me, of course, but I shan't belong. Alas!"

The Duchess was studying her bill and wondering how much to tip the waiter. She only answered absently.

"My dear Anne, you are talking quite foolishly. I wish I knew," she added plaintively, a few minutes later, "what you have been reading or whom you have been meeting lately."

"Don't bother about me," Anne begged. "What you want to do now is to tell Parkins to pack up your things and I'll come and see you off by the four o'clock train. Julien must wait outside for my future employer. What I really think is going to happen is that she's going to ask for my character. Julien, be merciful to me! Remember that above all things I have always been respectable. Remind her that if I were too intelligent I should probably rob her of her secrets or money or something. I am really a most machine-like person. Nature meant me to be secretary to a clever woman, and my handwriting - don't forget my handwriting. Nothing so clear or so rapid has ever been seen."

The Duchess signed her bill, slightly undertipped the waiter and accepted his subdued thanks with a gracious smile.

"I can see," she said, as they left the room, "that I shall have to wash my hands of you. Nevertheless, I shall not lose hope."

She shook hands solemnly with Julien, and he performed a like ceremony with Lady Anne.

"When shall I see you again?" he asked the latter.

"You had better question Madame Christophor concerning my evenings out," she replied. "It is not a matter I know much about. I am sure you are quite welcome to any of them."

Julien found a seat in the broad passageway. Several acquaintances passed to and fro whom so far as possible he avoided. Madame Christophor came at last. She was the centre of the little party who were on their way into the lounge. When she neared Julien, however, she paused and made her adieux. He rose and waited for her expectantly.

"We are to talk here?" he asked.

She nodded.

"In that corner."

She pointed to a more retired spot. He followed her there.

"Order some coffee," she directed.

He obeyed her and they were promptly served. She

waited, chatting idly of their luncheon party, of the coincidence of meeting with the Duchess, until they were entirely freed from observation. Then she leaned towards him.

"Sir Julien," she said, "I have read your articles, the first and the second. You are a brave man."

He smiled.

"Are you going to warn me once more against Herr Freudenberg?" he asked.

She shook her head.

"If you do not know your danger," she continued, "you would be too great a fool to be worth warning. Remember that Freudenberg came from Berlin as fast as express trains and his racing-car could bring him, the moment he read the first."

"I have already had a brief but somewhat unpleasant interview with him," Julien remarked.

"I congratulate you," she went on. "Unpleasant interviews with Herr Freudenberg generally end differently. Now listen to me. I have a proposition to make. There is one house in Paris where you will be safe - mine. I offer you its shelter. Come there and finish your work."

Julien made no reply. He sipped his coffee for a moment. Then he turned slowly round.

"Madame Christophor," he said, "once you told me that you disliked and distrusted all men. Why, then, should I trust you?"

She winced a little, but her tone when she answered him was free of offense.

"Why should you, indeed?" she replied. "Yet you should remember that the man against whose cherished schemes your articles are directed is the man whom I have more cause to hate than any other in the world."

"Herr Freudenberg," he murmured.

"Prince Adolf Rudolf von Falkenberg," she corrected him. "Do you know the story of my married life?"

"I have never heard it," he told her.

"I will spare you the details," she continued. "My husband married me with the sole idea of using my house, my friends, my social position here for the furtherance of his schemes. Under my roof I discovered meetings of spies, spies paid to suborn the different services in this country - the navy, the army, the railway works. When I protested, he laughed at me. He made no secret of his ambitions. He is the sworn and inveterate enemy of your country. His feeling against France is a slight thing in comparison with his hatred of England. For the last ten years he has done nothing but scheme to humiliate her. When I discovered to what purpose my house was being put, I bade him leave it. I bade him choose another hotel, and when he saw that I was in earnest, he obeyed. It is one of the conditions of our separation that he does not cross my threshold. That is why I say, Sir Julien, that you have nothing to fear in accepting the shelter of my roof."

"Madame Christophor," Julien said earnestly, "I am most grateful for your offer. At the same time, I honestly do not believe that I have anything to fear anywhere. Herr Freudenberg has made one attempt upon me and has failed. I do not think that he is likely to risk everything by any open assaults. In these civilized days of the police, the telephone and the law courts, one is not so much at the mercy of a strong man as in the old days. I do not fear Herr Freudenberg."

Madame Christophor shrugged her shoulders.

"My friend," she admitted, "I admire your courage, but listen. You say that one attempt has already been made to silence you. For every letter you write, there will be another made. At each fresh one, these creatures of Herr Freudenberg's will have learned more cunning. In the end they are bound to succeed. Why risk your life? I offer my house as a sanctuary. There is no need for you to pass outside it. You could take the exercise you require in my garden, which is bounded by four of the highest walls in Paris. You can sit in a room apart from the rest of the house, with three locked doors between you and the others. You may write there freely and without fear."

Julien smiled.

"I am afraid it is my stupidity," he said, "but I cannot possibly bring myself to believe in the existence of any danger. I will promise you this, if I may. If any further attempt should be made upon me, any attempt which came in the least near being successful, I will remember your offer. For the present my mind is made up. I shall remain where I am."

E. Phillips Oppenheim

She shrugged her shoulders.

"Ingrate!"

"Not that, by any means," he assured her heartily. "You know that I am grateful. You know that if I refuse for the moment your offer it is not because I mistrust you. I simply feel that I should be taking elaborate precautions which are quite unnecessary."

"I might even spare you," she remarked, smiling, "Lady Anne for your secretary."

"Even that inducement," he answered steadily, "does not move me."

She sighed.

"You will have your own way," she said, "and yet there is something rather sad about it. I know so much more of this Paris than you. I know so much more of Herr Freudenberg. Remember that there are a quarter of a million Germans in this city, and of that quarter of a million at least twenty thousand belong to one or the other of the secret societies with which the city abounds. All of them are different in tone, but they all have at the end of their programme the cause of the Fatherland. By this time you will have been named to them as its enemy. Twenty thousand of them, my friend, and not a scruple amongst the lot!"

He moved in his place a little restlessly.

"One does not fight in these ways nowadays," he protested.

"Pig-headed Englishman!" she murmured. "You to say that, too!"

His thoughts flashed back to those few moments of vivid life in his own rooms. He thought of Freudenberg's calm perseverance. An uncomfortable feeling seized him.

"I do not know," she went on, leaning a little towards him, "why I should interest myself in you at all."

"Why do you, then?" he asked, looking at her suddenly.

She played with the trifles that hung from her chatelaine. He watched for the raising of her eyes, but he watched in vain. She did not return his inquiring look.

"Never mind," she said, "I have warned you. It is for you to act as you think best. If you change your mind, come to me. I will give you sanctuary at any time. Take me to my automobile, please."

He obeyed her and watched her drive off. Then he went slowly and unmolested back to his rooms.

E. Phillips Oppenheim

CHAPTER X

THE SECOND ATTEMPT

The concierge of Julien's apartments issued with a somewhat mysterious air from his little lodge as his tenant passed through the door. He was a short man with a fierce, bristling moustache. He wore a semi-military coat, always too short for him, and he was so stout that he was seldom able to fasten more than two of the buttons of his waistcoat.

"Monsieur!"

"What is it, Pierre?" Julien asked. "Any callers for me?"

"There have been callers, indeed, monsieur," Pierre replied, "callers whose errand I do not quite understand. They asked many questions concerning monsieur. When they had finished, the man - bah! he was a German! - he thrust into my hand a hundred franc note. He said, 'No word of this to Monsieur Sir Julien!' I put the note into the bottom of my trousers pocket, but I made no response. I am not dishonorable. I keep the note because these men should think me craven enough to give them information, to hear their questions, and to say nothing to monsieur, one of my own lodgers! It was an insult, that. Therefore I keep the hundred franc note. Therefore I tell monsieur all that these two men did ask."

"You showed," Julien declared, "a rare and excellent discretion. Proceed."

"They asked questions, monsieur, on every conceivable subject," Pierre continued. "Their interest in your doings was amazing. They asked what meals you took in the house, at what hour you went out and at what hour you returned. Then the shorter of the two wished to take the room above yours. I asked him more than double the price, but he would have engaged it. Then I told him that I was not sure. There was a gentleman to whom it was offered. They come back this afternoon to know the result."

"If they find a lodging in this house," Julien said, "I fear that I must leave."

"It shall be," Pierre decided, "as monsieur wishes. I am not to be tempted with money when it comes to a question of retaining an old tenant. The room is let to another. It is finished."

Julien climbed the stairs thoughtfully to his apartments, locked himself in and sat down before his desk. For an hour or more he worked. Then there came a timid knock at the door. He looked around, frowning. After a moment's hesitation he affected not to notice the summons, and continued his work. The knocking came again, however, low but persistent. Julien rose to his feet, turned the key and opened the door.

"Mademoiselle!" he exclaimed, genuinely surprised.

It was Mademoiselle Ixe who glided past him into the room. She signed to him to close the door. He did so, and turning slowly faced her. She was standing a few yards away, her lips a little parted, pale notwithstanding the delicately artistic touch of coloring upon her cheeks. Her hands were crossed upon the jade top of her lace parasol. In her muslin gown and large hat she formed a very effective picture as she stood there with her eyes now fixed upon Julien.

"Mademoiselle," he began, "I do not quite understand."

"Look outside," she begged. "See that there is no one there. I am so afraid that I might have been followed."

Julien stepped out onto the landing and returned.

"There is no one about at all," he assured her.

She drew a little sigh.

"But it is rash, this! Monsieur Sir Julien, you are glad - you are pleased to see me? Make me one of your pretty speeches at once or I shall go."

"But, mademoiselle," Julien said, wheeling a chair towards her, "who indeed could be anything but glad to see you at any time? Yet forgive me if I am stupid. Tell me why you have come to see me this afternoon and why you are afraid that you are followed?"

"Why?" she murmured, looking up into his eyes. "Ah, Monsieur Sir Julien, it is hard indeed to tell you that!"

Mademoiselle Ixe was without doubt an extraordinarily pretty young woman. She was famous even in Paris for her figure, her looks, the perfection of her clothes, the daintiness and distinction of those small adjuncts to her toilette so dear to the heart of a Parisienne. Julien looked at her and sighed.

"Perhaps, mademoiselle," he said, "you will find it hard also to tell me whether you come of your own accord or at the instigation of Herr Freudenberg?"

She looked genuinely hurt. Julien, however, was merciless.

"It is, perhaps, because Herr Freudenberg has told you that I once lost great things through trusting a woman that you think to find me an easy victim?" he went on. "Come, am I to give you those sheets over there," he added, pointing to his writing-table, "and promise for your sake never to write another line, or have you more serious designs?"

"Monsieur Julien," she faltered, -

He suddenly changed his tone.

"Am I cruel?" he asked. "Forgive me, mademoiselle - forgive me, Marguerite."

She held out her delicately gloved hand towards him; her face she turned a little away and one gathered that there were tears in her eyes which she did not wish him to see.

"Take off my glove, please," she whispered. "I did not think you would be so cruel even for a moment."

He took her fingers in his, fingers which promptly

returned his pressure. His right arm stole around her.

"Monsieur Sir Julien," she continued very softly, "please promise that you will speak to me no more now of Herr Freudenberg. Tell me that you are glad I have come. Say some more of those pretty things that you whispered to me in the Rat Mort."

His arm tightened about her. She was powerless.

"Julien!" she murmured.

He laughed quietly. Suddenly she struggled to escape from him.

"Let me go!" she cried. "Sir Julien, but you are rough. Monsieur!"

He flung her from him back into the chair. In his left hand he held the pistol he had taken from the bosom of her gown - a dainty little affair of ivory and silver. He turned it over curiously. She lay back in the chair where he had thrown her, gripping its sides with tremulous fingers, her eyes deep-set, distended, staring at him. He thrust the weapon into his pocket.

"Really," he said, "I thought better of Herr Freuden-berg. Why doesn't he come himself?"

"Oh, he will come!" she answered.

"Will he?" Julien replied. "I should have thought better of him if he had come first, instead of sending a woman to do his work."

She sat up in the chair. Julien had known well how to

rouse her.

"You do not think that he is afraid?" she cried. "Afraid of you? Bah! For the rest, it was I who insisted on coming. He was troubled. I knew why. I said to myself, 'It is a risk I will take. I will go to Sir Julien's rooms. I will shoot him. I will pretend that it was a love affair. I will go into court all with tears, I will wear my prettiest clothes, nothing indeed will happen. An affair of jealousy - a moment of madness. One takes account of these things. Then Herr Freudenberg himself has great friends here, friends in high places. He will see that nothing happens.'"

"A very pretty scheme," Julien remarked sarcastically. "Supposing, however, I turn the tables upon you, mademoiselle. You are here and I have taken away this little plaything. Would Herr Freudenberg be jealous if he knew, I wonder?"

She glanced at the door.

"Locked," Julien continued grimly. "Do you still wish me to come and make pretty speeches to you?" he added. "You are certainly looking very charming, mademoiselle. Your gown is exquisite. What can I do more than echo what all Paris has said - that there is no one of her daughters more bewitching? Can you wonder if I lose my head a little when I find you here with me in my rooms - a visit, too, of pure affection?"

She rose to her feet. The patch of color upon her cheeks had become more vivid.

"You will let me go?" she faltered.

Julien unlocked the door.

"Mademoiselle," he answered, "I shall most certainly let you go. Permit me to thank you for the pleasure which your brief visit has afforded me."

The door was opened before her. Julien stood on one side. The smile with which he dismissed her was half contemptuous, half kindly. Upon the threshold she hesitated.

"Sir Julien!"

"Mademoiselle Ixe?"

"If there were no Herr Freudenberg," she whispered, "if it were not my evil fortune, Monsieur Sir Julien, to love him so foolishly, so absolutely, so that every moment of separation is full of pain, every other man like a figure in a dream - if it were not for this, Monsieur Sir Julien, I do not think that I should like to leave you so easily!"

Julien made no reply. She passed out with a little sigh. He heard the flutter of her laces and draperies as she crossed the passage and commenced the descent of the stairs. Julien was closing the door when he heard a familiar voice and a heavy footstep. Kendricks, with a Gladstone bag in his hand, came bustling up.

"Julien, you dog," he exclaimed savagely, "you're at it again! Why the devil can't you keep these women at arm's length? What has that pretty little creature of Herr Freudenberg's been doing here?"

Julien laughed as he closed the door.

"Don't be a fool, David! She wasn't here at my invitation."

"Tears in her eyes!" Kendricks muttered. "Sobbing to herself as she went down the steps! Crocodile's tears, I know. These d - d women, Julien! Out with it. What did she come for?"

Julien produced the pistol from his pocket.

"It was," he explained, "her amiable intention to please her lord and master at the slight expense of my life. Fortunately, the game was a new one to her and she kept on feeling the bosom of her gown to see whether the pistol was there still."

"What did you do?" Kendricks demanded.

"What was there for me to do?" Julien replied. "I took her little toy away and told her to run off. This is the second time, David. Estermen and Freudenberg have had a shy at me here themselves, and they'd have gotten me all right but for an accident. I won't tell you what the accident was, for the moment, owing to your peculiar prejudices. How are things in London?"

Kendricks threw himself into an easy-chair and began to fill his pipe.

"Julien," he declared, "you've done the trick! I'm proud of my advice, proud of the result. There isn't a club or an omnibus or a tube or a public-house where that letter of yours isn't being talked about. They tell me it's the same here. Have you seen the German papers?"

"Not one."

"Never was such a thunderbolt launched," Kendricks continued. "They are all either stupefied or hysterical. Freudenberg left Berlin an hour after he saw the article. You tell me you've met him already?"

"Yes, he's been here," Julien replied. "He offered to make me a Croesus if I'd stop the letters. When I refused, well, we had a scuffle, and by Jove, they nearly got me! He means to wipe me out."

"We'll see about that!" Kendricks muttered. "I'm not going to leave your side till we're through with this little job."

"Madame Christophor suggested that I should go there and finish," Julien said. "What do you think of that?"

"Madame Fiddlesticks!" Kendricks retorted angrily. "The wife of Falkenberg! Do you want to walk into the lion's jaws?"

"She is separated from her husband," Julien reminded him. "My own impression is that she hates him."

"I'd never believe it," Kendricks insisted. "The fellow has the devil's own way with these women. Look at that little wretch I met on the stairs. A harmless, flirting little opera singer a year ago. Now she'd come here and murder a man against whom she hasn't the slightest grudge, for his sake. I tell you the fellow's got an unwholesome influence over every one with whom he comes in contact."

"Have you read to-day's letter?" Julien asked abruptly.

"Read it! Man alive, it made the heart jump inside me!

I tell you it's set the war music dancing wherever a dozen men have come together. I always thought you had a pretty gift as a maker of phrases, Julien, but I never knew you dipped your pen in the ink of the immortals. I tell you no one doubts anything you have written. That's the genius of it. No one denies it, no one attempts arguments, every one in England and France whose feelings have been ruffled is already wanting to shake hands all over again. One sees that giant figure, the world's mischief-maker, suddenly caught at his job. It's gorgeous! How about number four?"

"Half written," Julien declared, pointing to his table.

Kendricks went to the door and locked it, went to the cupboard and brought out the whiskey and soda, undid his Gladstone bag, buttoned a life preserver on his left wrist, and laid a Mauser pistol on the table by the side of him.

"Julien," he said, "I feel like the biggest ass unhung, but I am here with my playthings to be watchdog. Get to your desk and write, man. One drink first. Come."

They raised their glasses.

"What have you called number three?" Kendricks asked.

"'A Maker of Toys!'" Julien replied.

"Here's damnation to him!" Kendricks said, raising the glass to his lips. "Now get to work, Julien."

CHAPTER XI

BY THE PRINCE'S ORDERS

Once more mademoiselle sat beneath a canopy of pink roses, surrounded by obsequious waiters, with the murmur of music in her ears, opposite the man she adored. Yet without a doubt mademoiselle was disturbed. Her fixed eyes were riveted upon the newspaper which Herr Freudenberg had passed into her hand. She was suddenly very pale.

"Send some of these people away," she begged. "I am frightened."

Herr Freudenberg smiled. With a wave of his hand they were alone.

"Dear Marguerite," he said quietly, "compose yourself. All those who stand in my way and the way of my country must be swept aside, but remember this. They have all received their warning. I lift my hand against no one who has not first received a chance of escape."

"He was a man so gallant," she faltered, "so *comme il faut*. Listen to me, please."

She laid the newspaper upon the table and kept the flat of her hand still upon it. Then she leaned towards him.

"You will not be angry with me?" she implored. "Indeed I did it to please you, to win, if I could, a little more of your love. I knew that this man Sir Julien stood in your path and that you found it difficult to remove him. An impulse came to me. We had talked together gayly as a man of gallantry may talk to a woman like myself. It might easily pass for flirting, those things that he has said. Although you, dear one," she added, looking across the table, "know how it is with me when such words are spoken. Well, I bought cartridges for my little pistol that you gave me, I thrust it into the bosom of my gown, I wore my prettiest clothes, and yesterday I went to his rooms."

Herr Freudenberg's cold eyes were suddenly fixed upon her face. His fingers stopped their drumming upon the tablecloth.

"Proceed!"

"I meant to shoot him," she confessed. "I thought that if I could not escape afterwards it was so easy for people to believe that he was my lover, that it was a crime of jealousy, a moment's passion. I said to myself, too, that you would help so that after all my punishment would be a very small affair. In no other way it seemed to me could he have been disposed of so easily."

"Sweet little fool!" Herr Freudenberg murmured. "Did it never enter into your little brain that you are known as my companion?"

She shook her head.

"That would have counted for nothing. People would

not have believed that I had any other motive. I should have declared that it was a love affair."

"What happened?"

"He was too quick for me," mademoiselle admitted. "He saw me feel the spot where the pistol lay concealed. He - he snatched it away."

"And afterwards?" Herr Freudenberg inquired, with the ghost of a smile upon his lips.

She raised her eyes.

"He let me go," she replied. "He threw open the door and he laughed at me. Forgive me, please, if I am sad, if indeed I weep. He was a gallant gentleman."

Herr Freudenberg sighed. Slowly he raised his glass to his lips and drank.

"It is an amiable epitaph," he declared. "Many a man has gone up to Heaven with a worse. Cheer up, my little Marguerite. A year or two more or less in a man's life is no great matter, and after all it was not one warning which this rash man received. You have not yet read the account of the affair."

Mademoiselle slowly withdrew the palm of her hand from the paper. The paragraph was headed:

SHOCKING EXPLOSION IN THE RUE DE MONTPELIER.

She looked up.

"I cannot read it," she murmured. "Tell me."

"It is simple," he replied. "This afternoon an unfortunate explosion occurred in the house in the Rue de Montpelier where Sir Julien had his apartments. The whole of the front of the premises was blown away. It is regrettable," he added, with a little shrug of the shoulders, "that in all seven people perished, including the concierge. Mr. Kendricks, an English journalist, was taken away alive, but terribly injured, to the hospital. His companion, who seems to have been within a few feet of him when the explosion occurred, was unfortunately blown to pieces. The details as to his fate might perhaps interfere with your appetite, but let me at least assure you, my dear Marguerite," Herr Freudenberg continued, "that such a death is entirely painless. I regret the necessity for such means, but the man had his chance. I regret, also, the fate of the other poor people who lost their lives. Unfortunately, it was necessary to remove Sir Julien in such a way that no suspicion should be cast upon any one person. The death of the concierge, for instance, was absolutely essential. He was suspicious about some of my men who had been making inquiries."

"But it is horrible!" she gasped.

"Little one," he went on, "life is like that. To succeed one has to cultivate indifference. Sir Julien Portel had many warnings. He knew very well that if he persisted in writing those articles, he was braving my defiance. Already he has done mischief enough. The whole series would have undone the work of the last two years. To-night," Herr Freudenberg continued, with a sigh of relief, "we may open the Journal without apprehensions. There are no more secrets disclosed, no more of these marvelously written appeals to - "

Herr Freudenberg stopped short. His eyebrows had drawn closer together. He was gazing at the sheet which he held in his hand with more expression in his face than mademoiselle had ever seen there before.

"My God!" he muttered.

She, too, bent forward. She, too, saw the article with its heading: "A Maker of Toys!"

Herr Freudenberg waved her back. Line by line he read the article. When he had finished, his face was almost ghastly. He drained his glass and called for the *sommelier*.

"Serve more wine," he ordered briefly.

"What is it that you have seen?" she asked.

"I was a fool not to have been prepared," he answered. "There is another article in to-night's paper, but of course he would have sent it off before - before the explosion happened. It is worse than the others!" he went on hoarsely. "Thank Heaven, that man is out of the way! I would give a million marks to be able to destroy every copy of this paper that was ever issued. It is not fair fighting!... It is barbarous! No longer can I hope for any privacy in this country. You see - you see, Marguerite? He has written of me openly. 'The Toymaker from Leipzig!' - that is what he has called me! These two, Kendricks and he, they saw through me from the first. They knew what it was that I desired. Damn them!"

Mademoiselle crossed herself instinctively. Once she had been religious.

"Poor Sir Julien!"

Herr Freudenberg sighed.

"To-morrow night, at any rate," he said, "there will be no article. We have made sure of that. I pray to Heaven that it may not be too late!"

She shuddered. The service of dinner was resumed.

"Put the paper away," she begged. "Don't let us think of it any more. After all, as you say, he was warned. Nothing that one feels now can do any good. Give me some wine. Talk to me of other things."

Estermen came in to them presently. Herr Freudenberg insisted upon his taking a chair. Once more he dismissed the waiters.

"All goes well," Estermen announced. "There is not an idea at headquarters as to the source of the explosion. I have been round with the newspaper men."

"How is Kendricks?" Herr Freudenberg asked.

"Alive, but barely conscious."

"It is a pity," Herr Freudenberg said coldly. "Kendricks is responsible for a good deal of the trouble. Did you see that to-night's article is here?"

Estermen nodded.

E. Phillips Oppenheim

"He must have been a day ahead," he explained. "It was probably a later one of the series upon which he was engaged when the thing occurred."

"This one will do sufficient harm," Herr Freudenberg remarked grimly.

Estermen shrugged his shoulders.

"It is true, and yet we have a great start. Public opinion is thoroughly unsettled. Even those who accepted the *entente* as the most brilliant piece of diplomacy of the generation, are beginning to wonder what really has been gained by it. If I were at Berlin," Estermen continued, with a covert glance up at his master, "now is the time I should choose. To-morrow *Le Grand Journal* will be silent. To-morrow I should send a polite notification to the English Government that owing to the unsettled condition of the country, and the nervousness of certain German residents, His Imperial Majesty has thought it wise to send a warship to Agdar."

"The German subjects are a trifle hypothetical," Herr Freudenberg muttered. "We had the utmost difficulty in persuading an ex-convict to go out there."

"What does it matter?" Estermen asked. "He is there. He represents the glorious liberties of the Fatherland. Millions have been spent before now for the blood of one man."

Marguerite sighed. She was leaning back in her place, watching the boughs of the lime trees swinging gently back and forth in the night breeze, the cool moonlight outside, refreshing in its contrast to the over-lit and overheated auditorium of the music-hall. On the stage a Revue was in full swing. Mademoiselle Ixe glanced at it but seldom. Her eyes seemed to be always outside.

"Tell me," she demanded almost passionately, "why cannot one leave the world alone? It is great enough and beautiful enough. Will Germany be really the happier, do you think, if she triumphs against England? It doesn't seem worth while. Life is so short, the joy of living is so hard to grasp. Don't you think," she added, leaning towards her companion, her beautiful eyes full of entreaty, "that for one night at least, all thoughts of your country and of her destinies might pass away? Let us live in the world that amuses itself, that takes the pleasures that grow ready to its hand, whose arms are not rapacious, and whose sword lies idle. Forget for a little time, dear friend. Let us both forget!"

Herr Freudenberg smiled as he finished his wine.

"Ah! dear Marguerite," he said, "you preach the great philosophy. We will try humbly to follow in your footsteps. Lead on and we will follow - up to the Montmartre, if you will, or down to the Rue Royale. What does it matter, sweetheart, so long as we are together?"

She shivered a little as his fingers touched hers, although her eyes still besought him. The *vestiaire* was standing by with her lace coat. She rose slowly to her feet.

"To the Rue Royale," she decided. "To-night I have no fancy for the Montmartre."

CHAPTER XII

DISTRESSING NEWS

Mrs. Carraby advanced into the library of the great house in Grosvenor Square. Her husband had risen from his desk and was standing with his hands in his pockets upon the hearth-rug. His dress was as neat and correct as ever, his hair as accurately parted, his small moustache as effectually twirled. Yet there was a frown upon his face, an expression of gloomy peevishness about his expression. His wife stood and looked at him, looked at him and thought.

"You are back early," he said. "What is the matter? You don't look radiantly happy. I thought you were looking forward so much to this bazaar."

"I was," she replied. "I am disappointed."

He saw then that her silence was not a matter of indifference but of anger.

"What's wrong?" he asked quickly.

Her lips parted for a moment. One saw that her teeth were firmly clenched. There was a wicked light in her strange-colored eyes.

"It was that woman again," she muttered, - "the Duchess!"

"What about her?" Carraby demanded. "She's bound to be civil to you now, anyway."

"Is she?" Mrs. Carraby replied. "Is she, indeed! Well, her civility this afternoon has been such that I shall have to give up my stall. I can't stay there."

"What do you mean?" he demanded.

"Nothing except that before everybody she once more cut me dead, cut me wickedly," Mrs. Carraby declared. "You don't understand the tragedy of this to a woman. You are not likely to. She did it in such a way this time that there isn't a person worth knowing in London who isn't laughing about it at the present moment."

"Beast of a woman!" he muttered.

Mrs. Carraby came a little further into the room. She sank into an easy-chair and sat there. Her hands were tightly clenched, her face was hard and cold, her tone icy. Yet one felt that underneath a tempest was raging.

"You know, Algernon," she went on, "we had some hard times when you first began to make your way a little. When we first took this house, even, things weren't altogether easy. Americans can come from nowhere, do the most outrageous things in the world, and take London by storm. London, on the other hand, is cruel to English people who have only their money. She was cruel to us, Algernon, but with all the snubs and all the difficulties I ever had, nothing has ever happened to me like to-day."

"You'll get over it."

"Get over it!" she repeated. "Yes, but I thought that that sort of thing was at an end. I thought that when you were a Cabinet Minister no one would dare to treat me as though I were a social nobody."

"You must remember that the Duchess has a special reason," he reminded her. "I suppose it's that Portel affair."

"Yes," Mrs. Carraby agreed, "it is the Portel affair."

They were both silent. There wasn't much to be said, for the moment.

"Have you heard," he inquired presently, "whether Lady Anne is with him in Paris?"

"No," she replied. "Somehow or other, people don't seem to talk scandal about Lady Anne. They say that she is staying for a time with an old friend there. Algernon!"

"Yes?"

"Is it true that you are doing so badly at the Foreign Office?" she asked bluntly.

A little flush mounted almost to his forehead.

"I have had the devil's own luck," he muttered.

"I can't take up a newspaper," she continued bitterly, "without finding it full of abuse of you. They say that during six weeks the *entente cordiale* has vanished.

They say that you have lost the friendship of France, that she trusts us no longer, and that Germany's tone becomes more threatening and more bullying every day, solely on account of your weakness."

"We can't afford to risk a war," Carraby explained. "I am a Radical Minister. I have represented a Radical constituency ever since I came into Parliament. What the devil should I have to say to my people if within a couple of months of taking office we were plunged into war?"

"I do not pretend," Mrs. Carraby remarked, "to be an active politician, but I have heard it said that the best way to avoid war is to show that you are not afraid of it. They say that that is where Sir Julien Portel was so splendid. Do you know that the leading article of one of your own papers this morning declares that Germany would never have dared to have said so much to us if she had not known that she had only a puppet to deal with in the Cabinet? You know what all the other papers are hinting at? Is it true, Algernon, that you gave two hundred thousand pounds to the party?"

"Whether it is true or not," Carraby retorted, "it makes no difference. I wanted this post, wanted it for your sake as much as my own, and I wish to Heaven that it was at the bottom of the sea! I'd resign to-morrow if I could do so with dignity. I can't now, of course. Every one would say I was chucked. To make things worse," he went on savagely, "there come these infernal letters of Portel's!"

Mrs. Carraby raised her eyebrows.

"Why, I've heard it said that those letters are the one

E. Phillips Oppenheim

hope this country has! I have heard it said that but for those letters France and England would be as far apart to-day as they ever were. I heard it said only this afternoon that those letters were our only hope of peace. They were compared with the letters of Junius, whoever he was. Lord Cardington told me himself that they were the most splendid political prose he had ever read in his life."

"That may be true enough," Carraby growled, "but they make it all the harder for me. No doubt Portel was a good Minister. No doubt he was doing very well in his post. Now he writes these letters every one remembers it, every one is asking for him back again. It's hell, Mabel! I wish to God we'd let the man alone!" Mrs. Carraby looked at her husband steadfastly. She was a little taller than he. She looked at him, from his well-brushed hair to the trim patent boots which adorned his small feet. She looked at him and in those strange-colored eyes of hers were unmentionable things. She turned away and walked to the window. In imagination she was back again in Julien's rooms. She lived again through those few minutes. If he had answered differently!

Outside in the square the newsboys were shouting. She had stood before the window for some time when a familiar name fell upon her ears. She turned around and touched the bell.

"What is it that you want?" her husband asked.

"A paper," she replied.

A very correct butler brought her the *Pall Mall Gazette* a moment or two later. She scanned it eagerly. Then it slipped from her shuddering fingers. She turned upon her husband.

"He is dead!" she cried. "Can't you read it? 'Death of an Englishman in an explosion in Paris. Mr. Kendricks, a journalist, seriously injured; Sir Julien Portel, the ex-Cabinet Minister, - dead!'"

She stood as though turned to stone. Then something in her husband's face seemed to bring her back to the present. She turned upon him. Her face was suddenly lit with some strange, quivering fire. It was one of the moments of her life.

"You miserable worm!" she shrieked. "You dare to stand there and smile because a man is dead! You!"

He tried to draw himself up, tried to rebuke her. He might as well have tried to stem a torrent.

"I've done my best to share your rotten, scheming life," she cried, "to help you in your dirty ways, and to crawl up into the places we coveted! Once I saw the truth. Once a real man was kind to me and I saw the difference. I've felt it in my heart ever since. For your sake and my own, for the sake of our rotten, miserable ambitions, I ruined him and sent him to his death. He is dead, do you hear? You and I did it! We are murderers! And to think that I did it for you! That you - such a creature as you - might take his place!"

She threw up her hands high above her head. There had been people who had doubted her good looks. No one at that instant would have denied her beauty. Carraby's eyes were fixed upon her and he was afraid. Even when she had cast herself face downward upon the couch, and lay with her head buried in her hands, he dared not go near. He stood there gazing at her across the room. Perhaps he, too, though his understanding was less, tasted a little of the poison!

In the splendid library of his palace in Berlin, the maker of toys leaned back in his chair after a long and successful day's work. There lingered upon his lips still the remnants of a grim smile, which the dictation of a dispatch to London had just evoked. His secretary gathered up his papers. His master was disposed to be genial.

"My young friend," he remarked, "those letters from Paris - they were stopped just in time, eh?"

"Just in time, indeed, Highness," the young man replied. "I have friends who write me from there. They assure me that their effect was tremendous. The cessation of them was indeed an act of Providence."

Prince Falkenberg's lips relaxed. There were hard lines at the corners of his mouth. Yet if this were indeed a smile, it was no pleasant thing to look upon!

"An act of Providence, without a doubt!" he exclaimed, - "Providence which watches always over the destinies of our dear Fatherland!"

"I shall bring you now, Highness, the foreign papers?" the young man suggested.

"If you please," his master replied. "I read them now, thank Heaven, with an easier feeling."

The young man retreated and reappeared in a few

minutes with a pile of newspapers. Prince Falkenberg rose and stretched himself, lit a long black cigar and threw himself into a comfortable chair before the high window.

"Your Highness will take some coffee, perhaps?" the young man asked.

"Presently."

The great Minister unfolded his newspapers. A reference in the English *Times* perplexed him. He turned to the journal which only a few days ago he had opened with almost a shudder. He undid the wrapper, shook it open and looked at it. Then suddenly he sat like a man turned to stone. The cigar burnt out between his teeth, his eyes were riveted upon that page, the black letters seemed to have become lurid. The sentences stabbed, he was face to face with the impossible. The paper which he read was dated on the preceding day. Before him was a fourth article, dated from Paris, dated less than forty-eight hours ago, signed "Julien Portel." The title of the article was "The World's Great Mischief-Maker!" He read on, read from that first sentence to the last, read the naked truth about himself, saw his motives exposed, his secret visits to Paris derided, his foibles photographed. He saw himself the laughing stock of Europe. Then he leaned over and rang the bell.

"Neudheim," he said, "let it be given out that I leave to-night for Falkenberg as usual. Let the automobile be prepared for a long journey. I leave in half an hour."

The young man stared. He had fancied that those flying visits of his master's for a time were to be discontinued.

"Your Highness goes south?" he asked.

"I drive all night," Prince Falkenberg replied. "See that the Count Rudolf is prepared to accompany me. Quick! Give the orders."

CHAPTER XIII

ESTERMEN'S DEATH-WARRANT

In the untidy salon of his bachelor apartments in the Boulevard Maupassant Estermen awaited the coming of his master in veritable fear and trembling. In all his experience he had never been compelled to face a crisis such as this. There had been small failures, punished, perhaps, by a sarcastic word or biting sentence. There had been no failure to compare with this one! Herr Freudenberg deliberately, and of his own free choice, was accustomed to take huge risks. When they came he accepted them, but when they were not inevitable he as sedulously avoided them. The wrecking of Julien's apartments in the Rue de Montpelier was by far the most hazardous enterprise which had been attempted since the days of the toymaker's first secret visits to Paris. Half a dozen human beings had been done to death in a manner which invited and even challenged the attentions of the French police. A terrible risk had been run and run in vain. The blow had been struck at the very moment when its object was unattainable! Estermen shivered as he tried to imagine for himself the coming interview. Gone, he feared, was his life of pleasant luxury among the flesh-pots and easy ways of Paris; his bachelor apartments, occupied in name by him but of which the real tenant was his dreaded master. And behind all this

E. Phillips Oppenheim

apprehension lurked another grisly and terrible fear! For the twentieth time during the last few minutes he peered through the closely drawn Venetian-blind, and his blood ran cold. On the pavement opposite, before the small table of a café, a man was sitting - the same man! For two days he had been there - a gaunt and silent person with a wonderful trick of gazing away into space from the columns of his newspaper. But Estermen knew all about that! He knew, even, the man's name! He knew that he was one of the most persistent and successful of French detectives. His name was Jean Charles and he had never known failure. Estermen looked at him through the blind and his pale face was ugly with fear.

The moment arrived. The long, gray traveling car, covered with dust, swung around the corner and stopped below. Herr Freudenberg was travel-stained and almost unrecognizable in his motor clothes as he stepped out and passed into the block of apartments. Contrary to his usual custom, he did not at once present himself before the man who awaited him in fear and trembling. Estermen heard him enter his own suite of rooms on the other side of the stairway and give a few brief orders. Then there was a peremptory knock at the door. Herr Freudenberg was announced and entered.

To the man who had been waiting for his sentence there was something terrible in the grim impassivity of Prince Falkenberg's features. His face was set and white and sphinx-like. Only his eyes shone with a fierce, unusual fire.

"What have you to say, Estermen?" he demanded.

"It was a miracle," Estermen faltered. "Sir Julien descended the stairs with the copy in his hand to speak to a caller. For seventeen hours he had been in his rooms, for the following seventeen hours he would probably have been there, too. For the intervening thirty seconds he happened to be upon the pavement. It was a miracle!"

This was the end of all the specious story which Estermen had gone over so often to himself! Yet he had done his cause no harm, for the few sentences he spoke were the truth.

"You have discovered his present whereabouts?" his master demanded.

Estermen hesitated. He feared that this was another blow which he was about to deal.

"He is at the house of Madame Christophor in the Rue de St. Paul," he faltered.

His news, however, did not discompose Prince Falkenberg. On the contrary, he seemed, if anything, to find the intelligence agreeable.

"Have you made any inquiries as to his condition?"

Estermen shrugged his shoulders.

"The household of Madame Christophor," he replied, "is, as you know, outside my sphere of influence. It is, besides, incorruptible. I myself am personally obnoxious to Madame. I could do nothing but wait for your coming."

Prince Falkenberg stood with his hands behind him, thinking. He had relapsed into his former grim and impenetrable silence. And while he waited the sweat stood out in beads upon Estermen's forehead. Greatly he feared that the worst was to come!

"Have you anything else to say to me?" his master asked.

"Nothing!" Estermen replied, with faltering lips.

Prince Falkenberg's eyes were fierce orbs of light and his servant quailed before him.

"Have you any reason to believe that the origin of the crime is suspected?"

It was the question which above all others he had dreaded! Estermen was a coward and a fluent liar. The latter gift, however, availed him nothing. He felt as though the nerves of his tongue were being controlled by some other agency. Against his will he told the truth.

"Jean Charles is watching these apartments!"

"Ah!"

Prince Falkenberg's single exclamation was the death sentence of his agent. Estermen knew it and his knees knocked one against the other.

"For six years," Prince Falkenberg said, after a moment's pause, "you have lived an easy and a comfortable life, Estermen, - a life, I dare say, spent among the gutter vices which would naturally appeal to a person of your temperament; a life, apart from the small services which I have required of you, directed altogether by your own inclinations. Be thankful for those six years. As you well know, but for me they would have been spent either in prison or in the problematical future world - a matter entirely at the discretion of the judge who tried you. It pleased me to rescue you for my own purpose. You were possessed of a certain amount of low cunning and a complete absence of all ordinary human qualities, a combination which made you a useful servant of my will. My one condition has been always before you. The present case demands your fulfillment of it."

Estermen began to tremble.

"The man may be there by accident," he faltered. "There is no certainty as yet that I am even suspected. I'm - I'm horribly afraid to die!" he added, with an ugly little laugh.

"So are most men of your kidney," Prince Falkenberg replied composedly. "Nevertheless, die you must, and to-night. Write your confession. Make it clear that one of the victims was your personal enemy. I'll dictate it, if you like."

"I can do it myself," Estermen muttered. "Let me - let me write the confession first and then make an attempt to escape," he pleaded. "If I am taken, the confession shall be found upon me. It will make no difference. Let me have a chance! I know the secret places of the city. I have friends who might help me to escape."

Prince Falkenberg watched his agent for a moment in contemptuous curiosity. Estermen was walking restlessly up and down the few feet of carpet, his fingers and the muscles of his face twitching. His words had come with difficulty, as though he had suddenly developed an impediment in his speech. His sallow complexion had become yellow. His carefully waxed moustache was drooping, a speck of saliva was issuing from his lips.

"The request which you make to me," Prince Falkenberg replied, "I absolutely refuse. I know you and your cowardly temperament too well to allow you to come alive into the hands of the French police."

"You value your own life highly enough!" Estermen snarled.

"It is not so," Prince Falkenberg asserted. "If I had ever valued my own life highly, there would have been no Herr Freudenberg; and if the whole history of Herr Freudenberg is discovered, I follow you, my friend, post haste. If I seem to be taking any pains to hold my own, remember that mine is a life which is valuable to the Fatherland. You have been and you are only a feeder at the troughs. One more or less such as you in the world makes just the difference of a speck of dust - that is all."

Estermen shrank cowering into his seat.

"I'd rather live - in torture - in prison or in chains - anywhere!" he gasped. "I can't think of death!"

Prince Falkenberg was becoming impatient.

"My dear Estermen," he exclaimed, "what prison do you suppose remains open for the murderer of seven men! You shrink from death. Yet let me assure you that the guillotine, with the certain prospect of it before you day after day through a long trial, is no pleasant outlet from the world for a sybarite. Be a philosopher. Go and die as you have lived. Write your confession, summon your dearest friend by telephone, give a little supper - you'll have plenty of time - but see that the affair is over before midnight! This is my advice to you, Estermen; these are also my orders, my final orders. If I find you alive when I return, or the confession unwritten, I will show you how death may be made more horrible than anything you have yet conceived."

Prince Falkenberg turned on his heel and left the apartment. Estermen remained for several moments shrinking back in the chair upon which he had collapsed. Then he rose and with trembling footsteps stole to the window, peering out from behind the blind. The man at the café opposite was still there!

E. Phillips Oppenheim

CHAPTER XIV

SANCTUARY

"This afternoon," Madame Christophor declared, looking thoughtfully at Julien, "I am going to send you a new secretary."

He turned a little eagerly in his easy-chair.

"Lady Anne!" he exclaimed.

"Are you glad?" she asked.

Julien hesitated. His eyes sought his companion's face. She was seated at the small writing-table drawn up close to his side, her head resting upon her left hand, the pen in her right fingers sketching idle figures at the bottom of the sheet which she had just written. She was wearing a dress of strange-colored muslin, a shade between gray and silver, but from underneath came a shimmer of blue, and there were turquoises about her neck. Her large, soft eyes were fixed steadfastly upon his. There was a sort of question in them which he seemed to have surprised there more than once during the last few days. A sudden uneasiness seized him. His brain was crowded with unwilling fancies. There were, without doubt, symptoms of coquetry in her appearance. He had spoken of blue as the one sublime color. As she leaned a little back in her chair, resting from her labors, he could scarcely help noticing the blue silk stockings and suède shoes which matched the hidden color of her skirt, the ribbon which gleamed from the dusky masses of her hair. Madame Christophor was always a very beautiful and a very elegant woman, and it seemed to have pleased her during these last few days to appear at her best. Julien gripped for a moment at his bandaged arm.

"You are in pain? You would like me to change the bandage?" she suggested almost eagerly.

"Not yet," he replied. "It is still quite comfortable."

She looked at him thoughtfully.

"You have the air of wanting something," she remarked. "Is there anything that displeases you?"

"Displeases me! If you knew how strange that sounded!" he exclaimed. "I do not think that any one ever lived with such luxury, or was treated with so much kindness, as I during the last few days. You make every second perfect."

Madame Christophor sighed. Almost as Julien finished his speech he regretted its conclusion. Madame Christophor, on the other hand, although she sighed, seemed vaguely content.

"You see, the fates against whom you have so great a grievance have done something to atone," she declared. "No doubt you hated to leave your work to come and speak to me in the street that afternoon. No doubt your red-headed journalist friend hated me also.

Yet if you had not come, if my automobile had been detained a few minutes on the way - ah! it is terrible indeed to think what might not have happened!"

She shivered. A moment later she raised her eyes and continued.

"I think," she said, "you must abandon a little of your hostility against my sex. It was a woman who worked this mischief in your life and a woman who was fortunate enough to save it. I think you can almost cry quits with us, Sir Julien."

He smiled. He was struggling to lead back their conversation to a lighter level. A certain change in this woman's tone and manner, a change which was reflected even in her appearance, disturbed him painfully.

"The balance is already on my side, dear hostess," he assured her. "You have left me an eternal debtor to your sex. I shall never again indulge in generalities or wholesale condemnation. It is, after all, foolish. But tell me why you are sending Lady Anne to help me to-day?"

She watched for any trace of disappointment in his tone. There was none. On the contrary, his mention of Lady Anne was accompanied by a slight eagerness which puzzled her.

"I have a few social duties to attend to," she explained a little vaguely. "Lady Anne is quite efficient. I like her handwriting, too. It is like herself - clean-cut, legible. There are no hidden pools about Lady Anne."

"Yet," he said, "a woman always keeps some part of herself concealed."

"You think that Lady Anne, too, has her secret?" Madame Christophor asked, raising her eyes.

"I think that if she has, she is quite capable of keeping it," he replied.

There was a knock at the door. Lady Anne entered. She came a few yards into the room with a slight smile upon her lips, and nodded pleasantly to Julien. In her slim stateliness, the untroubled serenity of youth reflected in her smiling face, she represented perfectly the other type of womanhood. Madame Christophor rose deliberately to her feet. For one swift moment she measured the things between them. She herself was conscious of a greater intellectual maturity, a more subtle quality in her looks, a beauty less describable, more exotic, perhaps, but also more provocative. The arts of her sex were at her finger-tips, the small arts disdained by this well-looking and perfectly healthy young woman. She turned her head quickly towards Sir Julien. It was the idle impulse of the man or woman who plucks the petals from a flower. Julien was gazing steadfastly at Lady Anne.... Madame Christophor picked up her belongings and moved towards the door.

"Be merciless today, my friend!" she exclaimed, pausing upon the threshold, - "virulent, if you will! *Le Jour* was screaming at you last night. Jesen has lost his head a little; or is it the lash of his master which he feels? How can one tell?"

"After tonight," Julien remarked, with a smile, "who will read *Le Jour*? I shall tell the story of the purchase of that paper by Herr Freudenberg. French people will not love to think that the pen of Jesen has been guided by the hand of Germany."

Madame Christophor made a little grimace.

"My friend," she declared, "my house is, I believe, the safest spot in Paris, yet there are limits. Remember that you have become a celebrity. There is an agitation in England to have you back at the Foreign Office. All Paris is divided upon the subject of your life or death. And there are men here in the city who seek for you night and day with death in their hands. My house is sanctuary, but no one can write such things as you are writing and deem himself secure against any risk."

He smiled at her confidently.

"Yet you would not have me leave out one single line, you would not have me lower the torch for one second! You suggest caution! - you, who haven't the word 'fear' in your vocabulary! It is your house, not mine. There are more bombs to be bought in Paris. Yet tell me, would you have me spare a single word of the truth?"

She flashed back her answer across the room. For the moment she forgot Lady Anne. They two were on another plane.

"Not one word," she assured him, with soft yet vibrant earnestness. "I would have you write the truth in letters of fire upon the clouds, for all Paris to see. You have a message. See that it goes out."

Madame Christophor closed the door softly behind her. Julien remained looking at the spot from which she had disappeared. Then he drew a little breath.

"She is wonderful!" he muttered.

Lady Anne took up her pen. She avoided looking at him.

"Let us begin," she said....

They wrote for hours. Julien was in the mood for this final and fierce attack upon *Le Jour* and all the powers that stood behind it. He held up Falkenberg to derision - the charlatan of modern politics, the Puck of Berlin, whose one sincerity was his hatred for England, and one capacity, the giant capacity for mischief! He wound up his article with a scathing and personal denunciation of Falkenberg, and a splendidly worded appeal to the French nation not for one moment to be deceived as to the character of this tireless and ambitious schemer after his country's welfare. All the time Anne took down his words in fluent and flowing writing. When at last he had finished, he looked at the sheetswhich surrounded her with something like amazement.

"Why, what a pig I've been, Anne!" he exclaimed, glancing from the table to the clock. "You must have been writing for nearly three hours!"

She was busy picking up the sheets.

"Quite, I should say," she answered, "but I loved it. Now I am going to ring for tea, and afterwards you must read it through. We might get the manuscript down to the office to-night."

E. Phillips Oppenheim

"I shall need you when I read it through," he reminded her. "There will be corrections."

"Either Madame Christophor or I will be here," she replied. "Madame Christophor may have some other work for me."

He looked at her curiously.

"Even you are different," he murmured.

"Tell me at once what you mean?" she begged.

"I wish I knew," he confessed. "To tell you the truth, Anne, a curious feeling of detachment seems to have come over me - during the last few days especially. It is such a short time since I was living the ordinary sort of mechanical life in London, engaged to be married to you, and my doings day by day all mapped out - a life interesting, of course, but without any real variation. And now here I am, hanging on to life by the thin edge of nothing, writing such things as I should never have dared to have said from my seat in the House, practically an adventurer. Do you wonder that sometimes I am not quite sure that it isn't all a nightmare? I am actually hiding here in Paris from assassins - in Paris, the most civilized city in the world - the guest of a woman whose acquaintance I made only because a little manicurist in Soho insisted upon it. And you, Anne, are here by my side, a professional secretary, the friend of a milliner, more intimate and on better terms with me than you were in the days when we were engaged to be married! What has happened to us, Anne? How did we get here?"

She laughed at him tolerantly.

"We've come a little into our own, I suppose," she remarked. "As for me, I feel a different woman since I stepped out of the made-to-order world. And you - well, don't be angry, but you're not nearly so much of a prig, are you, Julien? You're less starched and more human. Of course we are more companionable. We are both more human."

He nodded.

"I suppose that so far as I am concerned Kendricks had something to do with it - he was always trying to make me look at things differently. But it seems such a short time for such an absolute change."

She was balancing her pen upon the inkpot - keeping her eyes turned from him.

"It isn't always a matter of time, you know, Julien," she said thoughtfully. "You were never really a prig - I was never really a machine for wearing a ready-made smile and a few smart frocks. It took a shock to make us see things, but neither of us remained wilfully blind. You'll be back in your world before long and a better man than ever."

"And you?"

"I have hopes some day of becoming a perfect secretary," she confessed. "If I fail, I will at least make more bows than any one else in a day."

He leaned towards her, showing a sudden and dangerous forgetfulness of his bandaged arm.

"Anne," he said firmly, "if I go back, you go back.

Sometimes I think that I shall never regret anything that has happened if - "

The door was softly opened. It was Madame Christophor who entered with a little pile of letters in her hand. Lady Anne, with slightly heightened color, rose to her feet. There was something in Madame Christophor's eyes which was almost fiercely questioning.

"I am not disturbing you, I trust?" she asked slowly. "I bring Sir Julien some letters."

He caught up the sheets which lay by his side.

"I will not even look at them until I have corrected my article," he declared.

Madame Christophor settled herself composedly in an easy-chair.

"Lady Anne shall read it aloud," she proposed calmly, "and I will assist in the corrections. For the French edition I may be able to suggest. The papers today are most amusing," she continued. "The German press is almost unreadable. No wonder that there is a price upon your head, my friend!"

Julien moved restlessly in his place.

"I have had the most extraordinary luck," he remarked. "No other man, naturally, knew so much of Anglo-German and Anglo-French relations. And instead of being at home in Downing Street, and muzzled, I happened to be here on the spot, to run up against Falkenberg, discover his little schemes, and with my own special knowledge to see through them at once. No one else ever had such an opportunity."

Madame Christophor smiled enigmatically. She was looking thoughtfully across at her guest.

"It is not every opportunity in life," she murmured, "which a man knows how to embrace!"

E. Phillips Oppenheim

CHAPTER XV

NEARING A CRISIS

That night, for the first time since his arrival in the house as a guest, Julien dined downstairs. To his surprise, when he presented himself in the smaller salon to which he had been directed, he found the table laid for two only. Madame Christophor, who was standing on the threshold of the winter-garden opening out from the apartment, read his expression and frowned.

"You expected Lady Anne to dine?" she asked bluntly.

Julien was taken a little aback.

"It seemed natural to expect her," he admitted.

Madame Christophor moved towards the bell, but Julien intercepted her. He remembered all that he owed to this woman. He was ashamed of his lack of tact.

"Dear Madame Christophor," he pleaded, "forgive me if for a moment I forgot how altered things are. Indeed, it was not a matter of choice with me. Of course, it will give me the greatest pleasure to dine tête-à-tête with you!"

He was, perhaps, a shade too impressive, but Madame Christophor, as all women who greatly desire to read in a man's words what they choose to find there, hesitated. Finally, with a shrug of the shoulders, she turned away from the bell.

"Three is such an impossible number," she declared, with well-assumed carelessness. "Lady Anne has her own salon adjoining her apartment. She dines there always. If I am without company, I enjoy the rest of being alone. She is very delightful in her own way, your dear Lady Anne, but she and I have not much in common. Come and see my roses."

She led the way into the conservatory, a dome-shaped building with colored glass at the top, fragrant, almost faint with the perfume of roses and drooping exotics. A little fountain was playing in the middle. When the butler announced the service of dinner and they returned to take their places, she left the door open.

"Tonight," she announced, as they sat side by side at the small round table, "I am going to take advantage of the situation. I am your hostess and you are an invalid. It is my opportunity to talk. Are you a good listener, Sir Julien?"

She had dropped her voice almost to a whisper. Those beautiful deep-set eyes were challenging his. She seemed to have made up her mind that for that night, at any rate, her beauty should be unquestioned. She wore a dress of black net, fitting very closely, a wonderful background for her white skin and the ropes of pearls which were twined about her neck. He had never seen her _décolletée_, but he remembered reading in a ladies' fashion paper that a famous sculptor had once declared her neck and bust to be the most beautiful in Paris. She had even added the slightest touch of color to her cheeks. There was no longer any sign of the wrinkles at the sides of her eyes. She read the half ingenuous, half unwilling admiration in his face, and she laughed at him.

"Ah, my friend," she murmured, "I can see that you object to the rôle of listener! Very well, then, you shall talk. You shall tell me of your life in England. You shall tell me what dreams have come to you for the days when once more you shall help to shape the destinies of your nation. Tell me how you mean to live! Shall you be again - what was it Lady Anne thought you? - a prig?"

"I am like many other and more famous men," he remarked. "I have learned much in adversity."

"I read the English papers," she continued presently. "I have also a large correspondence. Do you know that there is nearly a rebellion in your party? Questions have been asked about you in the House. Both sides want you back. There is a feeling that you were allowed to go much too easily, that the indiscretion of which you were guilty was a trifle. This man Carraby is what you call - a cad! That does not do in the high places. Nationality cannot conceal a lack of breeding."

"I have thought over many things," Julien admitted. "If the way is made clear for me, I shall go back. Why not? I believe that I can serve my country, and it is the life for which I am best fitted. Carraby may have his good points, but his ambitions have been a little too extensive. He would have made a better mayor of the town where he was born."

"You are right," she declared. "There is no place for such men in the great world. You will go back. It is written. See - I drink to England's future Prime Minister!"

She raised her glass, which the butler had just filled with champagne. She looked into his eyes as she drank and Julien was conscious of a passing uneasiness. She set the glass down, empty. Her hand lay for a moment near his.

"You will go back," she murmured. "You will forget. The people whom you have met in your brief period of adversity will seem to you like shadows. Is it not so?"

He took her hand and raised it boldly to his lips.

"It will never be like that with you, dear hostess," he assured her. "There are things which one does not forget."

She did not withdraw her hand. Its pressure upon his fingers was faint but insistent.

"Do you remember when we first met," she said softly, "how bitter we were against the others - even at first against one another? You had been betrayed by that unimportant woman and the whole sex was hateful to you. I had just come from seeing the tragedy caused by a man's crass selfishness. I, too, was wearing the fetters. To me the whole of your sex seemed abominable.... You see," she went on, "my marriage was a terrible disappointment. I fancied that I was marrying a great man, a genius, an inspired statesman, and I found myself allied to a political machine. My wealth - have I told you, I wonder, that I am very

E. Phillips Oppenheim

wealthy? - helped him. For the rest, I was a puppet by his side. I lived in Berlin for one year. Official life in Berlin for an American woman, even though she be Princess von Falkenberg, is still intolerable. The men were bad enough, the women worse. I could not breathe. I was no part of my husband's life. I was no part of any one's life. The German women did not understand me. My husband - oh, he is very German in his heart! - only laughed at my complaints. He would have been perfectly willing to see me become as those others - *hausfrauen*, bearers of children, a domestic article. So we separated - divorce at that moment was impossible. I came back to Paris."

"You had no children?" Julien asked.

"One boy," she answered, her eyes becoming very soft. "Do not let us speak of him for a moment."

The service of dinner continued. Outside, the water from the fountain fell into the basin with a gentle, monotonous sound. The perfume of the roses stole through the open doorway. One softly-shaded lamp had been lit, but the rest of the lofty room remained in shadowy obscurity. The light from that one lamp seemed to fall full upon Madame Christophor's beautiful face.

"I loved my boy," she went on. "It was part of my husband's cruelty to detach him from me. He has the law on his side. I may not even see Rudolf. Very well, I do my best to steel my heart. I come here to live. I have many friends, but Falkenberg is the only man to whom I have ever belonged, and he has treated me as he would have treated one of those others - his companions for the moment. I have occupied myself here in work of different sorts. I have tried in my way to do good among women less happy, even, than I. Wherever I went I saw that every woman who has sinned, every woman who is miserable, every woman who has become a blot upon the earth, is what she is by reason of man's selfishness. Can you wonder that I have grown a little bitter?"

"I wonder at nothing in the woman who has been Falkenberg's wife," Julien replied. "He seems to me the most unscrupulous person who ever breathed. Yet in his way he is marvelously attractive."

"He is," she admitted. "I fell in love with him against my will. Directly my reason intervened, the madness was over. How old do you think I am, Sir Julien?"

Julien was a little startled.

"How old?" he repeated.

"A foolish question, of course," she continued. "How could you be honest! I am twenty-nine years old. I believe that I am the richest woman in Paris. I am tired of being called brilliant and cynical, of showing fortune-hunters to the door, of living my life in loneliness. Falkenberg has sworn that if I take any steps to make a divorce possible, I shall never see my boy again. I have not seen him, as it is, for nearly two years. The threat is losing its terrors.... You are listening, my friend?"

"Of course!"

She turned to the butler. The other servants had already left the room.

"Bring coffee into the winter-garden," she ordered. "Come, Sir Julien."

She lit a cigarette and threw it away almost immediately. Her eyes were gleaming like stars. She laid her fingers upon his arm as they passed out into the perfumed air of the conservatory, and he seemed to feel some touch of the fire that was burning in her veins. She swayed a little towards him. The color in her cheeks was brilliant. Her bosom was rising and falling quickly. She was splendidly handsome, nerved up to great things, a woman inspired by a purpose. Julien was afraid. He, too, felt something of the excitement of the moment, but his brain seemed numbed. There was nothing he could say. She threw herself back into a low chair and drew him down to her side. With her other hand she caught hold of a cluster of pink roses and pressed their cool blossoms to her cheek.

"Sir Julien," she murmured, "I have looked so steadfastly into life, I have striven so hard to find a place there. I have something to give. I do not come empty-handed. I can place offerings upon the altar of the great god. I have myself, my brains such as they are, and the golden key which unlocks the wonderful doors. Can you wonder that I ask for something in return? I have stood in the marketplace of life, I have passed down between the stalls, and I am humiliated. There is no life, there is no career upon this world for a woman. It is a strange doctrine, perhaps, to preach in these days, but I have searched and I know it to be the truth. Nature meant woman for man, and if she rebels there is no seat for her alone among the mighty places. Alone I can win none of the things I desire. You see, I talk to you like this, nakedly, because we are of the order of those who understand. You very nearly married a duke's daughter and became a middle-class politician. Don't do it. Don't think of it any more, Julien. You were meant for the great places, and I think - I think - that I was meant to hold the torch to light you there!"

"Madame Christophor!"

She started at his tone. In the splendid arrogance of her assured position, her brilliant gifts, her almost inspired individuality, failure had never occurred to her. Even now she refused to read the message in his set face.

"You feel, perhaps," she went on, leaning towards him, "that you are pledged to Lady Anne. Dear Sir Julien, rub your eyes! I want you to see - all the way to the skies. Lady Anne is a sweet girl who will look nice at the head of any one's table. She will read the papers and take an intelligent interest in her husband's work, and ask him trite and obvious questions to prove that she understands all about it. She will give you phenacetin when you have a headache, she will fill your house with the right sort of people. She will be very amiable and very satisfied. She'll always read the debates and she'll sit up for you at night in a pretty dressing-gown. And all the time the wall will grow, brick by brick, and you will look up to the skies and find them empty, and listen for the music and hear none, and a web will be spun about your heart, and your brain will be clogged, and the fine thoughts will go, and you'll never be anything but a successful politician. You know very well that all the paths to the great pit of unhappiness are crowded with men who have been successful in their profession."

E. Phillips Oppenheim

She swayed even closer towards him, her head a little thrown back, her eyes inviting him. He scrambled to his feet. Still she held out her hands.

"Won't you trust me?" she begged. "Believe me that I know the way into the great places, Julien."

"Listen!" he cried hoarsely. "You have offered me everything except your love. Thank Heaven you did not offer me that! I love Lady Anne."

"Everything *except* my love!" she exclaimed, with the first note of trouble in her tone. "Everything *except* my love! Are you mad?"

"I love Lady Anne!" he repeated, setting his teeth.

They stood facing one another. She tore a handful of the blossoms from a syringa tree and commenced crushing them in her fingers. The sound of footsteps scarcely disturbed her. The butler appeared, followed by Lady Anne. The former excused himself with a grave face.

"Madame," he announced, "the Prince von Falkenberg is here."

Madame Christophor turned slowly around.

"The Prince von Falkenberg! Where?"

"In the waiting-room, madame."

She moved away. She did not glance towards Julien.

"I come," she announced.

Lady Anne had some letters in her hand, which she handed to Julien. He threw them hastily aside and drew her suddenly into his arms and into the shadow of the giant palm.

"Anne," he pleaded, "not because of your mother, not because you would make me a suitable wife, but because I love you, will you marry me?"

He felt her relax in his arms.

"Julien!" she murmured.

"I didn't finish the sentence," he went on, - "to-morrow at the Embassy?"

"Absurd!"

"It's the only way," he insisted confidently. "We couldn't be married in London. All the tribe of Harbord would come and boo, and it would save no end of gossip and bother when we got back. Anne - I love you very much and I want you just as soon as I can get you!"

"Of course, if you put it like that," she said softly, -

"Well?"

"This is the only frock I have."

"The Rue de la Paix is at our gates," he reminded her.

"Be sensible," she begged. "You can't show your-self about Paris. Something terrible will happen."

E. Phillips Oppenheim

"Not it!" he replied confidently. "It's too late."

His arm crept a little further around her waist, he drew her even further back among the drooping palms.

"I think that I like this better than the last time you asked me!" she whispered.

CHAPTER XVI

FALKENBERG'S LAST EFFORT

"Madame," Prince Falkenberg declared, with a formal bow, "I owe you a thousand apologies for this visit."

Madame Christophor looked at him across the room, and in her eyes there was no welcome nor any anger - only surprise.

"You break," she reminded him, "the word of a prince!"

Falkenberg smiled icily.

"There are cataclysms in life," he said, "whirlpools into which one may sometimes be drawn. One's will is overborne. I myself am in that unfortunate position."

Madame Christophor looked steadfastly at her visitor. Was it her fancy or was he really growing older, this man of iron? The story of the last few weeks was written into his face, there were shadows under his eyes, a deep line across his forehead.

"Since you are here, be seated," she invited, sinking herself wearily into a chair. "Tell me as quickly as you can what has brought you?"

E. Phillips Oppenheim

"Portel has brought me," Falkenberg answered grimly. "They tell me that he has taken shelter under the shadow of your petticoats."

"Shelter from your assassins!"

"Precisely!" Falkenberg admitted.

"I do not admire your methods," Madame Christophor remarked. "They seem to me not only brutal but clumsy. You killed seven men and injured several others, to no purpose."

"Madame," Falkenberg declared, "to secure the death of that man I would have destroyed a whole quarter of Paris and every person in it."

Madame Christophor shivered.

"Thorough, as usual, my dear Prince," she murmured. "Nevertheless, I find such statements loathsome. We should have outlived the days of barbarity. I do not understand men who deal in such fashion with their enemies."

Falkenberg frowned.

"There is something between us greater than personal enmity," he retorted fiercely. "My personal enemy I would deal with in such a manner as I make no doubt would commend itself to your scruples. Julien Portel is more than that. He is the enemy of my country. Upon him, therefore, I shall have no mercy."

"I will not argue with you," she replied. "There is a plainer issue before us. In passing my threshold you have broken your word of honor. What do you want?"

"I want Julien Portel!"

Madame Christophor shrugged her shoulders.

"You have wanted him for some little time."

"Never so badly as at this instant," Falkenberg declared bitterly. "He has set all Europe in a ferment with those infernal letters. He knows too much. He knows whence came the money which bought *Le Jour*. He knows every detail of my campaign here."

"There are surely others," she objected, "who must have guessed -"

"But there was no one else," he interrupted, "who had the special knowledge which Portel has. He came from the Foreign Office, with the records of the last two years in his mind. At Berlin he and I crossed swords. He is the only Englishman who has ever caused me a moment's uneasiness."

"Are you sure," she asked, "that your campaign here has been a wise one?"

"The wisdom of Solomon," he replied grimly, "can be made to look like folly by the accident of failure. There is no doubt as to its wisdom. No one has studied these matters as I have studied them. No one has seen the truth more clearly. An alliance between England and America is a matter of a few years only, and when it comes the progress of Germany is set back for a generation. The one absolute necessity before me was to cut the bonds between England and France and to settle with England alone and quickly - diplomatically, if possible; by force of arms as a last resource. We don't seek war, Henriette. We are not really a bloodthirsty nation. We seek territory. We need new lands - fruitful lands, trade, the command of the seas. If we cannot get what we want by peaceful means, then it must be war. England for the present is weakly governed. She is in the throes of labor troubles. Her political parties are ill-balanced. There is a puppet at the Foreign Office. Now is the time to strike."

"Is it wise to tell me your secrets?" she inquired coldly. "I have no sympathy for you or your country."

"I have a bargain to strike with you and you must understand," he answered. "Twenty-four hours ago we dispatched a gunboat to a certain neutral port which comes under the influence of England. We paid a German to go there and send us word that he was in danger. We have sent an intimation to the French and English Governments. To England it is an insult. I have taken the chance that France has had enough of this *entente*. Now you understand why I must have Julien Portel before they can get him back to the Foreign Office, before he can do more mischief. A strong man in Downing Street at this juncture might upset everything."

"I understand well enough why you need Julien Portel," she admitted. "I am still in the dark, however, as to why you imagine that I shall give him up?"

"Because I am going to buy him from you," Falkenberg asserted.

She glanced across the room at him, half curiously,

half scornfully.

"Buy him! You!"

"Exactly," he replied. "You smile because you do not understand. I offer you a dispensation for your divorce, and your son."

A little tremor seemed to pass through her whole frame. For a moment she closed her eyes. Then she sprang to her feet and stood quivering before him.

"This is one of your traps!" she exclaimed. "You don't mean it!"

"To prove that I do," he insisted, "I have brought Rudolf with me to Paris. He can be in your arms in a few minutes. Look into the street, if you will."

She crossed the room hastily and lifted the curtain. A low cry broke from her lips. In the tonneau of the great touring car outside a little boy was lying back amongst the cushions, asleep.

"He is tired," Falkenberg said slowly, with his eyes fixed upon the woman. "He has come all the way from Berlin without an hour's rest. Am I to take him back to-morrow? It is for you to decide."

Madame Christophor turned toward the door. Falkenberg barred the way.

"Not yet!" he declared. "Do you accept my terms?"

"But he is hungry!" she cried. "I can see that he is hungry! And he is so pale - let me fetch him in."

"Of course he is hungry," his father agreed. "He has also been asking me questions about you all the way. He believes that he is going to see you. I, too, believe that. You consent?"

"Tell me exactly what it is that you require?" she demanded.

"Take me to Portel," he answered swiftly. "Inform him that you cannot any longer permit him the shelter of your roof."

She sat down and began to laugh, softly but in unnatural fashion. Falkenberg watched her with grim curiosity.

"And then?" she inquired.

He hesitated.

"I have made some plans," he said slowly. "If he passes outside your doors to-night, he will write no more articles!"

"But the whole of the English Press is clamoring for his return to power! There will be no need for his pen - he will take up his old position."

"Precisely!" Falkenberg assented. "It is not my intention that he shall return to that position!"

Madame Christophor sat with her eyes fixed upon the wall. Then she began to laugh once more in the same strange manner. Falkenberg was curious.

"You find my intentions amusing?" he asked.

"I find the situation amusing," she replied. "Half an hour ago I offered Sir Julien Portel what is left of my life."

Falkenberg stood perfectly still, watching her closely. Then his eyes filled with a sudden bright light.

"You!" he exclaimed. "You - Princess von Falkenberg - offered yourself to this man and were refused?"

"You are indeed a genius," she admitted. "I was refused."

There was a brief silence. Falkenberg waited. Madame Christophor remained silent. Her attitude puzzled him a little. He was afraid to speak for fear of striking the wrong note. Nevertheless, the onus of speech was thrust upon him.

"Madame," he said at last, "I anticipate your reply. This man has put an intolerable insult upon you. While he lives you could never forget it. There are some privileges still belonging to me. I claim the right of avenging that affront."

"It comes conveniently - the affront!" she remarked, through her clenched teeth.

"Conveniently or not, the affront exists!" he cried. "You cannot refuse me now! You would not have him go unpunished!"

"I am not sure that he was to blame."

"Not to blame?" Falkenberg repeated, with emphasis. "Would you have me believe that you threw yourself at

E. Phillips Oppenheim

his head unasked, without encouragement - you, the proudest woman in France? One does not believe such folly!"

"Nevertheless, it is the truth," Madame Christophor declared.

Falkenberg smiled incredulously, but he said nothing. Madame Christophor had found her way once more to the window. She stood there, looking down into the car. The boy was still asleep. She gripped the window-curtains with both her hands. He was so pale, so tired, and how he had grown!

"I give you even his heritage," Falkenberg promised. "Make of him a Frenchman or an American, if you will. He is your own son. Take him. I give my firstborn for my country. You will not refuse what I offer?"

Madame Christophor made no answer. Falkenberg, however, saw the longing in her face. It was enough! He suddenly changed his tactics.

"This Julien Portel," he said, - "it is another woman he prefers."

He saw her bosom heave. The storm against which she had been struggling all the time seemed on the point of bursting. The hot blood was singing in her ears, her eyes were aflame. She crossed the room and rang the bell. Falkenberg was content to wait. He felt that he had won! The butler appeared almost immediately.

"You will conduct the Prince von Falkenberg into the winter-garden," she directed. "He desires to speak to Sir Julien Portel."

"And you?" Falkenberg asked, turning towards her.

A swift gesture showed him her disordered countenance. It was reasonable.

"I follow," she announced.

CHAPTER XVII

DEFEAT FOR FALKENBERG

Among the palms of Madame Christophor's conservatory, Julien and Lady Anne were living through a brief new chapter of their history. The wonderful thing had come to them. It was amazing - almost unrealizable! A new glamor enveloped the merest trifles. They spoke in halting sentences, they were at times almost incoherent. The marvel of it was so great!

Lady Anne was the first to hear the sound of approaching footsteps. She listened. It was not Madame Christophor who returned. She laid her hand upon Julien's arm.

"It is Jean, the butler, who comes," she whispered. "He conducts some one."

On the threshold of the winter-garden, only a short distance away, they heard Jean's voice.

"Monsieur le Prince will find Sir Julien Portel a few steps further on."

"Monsieur le Prince!" Anne faltered, with whitening face. "Julien, what does it mean?"

Julien rose to his feet. The footsteps were close at hand now upon the tessellated pavement. Then through the drooping palm boughs they saw him. Julien was standing tense and prepared, his uninjured arm was ready to strike. Falkenberg was there.

"You!" Julien exclaimed. "Well?"

The iron prince had disappeared. It was Herr Freudenberg, maker of toys, suave, genial, fascinating, who bowed before them.

"Why so surprised, Sir Julien?" he asked. "You forget that this is my wife's house. The little difficulties which have existed between us have to-day, I am happy to say, been removed. I have restored her son to Madame la Princesse. We are reunited. Henceforth my wishes are the wishes also of madame. You will present me? It is Lady Anne Clonarty, I believe?"

They were both bewildered. For the moment Falkenberg was supreme. He bowed low upon the hesitating words of introduction.

"Dear Lady Anne," he murmured, "do not be prejudiced against me. Sir Julien believes that I am his enemy. I am not. I am his sincere and heartfelt admirer."

Lady Anne's eyebrows were slowly raised.

"You have surely," she remarked, "a strange manner of showing such sentiments!"

Falkenberg smiled whimsically. He had the expression of a penitent boy who has misbehaved.

E. Phillips Oppenheim

"It is at least consistent," he pleaded. "I admire Sir Julien's talents to such an extent that I am perhaps a trifle too anxious that he should not use them against my country."

"You haven't forced your way in here to bandy phrases," Julien asserted a little harshly. "What is it that you want?"

"You!" Falkenberg answered softly. "You, my friend! Madame la Princesse - my wife, whom you have known as Madame Christophor - finds it impossible, against my wishes, to offer you any longer the shelter of her roof. I am here to escort you, if you will, to your new quarters - to follow you, if I cannot reconcile you to my company."

Julien was startled, Lady Anne incredulous.

"I do not believe," the former declared, "that Madame Christophor intends any such act of inhospitality."

"As to that," Falkenberg replied pleasantly, "my wife will be here herself in a few moments. You shall hear what she has to say from her own lips. You must remember that I have paid a price. I have given up the guardianship of my son. You yourself," he continued, looking steadfastly at Julien, "may know if any other cause exists likely to have influenced my wife in granting my request."

Julien set his teeth, but he did not flinch.

"What is it that you want with me, Prince Falkenberg?" he demanded. "Another brutal attempt at massacre? I owe you this," he added, raising his bandaged arm.

"Do you imagine that you can continue to use the methods of other generations with impunity? The thing is absurd. There are too many who know already the secret of Herr Freudenberg, maker of toys! There are too many who will know, also, before long, the secret of the explosion in the Rue de Montpelier!"

Falkenberg nodded gravely.

"I understand," he admitted. "One moves, of course, always, with the knife at one's heart. Yet, until now, I, personally, am safe. Another man dies to-night, even as we talk here, and confesses himself guilty of the Rue de Montpelier affair. But let that pass. We have crossed swords, Sir Julien, and I frankly admit, although I have gained my end to-night, that I am worsted. The money I spent to purchase *Le Jour* has been thrown away. The months of careful intrigue, the sacrifices and efforts I have made to destroy the *entente*, have been rendered almost futile by your diabolical pen. Very well, for what you have done I will accept defeat - I will accept defeat without malice. But there is the future."

"What of it?" Julien asked.

"I do not intend," Falkenberg declared, in a low, firm tone, "to have you back, a member of any English Government. I prefer Carraby and such as he."

"You flatter me!" Julien remarked grimly.

"Not in the least," Falkenberg objected. "You know the position as well as I. The political party of which you are a member is in power for a long time. You have got hold of the middle class, you've bought the Irish vote, you've bought labor. In the ranks of your party there isn't a man whom I fear - only you. I will not have you go back."

"But as it happens," Julien announced, "I am going back. I have heard from England this evening. Your friend Carraby is resigning."

Falkenberg shook his head. He remained calm, but there was an ominous flash in his eyes.

"You would make a mistake," he asserted. "No one ever goes back - successfully. Do I not know - I who am twenty years your senior, I who have felt my way into all the corners and crevices of life? Listen to me, please."

He drew a chair towards them and sat down, crossing his knees and looking towards them both in friendly fashion.

"Sir Julien," he said, "and you, my dear young lady, your entire future depends upon this little conversation. Can you not put it out of your minds for a few moments that I am the dangerous Falkenberg, the mischief-maker, the ogre of all respectable Britons? Can you not remember only that I am a well-meaning, not unkindly old gentleman who has some good advice to offer? You at least will listen to me, Lady Anne. Do I look like an assassin by choice? Do I seem like the sort of person to indulge in these dangerous exercises for mere amusement? You are both young, you have both your lives before you. Why do you, Sir Julien, voluntarily put the yoke about your neck? Why do you, my gracious young lady, suffer the man with whom your life is to be linked to deliver himself over voluntarily into a state of bondage? Politics lose all glamor to those who have dwelt within the walls. Sir Julien has dwelt there and so have I. He knows in his heart whether it is worth while. One lives always amidst a clamor of evil tongues, a pestilent trail of poisonous suspicions. One gives up one's life to be flouted and misunderstood, to be accused of evil motives and every imaginable crime. When it is all over, when one has time to think of all that one has missed, one feels that all one has done could have been done just as well by the next man in the street. That is the end of it. And against all that, you two have the world before you. You can be rich - very rich indeed. You can make an idyll of this love of yours. You can travel around the world in your own yacht, you can visit all strange countries, you can wander where you will, and all the time affairs in the world will go on very much the same as if you had stayed and given the best hours of your life to the dusty treadmill. I am an old man, Lady Anne, and I have an evil name in your country. They call me greedy, subtle, and ambitious. I may be all these things, but let me assure you that if I had my time over again my master could find another servant and my country another toiler. There are fairer flowers in life to be plucked than any which can be reached from the high places in Downing Street or Berlin.... Let me, at least, Lady Anne, make sure of your support? Mind, I am not threatening now - I plead."

Lady Anne looked at him gravely.

"Sir Julien," she declared, "will answer you for himself."

"But I want your own decision," Falkenberg insisted.

E. Phillips Oppenheim

"I want you to see the truth as I see it. I want you to tell me that you agree with me."

She shook her head.

"But I do not!" she exclaimed. "To me you have spoken like a sophist. One does not gain happiness by seeking it. You may be honest in some part of what you say - I cannot tell. Only I think that you have mistaken Sir Julien's ideas - and mine."

"You disappoint me!" Falkenberg murmured.

Sir Julien smiled.

"Not very much, I think," he said. "You always did believe in trying the hundredth chance. Let us come back to the reasonable part of our discussion. Do you propose, then, that I should leave this house at this moment with you?"

"My car is entirely at your service," Falkenberg suggested.

"Do I seem to you so ingenuous?" Julien inquired. "I am wondering what resources are open to me. I might propose to Lady Anne here that she telephone for the gendarmes. Why should I not have an escort to take me to an hotel?"

Falkenberg shrugged his shoulders.

"I like the idea," he admitted. "By all means, do as you say. Only do me the favor to remember that this is my wife's house and with her authority I request that you leave it immediately."

"I wonder," Julien asked, "what may be in store for me? - what pleasant schemes you have hatched?"

Falkenberg shrugged his shoulders.

"Listen," he said, - "if you listen attentively you will hear the murmur of Paris calling you back. Almost you can hear the falling of a thousand feet upon the pavements of the boulevards, the voice of life. You may find an asylum there. Who can tell?"

They heard the soft swirl of a woman's gown passing over the marble floor. They all turned. It was Madame Christophor who stood there.

"Still here?" she remarked.

Julien frowned.

"It is not my intention to linger," he assured her. "Prince von Falkenberg has given me your message. I am prepared to go."

Lady Anne moved hastily forward.

"Do you know," she cried, "that they will kill him? Do you know that this man," she added, pointing to Falkenberg, "has admitted it? Would you dare to send him out to be butchered in the streets?"

"The young lady exaggerates," Falkenberg protested. "This is a perfectly respectable neighborhood. What possible harm can come to an English gentleman? Besides, I have offered him, if he will, the protection of my car."

Madame Christophor sighed. She waved back Sir Julien.

"Alas!" she exclaimed, "there has been a slight misunderstanding."

She touched a bell which stood on the table by her side. Almost immediately a tall, pale-faced man in dark clothes appeared, followed by Jean, the butler.

"My dear Prince," she said to her husband, "I do assure you that you need have no special anxiety. Let me present to you Monsieur Bourgan of the French Detective Service. Monsieur Bourgan - the Prince von Falkenberg - Sir Julien Portel!"

Monsieur Bourgan saluted. The two men looked at him, - as yet they scarcely understood.

"I suppose," Madame Christophor continued, "that I am a somewhat nervous woman, but you see I can always plead the privilege of my sex. I was delighted to have Sir Julien here with me, but in a sense it was a responsibility. It occurred to me then to send a message to the Minister of the Police, who happens to be a great friend of mine, and at his suggestion Monsieur Bourgan here, who is, as I have no doubt you both well know, very distinguished in the Service, has taken up his residence in my house. He has occupied, as a matter of fact, the next room to Sir Julien's. Forgive me," she added, smiling at them all, "if I kept this little matter secret, but I know that men hate a fuss. I propose, dear Prince," she added, turning to her husband, "that Monsieur Bourgan accompanies you to your rooms. You need not fear then any molestation."

There was an absolute silence. It was broken at last by the Prince von Falkenberg.

"I must confess," he said slowly, "that I do not altogether understand."

Madame Christophor faced him with a faint smile upon her lips. The smile itself told him all that he desired to know.

"But, my dear Prince," she declared, "it is my anxiety for your safety which induces me to propose this. Only a few minutes ago you were telling me that you feared that you had become an extremely unpopular person in Paris, and that the very streets were not safe for you. Under the circumstances, one can scarcely wonder at it! The French Government, however, is above all small feelings. A private citizen in Paris, even though he be an enemy of France, is a person to be respected. The protection of the detective force of Paris is at your service. Monsieur Bourgan, you will do me the great favor of conducting my husband to his rooms. Afterwards you will return here to continue your watch over Sir Julien."

"I am entirely at your command, madame," Monsieur Bourgan replied.

Falkenberg hesitated for one single moment. He seemed to be measuring the distance between Julien and himself. Under the pretense of picking up a match, Monsieur Bourgan was almost between them. Falkenberg laughed softly, then most graciously he made his adieux.

"Lady Anne," he said, bowing, "one is permitted to

E. Phillips Oppenheim

wish you every happiness? Sir Julien, let me assure you," he continued, "that it has been a pleasure to renew our acquaintance. Dear Henriette," he added, "this care for my safety touches me! And the boy?"

"He is safe in my room," she assured him. "It is absurd of me, no doubt, but I have turned the key upon him and placed a footman outside the door. Take care of yourself, dear Rudolf. Monsieur Bourgan, I know, will watch over you well. Yet you are one of those who take risks always."

Falkenberg raised her fingers to his lips.

"Almost, dear Henriette," he murmured, "you make me regret that I ever have to leave Paris at all."

She leaned a little towards him.

"I bear you no ill-will, Rudolf," she said softly. "Take my advice. Leave Paris quickly."

His eyes held hers as though seeking for some meaning to her words. She only shook her head. He turned and followed Jean. Monsieur Bourgan brought up the rear. Madame Christophor shrugged her shoulders.

"Really," she declared, with a sigh, "life is becoming altogether too complicated. Never mind, I have got rid of Prince Falkenberg for you, Sir Julien. Between ourselves, I think that he will receive a hint to leave Paris, and before very long. Listen - there goes his car."

"Dear Madame Christophor," Lady Anne whispered, "you are wonderful!"

Madame Christophor was already moving away.

"Not really wonderful," she replied. "Only a little human. I must go to my boy."

CHAPTER XVIII

THE ONE WAY OUT

Estermen started up from his chair. In the unlit room the figure of his master seemed to have assumed a portentous, almost a threatening shape.

"Who's that?" he cried out.

Falkenberg calmly turned on the electric light.

"Still here, my friend?" he remarked significantly.

Estermen began to tremble.

"There is plenty of time," he faltered. "I am not sure about the man opposite. It may be some one else he is watching."

Falkenberg walked to the window and stood there in the full glare of the light. The man opposite was still sipping his eternal coffee. He glanced casually at Falkenberg and back at his paper.

"You fool!" the latter said to Estermen. "Can't you see that he is waiting only to draw the others in? Do you know that I - I, Von Falkenberg, Chancellor of Germany, have received what they are pleased to call a hint from the French Minister of Police that it would be advisable for me to leave Paris? This is your blundering, Estermen!"

"Not mine only," the man muttered. "Do you know that there are those who wait for you in your rooms?"

Falkenberg turned away.

"Stay here till I return," he ordered.

He turned the key of his own apartments and entered. His servant hurried up to him.

"There waits for Your Highness," he announced, "the Baron von Neudheim."

Falkenberg started.

"Here?" he exclaimed.

"In His Excellency's private apartment. There waits also -"

Falkenberg had already departed. He opened the door of his room. His secretary rose hastily to his feet.

"What do you here, Neudheim?" Falkenberg demanded. "What has happened?"

"Excellency," the young man replied, "there is trouble. Within half an hour of your leaving, I had important news. I dared not telegraph. I have followed you. I took a special train from the frontier."

"Go on," Falkenberg said calmly. "It is something serious?"

"Indeed, yes, Your Excellency!" the Baron continued. "It is concerning the Agdar matter."

Falkenberg's face lit up.

"An ultimatum!" he exclaimed. "So much the better!"

Baron von Neudheim shook his head.

"For once, I am afraid," he said, "we have been trapped. His Excellency himself sent for me. The reply from Downing Street has been received."

"Well?" Falkenberg interrupted impatiently.

"Your Excellency, the reply to our note is exceedingly courteous. It states that the unrest referred to had already been reported to the British Government, and a warship which left Portsmouth under sealed orders some months ago was instructed to proceed to the port last week. The note goes on to state that no intimation was given to Germany, as the British Government was not aware that Germany had any interests, but it further contains an assurance that the welfare of all white men will receive equal attention." Falkenberg set his teeth.

"What battleship was sent?" he asked.

"The 'Aida,'" the young man replied slowly, - "a first-class cruiser, twenty-six thousand tons."

Falkenberg was silent for a moment. His face had grown dark.

"And ours," he muttered, "was a third-rate gunboat! Who in all Downing Street could have planned a coup like this?"

"It was Sir Julien Portel - his last official action," the Baron answered. "The papers to-morrow will be full of this. The Press of Germany and England and France have the whole story."

"Which is to say," Falkenberg exclaimed, "that we are to be the laughing-stock of Europe! Anything else?"

"There is an imperial summons commanding your presence at Potsdam at once," Neudheim acknowledged reluctantly.

"I start for the frontier in a quarter of an hour," Falkenberg decided. "I shall drive to Châlons and telegraph for a special train from there."

"You will let me accompany you?" the young man begged.

Falkenberg hesitated, then he shook his head.

"No, it is my wish that you return by train. Take a day's holiday, if you will. You will be back in time."

The young man's expression was clouded. He was obviously disappointed.

"But, Excellency," he pleaded, "there is trouble in Berlin. It is best, indeed, that I should be by your side."

Falkenberg held out his hand.

E. Phillips Oppenheim

"My dear Fritz," he replied, "you will obey my orders, as you always have done. It is my wish that you return by the ordinary train to-morrow night."

"There is nothing I can do - no message -"

"Nothing!" Falkenberg interrupted. "Look after yourself. Leave me now, if you please."

The young man moved reluctantly towards the door.

"Excellency," he protested, "I do not desire a day's holiday. Things in Berlin are bad. Let us talk together on our way north. You have never yet known defeat. We can plan our way through, or fight it. Don't tell me to leave you, dear master!" he wound up, with a sudden change of tone. "There are still ways."

Falkenberg laid his hand upon the young man's shoulder.

"Fritz," he said, "my orders, if you please! Remember that I never suffer them to be disputed. Goodbye!"

The young man left the room. As he passed down the stairs he shivered. Falkenberg passed into an inner apartment. Already he had guessed who it was waiting for him. Mademoiselle rose to her feet with a little cry.

"At last!" she exclaimed. "Dear maker of toys, how long you have been! How weary it has been to wait!"

She came into his arms. He patted her head gently.

"Dear little one!"

"You are taking me to supper?" she begged.

He shook his head. Her face fell, the big tears were already in her eyes.

"But you are troubled!" she cried. "Oh, come and forget it all for a time! Isn't that what you told me once was my use in the world - that I could chatter to you, or sing, or lead you through the light paths, so that your brain could rest? Let me take you there, dear one. To-night, if ever, you have the look in your face. You need rest. Come to me!"

He looked at her steadfastly, looked at her feeling as one far away gazing down upon some strange element in life. Then a thought came to him.

"Little one," he whispered, "you are irresistible. Wait, then. It may be as you desire. Only, after supper I pass on."

"And I with you?" she implored.

He shook his head.

"Wait here."

Once more he returned to Estermen's apartments. Estermen was still there, smoking furiously. The room was blue with tobacco smoke. Falkenberg regarded him with distaste.

"Make yourself presentable, man," he ordered. "We sup in the Montmartre and we leave in a few minutes."

"What, I?" Estermen exclaimed, springing up.

"You and I and mademoiselle," Falkenberg told him. "I have made plans. You may perhaps escape - who can tell?"

Estermen, with a little sob of relief, hurried into his sleeping apartment. Soon they were all three in the big car, gliding through the busy streets. It was getting towards midnight and they took their place among the crowd of vehicles climbing the hill, only wherever the street was broad enough they passed always ahead. At the Rat Mort they came to a stand-still. Falkenberg led the way up the narrow stairs, greeted Albert with both hands, nodded amiably to the *chef d'orchestre*, the flower girl and the head waiter, who crowded around him.

"For as many as choose to come!" he declared. "The round table! The best supper in France! It is a gala night, Albert. Serve us of your best. Mademoiselle will sing. We are here to taste the joys of life."

Albert led the way.

"Ah, monsieur," he said, "it is good, indeed, to hear your voice! There is no one who comes here who enters more splendidly into the spirit of the place. When you are here I know that it will be a joyful evening for all. They catch it, too, those others," he explained. "Sometimes they come here stolid, British. They look around them, they eat, they drink, they sit like stuffed animals. Then comes monsieur - dear monsieur! He talks gayly, he laughs, he waves salutes, he drinks wine, he makes friends. The thing spreads. It is the spirit - the real spirit. Behold! Even the dull, once they catch it, they enjoy."

Falkenberg took the cushioned seat in the corner. Close to his side was mademoiselle, her hand already clasping his. Estermen, gaunt, red-eyed, still haggard with fear, sat a few feet away.

"Wine!" Falkenberg ordered. "Pommery - bottles of it! Never mind if we cannot drink it. Let us look at it. Let us imagine the joys that come, added to those we feel."

Already the wine was rushing into their glasses. Falkenberg raised his glass.

"To our last supper, dear Marguerite!" he whispered.

She shivered all over. She looked at him, her face was suddenly strained.

"You jest!"

"Jest? But is it not a night for jests!" he answered. "Why not? Ah, Marguerite, I take it back! To our first supper! Let us say to ourselves that to-night we stand upon the threshold of life. Let us say to ourselves that never before have I seen how blue your eyes shine, how sweet your mouth, how soft your fingers, how dear the thrill which passes from you to me. Close to me, Marguerite - close to me, little one! Our first evening!"

"Dearest," she whispered, "first or last, there could never be another. It is you who make my life. It is you who, when you go, leave it desolate."

He held her hand more tightly.

"Ah, little friend," he murmured, "you spoil me with

E. Phillips Oppenheim

your sweet phrases! You set the music playing in my heart - the witch music, I think. Come, we must speak to Estermen," he continued, looking resolutely away from her. "We cannot have him sitting there glum, a death's-head at our feast. Estermen, drink, man! Is this a funeral party? Wake up. Mademoiselle who dances there looks towards you. Why not? You see, she waves her hand. You have waltzed with her before. Ask her to sit down with us. I have ordered supper. See, mademoiselle approaches, Estermen. More glasses, waiter. Open more wine. There is champagne here for everybody. Mademoiselle does us great honor. Permit me!"

The little dancing girl obeyed his invitation. She sat by Estermen's side, but she cast a longing glance at Falkenberg. Their glasses were filled. Estermen drank quickly, all the time looking about him with the furtive air of a whipped dog.

"To-night," Falkenberg cried, as he lifted his glass, "I have but one command - be joyful. Why not? To-night I have Marguerite by my side, and you - you can choose from the world of Marguerites. There is nothing in life like this - the hour of midnight, the music of the moment, the wine of the hour, the woman we love. Drink, Estermen, once more. Fix your thoughts upon the present. Mademoiselle looks around her. She finds you dull. She will seek for another admirer. Ah, mademoiselle!" he added, leaning across the table, "if the sweetest girl in Paris were not here already by my side, do you think that I would permit you to be for an instant the companion of a dumb admirer?"

Mademoiselle laughed back into his eyes.

"If monsieur's friend were but as gallant as monsieur himself!"

"He is depressed," Falkenberg declared, "but it passes. Behold! Another glass like that, Estermen! Drink till you feel it bubbling in your veins. Look at him now!"

Falkenberg leaned back in his place and pressed his companion's arm. Indeed, the wine was working its magic. The terror was passing from Estermen's face. Already he was becoming more natural.

"Leave them alone," Falkenberg said softly. "He will have no relapse. The wine is in his blood. Ah, Marguerite! never did you seem so sweet to me as tonight, when my face is set for the cold north! Have you joy in remembering, little one? Have you sentiment enough for that?"

"I have sentiment enough," she whispered, "to suffer every time you leave me. To-night I am afraid to let you go. Oh! dear - my dear - take me with you! I have begged you before, but to-night I beg you in a different manner. I am afraid to be left alone. I care not where or whatever the end of your journey may be. Take me with you, dear one. It is because I love that I ask this!"

He looked at her for a moment and there were wonderful things in his eyes.

"Ah, little girl," he murmured, "you teach one so much! One passes through life too often with one's eyes closed, one finds the great things in strange places, the rarest flowers even by the roadside. Drink your wine, press my fingers - like that. See, it is the *chef d'orchestre* who approaches. You shall sing - sing to me, little one."

He motioned to the musician, who with a smile of delight held up his hand to the orchestra. Mademoiselle hummed a few bars. The man who listened nodded his head. Then he raised his violin, he passed his bow across the strings. With the touch of his fingers he drew from them a little melody. Mademoiselle assented. Her head was back against the wall, her eyes half closed. Then she began to sing; sang so that in a few moments the passionate words which streamed from her lips held the room breathless. It was no ordinary music. It was the love prayer of a woman, starting in sadness, passing on to passion, ending in wild entreaty. As she finished she turned her head towards her companion.

"You shall not go alone!" she cried, and her words might well have been the text of her song.

Falkenberg shook his head.

"Something gayer," he begged, - "something more like the wine which foams in our glasses."

She obeyed him after only a moment's hesitation, yet in the first few bars her song came to an abrupt end, her voice choked. She leaned suddenly forward in her place, her face was hidden between her hands. They all gazed at her curiously.

"Nerves!" one declared.

"Hysterics!" another echoed.

"It is the life they lead, these women," an American

explained to a little party of guests. "They weep or they laugh always. Life with them quivers all the time. They pass from one emotion to another - they seldom know which. Look, it is over with her."

It was over, indeed. She raised her head and sang, sang ravishingly, charmingly, a gay love-song. Falkenberg was the first to applaud her.

"To-night, dear," he murmured, "you are wonderful. You sing from the heart, your voice has feeling, you bring to one the exquisite moments.... Behold, the supper arrives! Estermen has made friends now with his little *danseuse*. Sit closer to me, dear. These are the golden hours. Give me your hand, look into my eyes, drink with me.... How the minutes pass! There is magic in this place."

Towards four o'clock Falkenberg and his companions came down the narrow stairs, out into the morning. A fine rain was falling, the pavements were already wet. Falkenberg was still gay, still laughing and talking. Behind, a little company - the *chef d'orchestre*, the chief *maître d'hôtel*, the flower girl - wondering at his generosity, stood at the head of the stairs to bid him godspeed. He gave a louis to the *commissionaire* and called for a special carriage. He had almost to lift Marguerite inside.

"Dear child," he said, holding her hands, "here we must part for a time - not for so long, perhaps. Who can tell? It is a comfortable carriage, this. Here is a handful of money for the fare. It is of no use to me."

He emptied his pockets into her lap as she sat there. She made no effort to pick up the shower of gold

E. Phillips Oppenheim

and silver.

"What do you mean - that it is of no use to you?"

"We drive for home," he answered. "We shall need no money to take us there. Listen."

He drew her face very close to his.

"When you arrive at your apartment," he said, "you will find there a little packet from me. Be wise, dear. If chance will have it that we do not meet again very soon, may it help you to take all out of life that you can find. Only sometimes when the heart is joyous, when the wine flows and your feet are keeping time to the music of life, think for a moment - of one who dwells, alas! in a quieter country. Dear Marguerite!"

He kissed her, first upon the lips and then lightly on the forehead. Then gently he thrust away the arms which she had wound around his neck. He waved to the coachman to drive off. With a little shrug of the shoulders he took his own place in the great touring car. Estermen, too, clambered into the tonneau.

"You have supped well, I trust, Henri?" the Prince asked the chauffeur.

"Without a doubt, Excellency," the man replied.

"Then drive for the frontier," Falkenberg ordered. "We will stop you when we need a rest."

They left Paris in the semi-darkness. They were away in the country before the faintest gleam of daylight broke through the eastern clouds. Even then the way was still obscured. It was a stormy morning, and banks of murky clouds were piled up where the sun should have risen. The rain still fell. Soon they commenced to ascend a range of hills. At the summit Falkenberg pulled the check-string.

"Henri," he said, "come in behind here. I will drive for a time - it will amuse me."

The man descended. Falkenberg took his place at the wheel. Estermen, obeying his gesture, scrambled into the seat by his side.

"Go to the signpost," his master ordered the chauffeur. "Tell me exactly, how many miles to Rheims?"

The man clambered up the bank. The gray morning twilight was breaking now through a sea of clouds. From where they were the vineyards sloped down to the bank. A thin, curving line of silver marked the course of the river. Here and there a little gleam of sunlight fell upon the country below them. Estermen closed his eyes.

"It makes me giddy," he muttered. "I hope that you will drive slowly down the hill!"

Falkenberg glanced to the left - the chauffeur was still peering at the milestone. He slipped in the clutch and the car glided off, gathering speed as though by magic.

"You have left Henri!" Estermen cried. "He is running after us. Stop the car! Can't you stop it?"

Falkenberg turned his head only once. The stone walls now on either side seemed flying past them. Estermen looked into his face and quaked with fear.

"This ride is for you and me alone, my friend!"
Falkenberg replied. "Sit tight and say your prayers, if it
pleases you. This is better, after all, than poison, or the
cold muzzle of a revolver at your forehead. Close your
eyes if you are afraid; or open them, if you have the
courage, and see the world spin by. We start on the
great journey."

Estermen shrieked. He half rose to his feet, but
Falkenberg, holding the wheel with his right hand,
struck him across the face with his left so that he fell
back in his place.

"If you try to leave the car," he said, "I swear that I will
stop and come back. I will shoot you where you lie,
like a dog. Be brave, man! Be thankful that you are
going to your death in honorable company and in
honorable fashion! It's better, this, than the guillotine,
isn't it? Look at the country below, like patchwork,
coming up to us. Listen to the wind rushing by. You
see the trees, how they bend? You feel the rain stinging
your cheeks? Sit still, man, and fix your thoughts
where you will. Think of mademoiselle *la danseuse*,
think of her kisses, think of the perfume of the violets
at her bosom! You see, we arrive. Watch that corner of
the viaduct."

They were traveling now at a terrific speed, falling fast
to the level country. Before them was a high bridge,
crossing the river. On the left, a portion of it was being
repaired and a few boards alone were up for protection.
Falkenberg, recognizing the spot for which he had
been looking, settled down in his seat. A grim smile
parted his lips.

"Jean Charles will never place his hand upon your shoulder now!" he cried. "Can you hear the wind sob, Estermen? Soon you'll hear the water in your ears! Hold fast. Don't spoil the end!"

They were going at sixty miles an hour, and with the slightest swerve of the steering wheel they turned to the left on entering the bridge and struck the boards. Henri, in his account of the accident, declared that although the car turned over before it reached the river, Falkenberg never left his seat. Estermen, on the other hand, was thrown violently out, and struck the water head foremost. From the condition of his body it would seem that death was instantaneous. Falkenberg was found with his arms locked around the steering wheel, his head bent forward. He, too, seemed to have been drowned almost immediately. The steering wheel was jammed, the car wrecked....

The authorities, who had left only a temporary protection while they repaired the viaduct on the bridge, were severely censured. The makers of the car were subjected to a very searching cross-examination. The brakes and the uncertain light were blamed. Henri, who from the hillside a mile or more back had watched with ghastly face, was the only one who understood the accident, and he kept silent!

CHAPTER XIX

ALL ENDS WELL

The Duchess of Clonarty was famous for doing the right thing. Three weeks after the return of Julien and Lady Anne to London, she gave a large dinner-party in their honor. At a quarter past eight, a telephone message from the House of Commons was received, explaining that Sir Julien would be ten minutes late, owing to his having to speak at greater length than he had first intended upon the Agdar question. Lady Anne was waiting for him, and they would arrive together certainly within a quarter of an hour. The Duchess made every use of her opportunity. She was at her very best during that brief period which ensued while they waited for the delayed guests.

"You know, my dear Lady Cardington," she explained, raising her voice a little to indicate that this was not entirely a confidence, "I never dreamed that dear Anne had so much self-confidence and resolution. Even now I have scarcely given up wondering at it. If she had only told me that she was so sincerely attached to Julien, I would never have listened for one moment to that Harbord affair. It was a mistake, of course," she rippled on, "but then one learns so much by one's mistakes. Notwithstanding their wealth, they were most terrible and impossible people. I am sure the association would have been most distasteful to the Duke. Poor Henry used to lock himself in his study when any of them were about the place, and what it would have been if they were really able to call themselves connections, I cannot imagine. You were speaking of the Carraby woman a few minutes ago. My dear Eva! Of course, you have heard about her? Her husband, when he resigned, gave out that he was obliged to go abroad for his wife's health. My dear, his wife had already left him, three days before! She was seen in Paris with Bob Sutherland. I hear the divorce suit is filed. What a terrible woman!"

"A great escape, I am sure, for Sir Julien," Lady Cardington declared.

The Duchess drew a little breath.

"Poor Julien was always so chivalrous," she murmured. "How thankful your dear husband must be to think that at last he has one person in his Cabinet who does command some sort of a following in the country!"

The Duchess delivered her little shaft and moved to the door. Sir Julien and Lady Anne Portel had just been announced. It was almost a family dinner. The Duchess took Julien's arm and drew him into a corner while the others filed past.

"Is it true," she whispered, "that the Carraby woman has bolted?"

Julien nodded.

"I am afraid there isn't a doubt about it," he admitted.

E. Phillips Oppenheim

"How are things to-night? Anything new?" she asked.

"Quite calm again," he replied. "The trouble seems to have passed over. Falkenberg's death upset the whole scheme which was brewing against us, whatever it may have been. All the notes which are being interchanged at the present moment are perfectly pacific."

The Duchess sighed.

"After all," she said, "my little visit to Paris was not so wild. I don't think you would ever have found out about Anne but for me."

Julien smiled.

"If I really believed that," he assured her, "and I shall try to, then I should feel that I owed you more than any person upon the earth."

The dinner was a success. Lady Anne seemed certainly to have developed. She was looking wonderfully handsome, and though her eyes strayed more than once to the end of the table where her husband was sitting, she carried on her share of the conversation with just that trifle of assurance which marks the transition from girlhood to the dignity of marriage. After the women had left, conversation for a few moments was necessarily political. The Duke, who read the *Times* and the *Spectator*, and attended every debate in the House of Lords, spoke with some authority.

"I believe," he said firmly, "that we have passed through a crisis greater than any one, even those in power, know of. It is my opinion that Falkenberg was the bitter enemy of this country - that it was he, indeed, who kept alive all that suspicious and jealous feeling of which we have had constant evidences from Berlin. He was dying all the time to make mischief. I am sorry, of course, for his tragical end. On the other hand, I am inclined to believe that his departure from the sphere of politics was the best thing that has happened to this country for many years."

"There is no doubt," Lord Cardington declared, "that he was working hard to estrange France and England. Your letters, Sir Julien, made that remarkably evident."

"'The good that men do lives after them,'" some one quoted, "also the evil. I am afraid it will be some time before France and England are on exactly the same terms."

"I would not be so sure," Julien interposed, setting down his glass. "The politics of Paris are the politics of France, and the spirit of the Parisian is essentially mercurial. Besides, the days of the great alliance draw nearer - the next step forward after the arbitration treaty. Who can doubt that when that is completed, France will embrace the chance of permanent peace?"

The Duke rose to his feet.

"Five minutes only I am allowed, gentlemen," he said. "My wife wants some of us, some of us have to go back to Westminster. I shall ask you, therefore, before we separate, as this is in some respects an occasion, to drink to the health of my son-in-law, Sir Julien Portel. Though a politician of the old type, I do not fail to appreciate what we owe to the new school. I am a reader of the old-fashioned newspapers, but I recognize the fact that the modern Press sometimes exercises a new and wonderful function in politics. It is my opinion that by means of this modern journalism Sir Julien Portel has maintained the peace of the world. I ask you, therefore, not only as my private friends and relatives, but as politicians, to drink to-night to the health of my son-in-law."

They all rose.

"And with that toast," Lord Cardington added, as he bowed toward Julien, "let me associate the fervent pleasure felt by all of us in welcoming back once more the colleague to whom we have so many reasons to be thankful."

The party broke up soon afterwards. Lady Anne drove back with her husband to Westminster. She sat by his side in the closed car which had been her father's wedding present. Her hands, linked together, were passed through his arm. She was a very well satisfied woman.

"Julien," she declared, "it's lovely to be back here, but I wouldn't have been without those few weeks in Paris for anything in the world. I don't think we can ever get back down into the bottom of the ruts, do you?"

"If ever we feel like it," he answered, smiling, "we'll cross the Channel again, and take Mademoiselle Janette with us and seek for more adventures."

"Lovely!" she exclaimed. "I shall hold you to that, mind."

"No need," he replied. "Kendricks is going to stay there as correspondent for the *Post*. We must go and see him occasionally. There is no one who understands better the temperament of the Parisian than he."

"There will be no more Herr Freudenberg to circumvent," she remarked.

"Paris always has its problems," he answered. "Kendricks realizes that. The plotting of the world takes place within a mile of Montmartre."

They were nearing Westminster. Julien drew his wife towards him and kissed her.

"I shall only be about twenty minutes, dear," he suggested. "Why not wait?"

"Of course," she replied. "I have a little electric lamp here, and a book. I'd love to."

Julien walked blithely into the House. Lady Anne turned on the lamp, drew out her book, and leaned back among the cushions with a deep sigh of content.

*   *   *   *   *

That same night, wandering around Paris, Kendricks met Monsieur, Madame, and Mademoiselle.

"It is the gallant Englishman!" mademoiselle exclaimed.

"It is the gentleman who ate both portions of chicken!" madame cried, clapping her hands.

It was a veritable meeting. Kendricks willingly joined their little party and sat down with them in the

E. Phillips Oppenheim

brightly-lit cafe. Monsieur ordered wine.

"The business affairs of monsieur are prospering, I trust?" he said. "After all, the *entente* remains."

Kendricks lifted his glass.

"I drink to it!" he exclaimed. "It is the sanest thing to-day in European politics. Drink to it yourself, monsieur, and you, madame, and you, mademoiselle. You shall accuse us no longer, we English, of selfishness or stupidity. For what reason, think you, did we order a warship to Agdar and brave the whole wrath of Germany?"

Monsieur held out his hand.

"My friend," he declared, "it was a stroke of genius, that. It was what we none of us expected from any English Minister. It was magnificent. I confess it - it has altered my opinions. I drink with you now, cordially and heartily. I drink to the *entente*. I believe in it. I am a convert."

Kendricks shook hands with every one solemnly. He shook hands last with mademoiselle, and forgot to release her little fingers for several moments.

"Tell us of your friend, monsieur?" madame asked politely.

But Kendricks did not hear! He was whispering in mademoiselle's ear. Her dark eyes were fixed upon the tablecloth, her pretty lips were parted, a most becoming flush of color was in her cheeks. Monsieur looked at madame and winked. Madame smiled, well pleased.

"*L'entente!*" monsieur murmured.

Madame nodded.

E. Phillips Oppenheim

www.ingramcontent.com/pod-product-compliance
Lightning Source LLC
Chambersburg PA
CBHW030759260626
47169CB00001B/122